THE WEIGHT OF BETRAYAL

THE ANGELINA PIRRELLO SAGA

BOOK 2

SANDRA MONTANINO

EDWARDS PUBLISHING

The Weight of Betrayal

Sandra Montanino

The Weight of Betrayal
The Angelina Pirrello Saga Book 2
Published by: Edwards Publishing Provo, UT
Copyright © 2023 Sandra Montanino

Cover design by:
Bryan Heim Photography and Design - Bryan Heim
Interior print design and layout by:
Erika Kuta Marler
ISBN: 978-1-7345090-3-8 ebook
ISBN: 978-1-7345090-4-5 paperback
ISBN: 978-1-7345090-5-2 hardcover

Subjects:
FICTION / Romance. | FICTION / Historical. | FICTION / Coming of Age.
Author Sandra Montanino

-Sandra Montanino
AuthorSandraM@gmail.com

IN SUPPORT OF THE AUTHOR

In support of the author of The Weight of Betrayal, it would be greatly appreciated if you took a moment to leave your honest review on your favorite retailer's website.

-Sandra Montanino
SandraMontanino@gmail.com

It's with a warm heart, I dedicate this book to all my family—
those that are here, and those in the hereafter—
especially my grandmother, Angelina who left us with a rich
treasure chest of Sicilian stories. These tales, both real and
imagined, captivated and inspired me to write this book and those
that follow. I hope you will enjoy them as much as I have.

CHAPTER 1

Ybor City, Florida, 1910

The day had run out of hours. Darkness engulfed the night sky, and the modest house with six children and a father who shouted more than he spoke had grown quiet and fallen into slumber.

Alert to every sound, eighteen-year-old Angelina Pirrello remained saturated in a haze of panic. Careful not to ruffle the air and fearing discovery, she packed all her possessions into an old satchel, left a note, and cautiously made her way through the house.

Not until she reached the door, did she glance at the pendulum clock. It had tallied up all the years of her life and now appeared to signal a warning. She could abandon her plan right now, return to her bed, and no one would ever know what she had intended.

For an intense gathering of seconds, Angelina stood at the threshold of her home. This was the moment she had yearned for, planned out, and considered her absolute right. In a burst of nervous energy, she quickly closed the door behind her, and ran across the brick-laid street, passing the train station and the *casita* row-houses built for cigar workers.

With a strange rush of sorrow and joy, her breathing kept the same irregular pace as her heart. Nothing would ever be as before, and an inexplicable sensation came over her. Time had shifted. All that had existed in her present life now became the past.

Haunted by the escalating arguments with her father and frightened of her own boldness, Angelina made a nervous plea to God, "Please, don't abandon me."

She would not be at home when the sun arose, when her father, Domenico read her parting note, nor would she witness his anger and how the vein in his neck pulsated when he spewed Italian curses. His fist would slam on the table, and worse, his heart would harden against his eldest child.

Her eyes moistened. "And please, God, help Papa understand me."

A chill passed through Angelina's petite frame, despite Florida's summer heat. With only the shimmer of a solitary street lamp and the collision of her emotions, Angelina looked into the distance and saw the silhouette of her betrothed rushing toward her.

"Fabian!" She dropped her satchel, hurried into his arms, and released all her pent-up tears.

He held her close and whispered, "Shhh, it's okay, *mi amor*. I'm here."

Fabian had become her world. In his embrace, the wound between her and her father softened.

Hand-in-hand, beneath the stars, they walked while Fabian spoke of love. "These are our first exciting moments, the beginning of a new life. We'll be happy, Angelina. It's my promise."

His words were like balm on a wound, but her emotions

remained entangled.

Fabian pushed a lock of her long chestnut hair away from her face and gazed into the warm hue of her brown eyes. "Then I'll be happy for both of us, while you take your time to catch up?"

Although her apprehension persisted, Angelina appreciated his attempt to distract her from her misgivings and make her smile. She met the eyes of this young man she would soon marry and studied his features. Now and then, a few men emerge forged from the kiln of life and arrive flawlessly molded—so it appeared with Fabian. His defined jawline, rich dark hair, and magnetic gray eyes drew her and held her captive.

Angelina had never been a frivolous thinker, nor was she deceived by storybook descriptions of people and things. Good looks were not substance but a distraction. Throughout their time together, Fabian had been persistent in what mattered. He had ignited her love by proving he truly loved her.

Still, Angelina could not shake her anxiety. She glanced in the direction of the DiLeto's house as their large dog barked and jumped up and down in an effort to leap over the fence.

"Oh, no. What if the dog awoke my father?" The thought of a confrontation unnerved her, and she darted past Fabian.

"Angelina, stop." Fabian hurried to her side.

"You don't understand." She tried to pull away. "For my father, nothing could be worse than what I'm doing tonight."

"I understand," countered Fabian, "Even if your father awakes, he won't know you left the house."

"But I left him a note on the table. What if he gets up and sees it? He'll come down to the courthouse and stop us from getting married. I already told you about the marriage arrangements he made for me with men I could never love."

"Didn't one of them already have four children?"

"Yes. That was Umberto Rizzo, the baker. He's closer in age to my father, and the other was Rico Braccio. Both were well-established. My father wanted me to have a comfortable life, but what's comfortable about marriage to a man you don't love?"

Fabian let a moment slip away. "Then tell me, did everyone approve of your parents' marriage?"

Angelina had never considered the similarity. "They lived in Santo Stefano Quisquina. It's a long name for a small Sicilian village where the rich and poor never mix. Since my mother came from a family of significant money and my father had nothing, they only met by chance here in America."

Angelina looked out into the distance as if she were looking at a scene from the past. "My father always said, 'Only in America a man can dream.'"

"But they married." Fabian made his point. "In the end, that's what matters. People on each side of the road, the river, or the mountain think they are on the side that matters until they finally meet each other, fall in love, and run away together to get married." Fabian raised his eyebrows and looked secure. "So, there's the proof that each side can't be right. Right?"

Angelina appreciated his light-hearted way of analyzing the problem. "Right."

She raised her head and stared at the splendor of the stars. "I had no choice but to leave. Still, my father would consider this too great a betrayal and come looking for me."

"So, we're running off like Romeo and Juliet."

"That ended in tragedy, remember?"

Fabian kissed her cheek. "This is different. I'm promising not to take poison, and you must promise not to stab yourself to death."

They giggled. "It'll be our solemn vow," said Angelina.

CHAPTER 1 | 5

"Your father can return to his old-world ways, and we'll cast our nets out to sea and enjoy whatever wonders we pull in."

For a long time, they walked down the moonlit streets where legions of cigar factories stood at attention. They reached the bench outside the courthouse and sat together. Fabian put his arm around her as the evening's balminess embraced them. Love was not a quiet thing. It fell from the heavens, awakened the dreamers, and pressed against Angelina's heart.

"Do you ever think about your mother and how she would feel about us? Would she believe in us?"

"My mother wanted the very best for all her children. She would have encouraged our love, and she'd never stand in our way."

"Then we're not alone," he said.

The night loosened its hold on the darkness. Angelina and Fabian watched it take its final curtain call as the sun stretched its arms and arose with streams of tangerine and indigo at the edge of the eastern sky.

They had been up all night. Exhausted from the mixture of emotions, Angelina rested her head on his shoulder while the critical hours drew closer for the courthouse to open its doors and change their destiny.

Even in their young lives existed a powerful chronology of events. So, on this longest of nights, with only the sound of crickets and the dance of fireflies as company, Fabian and Angelina sat together and untied their parcels of poignant memories.

Angelina sensed a change in Fabian. "What's wrong?" she whispered.

He passed his hand through his thick, dark hair. "You shouldn't feel as though you've lost your family. It's not the same sensation as…."

Fabian smoothed the crease on his pants as if gathering his thoughts. "You know, Angelina, there's something I've never told you. Something I've never shared with anyone." He paused, looked up, and met her eyes. "Everyone believes I'm an only child." He paused again. "But once, I had an older brother."

Alerted to the sudden change in the tenor of his voice, Angelina could hear how his words cost him to speak and how he reeled them in from some far-off place in the past.

Fabian took in a deep breath before he spoke. "Diego was nine when he died, and I was seven."

Stunned, all her drowsiness left her. Wide awake now, Angelina could see the impact of the painful memory straining Fabian's face. She fumbled for the right words, but scattered thoughts toppled out instead. "Oh, Fabian, how horrible. I can't imagine how painful it is to lose your only brother. The thought alone is crippling."

Fabian appeared to be looking through the jagged edge of a broken lens, which had shattered his life forever and now existed in the archives of time. "I never speak of this." The softness in his voice did not conceal the strain in his words.

"Memories have two faces. They can bring comfort or make us cry. It's strange how we can carry such pain and then try to bury it to protect ourselves," said Fabian.

Angelina wanted to say something reassuring. "Then we have the same heartbreak. I lost my mother as she was giving birth, and my infant brother died with her. He was born dead or died moments later. No one seemed certain. At fifteen, I believed I would never recover. Maybe we never do, but we learn to keep going."

For a time, they were both lost in their thoughts as the leaves rustling about them made the only sound.

Angelina gazed up at the sky to stop her tears from falling. "Back then, one of us would cry, and then we all cried. It went on for so long."

"It's a terrible feeling and a high price to pay," said Fabian as he removed his arm from around Angelina and rubbed his hands together. "Have you ever heard the pounding of sugarcane fields blowing in the wind?"

She didn't allow herself to become distracted from Fabian and shook her head, yet the unrelated question puzzled her.

"It's like the sound of thunder. In Cuba, we lived next to a sugarcane plantation. My brother and I used to chase each other around, and even though we liked to hide, we never went into the fields. They warned all the children never to go there, but when do children listen to everything they're told?"

Again, Angelina wondered what had drawn Fabian to a conversation about sugarcane.

"The stalks can grow as tall as sixteen feet, and the rows go on and on, like a thick forest. Once you enter, you can't tell where you started. Every direction looks the same. Whenever I think of my life back in Cuba, I think of the tall sugarcane fields. I can almost feel the sensation of the broken stalks in my hand. Nothing ever changes. I see it in my mind, whether awake or in my dreams."

He looked away, and Angelina sensed his mood had grown more solemn.

"On the day my brother disappeared, the wind came up from the ocean and blew with such force. It's hard to imagine. Thick stalks of sugarcane swayed wildly and beat against each other like never-ending war drums. Sometimes grown men get lost in there and no one hears their screams. Some have been murdered in those plantations. It conceals the crime."

Angelina gasped. "I cannot imagine anything more frightening, especially for a child."

A desolate look crossed Fabian's face. We'll never know if someone chased him into the sugarcane fields or if he wandered in alone. So many came to help us search for Diego. Older people in the village told children stories of ghosts, fairies, and buried treasures among the stalks of sugarcane. My brother was only nine. He believed the stories. I think he wanted to find the treasure.

"So many came to help us search for Diego. They lit torches late into the night. Still, the wind kept its fierceness, running through miles of sugarcane stalks, thrashing and pounding, louder and louder, and blowing out some torches. After weeks of intense searching, they didn't find his body until the harvest in July, when the plantation workers cut down the sugarcane."

Angelina remained quiet and listened closely as Fabian continued to twist open the lock to the frightful events embedded in his heart.

The tragic story left Angelina spellbound and shaken.

Fabian paused the way people do when they want to resist what's on their minds. "When they found him, he remained curled up on the ground, like a baby sleeping, with his hands pressed against his ears to fight the thunderous sound. That's the way I saw him last. That's the way I still see him in my mind, and that's the way my father placed him in his coffin and buried him."

Angelina's mind raced at the number of things that could have killed the child: exposure, hunger, lack of water, and the added fear of being lost and by himself. "It's beyond dreadful."

"My mother fainted. My father never said a word." Fabian rubbed his forehead as if trying to fight the emotion. "Did you know people can scream without making a sound?" Fabian's breathing grew heavy, like he had to run back through time with no way to escape the memory.

"My father played the guitar for hours and hours until I realized the guitar cried for him. I must have reminded him of his greatest tragedy because one day, he hugged me tight, kissed me, and left the house. I never saw him again."

Angelina could see a part of Fabian remained trapped in the same catastrophic tragedy.

"My mother used to sing all the time." His eyes glistened, and he squeezed them shut to contain his tears. "After my brother died, she never sang again." Fabian shook his head as if trying to erase the memory. "Yet, every meal, my mother would set a place for my brother at the table, as though she couldn't bring herself to believe her first-born child was not coming home." He hesitated as if the recollection had become too vivid.

Angelina gazed at the man she intended to make her husband. Fabian had never spoken much of his past. "Is your mother still in Cuba?"

At first, Fabian didn't answer. His eyes fixated on the ground. He pushed away a strand of his thick, dark hair that had fallen across his eyes. "She lost her ability to distance herself from those memories. It was the source of her great sadness. I think my mother built a house inside herself. When things became so bad, she'd go into that house where no one could reach her. Then, one day, she never came out. I could almost see her frail spirit leave her body, and I shouted at her not to leave me, but she vanished like mist. I tried to catch her spirit and keep her from going. They said she died from a broken heart."

Although he remained blameless, Angelina hoped his telling the story might release some of its power over him, and become a form of absolution he needed. She understood loss and heartbreak and how life could come to a sudden stop.

"Forgive me, *querida*, for telling you this on such a special day. Perhaps after all the bad, I never imagined finding such happiness. You're my jewel, and because of you, the sound of sugarcane stalks drumming in my head will grow silent. This is our beginning."

"It's a blessing to recall the past, but now and then, it's a blessing to let it go."

Angelina scooted closer to Fabian and once again rested her head on his shoulder. One thing she knew for sure, even when her mother died, her father would never have abandoned his six children.

"So, these are our yesterdays," she said. "Those who were once in our lives and loved us would not want us to live in sadness."

Angelina and Fabian sat alone in silence and watched as the world stretched its arms, yawned, and the spectacle of the city came alive. Its musical serenade of wagon wheels, carriages, pushcarts, and the occasional Model-T filled the streets and announced a new day. Still, no one seemed distracted by the couple on the bench.

Fabian stroked Angelina's cheek. "From now on, we won't let our yesterdays darken our tomorrows." His expression and words were warm and encouraging,

But it's what you don't expect that can destroy you, she thought.

"Look, the courthouse doors are opening," said Fabian.

Angelina inhaled deeply, and when she put her hand below her throat, she felt the St. Jude medallion around her neck. It had been a gift from Rolando Aguirre to hold as his promise to return to her. But the wild roses had bloomed. The following year, they bloomed once again. And after all the petals had fallen to the earth, along with her tears, did Angelina believe Rolando had released her from his heart and forgotten her.

CHAPTER 2

THE SUMMER HEAT of 1910 had no mercy. Halley's Comet raced across the sky. William Taft was the 27th President, and John D. Rockefeller, thought to be the wealthiest man in the country, announced his retirement. The world had turned a page, distanced itself from the nineteenth century, and eagerly stepped into the booming industrial revolution. But Rolando Aguirre's world remained abandoned by time and detained unjustly in the most infamous prison in Barcelona, Spain.

"*¡No soy culpable de lo que paso! Vengo de América.*" Rolando repeated his loud outbursts of wrongful imprisonment. But his shouts collided with those of other inmates, and both fell upon the ears of the prison guards, who had neither interest nor compassion for anyone.

Had Rolando arrived a day sooner or a day later, he would have avoided the young men in the disastrous insurrection to overthrow King Alfonso XIII of Spain. Instead, he was beaten, dragged away, handcuffed, and arrested.

Angry, Rolando squeezed his hands around the bars of his cell. Most unbearable of all, they were denied communication. His plans and life revolved around returning home to Ybor City and marrying Angelina, not languishing in a Spanish prison.

Not Angelina, his family, nor the Cigar Makers International Union that had sent him to Spain as their representative knew what had become of him.

Angelina would think he had forgotten her. What else could she believe? Day and night, the frustration consumed his thoughts and infused his determination to return and find her the moment the cell door opened to set him free.

He carved another mark on his cell wall, one for each day spent in Barcelona's most inhospitable accommodation prison. It had been two years of mistaken incarceration, with no one willing to verify his wrongful arrest. Rolando doubled his fist and pounded it so hard on the stone barrier that confined him that his hand bled.

The guard rattled the door's bars with his gun. "*Oye*, you, *Américano.* Come and get your steak dinner and fine wine." The man's enormous belly shook as he laughed.

Rolando grabbed the tray and looked over the unappetizing meal of stale bread and something indescribable. "What's wrong with you, *tío*? Don't they teach you to say *gracias* in that America of yours?"

"For what? Food made for roaches and rats crawling all over this place? They're the only ones getting fat around here." Disgusted, Rolando shouted, "When am I going to get out of this hellhole?"

The guard walked away, laughing.

"*Soy inocente. Pertenezco a la Unión de Cigarros.*" Once again, Rolando shouted his innocence, his reason for arriving in Spain, and his affiliation with the cigar union in America. He was young, looked no different from the revolutionists, and even more incriminating, Spain was the country of his birth, which tainted his alibi. He did not appear the foreigner he professed.

After weeks without jailers providing those confined with sufficient food, punching them, and breaking their spirits, Rolando had weakened and lost body mass.

He laid down on his stiff cot, too short for his tall frame, and gazed at the discoloration and neglected cracks in the ceiling's paint. The lines meandered aimlessly and then spilled down the walls. It seemed a road map of the incarcerated life of every prisoner.

He thought of his family. They were used to his absences, extended travels, and the lapses of time before they heard from him. Although it had been far too long since they'd received a letter, he counted on their belief that no news was good news. Had a severe injury or death occurred, they would have received word.

But then there was Angelina. With no idea what had become of him and no way to reach her, his only release came when he recalled their days together filled with depth and breadth—and wonder. How did the miracle of their meeting occur in the panic and midst of Florida's greatest and most horrific fire? He remembered looking up and meeting her eyes as her uncle introduced them, and for the first time in his life, he saw his destiny before him.

His mind drifted back to that last day he'd held Angelina in his arms at the train station and felt her heartbeat next to his. He thought of her beauty, the love in her eyes when she looked at him, and the softness of her lips.

He had lost so much in the dark confines of this cell. But one thought remained clear and bright—Angelina.

They could not keep him incarcerated forever. He had no weapon or traitorous materials when captured and still arrested, although he hadn't stolen or killed, and no one testified against him.

Hear my thoughts, Angelina. Please wait for me. I promised I'd return to you, and when I do, nothing will ever separate us again.

Nothing.

Someone coughed in the next cell, then coughed louder. Rolando looked up.

"*Psst. Oye,* Américano, *es* Javier Rivera," came a whispered voice.

Rolando rose and pressed his frame against the bars that separated the cells.

"We know you're not one of us, but they'll never believe you or stop knocking you around. So, stay close to me tomorrow if you want to get out of this devil's den. We have a plan."

"Tomorrow, where, how?" Rolando kept his voice just as low.

Javier stepped back and winked.

For just a few blessed moments, Rolando felt his muscles release the tightness that had tormented him since his arrest. In that sliver of time, he imagined breathing air untainted by confinement.

Javier Rivera walked away from the corner of his cell, apparently unwilling to say anything more. It left Rolando in a frenzy of emotions, trying to decrypt Javier's escape plan. *Would they be crawling through a collapsing tunnel of dirt, running through a spray of bullets if discovered, concealing themselves in trash barrels, placed on wagons, and driven away from the prison's walls?* He had seen the wagons leave but not where they went. *What if they rid themselves of the trash by rolling the barrels into a fire?* Rolando's imagination went wild, but he could not conceive of a

foolproof way to escape the prison without threatening their lives.

Three men shared Rolando's cell, but they committed violent crimes. But Javier and himself fell under the category of political prisoners and were treated far worse for daring to defy the King.

The afternoon and the night commingled and stretched until the *tomorrow* Javier had spoken of had arrived. The morning sun had risen, but no prisoner had ever seen its brilliance from their cell.

Rolando remained uneasy as the morning came and went. Javier said nothing more, but gave Rolando an occasional nod.

That afternoon, a startling horde of thunderous chants penetrated the cell walls. "Open the cells and let them out." The mob demanded the release of the political prisoners and kept the prison guards busy.

Rolando looked through the bars at Javier, who winked and again nodded.

The prison erupted with a swarm of fuming voices and, growing louder, echoed through the walls. The gathering grew momentous and the shouting louder as the warden summoned guards to join forces outside, but that was a mistake.

An inside guard with a connection had bribed the revolutionaries. His part in the conspiracy was to leave the keys to Cell Block C. He would later claim he'd dropped them in his haste as he hurried out to offer support.

They fired guns into the air to break up the mob uprising outside the prison wall, but the mob also came armed.

"Suelta tus armas!" The warden's cry to those at the gate to drop their weapons met with curses.

The guards now stood shoulder to shoulder at the gate with their guns drawn. "Open your cells and release the men!" The chanting to release the political prisoners grew stronger.

Inside, cells had been unlocked, and prisoners stormed into the courtyard.

Words and anger mounted. Several guards were captured as hostages. Nothing defused the mob.

The standoff and chaos on the outside were planned distractions for those escaping on the inside.

"Vámonos!" shouted Javier.

Rolando did not hesitate to act. They sprinted from the filthy cells, down the prison halls, and past the torture rooms where beatings and solitary confinement occurred. As they ran past the kitchen, they saw the abundance of food with- held from the prisoners.

"This way," said Javier, rushing past the main office, momentarily abandoned but filed with prison records.

"Wait!" said Rolando. "Let's take our files and destroy them, or they'll destroy us."

Javier's eyes opened wide. "Brilliant! But move fast."

Rolando pulled open the file drawer with the letter "A." He grabbed a handful of folders with the same last name as his, as did Javier, and they jumped out the office window.

Amid the growing band of raging rioters fighting and shouting, Javier and Rolando ran behind the building, around the outskirts of the bloody scene, and escaped over the back gate.

Outside, they ran through a wooded area and remained concealed until they reached a narrow clearing.

Though winded, Javier kept running. "Don't stop. The sea is only 3.8 kilometers from the prison. When the dirt turns to sand, we made it."

"Then what? We swim?"

"We planned this breakout for weeks. My cousin has a fishing boat. He's waiting for us."

Rolando laughed. "You've thought of everything. You should be the King of Spain."

"That *bastardo* sitting on the throne spends hours admiring his collection of riches but can't see his homeless and hungry subjects."

They reached the sea, and Javier waved to his cousin standing on the deck. "We're saved. Let's go. More boats are coming and you will return to America." Javier glanced back at the prison. "Did you know they never meant for us to get out of there? And all they had to do for your release was to notify the cigar union, and you would have walked out, but justice doesn't exist in prison. Today these *compañeros patriotas* created a huge distraction and gave us back our lives. So let's make sure it wasn't in vain."

Together, they ran down the pier and jumped into the boat. Javier threw up his hands. "Breathe in the sea air, *amigo*. I won't forget you, Rolando Aguirre, and don't forget me, Javier Rivera. We'll meet again."

Rolando laughed a hardy laugh, saturated in relief and the independence he had almost forgotten existed. They went through the files they'd been carrying, and Rolando pulled out all his vital identification. Everything else, they burned.

"As long as I live, I will not forget the name Javier Rivera. Fill your lungs, Javier. It's thick with freedom."

"And for you, the cigar union will know where you've been. You'll catch a boat to America, and your arms will hold in your arms that Angelina you call out to in your sleep."

CHAPTER 3

Fabian stopped just before they entered the courthouse. "Wait right here. I'll only be a moment."

"Where are you going? What are you doing?" said Angelina, puzzled.

"I'll be right back. Something's not right."

Angelina thought of how she'd dared to leave her home and run off, to get married. So much wasn't the way it should be. "What's not right, Fabian?"

"I'll be right back."

Already nervous, he left Angelina unsettled and confused. Then, moments later, he returned with freshly picked flowers. "How can we marry without my bride holding flowers as beautiful as she is?"

The gesture gave her the encouragement she needed at this crossroads in her life. Angelina put her arm through his. They kissed, and its sweetness calmed her.

"We'll stand before the Justice of the Peace, say our vows, and you'll become my wonderful *esposa*," Fabian spoke with a wide smile.

He sported the customary dress of a cigar maker—dark

pants, white shirt, and tie, topped off with his familiar brown cap.

Angelina wore the same blue dress she'd worn when they first met. Her mother had owned it, Signora Bertelli had altered it, and her father had refused to replace it. Hers could not compare to the grand wedding of her friend from work, Rosa Caprici, with an abundance of decorations, banquet tables, and a large gathering of friends and family. Angelina had no father to gaze at her with pride and love as he gave her away. No mother to smile at her and wipe away her tears. No church, priest, High Mass, wedding gown, or attendants.

Now, her blue dress upheld almost all traditions—something old, something borrowed, and something blue.

A young couple walked in. The man was tall and red-headed, like Rolando. Struck by the unexpected resemblance to the young man who had stolen her heart, Angelina shook her head in anguish to allow such a powerful memory to resurface at such a moment in her life.

Angelina took a deep breath to calm herself. Without thinking, she raised her hand to her throat, and touched the chain of the Saint Jude medal around her neck. He was the saint of miracles and stirred another memory. Rolando Aguirre had given it to her the last time they saw each other. They stood at the train station, where he kissed her and promised to return in two weeks, but the weeks had overflowed into months and seasons without his arrival.

She'd worn the medal for so long, it became a habit. Perhaps the miracle belonged not for Rolando, but to Fabian. He was her miracle. She looked at the clerk and pointed to an empty seat against the wall. "I feel dizzy; may I sit a moment?"

"Of course. It's there for the brides." He appeared amused. "Sometimes for the grooms."

"Are you alright, *querida?*" asked Fabian.

"Yes. It's just that so much is happening so fast."

Fabian sat next to her and put his arm around her. "Our lives together are about to begin, and we'll be happy. You'll see."

She reached for Fabian's hand and squeezed it. Life navigates through dreams and tempests, and Fabian claimed her heart. She loved him and could not imagine what had possessed her to think of the young man who had broken her heart.

Fabian's voice tore through her thoughts. "We'll sign the marriage license right after the ceremony."

Angelina nodded. The desk clerk tore open a new box of paperclips and slid it near their forms.

"May I have a paperclip?" asked Angelina.

The man shrugged his shoulders and pushed the little box toward her. She reached inside and took out a single paperclip. This tiny piece of wire completed her wedding tradition. She had her hand clasped around *something new*—a paperclip.

Angelina looked around. The uninspiring courthouse had not one embellishment, but that didn't matter. She stepped through the adjacent doorway and stood in line among strangers with Fabian's hand in hers.

"Fabian Dominguez and Angelina Pirrello. We're ready for you," said a stoic and clearly disinterested civil servant.

They stepped forward, but Angelina's mind wandered back in time and how she had arrived at this moment, how she tried to ignore Fabian at first, how she had resisted his charm and classic good looks. Still, as weeks became months, he remained undaunted, made her laugh, appeared often, declared his love, and in the end, stole her heart.

"I will always remember this day as perfect, Angelina," he said.

His words eased Angelina, but she would remember the

day differently. She could not overlook its complexities that weighed on her mind.

Surrounded by reams of paperwork, desks, files, and somber employees hired to witness redundant vows of love, Fabian whispered words she needed to hear. "Nothing can stop now. We'll have a wonderful life."

The Justice of the Peace stepped before them, wearing a brown suit with an oblong stain on his lapel. He was a short angular man with hollow cheeks, as though, over time his features had worn out, grown lazy, and lost interest in impressing people.

He cleared his throat. "Do you, Fabian Dominguez, take thees woman, Angelina Pirrello, for you lawfully wedded wife? *Sí o no?*" Known for its abundance of immigrants, Ybor City remained cradled in foreign accents and none more prevalent than Spanish. Nevertheless, Angelina had no trouble understanding him.

Fabian's face lit up, and his perfect smile returned and glimmered. He met Angelina's eyes and squeezed her hand.

"*Sí*, I do. Yes." He further emphasized his response by nodding his head.

Angelina believed the logical destination for falling in love led to marriage. These were the vows that withstood time and created families. In her mind, she painted a picture of growing old with Fabian, which comforted her.

"And do you, Angelina Pirrello take thees man, Fabian Dominguez to be you lawfully wedded husband? *Sí o no?*"

The pivotal moment had arrived powdered and polished in ancient words that sounded a trumpet. For the first time, Angelina had made a monumental decision of her own. Still, she loved her father, but all their arguments churned inside her.

"*Sí o no?*"

Angelina did not consider the question. Instead, like a dot

on a sheet of paper, a once-faded memory returned—a nest under the eaves of her father's porch where a tiny bird flapped its wings until he gained strength and took flight. She had become that bird; her time came to fly away.

The small man wrinkled his brow and raised his voice. *"Sí o no!"*

Angelina had become stronger than she thought. She could have left home and run off on her own, but when she met Fabian's eyes, this became her greatest decision, the right decision, the only decision.

The tiniest single word would change her life forever. *"Sí,"* said Angelina.

With a noisy exhale, the Justice of the Peace instructed each one to promise to keep the other for better, for worse, for richer, for poorer, in sickness and health, and cherish the other till death do they part.

"Fabian, repeat after me. I give you thees ring as a token of our love."

Fabian slipped a simple gold band on her finger. "I give you this ring as a token of our love, Angelina."

"You are now man and wife. Till death do you part. Kiss de bride—*por Díos!*" And then he coughed.

Fabian took Angelina in his arms, bent her backward, and kissed her. "I've been poor, but now I'm rich. You're my jewel, Angelina."

"I love you, too, and thank you for being so patient with me." They kissed again, and those at the desks and counter gave weary nods of congratulations while those who remained in line wore wide grins.

The scale had tipped away from a large church wedding and her father's choice of a man she didn't love to a simple exchange with one she did. Fate and circumstance had prevented her family from attending. Still, she kept them in her heart.

Fabian gazed into her eyes like Ybor City had become a glorious kingdom filled with endless possibilities. "We're perfect together." Fabian tightened his arm around her waist and whispered words of love as they left the building and walked down the street. Angelina glanced over her shoulder at the unimpressive brick structure they had entered and considered how quickly her life had changed. Still, for a reason she couldn't fathom, it gave her a strange sense of foreboding. She rubbed the chill from her arms.

Fabian had not lost his enthusiasm, oblivious to her momentary change in demeanor. "We'll have our first meal together at the finest Cuban restaurant, *mi amor,* and then we'll move into the *casita* I rented, and we'll be happy. I made all the arrangements yesterday."

Her father's greatest fear was that she would end up living in a little rented *casita* when he had twice tried to secure her future in arranged marriages.

Fabian kissed her cheek, her forehead, and then her lips. Love had materialized for Angelina, and she allowed herself to bask in the wonder of it. Nothing else seemed to matter.

THEY ENTERED THE RESTAURANT, *El Cubano,* and sat together at a small table. A waiter appeared and placed a napkin and tableware in front of each one. "How may I help you?"

"Senor, allow me to introduce my wife, Angelina Dominguez. We were just married, and this is our first meal together," said Fabian as he beamed, and Angelina blushed.

"Well, allow me to offer my congratulation." He nodded approvingly.

"Thank you," said Fabian. "We'll have the Cuban feast of shredded beef known as *ropa vieja* or old clothes, and *Moros y*

Cristianos, the Moors and Christians, another name for black beans and white rice."

The waiter served them, and Angelina offered a brilliant smile. "It looks delicious." Overwhelmed now by her own daring, her stomach constricted a bit. She ate slowly and gazed at Fabian. "So much has happened. I almost can't believe it."

"It worked out the way it should have."

When they finished their meal, the waiter returned and set a piece of cake in front of them. "All of us here from *El Cubano* would like to offer you a slice of cake to celebrate your marriage and offer our congratulations. May you have a long life together."

They both looked at each other in surprise. "Thank you so much," they said in unison.

Fabian stood up, shook the waiter's hand, and thanked him again.

"That's so kind of you," said Angelina.

When they left the restaurant, they walked through the park hand in hand, and Angelina shared how she had hoped to enter college one day.

"And you shall. Like I said, anything for you."

The afternoon sun was high when they arrived at a whitewashed row house, where Fabian lifted her over the threshold.

"One day, we'll move into a mansion with servants to carry our bags. But for now, I'll do everything." He set her down, took her hand, and quickly bowed. "*A su servicio, Señora Dominguez.*"

"*Muy amable, Señor Dominguez.*"

Angelina set down the flowers, and Fabian picked them up. He poured some water into a glass, placed the small bouquet inside, and set them in the center of the table.

"Our first beautiful decoration," said Fabian.

"You know they are going to die soon."

Fabian smiled. "But their memory will live forever, my wonderful wife."

Angelina beamed at her new husband and the gallant way that he addressed her. She then gazed around their small, three-room, furnished home with wonder. She tested the parlor's overstuffed chair, stepped into the kitchen, opened a few drawers and cupboards, and then carefully placed her new paperclip in the far corner of a drawer for safekeeping.

She turned around, took in her new home, and saw her husband in their bedroom's doorway. Angelina had only the vaguest idea of what to expect. Italian mothers never spoke about such things with their daughters, and after her mother died, her elderly neighbor Signora Bertelli filled the role. She had also distanced herself from such a discussion. Angelina had heard only one reference on the subject. *The marriage bed is meant for the fulfillment of God's will, to be fruitful and multiply.*

Fabian reached out, "Come, *mi amor.*" They entered the bedroom. Fabian put his arms around her and held her close. "Señora Dominguez," he whispered. He kissed her again and again with such passion that a fire ignited deep inside Angelina, and she didn't want it to end. He lifted her off her feet and placed her atop the freshly made bed. Love was alive. It had a pulse and blossomed.

"Te amo, Fabian," Angelina whispered the ancient words as the world beyond faded away. Fabian bore his tenderness when he looked into her eyes.

"Te amo, querida." Fabian's voice had a lyrical timbre, and she felt loved.

An ageless incense stretched the depth and breadth of the room, and Angelina inhaled its alluring fragrance. This secret world unfolded and left her wrapped in wonder. She could find no words in any language she knew that did justice to the sense of serenity she had in Fabian's arms.

Somewhere in the recesses of her dream-like state, she heard Fabian's voice, *"Te amo,"* he said again and stroked her cheek. "Always remember, I fell in love with you first." The warmth of his words spilled over her like a warm mist.

Angelina sensed she'd been transported to another world she had never known existed. Although still daylight, she had the sensation of being aroused from a deep sleep.

When Fabian carried her into the house, she was far too nervous to notice her surroundings. Now, as she basked in his arms, she gazed about their little *casita.*

Blue-flowered wallpaper graced the room, a sliver of daylight peeked through the edge of the window shade, and the furnishings, though simple, appeared extraordinary to Angelina.

All the planets had aligned with the earth. It would have been a tragedy never to have known love. She was right to seek it, blessed to find it, and she would hold on to it forever. With her whole being, she believed the words: *Till death do you part.* Still, it seemed a strange thing to mention death when uniting couples in love.

CHAPTER 4

ANGELINA SAT in the grand *galeria* of the Cuesta Rey Cigar Company, where she rolled together the three kinds of tobacco leaves that made up a good cigar. It had only been a week since her marriage. She returned to work elated and wrapped in the belief that from now on, her days were wide and tall and filled with wondrous possibilities. She had a handsome husband, a home, and freedom from her father's unreasonable demands. The light in her life had grown brighter, and her dreams had become a reality.

Carmen rushed into the factory, sat next to Angelina, and smiled. "I'm late, but it was not my fault."

Angelina nodded. "Sometimes, the world keeps spinning, and we can't catch up. I was almost late."

Carmen grinned. "Really? Fabian must be doing something right because you've never been *almost* late. You're almost always early, but never mind all that. I'm dying to know everything. So, is married life as glorious as you look, or is it what my mother says it is?"

Angelina shook her head. "I don't know what your mother said, but my marriage is beautiful." She closed her eyes and sighed. "Fabian showed me a love I never knew existed. The ocean never looked so majestic, and the sky is higher, wider, and bluer than I ever knew."

"And?"

"That's it."

"That's it?" Carmen teased, as if unimpressed. "My mother said she received two rings from my father, a wedding ring and some suffe-ring."

Angelina suppressed her smile as she rolled the last leaf on a cigar, trimmed the end, and placed it in a humidor. She hummed as she selected three more grades of tobacco leaves for her next cigar.

Carmen sifted through the piles of tobacco leaves, made her selection and expertly rolled the product that famously dubbed Ybor City, the Cigar Capital of the World.

"Well," said Carmen. "You make marriage sound so romantic, unlike my mother. I'm so happy you found love again. I want to feel like you do one day."

"I know you will. What is it that your mother told you?"

"She explained it like this. It starts with both sides equal in the give-and-take department. Then one day, there's give on one side more than on the other; a bit later, the two sides try to sneak an extra *take*. After that and from then on, it's give, give, and give, on one side—almost always the wife's side—and the other side takes, takes, and overtakes. It goes on until give and take pulls out their weapons and goes to war."

"With that description, no woman will ever want to take a chance and get married."

"My point exactly."

The floorboards quivered. Heavy footsteps grew louder, crossing the wooden planked floor. Lopez, the new supervisor with the scruffy mustache, headed toward Angelina.

"Angelina Pirrello?" His voice grated on everyone's nerves.

It seemed ridiculous to hire outsiders to oversee cigar makers. Cigar factories were quiet, and this man shouted as if he worked in a noisy machine-driven factory. Far more offensive, he had no respect for the product they produced. How can anyone trust a man who smokes a pipe in a cigar factory?

"I'm married now. My last name is Dominguez."

"Since when do women change the name they were born with when they marry?"

"This is how we do it in America."

Lopez rolled his eyes. "All right then, Señora Dominguez." He spoke as if his energy might evaporate. "A man is waiting to talk to you outside. Take your break now and go see him."

No one had ever sought her at work. "A man? What man?"

"He said his name was… I don't know, Pedro, Paolo…."

Angelina wrinkled her brow. "I don't know a Pedro or a Paolo." *How hard is it to remember one name?* "What does he look like?"

"Older and speaks with an accent, like someone who just got off the boat."

She stood up. "What kind of accent? A boat from where?"

"Maybe Italian."

"Pasquale?"

The man nodded. "That's it."

Angelina could not contain her delight. She even grinned at this annoying man with the problematic memory. "Carmen, my uncle's outside!"

"Is that the uncle that makes you laugh? Your dad's older brother?"

"Yes. That's him." Overjoyed at seeing her uncle, Angelina put down her half-rolled cigar, rushed across the room, down the stairs, and pushed open the building's heavy wooden door. Under a large tree near the entrance stood her Zio Pasquale. He waved, and his endearing voice greeted her.

"Angelina, I think you gotta still work at Cuesta Rey, so for sure, I come to see you!"

Angelina lost no time. She threw her arms around her uncle. "Yes, yes. I still work here. Oh, Zio, you have made me so happy. I've missed you and everyone so much."

"And we miss you too much, too. I wanna be sure you okay and tell you everybody love you, even you Papa."

A great sigh of relief escaped Angelina. "Did he say that, Zio?"

Pasquale kissed her cheek. "You Papa no like anybody to know how much he miss you."

Angelina sobered. "Sometimes, Zio, there are people we can love up close and some we have to love from a distance, but every night I pray for everyone, especially Papa." What more could she do?

Pasquale had a tender heart, and he understood such things.

"How's my sister, Lily, and all my brothers? How's your son?"

"Everybody is for sure okay, but nobody like that they no see you. Pasqualino is a okay, too. He learn to swim and he go to school every day. He is a so smart."

Angelina smiled as she remembered the day her uncle adopted a homeless Chinese boy and gave him an Italian name to make him feel we were his family. "I miss all of you so much, but I fear Papa."

"I work in Key West, but I no like I no see everybody."

"Please tell everyone how much I miss them, and I promise I will come and give them a big hug and kiss, but not yet. It's too soon. Papa wouldn't like it."

Pasquale gave her arm a reassuring squeeze as she

spoke. "Don't go away too long. A family is always a family, Angelina. Maybe you Papa no so happy, and maybe that make you no so happy. Why you no go to see him?"

Angelina imagined the angry scene. "I know his temper. It's too soon and will end even worse right now. I left in the middle of the night to escape his control. He will not forgive that, or that I'm married, or that my husband is Cuban and not Italian. It's not the time to find out what he'll do or say. I'm happy in my marriage, and I don't want that to change."

Without hesitation, he threw his arms around Angelina and kissed her again. "I so happy you find someone you love, Angelina. It's more special he love you, too."

"You and Papa are brothers and you're so different."

"Sometime Domenico, he getta mad, and he forget he love you so much, but one day, everything will be happy again."

"I wish I could believe that." Her uncle's tender expression, the softness in his brown eyes, and the way he raised his shoulders dispelled some of her sadness, but the wound had lodged deeply.

Pasquale tapped his forehead, the Italian hand gesture to pay special attention. "I tell you a story."

She knew her uncle well enough. He told stories as his gentle way of trying to help.

"We have a *paisano* Luigi who live in our village. One day, Luigi he see a wolf in the mountains. He run so fast to get away, he fall down, and he get cut and scratched and you can see blood. Luigi run to the piazza and he tell everybody what happen, but no one say too much. They said, 'It's okay, Luigi. You gonna be fine.' Luigi can no believe nobody believe him. Then the winter come. It'sa so cold, everybody wanna stay inside. So, they sit'a by the fire and talk and talk, and pretty soon, they talk about what Luigi say happen to him. They all see Luigi have cuts, scratches, blood, and he look nervous."

Pasquale's accent only flirted with the English language. Yet, it somehow emphasized the moral of his stories.

"You no believe, Angelina, all winter, they tell the story of what'a happen to Luigi. Now, they say, Luigi saw the wolf, the wolf he jump on Luigi, but he no just fight the wolf with his two hands, Luigi choke the wolf to death. That is a why he come back to the village all cut up."

Angelina smiled. She hadn't heard this story but expected its happy ending.

"In the spring, when everybody come out to go work in the field and so happy to see Luigi. Everybody wanna shake his hand. Luigi, he so surprised. And that's how Luigi Franciamore, he become the mayor of Santo Stefano Quisquina."

No matter the subject, Pasquale could make Angelina laugh. "I love you, Zio Pasquale, but what is the likeness between Luigi and me?"

"You papa no wanna believe when you tell him the truth. Nobody wanna believe Luigi when he tell everybody the truth. Everybody believe what they wanna believe. You marry and you happy and Luigi is the mayor. It no matter who believe what. Something good happen from something bad."

Angelina hugged her uncle. "I hope you're right, and Papa will one day see he gave me no choice."

"Angelina, you love someone. That's a good." He wore his usual smile.

Angelina had no desire to resume the battle. Even after running from her father and his control, his dark shadow lingered with uncertainty.

CHAPTER 5

ANGELINA DREAMT OF HER FAMILY, the store, and everything that surrounded it. Still, in that haze between awake and asleep, she knew it couldn't be real. The DiLeto's dog would be barking at the Castellano's crowing rooster and lacked the clanging sounds of morning trains. Her siblings weren't chattering, and the aroma of her father's cooking had not filled her lungs and permeated throughout the house.

She blinked away the remnants of her dream, looked around the room, and sighed. She missed her old life. Her world had now recalibrated again.

"I'll see you later today, *mi amor,*" Fabian blew her a kiss. "I love you."

"I hope so."

Angelina rose, dressed, pulled open the curtains, and looked out. The sun had decided to take a nap. She grabbed her shawl, and just in case, an umbrella and left the house.

Sacred Heart cast an imposing shadow on the sidewalk as she turned the corner. She paused to admire the majestic, multi-colored Rosetta window designed to catch the morning and afternoon arc of the sun and inspire parishioners.

In need of spiritual guidance, she climbed the few steps to the entrance and opened the heavily carved door with symbols of Alpha and Omega, a church's way to remind parishioners that God is the beginning and the end of all creation. She dipped her hand in holy water at the entrance and blessed herself again.

The pews were almost empty except for an older couple seated at the back. Angelina walked toward the altar, genuflected, blessed herself, and entered a pew.

Soft footsteps grew louder and stopped when they reached her. She looked up and saw Father Cavalli. She had no illusions that this would go well. They had never seen eye to eye on any of the sacred doctrines, and with his face red, his posture stiff, something new would erupt.

"Angelina, I hear you are living in sin. Your marriage is completely invalid in the eyes of our precious Lord." The priest made no effort to lower his voice. She glanced at the older couple at the back of the church. They appeared oblivious or disinterested.

Nothing had changed. Once again, Angelina and Father Cavalli were on different sides of the fence. Her mind reeled as she thought of how the priest declared her infant brother stillborn and baptism futile. This priest also prevented the employer of her previous cigar factory, Claudio Garcia, from High Mass at his funeral because he committed suicide. Perhaps, in the last moments, Claudio changed his mind, didn't want to die, and asked the Lord for forgiveness. Father Cavalli should have considered the possibility.

All these things raced through Angelina's mind, and she ignored the comment about her marriage. "Hello, Father. I hope you're doing well."

"The answer to that is *no!* I'm not doing well, and you are not doing well either." He raised his hand to the sky like a lightning rod and pointed to the Heavens as if a reminder in which direction Angelina would be barred from entering. "It is shocking to hear that a good Catholic family has a daughter who defies the sanctity of the Holy Catholic Church. Marriage is a sacrament, a way to receive God's graces. It's a sacred pact, a permanent and unbreakable pledge between God and his children. The church is most explicit on this issue. Marriages outside the church aren't recognized, therefore, invalid. A reckless act that puts you in a state of living in sin."

The priest did not refrain from lowering his voice. Angelina glanced again at the older couple at the back of the church. Perhaps they had some hearing loss.

"Sin?" Angelina considered the torment of hell's eternal flames and could not imagine herself in the same place as assassins, thieves, the unscrupulous, and the like. She simply married at the courthouse, which is perfectly legal in Ybor City, Florida, United States of America.

"I understand your desire to save me, Father Cavalli, and I will tell my husband that if we expect to go to heaven and live the rest of our lives together, we must marry in the church."

The priest exhaled. "It's quite necessary." He turned away and then turned back to face her again. "And all your children are to be baptized and raised in the Holy Catholic Church. You have known all your life; it is my sacred duty to see that our parishioners make their way through the gates of Heaven."

Angelina believed in the church and did not want to contradict its doctrine, but she did not see the urgency since she had no children, which brought up another question. "How did you know I had married?"

"You are not married, and that is my point. Ybor City's a small world, and God sees everything and is everywhere."

Angelina considered it unlikely God told Father Cavalli she had married at the courthouse.

Although not the best place to stretch the truth, but sometimes things are necessary. "It's always so wonderful to see you, Father." She tried to look contrite. "But I have to get back."

"I expect to see you married shortly into God's good grace."

Angelina nodded, took a few steps back, and knelt before the altar as she made the sign of the cross. "Goodbye, Father Cavalli." Then she hurried out, with the priest's voice trailing behind her.

"Remember what I've said! You are not married in the eyes of the church, Angelina Pirrello—more important, in the eyes of God."

The priest made his point. She remained unmarried.

Angelina hurried along the sidewalk, lost in her thoughts. She loved the Lord and had nothing against a church wedding, but in her case, she saw no other solution, especially since her father and Father Cavalli had conspired to arrange her marriage to Rizzo, the baker.

A disaster would have erupted if she had contacted the priest to marry her to Fabian. He would have informed her father. There would have been a terrible scene at the church. She shook the troubled thought from her head. On the other hand, it also seemed highly unlikely that couples married by the Justice of the Peace went to Hell or Moses would have added it to his list of dos and dont's.

Angelina gazed at those walking along the avenue. Most in Ybor City were Catholic, atheists, or something in between. Either way, everyone uttered His name in high regard. *God bless,* they said over their meals. *God willing,* they said in the hope of something good. When in fear, they said, *God forbid,* and in court, with one hand on the Bible, they said, *so help me God.*

When Fabian came home, Angelina told him about her encounter with the priest. "How do you feel about this?"

"Our marriage is legal, binding, and recorded. How is that illegitimate or sinful? Tell Father Cavalli that when the police arrive at our home to arrest us, we'll let him know, and he can come to the jail and marry us."

Angelina visualized the scene and giggled. "The priest and I have never agreed on anything, so I'm sure he thought this was my chance for salvation."

Fabian put his arms around her. "Don't worry. I'm not going to let the devil take you."

Angelina pushed him back and laughed. "You are not Mr. Innocent. I didn't get married to myself. If I'm living in sin, then so are you."

"Well, we'd either better start preparing for an unpleasant hereafter or we'd better get married again in church," said Fabian.

"I pick the second option."

"Then that's what we'll do."

"When?"

"For sure, before we die—and not a moment later." He winked, blew her a kiss, and slipped out the back door to work in the garden.

ANGELINA SPENT the afternoon shopping among pushcart vendors and talking with neighbors. She loved the busy marketplace, merchants shouting in various languages, each selling household goods to housewives and claiming to have the best guavas, mangos, and black beans. Lively energy infused the air. People from all stations came with empty bags and left with full ones on their arms or balanced them on their heads.

As Angelina made her way through the crowd, she caught a glimpse of a man with a cane coming out of the Alvarez Cigar Factory and immediately recognized him.

"Señor Don Carlos Madrid!" Angelina called out his full name several times above the street noise until he turned around. It had been so long since she'd seen her old friend.

"Señorita, Angelina Pirrello!" He waved and appeared genuinely happy to run into her. "It's been such a long time, like water vanishing in the sand, with no way to catch it again."

Don Carlos leaned on a walking stick, something he hadn't needed the last time she saw him. He took off his hat. His salt and pepper hair had turned to silver. His eyes, always clear, intense, and focused, now appeared strained.

He slipped his book under his left arm and reached out to shake hands with Angelina. "As always, I carry something to read. It would seem uncivilized for a man who spent a lifetime reading to thousands of people to walk around empty-handed. It also reminds people who I was once."

He lifted his walking stick and pointed to the entrance of Alvarez Cigar Factory. "It's where I worked before the Garcia-Marcos's Cigar Factory where I met you. We can sit and visit there for a bit. They have a new reader who always asks to borrow one of my classics. I have enough to fill a small library." He appeared pleased. "Ah, but those were the days when I was *el lector*. Weren't they, Angelina?"

"Yes. Oh, yes!" Angelina answered quickly, sensing he lived amid a mist of memories. "I remember you sitting high on the podium in a room filled with rows of anxious cigar makers. You raised your hand as if conducting music to emphasize the rhythm of the author's words. Those in the audience would go home and retell the stories over dinner. Their wives and children would discuss it the next day. And so it went. Some would even bring their lunch and sit outside the open windows to hear your stories." More famous and respected than most *lectors*, Don Carlos Madrid had a reputation as a man of countless tales and unsurpassed wisdom.

"I remember every book you read and everything you taught me. I wouldn't change one moment of it." Angelina had known him a long time and might have called him by his first name, but with his popularity in the city, that might others might take as a lack of respect, and nothing could be further from the truth.

Although he had suffered lost his purpose, which saddened her, he seemed pleased by her answer.

They walked inside the factory, and he waved through the glass-paneled office at the man seated at the front desk. He then led Angelina to a small reception room, where he set down the book he carried on a small table. A display of several early photographs of the factory and the present day hung on the wall. Don Carlos held out a chair for Angelina and then took a seat. He moved slowly, more carefully now.

"I feel more at home in a cigar factory with a book than anywhere else. I've lived vicariously through stories, traveling worldwide, and in many centuries. I've known love, war, betrayal, mystery, heartbreak, and joy." He sighed. "I enjoyed our Saturdays in the park for your lessons on great literature."

"I couldn't wait for Saturday to come."

"Aye, yes, I remember you wanted to be a writer. And you can do it. Stories exist everywhere in the past and the present. All it takes is someone like you to write them down."

"I've been keeping notes on my thoughts and experiences."

"Every novel began as a thought or experience, like every bloom started as a tiny seed."

"I wanted to study writing and I was even accepted at a college, but my father never showed me the letter. I found it accidentally, but by then, it was too late. He not bad, but he's disciplined, stern, and not tolerant of women finding a new way to mark the world. He lives in the past."

"It's easy to think of the past as heroic, or pretend it's heroic, or try to seduce us into believing it's heroic." Don Carlos' words were never frivolous. "But clinging to something long ago shuts the door on today. But tell me, Angelina, how have you been?"

The short question had a long, entangled spider's web of an answer with no reason to elaborate. "I've been married to Fabian Dominguez for almost three months."

"Congratulations! My best wishes. I must remember to call you *Señora!*"

"Thank you." A moment lapsed with only the sound of horses' hoofs and carriage wheels seeping through the open window.

"By his name, I see he's not the Italian your father had insisted you marry. You are indeed an independent thinker." Don Carlos pushed his glasses up the bridge of his nose before he met her eyes. "Most young women these days would have obediently followed their father's order and married the man he selected, but you've carved your path."

"It wasn't bravery, but fear of being trapped in a loveless marriage. My father never understood that." The subject caused her voice to quiver.

El lector rubbed his mustache. "Each day brings a new chance for forgiveness. It's a lot of hard work to remain angry. Most people cannot sustain it."

Angelina shook her head. "My father is not like most people."

"You have conviction and hold to your principles regardless of cost, much like your father, I see."

Angelina preferred to believe any similarity between her and her father rested in the color of hair and eyes, not temperament.

Don Carlos exhaled a heavy sigh. "The only family that does not quarrel is a family of one. While it makes for a more tranquil life, it also has disagreeable moments."

"I honestly don't know what to do now."

El lector held a thoughtful expression. She could see it in his eyes.

"Yes. That day will come. I once read a story at the factory written over three hundred years ago. It's about an ancient warrior who led his men across the sea into battle. When their ships landed, he saw they were greatly outnumbered and ordered his men to disembark and then set fire to their ships. Desperate and with no way to return, the men's lives depended on winning the battle they'd come to fight and take command of their enemy's ships or perish. They fought long and hard, and won."

Angelina didn't respond right away. Instead, she allowed the story to simmer inside her. "So, the moral is to fight like your life depends on it."

"Like the ancient warriors, you burned down your ship when you left your father's home."

"What if there's no other ship to return to?"

"Life has taught me there's always a way. You'll find the path back to your father's heart."

Angelina clenched her hands. Her father had two traits, proud and unyielding.

CHAPTER 6

ANGELINA CAUGHT the last trolley and gazed out at the street. It was unusual to see out so clearly, as though the window had remained open. Someone had finally washed the layers of smudges off the glass.

She took in the view and saw a young couple walking together and laughing. A yearning ignited inside her. Over the past two months, she'd sensed a slight distance between her and Fabian. Although hardly noticeable, like not always kissing her goodbye or not always greeting her with his usual broad smile when he came home. Maybe he had encountered trouble at work or with someone and didn't want to talk about it. Perhaps he didn't feel well. He kept a lot inside, like withholding what had happened to his parents and brother. Angelina quickly rid herself of any negative thoughts. She was grateful for so much more.

She continued to look out the window and noticed how people passed each other in the street without a smile. Unlike Zio Pasquale's stories about his Italian village. *Everybody say hello to everybody, because everybody know somebody who know somebody.* Angelina could hear his voice in her head and smiled. She missed her uncle, but this wasn't a small village in Sicily. America had an unprecedented influx of immigrants arriving daily. Most couldn't speak English and were probably lonely, even in a crowd.

As the trolley pulsated down the street, Angelina persisted in surveying those strolling along the avenue. She observed how many men enjoyed smoking cigars, and unlike the upper part of town, how few women wore hats. Perhaps because some newly arrived women still balanced their bundles on their heads.

A tall, young man with red hair caught her attention. She focused on his familiar gait until astonished. Angelina jumped up from her seat while the trolley kept moving, then fell back down as it jolted. It had to be Rolando. He turned his head, and in that fraction of a second, she saw his face. It was him.

Angelina quickly forced the window open.

"Rolando!" she shouted. "Rolando!" she called again, but the clanging of metal wheels, the honking of an automobile horn, and the growing distance between him and the moving trolley masked her voice.

"Sixth Street!" The conductor cried out.

A line of passengers ready to exit had already formed. Angelina stood impatiently, waiting her turn. As soon as she darted off, she hurried across the street and searched in every direction for him. Had he turned a corner, entered a store, or caught a ride? She moved as quickly as she could and continued searching, even looking in stores, until it became apparent, he had once again vanished.

She had reacted without thinking. If it had been Rolando, and he cared so much for her as he had professed, why had he disappeared in the first place? Even after meeting Fabian, she had waited. Why had he never returned, sent word that he never planned to return, or that he still cared, or didn't? She took in an exasperated breath.

All the nights of crying and praying. All the beautiful memories of their growing love followed by the tormented heartbreak of searching for answers. Months grew more months. All those times, she had sat at home across from the train terminal, gazing out the window at passengers and searching for his familiar figure over all the rest. Would he step off the train? Was he alive, dead, or injured? Did he lose his memory? Did he love someone else? The memory returned encased with that same crushing fear and hurt that broke her heart.

Angelina shook her head, ashamed of herself. She had reacted without thinking. What would it matter now? Whatever he could say to her after so long would have meant so much back then, but like the fragrance of a lovely perfume, the irresistible scent of what had once been between them had dissolved and nothing remained.

CHAPTER 7

FABIAN BROUGHT Angelina flowers every Friday and took her to the Cuban restaurant, where they had eaten on their wedding day. They sat and talked about little things that had become big memories, how he had seen her every day walking to work, how they met at Rosa's wedding, how all the girls gathered around Fabian to get his attention, and she ignored him. Each recalled something different about the events, and they laughed. Now, the concern was what to plant in Fabian's vegetable garden and which tobacco leaves to use, and rolled into the finest cigars.

But there were two subjects that neither touched on. Other than the drinking, Fabian spoke vaguely about how he and his friends spent their time together. Angelina decided if she had to trust him, then he should also trust her.

Since her long-ago experience with the Suffragettes, she had continued to be supportive and drawn to the posters announcing their meetings. Equality for women was a major problem. However, unsure of Fabian's reaction to the movement, she decided not to discuss her feelings—at least not yet.

Saturday came, and Angelina went straight to where she'd seen some picture frames displayed in a store window.

As soon as she entered the store, an older woman in a high-collared green dress with rows of endless buttons greeted her. "May I help you?"

"Oh, yes." Excited, Angelina rushed to explain. "I'm looking for a nice frame to hold my marriage license."

"That's very sweet. It's easy to recognize true love."

For a swift moment, Rolando Aguirre's face flashed before Angelina. He had once said those very words. She dismissed the thought.

Angelina selected the frame with an attractive geometric design and painted gold. She handed it to the salesgirl with her money. "It's not just a piece of paper that sealed my husband and me together. It's that special way he looked into my eyes, like the world had become magnificent. I want to preserve the memory."

"I've never heard anyone put it that way. You must have many remembrances of your lovely wedding."

Angelina nodded. Their wedding had one bride and one groom, with only this one reminder of her big day. How strange, it had not occurred to either of them to at least have stopped at Nuñez Photography.

Thrilled with her purchase, Angelina hurried home, slipped their certificate inside the frame, and stepped back to admire it. Every evening and morning, they would see it and remember their vows. Nothing else on the wall would distract them. *Fabian is going to love it.* She wrapped the frame in newspaper and tied it with string.

When Fabian's key rattled, he stepped inside, and Angelina rushed into his arms. "I'm so happy, Fabian."

"Now, that's the way to greet a husband." He held her tightly and kissed her.

"Sit down. I've been waiting to show you something beautiful."

"I'm already looking at something beautiful."

Fabian's flattery assured her she had found the right man and made the right decision. She handed him her surprise. "Open it."

Fabian thanked her with a kiss and tore off the wrapping. "What have we here?"

"It's our marriage license. I'm hanging it on the wall in our bedroom to remind us of the day we began building our life together."

Fabian held it up and grinned. "It's a work of art, and the frame is nice, too."

Angelina laughed.

"From now on, we'll hang up all our memories. So, we better start looking for a home with more walls," he said.

"And I'll start looking for more frames."

Fabian sat down and pulled her toward him. "Sit on my lap, *esposa,* and I'll tell you about an island in the sun. Forget Sicily. This island is Cuba."

"At least it's closer."

"There were seven of us on the fishing boat. The sea was rough, the clouds dark, it rained, and then I caught *el premio* —a prince among fish—the ultimate ambition of every fisherman worth his bucket of bait."

Angelina's grin widened. The best stories had no proof.

"But my best catch is you." He pressed his lips against Angelina's. She came to believe that love could become perfection—how one is cleansed after confession and blessed after communion.

She embraced her husband. "At last, I have someone to share my dreams. Even my father would have to admit he was wrong about my marrying a man I didn't love."

"Well, as long as that's how you feel, let's not worry about how he feels. Forget your father."

"But he's my father."

"And I'm your husband. It's our turn in life. He'll come around, maybe not today, but one day." He kissed Angelina again. "I have some good news. My mother's sister, my Tia Lourdes is giving us a bureau, and my cousin Bertha's *novio* is helping me bring it home. So I'll be back soon."

"Bertha's boyfriend? Is that Alejandro?"

"That man was last month. This new boyfriend is José Valle. He's waiting for me." Fabian gave her a peck on the cheek, and slipped out the door.

Angelina glanced out the window and watched him walk away. *This is our turn in life*. Fabian's words echoed inside her and she wanted to make the best of it. She looked around her home with a critical eye. Intent on impressing her new husband with her skill for keeping their house tidy, filled a bucket of water to wash the floors and began cleaning out the cabinets.

To her surprise, Angelina found a full bottle of whiskey when she reached the back of a lower cabinet. The last tenant must have left it, so she placed it inside her trash basket. While cleaning, she wondered how much a bottle of whiskey cost. Perhaps the old tenants may return and ask for it back. After much consideration, she pulled it out of the trash, wiped it off, and returned it to the back of the lower cabinet.

Now on her hands and knees, she scrubbed the floor and hummed a funny song Zio Pasquale had taught her. Her confidence surged, and she sang Verdi's Rigoletto as her mother had taught her.

"Hello, inside!" Came a woman's voice.

Angelina jumped. She'd forgotten how close together these narrow *casitas* stood. Someone's complaining about her singing. She dashed to the door. "I'm sorry," she said as she pulled it open.

"You're Sorry? Interesting name, Sorry." Carmen chuckled. "Well, 'Sorry,' I'm Carmen, and this is my cousin standing right before you."

"Carmen!" Angelina's eyes widened, and she hugged her friend. "I forgot you said you lived in this neighborhood. You never said exactly where."

"Well, unlike me, you told me exactly where you live, and as it happens, I decided it's time you had guests."

At last, Angelina had a home where friends could visit without the constant interruptions of children running back and forth, her father calling her to help with something in the store or the endless housework.

"And my name's Ophelia. That's Ophelia spelled with a *ph*, like in Shakespeare, not an *f*, like in Spanish. And that's because my mother fell asleep reading Hamlet and never got to the part where Ophelia commits suicide. So that's where my namesake and I part ways."

"I'm so happy to meet you, Ophelia." Angelina grinned at the strange introduction. "Please, both of you, come in and sit down. So, does your mother read much Shakespeare?"

"Only when she has insomnia."

Angelina giggled. "It's nice to meet someone in your family."

Ophelia stood taller than her cousin, and her eyes were hazel, not the rich brown of Carmen's. But there remained something indisputably familial about the two, like the snappy and quick-witted way they spoke.

"We are here to help you," said Carmen as she stepped through the nonexistent partition into the kitchen, grabbed the broom, and placed it behind the front door.

Ophelia nodded. "That's right. Don't take any chances. If you're unsure of someone you meet, don't talk to them until you consult us. And should someone come to your home and you want them to go, put your broom upside down behind the door, and they'll leave in a hurry."

"I'm not sure how it works, but it never fails," said Carmen. The young women had already taken their seats on the sofa.

"Hey, this is comfortable," said Ophelia as she bounced on the cushion.

"I know. No telling how old it is, but it's broken in just right."

"If only you would have come to all those Saturday night dances, you would have met my cousin Ophelia, long ago. Not to mention, you'd have learned some great salsa moves."

Angelina shuddered, another reminder of how her father controlled her life.

Carmen pointed to her cousin. "And guess what, Señora Angelina? Ophelia with a 'ph' lives right next door to you."

"Next door? Which way?"

"Where the flowers bloom, a swing sits on the porch with two small pillows, and four bricks are missing in the walkway. I live there with my parents and a hussy of a female cat who roams around all night but never produced a single kitten."

"That's because your female cat is a male," said Carmen.

Ophelia opened her eyes wide. "So that's it?"

Once again, Angelina giggled. She had needed a little company to lighten the day. "Then you're not married, Ophelia?"

"As it happens—no. I need someone who is not an anarchist. The men rolling cigars get all fired up, argue, and complain. Anarchists make bad husbands. They're more interested in causes, distracting them from showering their wives and girlfriends with lovely gifts—the way God intended."

Afraid someone might trip, Angelina opened the front door and set out the water bucket she used.

"Next time, we'll help you clean," said Carmen. "By the way, no one around here runs to *la panadería* for bread. Your milk will be delivered on the porch. Get that man of yours to drive a big nail into your doorframe about eye level and the bakery deliveryman will force a fresh loaf of delicious Cuban bread right through the nail each time he comes. Easy, huh?"

Angelina tried to envision a long loaf of Cuban bread impaled between her door jamb and mailbox.

Carmen gazed around the home. "So, do you approve of marriage, after all?"

Angelina beamed. "So far, give and take is even. Fabian is wonderful, but sometimes…." Her expression lost a bit of excitement. "I still think of my father, and I feel sad he never understood my feelings."

"Now that's a mistake," said Carmen.

"That's right," said Ophelia. "Never mix up happy with unhappy, like the centipede and the spider."

Angelina shook her head. "The what?"

"The happy little centipede, minding his own business, took an afternoon walk."

Carmen winked at Angelina. "It's a good story. You'd be surprised how often it comes in handy."

"Please, no interruptions, Carmen." Ophelia cleared her throat and looked up at the ceiling as though trying to regain her focus. "A spider came along and asked the centipede: How do you walk with so many legs? And the centipede answered: It's simple. First, I start with this leg, and he put out a leg. No, no, that's not right. It's the other leg. Yes. No. I mean, I put out this other leg first. No, it can't be that one. And no matter how hard he tried, the centipede could never walk again."

Carmen gave another knowing wink. "See that? I told you

it was a good story. If everything is going well—don't analyze it until it doesn't make sense."

"You're right. I will never question my happiness again." Angelina grinned and glanced over at the kitchen. "I have some *pignolata.* They're Sicilian honey balls. You'll like it."

"Gracias, but we can't stay. Ain't got no time," Carmen said.

"And ain't got no money." Ophelia threw up her hands. "Which is worse."

Angelina already liked her new neighbor. "But you'll insult me if you don't taste them." Angelina knew well the power of old Italian sayings, and this one on how to shame guests into eating had been around for centuries.

"Well, if you insist." Carmen looked over the tray of honey-covered balls stacked like a pyramid, made her selection, and took a bite. "Hmm," she said, licking honey off her lips.

"Don't mind if I do," said Ophelia eyeing the doughy delights. "The best thing about living in Ybor City is the world of immigrants meets here, and they brought their recipes."

Ophelia bit off a corner of the delicacy, closing her eyes and took another bite, and then another. "I love honey. So nice of God to invent bees." She then fumbled around in the deep pocket of her skirt and pulled out a long-necked bottle with a tint of emerald green liquid. "We are here on a mission. My mother wants you to have this."

Angelina accepted the bottle with an appreciative smile. "That's very nice of your mother. What's it for?"

"Ay, *chica*," said Carmen. "'What's it for?' How can you say you were born in Florida and don't recognize Florida Water? It's like not realizing we have the Gulf of Mexico, the Atlantic Ocean, or alligators."

Ophelia pointed to the bottle. "What you have in your

hands is a genuine bottle of Florida Water straight from Ponce de Leon's Fountain of Youth! We use it for everything but drinking." Her new neighbor looked around the little *casita*. "Let's see. We need to find a special place to put it, so anyone who enters will know that you know about its power."

Angelina placed it on the kitchen table and glanced back at Ophelia, who shook her head. She tried a few other spots and then set it on the small coffee table in front of the sofa. Carmen's cousin smiled and nodded.

"That's right," said Carmen. "Florida Water's the answer to a prayer, a gift from Greek gods, a winning *bolita* ticket!"

Angelina considered the only plausible explanation. Their Florida Water had become a superstitious concoction. Strangely, her old Italian neighbor, Signora Bertelli, known for her proficiency in spells and *malocchio* the evil eye, had never spoken of its merits.

"Sprinkle it in every corner of your house," said Ophelia. "It rids the house of the evil the last tenants forgot to take with them. Although we have nothing to report, protecting yourself against curses and bad omens never hurts. Also, this bottle has the power to bring you good luck. If you get sick, rub it all over yourself. Pour it on a cloth and place it on your forehead when you have a fever. Inhale it if you need to be revived and wear it as a perfume. It refreshes on hot, sticky nights and cools your skin."

"And as an added benefit, it repels insects!" said Carmen.

"That's a fact," said Ophelia.

This type of declaration sounded somewhat familiar to Angelina. She'd add Florida Water to Signora Bertelli's long list of Sicilian repellents of bad luck. "Did you say the last tenants were evil?"

Ophelia shrugged. "Maybe yes, maybe no. Who knows what people do behind closed doors?"

Angelina held up her gift and stared through the clear glass with renewed interest. "The Fountain of Youth, huh?" She grinned. "I thought Ponce returned to Spain wiser, with gray hair and wrinkles."

"That depends on who's telling the story." Carmen seized the bottle from Angelina and twisted open the lid. "Smell it. It's made with lavender, rose petals, and cinnamon." She put some behind her ears. "Splash yourself, your bed, and use it in bathwater. It even attracts men, but you already have a man, so that's not your problem, right?"

"By the way," said Ophelia. "Because you've only recently moved into this neighborhood, here's some valuable advice: look out for Lupe Rios, who lives around the corner. She borrows everything and returns nothing. I say get rid of her right away."

"And how do you suggest I do that?"

Carmen narrowed her eyes. "Tomorrow, say hello, and when she asks to borrow a little money, which she will, say yes."

Ophelia nodded. "That's true, but tell her you need it back next week. From that day on, you'll never see her again. She'll avoid you at every corner. That's a blessing."

"Amen!" said Carmen, wiping the pastry's honey off her fingers. "It's worth the price, a solid investment—like buying an insurance policy!"

"That's very clever."

"No sense in learning things the hard way," said Carmen as she went to the window and pointed. "You see that house with the blue porch? That's Elvia's house. The woman's jealous of everyone. At weddings, she's jealous of the bride. At baptisms, she's jealous of the baby, and at funerals, the dead roll over in their caskets when they hear her coming. You have no time for her."

Carmen hooked her arm in Ophelia's and pulled her

toward the door. "In this neighborhood, it's much easier to make friends than to get rid of them." Carmen nodded.

"Gotta go now," said Ophelia.

"Wait. Here's a plate of *pignolata* to take with you. Give some to your mother, Ophelia. My father always taught us never to return an empty plate. Thank your mother for the Florida Water."

Carmen hugged Angelina. "Guess what, Ophelia? Angelina used to be one of the Italians on the other side of town, and now she's converted to Cuban."

Ophelia shook her head. "Who could have imagined such a thing? Like changing sides in the middle of a war."

The two were gone as quickly as they'd arrived. Angelina held up the mystical Florida Water and inspected it. *It rids the house of evil,* Ophelia had said.

CHAPTER 8

ANGELINA GLANCED AT THE TIME. It had been an hour since Carmen and her cousin left. She smiled, thinking of the funny ways they described the neighborhood. Before Fabian arrived, she stole a moment, reached for her book of Shakespeare's Works, and turned to *A Midsummer Night's Dream.* She had an affinity for the story. Hermia loves Lysander and must resist her father, who has arranged her marriage to Demetrius. This had problematic for girls throughout the ages.

"Mi vida!" Fabian's voice drifted from the front door. "Come say hello to José Valle. He's been helping me move this pirate treasure we've been given—Tia Lourdes' bureau."

Angelina set down the book, rose quickly, and rushed to greet her husband and his friend. Fabian entered, accompanied by a tall, bearded man with weathered skin, though she suspected he could not be much older than Fabian's twenty-two years. The smell of liquor on José caused her to step back instead of forward to greet him.

"Welcome, José. It's nice of you to help us. *Muy amable.*"

To show her appreciation, Angelina reached out to shake his hand. Everything about José reflected a harsh life, and when he gripped his hand around hers, his grasp could crush bones. *Yet, did he know his strength? He must be a wrestler.* Perhaps she exaggerated, but she could not rule out the possibility.

Angelina rubbed the numbness from her hand and turned to her husband. But Fabian's attention was on retrieving the drawers he'd pulled out to lighten the chest's weight.

"Where do you want us to put this magnificent example of fine furniture, *mi amor?*" he said with his back to her.

Angelina looked over the carved mahogany with its rows of drawers, and the two cabinet doors on the upper half with figures of ornate vases filled with flowers. She had to agree this gentlemen's wardrobe gave an impressive refinement to the room—to any room. "How could your aunt bear to part with it?"

Fabian turned around. "She told us the first to marry would get it."

Angelina giggled. "So, did you marry me to beat the others to it?"

"To keep me warm at night."

"Oh, too bad. We don't live in Alaska." She smiled, entered the bedroom, and pointed to the far wall. "I think over there is best. No. It'll be hidden. This furniture is the most beautiful thing we have. Let's put it in the parlor where everyone can see it."

"Did you hear that, José? My little wife has incredible taste in furniture and men."

José laughed. "If she had good taste in men, she would have married me instead."

Uncomfortable with the remark, Angelina could not think of a proper way to respond, so she smiled.

José pulled out a handkerchief and blotted the sweat from his forehead before they moved the large piece. When they set it down, the bureau claimed its spot as if it had always been there, like a cat curled upon its cushion.

Angelina thanked them both but couldn't help noticing José once again. He couldn't be a cigar maker. They were artisans and always appeared distinguished with a white shirt and tie. José looked more like an unmade bed. Her father would never have brought home a man so clearly drunk and exposed him to the family, but she appreciated his efforts. Still, he must be able to control his liquor or he couldn't have helped carry in the large piece of furniture.

"Would you like something to eat, Señor Valle? Perhaps I can make you an Italian or Cuban sandwich or some soup."

He looked at her as though trying to decide, and shook his head. *"No, gracias."*

Fabian patted him on the back and thanked him. José moved to leave, but stumbled when he reached for the door. Her husband helped steady him.

Angelina noticed the edge of a newspaper inside the man's shirt. She could not imagine a reason to stuff a newspaper beneath a shirt. So when he left, she waited for an explanation about the strange man. But Fabian stood before the tall bureau and said, "Well, what do you think? It's beautiful, no?"

"It's a treasure, and I'll take special care to keep it that way." Angelina had never had an angry word with Fabian, so she eased into her question. "Why did José have a newspaper underneath his shirt?"

"It's a habit. I observed it in my childhood. Newspapers keep people warm when they're cold and poor."

"But the weather's mild."

"As I said, it's a habit."

"What about his bloodshot eyes, swaying, and the smell of liquor?"

"That's another habit. But why waste our time talking about José?" Fabian looked more interested in the bureau than José.

She had to agree. José had the problem, not Fabian.

Her husband pulled her into his arms, unanswered questions washed away.

THE NEXT DAY, Angelina arose early. She busied herself in the kitchen and baked a tray of desserts. Fabian entered the kitchen.

"What's this?" he asked, reaching for the tray.

Angelina batted his hand away. "These are for your Tia Lourdes as a thank you for the beautiful wardrobe. We could leave together and visit her for a bit."

"For you, anything." Fabian went to the door and held it open.

On the way, Fabian sang a lively Cuban song as they walked to Lourdes' home. He only paused when he saw someone he knew and shouted a greeting. "Everyone has a white home on this block except Tia Lourdes. She had us paint hers bright yellow, so that no one would miss it." Fabian knocked on his aunt's door, imitating the drumming rhythm of bongos.

The door opened, and a short-stature, gray-haired Lourdes greeted them with a brilliant smile. *"Bien venidos, niños."*

Fabian kissed his aunt and then pulled Angelina closer. "Here she is. The one that stole my heart, Angelina Pirrello Dominguez."

"Come in, Angelina. Finally, we meet!"

Angelina grinned at her new aunt. They hugged, and she appreciated the welcome. "Here, I brought you some Italian pastry. I hope you like it. It's very fresh; I made it this morning. We call them *cannoli.* I added some crushed roasted almonds and some chocolate."

"*Gracias, niña.* I can see you will be a wonderful wife to my nephew. Everyone in this family loves pastry. Please, sit down. *Mi casa es su casa.*"

Angelina liked the warm feel of the room, like the center of many happy gatherings. She admired the small collections of keepsakes, tintypes, and family photographs.

Lourdes turned to Fabian. "*Hijo,* please, run next door and help Ignacio pull his wagon out of the street. It's piled high with lumber, missing a wheel, and sitting in front of my house. It's tilted and might fall on someone."

Fabian laughed. "I noticed that when we arrived; but thought it was an ugly decoration."

"Yes, a decoration waiting to bury someone under a pile of lumber."

Fabian smiled and headed for the door.

Lourdes placed the plate of cannoli on the kitchen table and turned to Angelina. "You are certainly a lucky girl to have captured my nephew. He is so handsome, isn't he? So many women have been after him for so long, sending him gifts and even coming to my home to tell me they would be devoted to him. A lot of hearts will break when word gets out he has married. But I have every faith that you will be dedicated to his happiness, Angelina, and be a good, little wife."

Dedicated to his happiness? Good little wife? That phrases had an awkward ring to it. Surely, Tia Lourdes didn't mean it was subservient. The statement floated around in Angelina's mind, with no comfortable place to settle.

"It's always wonderful when the couple becomes equal partners. Fabian is a treasure. We are so much in love and committed to each other's happiness." Angelina folded her hands in her lap and smiled warmly. "He is even very supportive of me furthering my education."

The woman ignored Angelina's last comment and pointed to a framed picture. "This is our Fabian when he first came to live with us. Everyone is smiling in the picture but him. See the full head of hair he had? Some thought him a girl, and he was a real *flaco*, so skinny and refused to eat much. His eyes were always red from crying. You can see the difference between him and my boys, who would never pass up a meal." She then reached for another picture placed in a frame and sat prominently on the coffee table.

"See the difference after only living with us for a year? He put some weight on those little bones, has a beautiful smile, and is so happy. If only my sister could see him now. She would be so proud."

"He's fortunate to have you and your family to love him."

"And we do. We are all very protective of Fabian, as I'm sure you'll become. After all, men are heads of the household as God is head of the church." Angelina realized Tia Lourdes gave her the *golden rule.*

Without a mother, Angelina wanted nothing more than to be close to Tia Lourdes. Still, many older women had grown accustomed to and accepted the misconception that everything should remain the way it had been in bygone times, all the way back to cave dwellers dragging women by their hair—allegedly.

Angelina needed to clarify this, yet appear pleasant while not offending her new relative. "Oh, Tia Lourdes, have you read the newspapers lately? It's so exciting. The Suffragettes are gaining more and more support every day. I feel one day soon women will have the right to vote."

Tia Lourdes waved her hand dismissively. "A hopeless cause. There is so much to do in the home with washing, cooking, cleaning, and caring for children—even when they grow up; they need our help and support. We already have a full-time job. We need our men to run the country and the world."

Angelina had to fight through the clutter of Lourdes' words, but the woman had not finished.

"Men rule the house," Fabian's aunt continued. "We women must be realistic and follow our lot in life. That's what creates a happy household."

Angelina kept herself calm. Taught all her life to respect her elders, she hesitated. But this could come back and snap at her if she didn't make her point.

"I believe women are equal to men. The best marriages are the ones where both respect each other. We share our dreams, and it's been mine to attend college one day. Fabian says if I still feel that way in another year, he thinks I should do it."

The woman shook her head. "I fear you are misguided, *querida.* Women have a place in the home, and men have theirs outside from the very beginning of time. How will it look if you are far more educated than your husband? You will disrespect him, bring him shame. It's the way it's supposed to be, from the time of Adam."

Angelina tried to keep her smile. "Don't you wonder, Tia Lourdes, if Adam was smarter, more masterful than Eve, and more obedient to the Lord, then why didn't he refuse the apple when Eve offered it to him?"

"Well, maybe he trusted her."

"Or maybe he saw her as his equal, and that's why he took a bite."

"Oh, Angelina, Angelina." The woman looked at her with such sympathy. "Fabian told me you lost your mother. I'm so sorry. I'm certain she would have explained the way things are to you. We are a delicate race and destined to be protected by our men. I'm sorry, but Paradise lost is Eve's fault."

Angelina choked on her simmering anger. To begin with, her mother never believed women were inferior to men and pushed her daughter to reach every height academically and otherwise.

Angelina met Lourdes' look of unwarranted sympathy. She had escaped the control of a dominating father and was unwilling to submit to another controlling family member.

"You know, Tia Lourdes, I think God was angry with Adam for pointing his finger at Eve, so he marked men for all eternity as a reminder to the women not to believe everything men say."

"What are you talking about? Men are not marked." Lourdes' comment came quicker than before and more ruffled.

"Perhaps you never noticed, but I have four brothers, and the moment they stop being sweet little boys and start reasoning for themselves, God marks all their throats with an *Adam's Apple* for the lie Adam spoke about Eve. Appropriately named, don't you think? I mean, Adam had the choice to be chivalrous and take full responsibility, but instead, like a coward, he pointed his finger at Eve."

Fabian's aunt scrunched up her nose, but before she could answer, the door opened, and Fabian burst inside. "Well, ladies, now that you've made your acquaintances, let's celebrate with the pastries Angelina made. She's a wonderful cook and always has something special for me."

Tia Lourdes turned to Angelina, "Ah, so you bake delicious pastries and are a wonderful cook for my nephew." The woman grinned. "You almost had me fooled, Angelina. I thought you were serious for a moment. Adam's apple, *por Dios.*"

She laughed out loud and pinched Angelina's cheek as though she had made her point with her new niece.

Angelina crossed her arms. Tia Lourdes sought to control her behavior, but if she had resisted her father, she had no intention of allowing Fabian's aunt to do the same.

CHAPTER 9

Hours had passed since the night deepened into waves of velvet black and scattered its tranquility on those who dream. Once again, Angelina had awoken to Fabian's stirring in bed. Even in his sleep, he placed his hands over his ears, reliving the torment of the sugarcane fields.

Angelina nudged him. "Fabian, wake up," she spoke softly to lure him gently from the terror of his nightmare. "Fabian, it's only a dream."

He moaned, and the sounds grew louder until Angelina had to raise her voice and shake him. "Please, wake up."

Fabian's chest heaved. His breathing became labored, heavy, and erratic. Finally, he opened his eyes and looked around the shadows of the darkened room in confusion.

"Are you alright?"

Seemingly still readjusting, he didn't answer.

"It's that nightmare again about the sugarcane fields, right?"

He ran his fingers through his hair and, for a moment, did not answer. He then fumbled for the kerosene lamp, lit it, and shook his head. "It's always there, waiting to haunt me, like a demon in the dark. How am I supposed to fight a nightmare? There's no way to stop it." Fabian made a fist, socked his pillow, got out of bed, and began pacing.

"Please come back and try to rest. We have to work tomorrow. You'll be so tired."

"It's not that simple." He rose from the bedroom, took the lighted lamp, and entered the kitchen. Angelina could not imagine how to fight the demons of the dark. Dreams were a product of a mysterious world where they remained untouched and undisturbed throughout the millenniums.

Fabian made little trinkets of sounds in the kitchen as the night wore thin. Once again, Angelina grew sleepy and closed her eyes. She had been vaguely aware that her husband had returned to their bed until the scent of liquor seized the room. After that, she couldn't sleep.

ANGELINA HAD long since disciplined herself to give most of her earnings to her father to help with the family. With Fabian, they agreed to join their funds, pay their bills, and take a reasonable amount for each of them to spend. The rumor about a union strike percolated through every cigar factory. Angelina took it as a warning to prepare.

Fabian entrusted her with establishing a saving for their future and a bit for her college. This money she hid behind Tia Lourdes' bureau, rolled up in her stockings, under the sink, or wherever she thought safe, until her bi-weekly trip to the bank.

"You change your hiding place every week," said Fabian with a smile.

"But I'll tell you where it is. The union could call a strike at any time. So it's a warning to save."

"There's nothing to worry about. With you saving and me

buying *bolita* tickets from Bolita Bernardo, I'll win a fortune soon, and we'll retire."

"Just in case, let's keep saving."

"You've got to change the way you think." Fabian grabbed a pastry from the counter and took a bite. "Hmm. Very good." He finished it. "So, when we were at Tia Lourdes' last month, she asked me to do a few repairs for her. I can't put it off any longer, and we have an abundance of vegetables in the garden. I will take her some. Do you want to go with me?"

Angelina had no desire to visit someone who clearly did not support the advancement of women in government, society, or at all. "No. She's very sweet, but we don't have much to talk about. I honestly think your aunt would prefer a conversation with my father over me. They think alike. They both think women should hold a baby with one hand and a washboard with the other. One day, women will get the right to vote, and it will kill both of them."

Fabian grinned. "Okay. I'll tell her you are busy working on a speech for the next Suffragettes' meeting."

Angelina threw a dishtowel at him. "No, you will not."

He laughed, kissed her, and walked out the door.

"Just buy a couple of chance tickets. The odds are against you."

"The odds are against everyone else, not me."

ANGELINA TOOK pride in preparing meals for her husband. She stood at the stove stirring her specialty, pasta 'ncasciata, passed down to her by her mother and altered by her neighbor Signora Bertelli.

Fabian's key clicked as he turned the door latch, and she quickly removed her apron. "Fabian!"

"Something smells wonderful." Fabian crossed the room to the kitchen, lifted the lid, and glanced inside the pot and then at his garden outside the window. "Do we need a bushel of tomatoes, thirty-two onions, and three types of yucca root to go with tonight's dinner?"

"Only if we're trying to get fat or sick or both. Besides, I've already made Sicily's most famous pasta dish."

"It smells like a feast. I'm famished."

Angelina set the table. After they ate and Fabian properly raved about the meal, he walked toward the back door and entered the garden.

When he returned, he held up an entire bag of his produce. "I'm going to give some to the Martinez family around the corner. Be right back."

"Be right here."

He closed the door behind him, and a sensation of softness engulfed Angelina. Without Fabian drawing her into a lively conversation, the house stood quiet. Even the mantle clock remained still. Engrossed in life with her new husband, this had not been the first Saturday Angelina forgot to wind up the clock. She turned the key until the mechanism held tight and matched the time with her treasured pendant watch sent from Sicily by her grandmother. She gave the pendulum a slight push, and like an obedient soldier, the clock resumed its march of the minutes.

After six months of marriage, good minutes and bad, careless, careful, and confounded, their time amounted to a sense of peace she had never known.

Angelina had a secret—a secret she could not hide much longer. The day began fresh and perfect. But years and years from now, when this day and Angelina and Fabian's tomorrows grew old and became their yesterdays, she intended to remember the look on Fabian's face and the touch of his kiss when he heard the news.

Still lost in her thoughts, the door slid open, and Fabian appeared. "We don't work tomorrow, *querida*. Let's sleep in late and then walk along the beach."

His suggestion could not be more perfect. "That's a wonderful idea."

The sun broke early, and they meandered along the beach. The weather appeared flawless, with the right amount of breeze, and the sky gave only a lethargic offering of a billowy cloud.

The soothing ebb and flow of the waves and the warmth of the sand beneath her feet had a calming effect on Angelina, and she reached for Fabian's hand and stopped walking. "You know, when I was a child, I believed the blue of the sky came down and spilled its blue into the sea."

Fabian pulled her closer and put his arm around her shoulder. "Maybe you were right. Maybe Heaven and earth are the very same place."

A quiet moment passed between them. "There is something I need to tell you," she said.

"Did you find a pirate treasure under the tomato plants?"

Angelina grinned. "I tried, but it wasn't there."

"Well then, you need to keep digging. Gaspar, the pirate, jumped from his ship to avoid capture, and his immense fortune lies buried somewhere around here. There could be a chest of gold underneath our toes right now."

She enjoyed Fabian's lively imagination. "I'll keep that in mind. Try again."

He met Angelina's eyes. "It doesn't matter. I've already found my treasure." He took her hand and raised it to his lips.

"Then you give up?" she said.

Fabian shook his head. "I don't remember saying that."

Angelina had his full attention. She turned around and

looked at where they had been walking. "See our footprints in the sand?"

"Sí."

"How many footprints do you count?"

Fabian glanced behind him and raised his hand to shield his eyes. "Hmm. Now, let me see. I count one, two, three, and four footprints wide. If I divide them into pairs and multiply them by how far we have come, remembering I had to hop that one time, I stepped on a shell." He looked at Angelina, awaiting confirmation. "I hope there is a prize for this?"

"A big one." This moment meant everything to Angelina. She intended to remember it all her life and capture every particle of his reaction. "Soon, there will be three sets of footprints, one very small." Her words were soft, as if the breeze had caught them, and they encircled Fabian until he grasped the fullness of what she had said.

At that instant, his grin grew into a wide, booming shout of joy. *"¡Aye, Dios mío!* Are you sure? I mean, are you certain?"

The absolute delight on his face caused the tension inside Angelina to ease. They had never discussed children one way or the other, but it was always a possibility.

Fabian lifted her off her feet and kissed her passionately. All doubts about leaving her father's home vanished. He kept her in his embrace and danced around with her in his arms. Every movement he made and said reassured her of a blissful life.

"It's the best news I've ever heard." He paused as if to let the revelation run its course through his veins and to his heart. "It's a boy!"

Angelina laughed. "Maybe, or maybe not." All the men she knew wanted boys, but a girl would be a blessing.

"No, I'm sure it's a boy," said Fabian. "The chances are very high. You have four brothers, and my mother had six brothers."

Either way, it made no difference to Angelina.

"A girl is good, but it's a boy. I can see into the future. We'll dine out tonight to celebrate at the best Cuban restaurant."

"Or an Italian."

"We'll flip a coin to see if it's *arroz con pollo* or lasagna," said Fabian.

It didn't matter who won. Angelina could see into the future, as well. She spoke Spanish and Fabian's knowledge of her world remained limited to the names of Italian dishes. She concealed her amusement, certain their child would babble in Sicilian before he learned a word of Spanish.

Fabian pulled out a coin. "What will it be, little Mama?"

"I pick heads."

The coin spun through the air, and he slapped it on the back of his hand. "Heads!"

"Before you look, promise me we will work together and become the best of parents so our child will feel loved, happy, and safe."

Fabian nodded. "It's sad, but I hardly remember my father. One thing is certain, I will never turn my back and leave my child. Never."

"Our hearts are bigger than we think."

They spoke of a long life together and glanced out to sea. For a time, they listened to the sound of the waves while the sun threw its diamonds upon the waters, and the day slowly melted away.

And yet, for no apparent reason, an unexplained sensation washed over Angelina, and she cried.

CHAPTER 10

ANGELINA'S ANTICIPATION of holding her newborn in her embrace grew stronger. As she crossed the street, she thought more and more about the miracle of a child growing inside her. She made the sign of the cross on her belly and said a quick prayer for the Lord to grant her child good health and a kind spirit.

Still lost in the wonder of it all, she couldn't contain her excitement and took a quick trolley ride to Steinberg's Dry Goods Store. There she could look over all their displays of baby items.

She stepped inside and right away saw a familiar face. If she had lived, Angelina's mother would have been the same age as Vincenza Zoleo, but the woman always looked much older with her prematurely gray hair.

"Signora Zoleo, I am so happy to see you." Angelina could not have been more pleased with the chance meeting.

"Little Angelina, why haven't you come to visit? I am still in the same house. Nothing has changed. Where have you been, *bella*? Every time I ask your father, he gives an answer that is no answer at all."

Angelina's eyes widened. "What did he say?"

"Only that you ran away, and that's the end, but I can tell you that your brothers and little Lily miss you and want to know all about you."

Signora Zoleo talked of the price of eggplants, the Castellano's twins, and the Dileto's noisy dog digging holes in the yard, but Angelina's smile had lost its vitality thinking of her father and could not give the conversation her full attention.

"Please, *bella*, I will tell them that I saw you. Tell me something to share. I will do it when your father is not listening." She paused. "No, I will do it when he is listening. I know these Sicilian men. They want something, but they are too stubborn to admit it."

Angelina's need to communicate with her family grew more intense. "Tell them they are all in my heart, I love them, and I will love them forever. Say I'm happily married to Fabian Dominguez, and I will see them as soon as I can, but for now, I will see them in my dreams." Angelina wanted to say more, but the mere mention of her marriage would infuriate him, although he had to know already. To tell him she expected a child might be too much for him to tolerate.

"Tell me, *bella,* you are such a little thing. Are you expecting a blessing?" asked Signora Zoleo.

The question lingered, and Angelina did not answer the woman for a few nervous heartbeats. There appeared no graceful way to avoid the question, and it did not feel right to deny her unborn child. "Yes, I am. I hope my father will be as happy as I am about his first grandchild."

"Your mother is looking down from Heaven and smiling. I can feel her all around you."

"I hope so, Signora, I hope so."

All the way home, Angelina's thoughts wrapped around her father. Of all the things she could say to him, to announce he would become a grandfather should be the most stupendous. Surely, his heart would melt, and all would be well once he held the baby. The news burned inside her, but she would have to fight through a forest of his angry words to deliver it.

At home, Angelina sat at her kitchen table to compose an overdue letter to announce she loved her family and wanted to visit. She'd keep the letter and mail it later before she visited with her child. This would give her time to write and rewrite it to perfection.

As she contemplated how to begin, she pressed her pen against the paper and wrote *Dear Papa.* Over and over, she penned her feelings, scratched them out, and started anew. Each heartfelt sentiment, although unstable, stumbled precariously onto the page. Her words needed to be better and stronger. Why should she sound contrite for refusing to marry the men her father chose?

Angelina could almost see her father's when they last argued, and he struck her—something he had never done before and for her refusal to marry Rizzo, the baker. The memory of that moment remained frozen in her mind.

She loosened her grasp on the pen and let it slip onto the table. She could not bring herself to send her father a letter, and she doubted he had the resilience to receive it.

Angelina twisted the simple gold ring around her finger as she thought of her situation with her father, her love for Fabian, and the blessed event of having her baby. With every blessing, she feared a hidden thorn. This strange interplay between living on her terms and forfeiting contact with her younger siblings gripped her heart. She'd find a way to reach them. This time in her life would revolve around happiness, not anguish.

Her mother had always said *God listens to those who have faith.* But her mother had died, and her father also had a saying about God. *God forgives. Italians do not.*

~

A FLURRY of winds embodied Sunday morning, but by the arrival of the 10:40 train, the wind had withered into a soft, silken breeze as the train rumbled in and screeched to a halt.

The doors rattled open, and passengers hurried onto the platform when the tall figure of Rolando Aguirre stepped off. He focused on the house attached to the little grocery store across the street.

This is where Angelina had pointed out her home, where he put his hand on her long chestnut hair, looked into her bright dark eyes, and pulled her close to kiss her goodbye. Where he had vowed to return to her and where she promised not to fall in love with anyone else. It had been a warm summer day, but summer had gone and come again, and so had the days of autumn. Without word, how could she know what had happened to him?

Rolando laid in bed the night before, anxious and unable to sleep, listening to the murmur of the night and reliving his time with Angelina. From the moment he first saw her, Rolando remembered being struck by a powerful emotion he had never known. Circumstances had separated them, but he refused to release her vision from his mind. His need to see Angelina had remained strong and impassioned. Rolando would not rest until he found her—even if it lasted only a few moments, even after if she turned away.

Now, the moment had come. Rolando arrived early at the train terminal, and with a clear view of Angelina's home, he stood alone, collecting his thoughts.

Domenico had built the home as an afterthought, unconventionally adjoining the store's north wall to the house. Its design would unlikely be mistaken for any other home or easily forgotten.

In the store's large window, the oversized print of the

menu could be seen, along with a display of cans stacked in the shape of a pyramid, and several hanging rolls of dry salami. It would be so simple if Angelina opened the door, ran out, and threw herself into his arms.

Yet, after so much passing time, only one thing remained certain—her home sat across from the train station.

Rolando sighed deeply. He had tried two days before to see Angelina, but Domenico erupted into anger when Rolando mentioned her name.

Forget her, her father had shouted. *Impossible,* he thought. He had to find her. How many times had her memory given him the strength to endure another day and comforted him through the bitter torments in the most horrid prison in Spain?

He had practiced what to say so many times, continually rearranging the order of his words, always searching for a better way to offer his heart. Still, he grew more agitated. Words hadn't made the difference in his life, but time—lost time.

Rolando stared at the house like a mirage in his desert of despair. Bushes with soft pink roses encircled the porch and bordered the steps. He could almost see Angelina planting them.

He lit a cigar, took a few puffs, and then nervously put it out. Unwilling to waste another minute, he crossed the street, stepped onto the walkway, knocked on the door, and waited for an eternity. No one answered. He knocked again.

A boy, almost the same height as Rolando, answered the door. "If you're hungry, the store's entrance is over there." He pointed to his right.

"No," said Rolando. "I'm here to see Angelina. Could you get her for me?"

"Angelina?" The boy showed more interest in Rolando.

He stepped out onto the porch and closed the door behind him. "Who are you, anyway?"

"Rolando Aguirre. I'm a friend of Angelina's. Is she here?"

"No. I'm Angelina's brother, Vincenzo, but you can call me Vinny; everyone does, except my father."

"You're quite tall. If I didn't know better, I would think you were the oldest."

"Yep, then comes Sal, he's almost eighteen, I'm sixteen, but almost seventeen, then there's Filippo, Lily's our other sister, and the youngest is Giuseppe. Anyway, Angelina hasn't lived here for a long time. So, if you find her, tell her Vinny says, *Hey, what's up?*"

Rolando had a rash of questions but remained cautious about how to ask them. "You said she hasn't been living here for a long time? I sent her several letters the moment I was able. Perhaps she didn't get them. Do you know why she left?" It would not have been right for Rolando to frighten Vinny and tell him he'd been in a Spanish prison.

"Letters? Nope. Never saw them." He glanced toward the store's entrance as a customer opened the door and walked out. "Hey, let's get off the porch. It's better if my father doesn't see us. Whenever someone mentions Angelina, his face turns red, like he's about to have a heart attack or something." Angelina's brother looked pensive. "Of course, I've never seen anyone have a heart attack, but I bet their face turns red."

Vincenzo's innocence reminded Rolando of how quickly the world's heaviness can soil a youth. He was no closer to seeing Angelina than he had been across the sea.

The boy gestured for Rolando to follow him. They walked a half block to *Setima* Street, with Rolando remaining focused on why he had come.

"Vinny, I've been away a long time, and I've come a long way to see Angelina. Can you help me?" He glanced back at the grocery store. "I won't waste time speaking to your father again. The last time I came and mentioned your sister, he wouldn't listen to another word. I left. And you're right, your father's face did flush when I said, 'Angelina.'"

"I told you."

A vein of panic quickly built up inside Rolando. "Tell me the truth. Has something bad happened? I must know."

"Something bad is always happening, but I don't know—exactly. It started with this Rizzo guy. He's the baker, and it's where we get all our bread to make sandwiches for our customers. My father makes me, or my brother Sal, to go pick up the rolls, but now and then, he would send Angelina. When Rizzo saw her walk in, he'd give her free Italian pastries and cookies. So, Sal and I aren't dumb. We became hard to find when it was time to pick up the bread." Vinny nodded with a wide grin. "Next thing you know, Rizzo's wife dies, and he wants to marry Angelina. He already has four kids, and my father thinks it's a good idea."

Rolando pulled out a handkerchief and wiped the sweat from his forehead. "What happened after that?"

"Angelina said, 'No,' in Italian, English, and Spanish, but my father did not like that answer in any language."

Rolando eased a bit. "Well, that's good, but it's the same word in all three languages."

"Yeah, that's what I was thinking. Anyway, Angelina ran away in the middle of the night. I know because Angelina got mad at the priest for planning her wedding without her consent. Rizzo got mad at my father for not making Angelina marry him. My father got mad at Angelina for the same thing, and in the end, she got mad at everyone and left."

Rolando tightened his hands into fists, relaxed, and then tightened them again. "You must have some idea where she went. Did she say anything?" Rolando remained visibly nervous, speaking more quickly and in a more urgent tone.

Vincenzo rubbed his chin. "So, why did you say you want to see her so badly?"

"It's a long story, Vinny."

The boy raised his eyebrows. Clearly, this did not satisfy him.

"Angelina's an extraordinary friend of mine. I care for her." Rolando hesitated and waited to see if Vinny might ask another question. "I need to see her."

Vinny paused, as though not sure what to do with this information. "Well, I heard she might have gotten herself married."

"Ma-married?" The word caught in Rolando's throat, unable to mask the powerful emotion that jolted him.

Vinny noticed the change in his demeanor. "Hey, maybe I'm wrong. I'm wrong all the time. I mean, I couldn't swear to it, but my father believes it because he said my sister is dead to him. If someone is dead to you, that's probably not too good, right?"

Rolando concealed his true reaction to this news. He loved Angelina. She became his reason to keep breathing, his will to endure. Worse, when you long for the one you love, the hours and days multiply, a month becomes a season, and a season draws into a year, and one year becomes two. After so much passage of time, how could Angelina possibly know what had befallen him or how much he needed her love? And how could he think no one else would have noticed her beauty, kindness, quick wit, and spirit?

"Are you sure?" said Rolando deflated.

"Huh?"

He cleared his throat. "Are you sure about Angelina, Vinny?"

"No. I'm not sure of anything, but Signora Zoleo, a nice lady, but likes to talk and talk, came into the store. Usually, I run out, but this time, I was trapped stocking shelves. I heard her say to my father she saw Angelina, and Angelina told her she was married to some guy named Fabian Dominguez and she's even having a baby. I never heard of the guy. Do you know him?"

Wounded by Vinny's revelation, Rolando shut his eyes to block out the scene forming in his mind. "Yes, I know Fabian Dominguez."

"Hey, are you okay? You don't look so good," said Vincenzo.

Shaken, Rolando pulled on his collar. "Please don't forget I came to see your sister, Vinny, or my name is Rolando Aguirre. Can you remember that?"

"Yeah, sure... What is it?"

"Tell her that her good friend, Rolando, who worked with her in the cigar factory, came by."

"I know. I'll say you have red hair."

If the boy remembered any part of their visit, Angelina could figure out the rest. Unable to conceal the strain on his emotions any longer, he shook Vinny's hand. "It was good meeting you, Vinny, but it's better if I leave."

"Yeah, I gotta get back, too. Because of Angelina, now Sal and I gotta walk five more dumb blocks to another baker for bread rolls." He sighed. "I get she didn't want to marry the baker, but you gotta admit, if she had, we'd have our pick of free pastries every day. I don't understand how Angelina didn't think of that before she refused to marry the guy and left."

Married and pregnant, and of all the men in Ybor City, it's Fabian Dominguez. Rolando's thoughts went wild. He knew Fabian—both sides of his personality. The thought of Fabian twisting his charming web around Angelina plummeted Rolando's anxiety even deeper. He saw no way to corral his anger for the incredible misstep that had caged him for nearly two years and redirected his life—and Angelina's.

He leaped onto the trolley but couldn't sit still. He returned to the exit door and jumped off at the next stop. It didn't matter which way he went, where, or how long it took. Why rush to reach nowhere?

Rolando, the Cigar Makers International Union, originated in Spain. Negotiations are growing more threatening. They speak your Castilian dialect. They'll listen to you. These words from the union leaders left a deep scar and derailed his life. The union had to know about the unrest in a country on the brink of a revolution. Yet, they put their needs ahead of his safety.

Rolando faced the barrel of a gun the moment he stepped onto the main street of Barcelona. Questions brought more questions, and his anger compounded. Did anyone in Florida search for what had become of him?

For months Rolando thought of Angelina. Tormented by the news he had lost her, he walked for hours in defiance of what had become of his life. When he finally sat on a bench, Rolando gazed up at the azure sky. After all the millions of years man had existed, why had no one discovered the means of restoring a shattered heart?

CHAPTER 11

Don Carlos Madrid is blind! Of all people to suffer such a fate, why him? Angelina's mind raced. The sad news about the beloved *lector* traveled quickly throughout the factories. He had made his living reading to and distracting thousands of cigar workers from the monotony of rolling cigars. She could not believe the shocking injustice of such a man losing his eyesight.

Angelina arrived out of breath at Señor Alvarez's cigar factory, grateful she was not too late to collect Don Carlos' address. Even if she only visited her friend briefly, she wanted to offer her support. He might need something or someone to run errands.

She hurried to the home specified on the slip of paper and knocked. The door swung open, and she blurted, "Señor Madrid, I'm so happy to find you."

A thin film covered his eyes. Perhaps she had refused to notice anything wrong in her excitement at meeting him the last time. "I'm so terribly sorry that... It's not fair...." Her words spilled out in splintered fragments. "Why you? You gave us so much joy reading."

He had always been a serious man, scholarly, and careful not to squander his words or a smile, but Don Carlos Madrid gave her a warm grin and opened the door wider. "Come inside, and please have a seat, Angelina. I only need my hearing to know it's you and my voice to welcome you. Unfortunately, my eyes are no longer of much use, but I am indeed happy you came. My vision is dim, yet I still see forms and shadows; and can still light my cigar."

Angelina came to console him, but he was now calming her fears. She followed him as he used his hands to guide himself to the sofa. He always appeared well-dressed, almost formal. But as if it made all the difference, it charmed her he took a moment to put on his suit jacket before he sat down.

"I've been losing my eyesight for a long time, but I have no one to blame."

"How long have you known?"

"It's always been a fear. As a boy in Spain, we were fascinated by the day that turned into night. We all looked up to see what had become of the sun when it went behind the moon. Some thought God was angry at the world, and he took back the sun to leave us in darkness. Others said the moon was hungry and had returned to devour the sun, but it was an eclipse. There are always consequences for staring at something that powerful. Or, perhaps, my eyes are exhausted and wore themselves out." He shrugged and took a puff from his cigar before continuing.

"I've used my vision well. At a young age, I read the classics. I read the novels so many times and became the storyteller in my village. As a child, I would stand on a street corner and tell stories. Then, as an adult, I went to Cuba and became *el lector* in one of their prisons."

"A prison?"

"That's where it all began. They imprisoned Vicente Martinez Ybor in Cuba, where the prisons hired *los lectores* to read to the inmates. When they released Ybor, he came to Florida, he opened a large *tabaquería* he brought in lectors. Immigrants were coming into America in huge numbers, looking for work. They came to Tampa and asked for Ybor's City."

"But there's still a Tampa."

"That's true. However, northeast Tampa will always be Ybor City—a city within a city."

It struck Angelina that he seemed far more relaxed than she remembered or expected in his present condition. "Ybor would be proud of you. You're a master *lector*. Most people could never have held the worker's attention the way you did and the way you changed the pitch of your voice to distinguish characters."

"And because of it, I have kept a lifetime of stories in my head to keep me company. We, lectors, realized all stories are the same. Only how it's told is different. We are born, love, and laugh. We fear, suffer heartbreak, and everything in between. All that happens has happened before and will happen again." He appeared lost in thought.

"I've never seen it that way."

"This is our moment, but time will go on without us. Books are our record keepers. Read as many as you can. Though frayed, they never grow old, and unlike people, books will not desert you."

"I believe that. I still have the book of Shakespeare you gave me, and I'm always reading and rereading his works."

"With only twenty-six letters in our English alphabet, come hundreds of thousands of words that name everything and every emotion and so much more." Don Carlos appeared thoughtful and sighed. "I am an old man now, older than my father was when he died, older than my grandfather was. I don't know if there's a library in the next world, and I would hate to go to an eternity without books." He chuckled.

Angelina looked around at the collection of books displayed in almost every direction and giggled. "That would take an enormous coffin."

"In that case, I'm leaving instruction that I'm to be cremated to allow more room in the coffin."

Angelina shook her head. "Still, no way to close the coffin, but if you are cremated, I'll take you to a library, and when no one is looking, I'll carefully sprinkle you little by little around their finest classical literature."

Don Carlos Madrid's solemn expression vanished, and he burst into laughter. Angelina laughed with him, delighted she had said something that amused him.

"An appropriate farewell for a devoted *lector*," Don Carlos said, still tickled at the thought.

"But to see you go would break the hearts of the hundreds, maybe thousands, that love you."

"Death is a certainty. We can only control the way we live."

For a moment, Angelina thought of Fabian, who seemed to have missed this revelation completely.

"I hope you don't mind my asking you a question, Señor Madrid, and you don't have to answer if you don't wish, but you always tell me such powerful things about life. I wondered, have you ever married or had children? I hate to see you alone."

"It's a good question because you possess a good heart and are concerned." He kept silent and appeared to mentally flip through the pages of his life, searching for a bookmark that held the spot where his life had changed.

The stillness grew louder. Already sorry to have asked, but too late to withdraw it. She waited for his answer.

"Love is one of the most powerful forces in the universe. When it happens, we feel so alive and think of no one else. I was in love once, long ago, and she loved me, too. I would grow impatient when we were apart. The only way I knew to measure time was from the moment I saw her to the moment I saw her again. We married, but It sadly didn't work out."

Angelina had heard Don Carlos Madrid tell so many stories and knew well the changing intonations in his voice. He had fallen into a place of sorrow, and she didn't know how to rescue him.

"We all have our challenges, but we learn to adjust. Better men than me have lost their vision; Homer, Galileo, John Milton. It's reported that Claude Monet, the famous impressionist, is losing his eyesight and the vibrancy of his paintings has paled. But no matter the heartbreak, life goes on."

"It seems ironic, does it not, that it takes strength to have strength?"

"That's the challenge. Please tell me what you see, Angelina. Describe it with passion because your words are my eyes and the paintbrush, I use to create the image in my mind. But I must warn you that even the way you say a word adds light and shadows to the scene. My world grows darker, but you're holding the lantern."

Angelina had never thought about the seriousness of a description or how random words carelessly tossed around held such power. She needed to become far more observant with her descriptions. This habit would give her writing far more substance when she wrote the novel ripening inside her. She glanced around the room and focused on the fireplace. "I see a fireplace." She turned to face *el lector*.

"Yes, but I see nothing."

Angelina glanced back at the fireplace. "It's beautiful."

"What's beautiful?"

"It has a carved wooden mantel with an attractive clock in the center, like a king on his throne. Below it, a black metal screen over the hearth and emerald green tiles decorates the face of the opening." Angelina stood and passed her hand over the tiles. "Oh, wait, they aren't flat tiles, all are curved at the center. And to the right, on the floor, leaning against the tiles, there is a somewhat tarnished brass poker."

"That's a starting point, but it's what I might expect from someone else. Not you, Angelina. From you, I expect you to describe a Rembrandt to lighten my darkness. Hold your lantern higher and closer. Please tell me what you see, Angelina. Tell me."

She leaned forward a bit and looked again. She wanted to offer him the sense of the item, something more than a sketch in words.

"On the right, I see a long and narrow dark stain on the oak mantle, like something had spilled and left neglected. Then I see a carving of three oak leaves at each end." An unexpected moment of sorrow washed over her. "When I go to the cemetery to visit my mother's grave, I've seen this same design on gravestones."

"That's because the oak tree symbolizes strength and endurance. It's the king of trees. People put it on headstones as a reminder their loved ones lived long, endured much, and will live again." He paused. "What else do you see?"

Angelina cleared her throat. "I see something very pleasing. It's a large, ornate clock that sits regally displayed on the mantle, as though ready to draw notice and compliments each time it chimes. The pendulum is made of brass, as are the brass heads on each end portraying Mercury with wings on his helmet."

"It seems a contradiction, does it not, that Mercury, representing speed is depicted on a clock whose sole purpose is to account for each passing minute without rushing," he said. "What else do you see, Angelina?"

Angelina glanced again at the clock.

"The body of the clock is green marble, with dark, wavy veins running through it. It sits on four legs of brass, each decoratively carved to look like dolphins. It's quite impressive."

"What about the weight of the clock?"

"Oh, it's heavy. Marble is always heavy."

"Now lift it from the mantle and tell me what is wrong with your description."

Angelina saw nothing wrong with her description. As far as she could see, she had been thorough. Still, Angelina did as he asked.

"What do you know about the clock now?"

Embarrassed, she said, "It's not marble."

El lector nodded. "That's right. It's wood painted to look like marble. Remember this lesson. Just because you have vision doesn't mean you see what's there. Even the sighted are often blind. This clock's design played a trick."

Each time Angelina met with Señor Madrid, she learned something to enrich her thinking. "You're the most knowledgeable person I have ever known. No one can take that away from you, sighted or blind."

"Even so, I sense you feel sorry for me. You mustn't. Most of my life is behind me, and it was a good life." He took several slow, pensive puffs on his cigar.

"If I may, I'll share some insight. Life is far too short. Don't waste time reading *good* books. Read only the great ones. They are filled with magic and come alive. Each time, you'll learn something new. This is why we lectors read so much Shakespeare to the workers. These stories have endured *the slings and arrows* of time."

Once again, Angelina absorbed her friend's knowledge.

"Tell me, has anything changed with you and your father?"

The mention of her father deflated Angelina. "I don't understand him. He tells us stories of how desperate life was

CHAPTER 11 | 89

in Sicily and how they escaped for a better life in America. Yet, he thinks like he's still in the old country."

"'To be ignorant of what occurred before you were born is to remain always a child.' These are the words of Cicero, who lived before the time of Christ and left us with this one great pearl of wisdom. Everyone who has ever lived, whether prince or pauper, knows something we don't know. Your father has experienced many things. There is a famous Spanish saying, *El diablo sabe más porque es viejo, no porque sea diablo."*

"'The devil knows more because he's old, not because he's the devil.' I remember my friend Carmen saying this once."

"Your father's experienced something, and that is why he thinks the way he does."

The mantle clock chimed and drew Angelina's attention. "Oh, I didn't mean to stay so long. Unfortunately, I must go. Do you need me to do anything for you, clean, wash, run to the store, anything?"

Don Carlos stood up. "Your visits are always a gift and welcome, but you don't have to bring me anything or do anything. Alvarez has seen to everything. We are from the same town in Spain, and he has been the best of friends."

"It's wonderful to find an old friend so far away from home. And you'll soon know what an excellent cook I am, not because you're the devil, but because old and tasted the difference."

Don Carlos burst into laughter.

Angelina giggled and hugged her old friend. "I can't wait to see you again soon."

"And I wholeheartedly look forward to it."

CHAPTER 12

ANGELINA OFTEN THOUGHT of her friend Don Carlos Madrid. His advice and stories were like the refrain of a song, and the lyrics played over and over in her mind. *You have conviction. Hold to your principles.* He'd infused her with fortitude.

The next day, Angelina entered the factory, took her place, and began her task of turning tobacco leaves into cigars. She watched the clock until she couldn't sit still and found Lopez at his desk. He lit his pipe and looked at her with indifference. "I'm going to leave work for only an hour today, Señor Lopez."

"We don't pay cigar makers for not working." He puffed several times on his pipe.

Angelina rolled her eyes. "I did not expect you to pay me. There's just something I have to do."

"Then do it. But remember, there are others who want your job."

The comment infuriated Angelina. "Yes, but will they work as fast and efficiently as I do? I never waste materials, work all the hours I'm asked, never late for work, and never take long lunches. I'm leaving at 2:30, and will return in one hour at exactly 3:30." Angelina grew impatient with Lopez' assertion of power. "If you like, I will address this matter with Señor Cuesta. He knows me and my work pretty well."

Lopez pulled the pipe from his mouth and coughed. "That's not necessary. I give my permission." He rose from his chair and walked out.

Angelina went to her usual seat at the worktable and told Carmen about her encounter with Lopez.

"But where are you going?" said Carmen.

"Where I should have gone long ago." She looked at the clock and back at Carmen. "I'll tell you all about it when I return, but I must leave right now."

Angelina cleaned off her section of the long table, dashed out the door, and down the stairs. She hurried to reach the school where she had spent so many happy years and just in time to hear the principal ringing the bell announcing the school day had ended.

She stood outside by the sidewalk until she heard her sister Lily scream her name. All her younger siblings came rushing over. Lily reached her first, and Angelina scooped her up in her arms. Angelina could not hold back her tears as she took turns and hugged everyone. "You will never know how much I've missed all of you."

"Where have you been hiding?" said Filippo.

Angelina ruffled his hair. "Where are you hiding? This can't be my little brother. You're too tall!"

Filippo grinned, and Giuseppe came running. "Angie, Angie!"

As the oldest, Angelina rushed to meet her siblings. "I can't believe how happy I am today."

With Sal and Vinny closest to her in age, her happiness would have been incomplete without seeing them, even after all the teasing and pranks they put her through.

"Angelina!" Their voices came in unison.

Angelina laughed when they hurried over and hugged her. "So, you loved me after all."

"Of course," said Vinny, "you don't think we would have wasted all that time tormenting you if we didn't love you?"

Sal nodded. "Yeah, what kind of brothers do you think we are?"

Angelina beamed. "I'm so happy. Seeing all of you means so much to me."

Vinny put his hand on her shoulder. "But hey, Angie, what's going on?"

Certain that Vinny was referring to her pregnancy, she thought long and hard about mentioning discussing it. Things were bad enough.

She raised her hand and messed up her brother's hair. "I grew up. One day you will too." She rolled her eyes. "Well, maybe not." And she laughed.

The younger children still had their arms around her and pulled her skirt.

Sal stood over her and kissed her forehead. "That's letting you know I'm taller than you, and you'll never catch up."

Neither one of her brothers enjoyed schoolwork as she did. Angelina pinched Sal's cheeks. "Yes, but I know more than you do, and you'll never catch up."

Vinny turned to Angelina. "Okay, this guy comes to the house, says he's your friend, and asks me three questions. 'Where are you? And where are you? And like where are you?'"

"What are you talking about? What guy?"

"He told me not to forget who he was, but I can't remember now."

"Well, I see some things haven't changed."

"He was taller than me, which isn't easy, and he looked nice, like he didn't work in a coal mine or something."

Angelina shook her head. "And who do you know in

Tampa who works in a coal mine?" Still, something tugged inside her. "Well, if you can't remember who he was, can you remember what he looked like?"

"Oh, yeah, now I remember. He had lots of red hair. But if he worked in a coal mine, it would be black, right?"

Stunned, *it couldn't be.* Instead, the strangest mix of sensations passed through Angelina, both stirring and frightening.

"He said he was a very good friend of yours. Do you know him?"

Do you know him? She froze at the sound of the question, and an avalanche of memories engulfed her. If she met him on the street when she was sure she saw him from her seat in the trolley, then that would have just been a chance encounter.

But why is he going to my father's house and looking for me?

Angelina crossed her arms over her waist and tried to remain calm as she fought off the sudden return of powerful memories. Still, they flooded her mind. Rolando said he loved her, and he believed the feeling to be so strong that they must have known each other in another time and place. In his embrace, the world around them slipped away.

He gave her the St. Jude medal to remind her of his return, but not for two unbearable weeks. Angelina recalled the last thing she said to him. *I promise I will wait for you.* Those words had returned to haunt her, but there was something else far more frightening. Rolando had said, *I sense I'm being warned not to go or something bad will happen.*

Shaken by the rush of memories, she turned once again to her brother. "What else did he say, Vinny?"

"Is it important?"

"Yes."

"I donno, I guess he wanted to find you and kept asking questions. Only…"

"Only what?"

"Only he really wanted me to tell you he came to see you. Anyway, that's all I remember."

Angelina knew this would play on her mind for a long time, and hard to forget. *What possible reason would Rolando want to seek me out after more than a year and a half.*

She cleared her throat and didn't want to draw attention in front of her brothers.

"Hey," said Vinny. "Remember that story Mama used to tell us about the wolf that refused to enter the lion's den? The wolf saw many footprints going inside, but only the lion's coming out."

"Hey, I remember that story," said Sal.

Vinny put his arm around Angelina and whispered so only she could hear. "Right now, don't come to the house. It's like the lion's den. Papa's still so mad. He'll swallow you in one gulp."

Angelina's expression sobered, and she also changed the subject. "I came to hug and kiss all of you. I love all of you; and I will love you forever, but I also have to get back to work."

She nodded at Vinny, kissed each one of her siblings, and turned away to leave. She stopped and shouted back, "I promise to see you soon."

"Soon?" echoed Sal.

"Yes. Soon." Angelina hurried back to work, blinking away her tears.

CHAPTER 13

ANGELINA HATED those first moments when she opened her eyes in the morning. Nausea and retching accompanied the great miracle of creation.

"Don't worry. It's nothing," said Fabian

"I wouldn't be this sick if it was nothing."

None of this fazed Fabian. If only he understood how much she suffered every morning and how sometimes the uneasiness lasted until early afternoon. "Why don't you get sick tomorrow morning instead of me?"

Fabian laughed. "I hear it doesn't last forever."

"Maybe you heard wrong."

"If men had morning sickness, I bet the human race would have died out by now."

Fabian kissed her. "Such an imagination you have, but I can't stay to hear your other thoughts. Tia Lourdes says one of her pipes clogged. I won't be long." He waved goodbye at the door.

After some thought, Angelina decided the outdoors would do her good. So, she left the house and walked through the park. The day was tall and wide and full of possibilities. She inhaled the fresh air and relished the contrast from the strong scent of tobacco leaves. Angelina contemplated the wonder of life with a child to love.

"Angelina, is that you?" The familiar voice came from behind. Angelina turned to see the face of her oldest friend from childhood. They had been more like sisters than friends.

Sophia Esposito hurried over and threw her arms around Angelina. "I thought I'd never find you. They told us in school that Ybor City was 40 square acres, but that was then. It's grown so big or I would have found you sooner."

"I've missed you."

"Time is such a thief. It goes by so fast, and there's no way to catch that bandit."

"I hate we lost contact. It's a wonderful surprise to see you and look at you." Angelina took in the sight of her long-time friend, her violet-colored dress in a lovely silk fabric, her stylish hat, and her radiant glow. "You're so stylish. Where have you been, modeling for a fashion magazine?"

"And where have you been? I could ask you the same question. I wrote you to let you know my new address, but my letters were never answered. As soon as I arrived from New York, I went straight to your house. Your father was no use. He wouldn't tell me anything." Sophia hooked her arm in Angelina's and they began walking together.

Angelina's smile faded. "We live here in America, but in his mind, Papa still hasn't left his small Sicilian village." She described her situation with her father and could easily imagine the scene Sophia had with him. "He's very strong-minded. Yet, I know that inside, he still loves me."

"After I saw your father, I went to your old neighbor, Signora Bertelli. She remembered me and told me where to find you. She also described the argument you had with your father and how you left." Sophia shook her head.

"Yes. It was very emotional. Sometimes, the ones that love you can almost destroy you." Angelina waved her hand as if to send her troubles away. She didn't want them to tarnish her excitement at seeing her friend. They stopped, and Angelina smiled at Sophia. "Look at you. You're radiant. You must come to my home. I live right around the corner. We can sit and visit."

"I'll walk with you, but I can't stay long."

In a neighborhood of so many hard-working locals and immigrants, those passing them in the street glanced twice at Sophia's elegant appearance.

"I am so happy about your good fortune. Your dress looks like one I've only seen in a glamorous monthly magazine. That color is so striking, and the needlework is beautiful."

"When we announced our nuptials, my fiancé had several dresses made for me in New York. We're marrying when he finishes medical school and joins his father's practice. After that, we'll be living in Albany." Sophia held out her large diamond ring for Angelina to see.

"Oh, my goodness. I've seen nothing like it. It's truly stunning. I hope this fiancée knows he's getting a wonderful wife."

Angelina kept her hand at her side. She loved her old friend, but it would have been foolish to compare rings.

Sophia beamed, and it pleased Angelina to think her childhood friend had done so well. "So, what is the name of your prince?"

"John Greenfield—soon to be *Doctor* John Greenfield. We met in college."

"That's a wonderful name, like a green garden or a lovely pasture."

Sophia winked. "Or like greenbacks."

Angelina grinned, but ignored her reference to money. "It's wonderful when your dreams come true."

Everything had gone right in Sophia's life, as if she'd planned every detail. Angelina had not followed such a privileged path. "I plan to go to a local college and won't be needing a husband. I already have one. I can't wait for you to meet him. Fabian is good to me, and we're so excited. We're having a baby."

"Congratulations! I can't believe it," said Sophia. "It seems like yesterday we were sitting in school passing notes."

The memories came rushing back, and Angelina laughed. "You passed notes, asking me for the answers."

"I loved those days," said Sophia.

Angelina sighed. "All I wanted was to study and go to college, and I intended to stop at nothing, but *La Mano Nera* came into our store one day, and my father had me quit school and go to work. It changed my life."

"The Black Hand? Everyone knows how violent the Mafia is. When I was still a child, they put a baker in his oven."

"Just horrible. Everyone talked about it."

"See, that's your problem, Angelina. You need to throw open the windows and doors and free yourself. Go to college if that's what you want!"

Angelina put her hand on her stomach. "With a child growing inside me, it would not be logical to stop working, start college, and then quit to have a baby. Besides, I get so sick in the morning."

Angelina stopped in front of the little white-washed *casita* indistinguishable from all the others standing in a straight row. "I live here. Come inside, Sophia. I'll make you something wonderful to eat."

Sophia glanced at the little *casita* without expression. "I wish I could chat longer, but do you remember what today is?"

Angelina shook her head.

"It's my mother's birthday, exactly a month after your

mother's." She paused. "Oh, Angelina, I'm sorry to remind you."

"It's fine." Angelina never forgot her mother's birthday, but instead of a celebration, it became a day of reflection and a private thing.

"I'm here in Florida to help with my mother's party. How will it look if I miss the trolley and show up late? Let's sit on the porch, so that I hear its bell in the distance."

"All right, but let me offer you something?"

"No, no. I'm fine." Her friend opened her bag and pulled out a little book with embossed pink flowers and a small pencil. "Here, write your address, or I'll forget where we are. I can't visit long this time. I'll be back, but I don't know when."

Angelina flipped through the pages and saw a few women's names. She turned the pages to the letter *D* but asked, "In Italy and Cuba, a woman keeps her maiden name, but in America, we take our husband's last name. Will you remember my name is now Dominguez?"

"Probably not. Write it under 'A.' I'm terrible with last names. Anyway, I write everyone down under their first name except for Graciela Muni. You remember her, don't you? She used to call us names when we were children and even once threw a rock at us. She heard I'm marrying a doctor. Now she wants to be my friend, so I put her under *N*."

"*N*?"

"For *No good.*"

Angelina suppressed her smile and wrote her name larger than usual, so that it wouldn't be lost between Alberto and Antonio. "Don't you have any idea when you're coming to visit Sophia? I want to prepare something special for you to eat."

"I'm never certain about anything." She took back her

address book, scribbled her address on the last page, ripped it out, and handed it to Angelina. "Here's where I live. Be sure and let me know when you have your baby. Better yet, you and your husband should bring the baby to New York and visit John and me. We have lots of room. You'll like him, and you'll love New York."

Angelina could not imagine the first-class, extravagant fare to New York on a passenger train where you slept, and they served meals with real silverware and porcelain. "One day, Fabian and I and our baby will visit you, I promise."

"You know, Angelina, you were always the smart one, maybe the smartest in the entire school. I remember how you pushed me to open my schoolbooks and learn something new. You'd tell me, 'You can't eat the egg unless you break open the shell.'"

"My mother always said that." Angelina recalled her mother's calming voice of wisdom. "I can still hear your usual answer, 'But I already read it, and I don't understand it.'"

"And then you'd say, 'If the egg doesn't crack open on the first try, you don't go hungry, do you? You try again.'"

"My mother always said that, too. In everything, the power to win or lose in life is up to you only." It had been a long time since they'd talked about school and the wisdom her mother had left them. The years had blown far away, and Angelina missed it all—what good friends they'd been as children, all those years before she'd lost her mother and her father, forced her to leave school.

"I remember all your lectures, Angelina. Even now, when I struggle over a problem, I force myself to think of something wise you once said. You had an answer for everything. It would have been so wonderful if you had gone away with me to get an education."

In the distance, the faint sound of a trolley's whistle sounded. "Oh, I have to go, Angelina."

"Just go down this street, and you can catch the trolley."

They hugged quickly, and Sophia hollered, "I'll be back."

Angelina watched her go. She vowed that one day she would receive her education. Perhaps it *was* a great misfortune that she hadn't attended college with Sophia. At that moment, she felt her baby kick. *Perhaps not.*

CHAPTER 14

"TODAY'S THE DAY, Fabian. Please come with me. I've made *pasta alla Norma* for Don Carlos and promised to bring it today." Angelina gave a brilliant smile.

"And what did you cook? In English, please?"

"It's the most legendary pasta dish in Sicily named after a famous opera. It has tomatoes, basil, ricotta, eggplant, simmered in garlic, and anything else I can think of. I made a large plate for us."

"You're making me hungry, but why must I go along?"

"You only know him by reputation. Here's your chance to meet Don Carlos Madrid in person—the greatest *lector* Ybor City ever had. Besides, you can carry the food."

"Ah, so that's it."

Angelina giggled. Along the way, they spoke of the day they met and how long it took to convince her to pay attention to him. They spoke of their future, what it might be like if their child was a boy, a girl, twins, maybe triplets? They talked and laughed until they came around the last corner and saw Don Carlos in the distance, about to cross the street to his house. He held the tip of his walking stick before him, waving it from left to right near the ground.

"That's him," she told Fabian. "Don Carlos!" Set on getting his attention, she shouted and walked faster. "Let's catch him." The street seemed asleep, with no one coming or going in either direction. As always, he appeared taller than his stature, with his back straight and his head held high. Well-dressed in a white suit, the most admired *lector* in all of Ybor City tapped his cane on the curb and stepped out onto the street.

Angelina called out to him once more. This time, he turned his head toward the sound of her voice.

"It's me, Angelina." She waved.

He smiled and waved back, but before he could answer, a Model-T sped around the corner, honking and screeching but not stopping or turning its wheels to avoid a collision. The automobile struck Don Carlos Madrid so hard his walking stick flew into the air, and the impact forced his body against the harsh, unyielding brick-laid street while the weight of the vehicle rode over him.

Angelina screamed and darted toward the terrifying scene where her beloved *lector* lay covered in blood. Fabian ran with her.

The driver of the vehicle jumped out. Then, with only a glance at his victim, he ran to one side of the street and back again, shouting in a deep baritone voice that rose and fell, declaring himself blameless. Others in the street rushed toward the injured man.

"All of you saw him. It's not my fault. Out of nowhere, he stepped in front of my Model-T, like he was blind or something. I was going slowly."

Fabian spoke up. "If you were going slowly, you would not have hit him."

Angelina paid no attention to the driver's ravings. With

blood splattered everywhere, her fear intensified. Fabian and three men that came running tried to lift the car off of Don Carlos. After a few attempts, they succeeded and pulled him out from under the automobile.

"Oh, please, God, help him." Angelina cried as she tried to stop the bleeding by pressing the folds of her skirt against his open wound.

His stomach rose as he gasped for air. "I can't," he said. "I can't breathe." His voice had become hoarse, unrecognizable. "My chest…"

She gazed in horror at his crushed chest. Fabian returned to her side.

"Someone is running right away to get help. There's a doctor close by."

Don Carlos moaned, shook his head, and grimaced in pain.

Fabian looked behind him. "The doctor's office is just around the corner. Just hold on. He'll be here quickly."

Angelina sobbed hysterically. "Please be strong," she begged. "Did you hear Fabian? Someone is bringing the doctor. He's not very far, and he'll take care of you. Hold my hand."

In a panic and panting in near hysteria, Angelina knelt next to him as he bled from his head and chest.

"Please, God, save the good man," she whispered.

He tried to speak, and Angelina leaned closer to hear his feeble words and to tell him what she wanted him to know.

"I love you, Señor Madrid. I need you. Please don't leave me." She shuddered as she spoke, and her words came out etched in agony. Unable to sustain the pain tearing at her heart, she put her arms around him. "I'm here. I won't leave you."

"Help is on its way," repeated Fabian as he bent down next to Angelina.

People filled the street, some running for help and others toward the accident. Everyone shouted questions or orders. The alarm to help reigned everywhere. The bleeding didn't stop. Again, she placed her head closer to hear him, but his voice had slipped into an ethereal fragility, as though he'd accepted this fate and drifting away.

"Follow… your heart, Angelina.…" His chest heaved, and his words were strained and faint. One arm had twisted in an unnatural position. She reached for his free hand and held it for support, trying to comfort him. He took one long, breath, exhaled, and looked up at the sky with wonder as though he had regained his vision.

"No! Oh, please, God, no. Don't take him!" Angelina screamed. She threw her arms around her old teacher and cried hysterically on his chest. But Don Carlos Madrid never moved again. Fabian didn't know how to comfort her.

Two men approached. One gently closed *el lector's* eyes, and Fabian lifted Angelina from his body. Then, bathed in his blood and too stricken and unsteady to walk on her own, Fabian led her out of the street, where she sat on the curb's edge crying.

"Are you family?" said one man.

Angelina could not control the shock that had overtaken her. Fabian shook his head. "No, but my wife knew him very well," he said.

"Perhaps it's a blessing," said the other man. "His suffering might have been too great to endure."

The knot in Angelina's throat tightened. The men turned away, and together, they lifted the broken, lifeless body of Don Carlo into a wagon. Angelina stood transfixed as the wheels turned unhurriedly down the street, carrying away the finest lector Ybor City had ever known.

She hung her head in utter shock while the man in the Model-T told the police that nothing had been his fault. It didn't matter anymore. Nothing was going to bring back her dear friend.

Fabian put his arm around her. In the excitement, he had put down the dish Angelina had made to give Don Carlos, and now trampled by all who came out to see the tragedy.

"Oh, Fabian, if only I could roll back time. He meant so much to me. You will never know." Now she witnessed the last of his heartbeats.

"Nothing can stand in the way of fate. When his time came, it was our destiny to witness it. Maybe it comforted him to see you there."

Angelina's breathing came in nervous, uneven gasps with no way to calm herself. Her dear friend now carted away unceremoniously. How could the world ever be the same again? He had never been a simple or ordinary man, but one with vast knowledge and great wisdom. She sat on the curb sobbing uncontrollably, painful, soulful tears while trying to catch her breath.

Fabian stroked her head. "It's best to cry it all out. I know you cared for him. I'm glad I was here for you." He spoke tenderly.

"The Italians have a saying about death. My father said it when someone died. 'In the end, we are all the same. When the game is over, the king and the pawn go into the same box.'"

IT TOOK many weeks before the tide of her immense grief over the death of Don Carlos Madrid subsided. At first, Angelina was consumed in her own sorrow and had not real-ized the death of her beloved friend had affected Fabian also. It must have triggered the memory of his own loss. His nightmares and drinking increased. She'd see him place his hands over his ears as though trying to drown out the drumming sound in his head.

All death is painful to loved ones left behind, but there is something worse about an unexpected death. It's wrapped up tightly in shock and it's that disbelief that makes it all the more painful.

CHAPTER 15

THE LONG-AWAITED DAY HAD ARRIVED. The leaders of the Cigar Makers International Union now had to explain how they managed to lose contact with Rolando Aguirre, their emissary to Spain.

Rolando walked into the building, angry and self-assured. He headed straight for this critical assembly of union officers and those who thought it wise to derail him from his *two-week* mission to Key West, redirect the plan to Barcelona, Spain, and then forget him.

Rolando raised his chin as he walked into the meeting room and approached the young man seated at a table near the entrance. "My name is Rolando Aguirre. I'm here to meet with the committee." His voice was clear and unmistakable.

"Please sign your name and state your reason for your meeting in our ledger."

Rolando dipped the pen in the inkwell, and with a few drops of ink still dripping, he wrote his name and stated his reason for being there as *anger*.

The young man glanced at the words and then at Rolando. "This doesn't give an actual reason."

"If anger is a good enough reason for countries to declare wars, it's a good enough reason for this cigar union to hear what I have to say."

There were no further questions.

Manuel Castillo held the gavel, and as soon as they announced Rolando's name, he approached the long table where the twelve heads of the union had seated, but instead of taking the chair offered, Rolando remained standing. He was not there to ask forgiveness; he arrived to demand answers.

"I know every one of you, and you must all know me by my unfailing dedication to this union, but for the record, my name is Rolando Aguirre. I was born and raised in Vizcaya, Spain. More importantly, I was the logical choice to return and discuss certain critical issues with our union brothers in Barcelona, Spain, show our strength, and seek their support to help us make our voices heard."

"That is true, Rolando," said Manuel Castillo. "And the Cigar Makers International Union appreciates your service." He paused and cleared his throat before he answered. "Since the establishment of this union in 1864, nothing like this has ever happened in our history. It was a disastrous incident, and for this, we are truly sorry."

"I'm here to tell you that you destroyed my life. You sent me to Spain to seek help and apprise the heads of the union of our troubles with the Mafia and the cigar barons. You had to know the gravity of arriving amid an angry insurrection of young men my age rebelling against the government. The authorities arrested me when I stepped onto the *Gran Via*, the main street where the rioting erupted." Rolando raised his voice and kept his eyes and fury on Castillo.

"You're a very valuable and intelligent member of our union. We had men searching for you everywhere. But, in the chaos and revolt, no one had any idea what had happened to you." Castillo spoke in a softer tone, as though trying to calm down Rolando.

"This committee told me I was to go to Key West for two weeks, and then you sent two men to interrupt my journey, and I was boarded on a boat to Spain."

"Secrecy was imperative. You already knew that union leaders were being separated from their families and taken out of the country—some abducted to Spain. If word had leaked out about this, it would have caused panic, and we could not accomplish our goal and keep our members out of danger."

"Everything with these big cigar magnates is about profits, profits, and more profits," said Rolando. "But I have a life too, and I was robbed of it all."

Castillo rubbed his hands together as though ridding himself of the blame. "Please understand, we never gave up our search for you, and those sympathetic to our cause went to the hospitals and read through the prison's records."

"You should have asked to see the young men arrested. I was incarcerated—not hiding." Rolando's words were quick, sharp, and to the point.

"Florida has a ruthless and powerful association of factory owners who want nothing better than to cripple the union. They pay off politicians, and use whatever tactic to break the union's back, including the forced deportation of union leaders. But our union is international and was founded in Spain. So, we can play their game."

Rolando remained stiff and unaffected by Manuel Castillo's words. "If you knew how to play, I would not have been arrested."

"We have a strong brotherhood in Spain and the utmost respect for you, Rolando. If we sent a Cuban there, he would not have had the impact you have in the country of your birth. We needed someone with your skill to convince the

Spaniards to join our cause. There are nearly two hundred cigar factories, powerful enough for factory owners to entice the Mafia for help."

The room and the conversation grew more stifling while the fragile breeze from the open windows did nothing to combat the heat.

"Now let me tell you what you did to me. I was abruptly redirected to Spain and arrived amid a revolt of mostly young men like myself. The military was called out. Guns were used and we were beaten with clubs." The memory infuriated Rolando.

"Along with so many others, I was captured and thrown in jail and no one came to my rescue. I suffered in that prison for two years I went hungry and lived with rats. I never saw the sky. And worse, I told the girl I loved I would be back in two weeks. She had good reason to believe I lied to her, abandoned her, and she married someone else. She meant everything to me." Roland's throat tightened. His breathing grew heavy and for a moment, he couldn't continue. "This union has destroyed my life."

The committee's faces appeared the same, not in looks but in blank expressions. No one had a reasonable answer, and no excuse given to appease Rolando.

The foreman reached for a glass of water and took a drink. An uncomfortable quiet permeated the room while clear he tried to gain some time to consider his response. At last, he looked up at Rolando. "I can only imagine what you went through, but this is not the committee's fault. We tried to find you."

"Not hard enough, or you would have found me. Knowing so many were arrested, you should have gone to the prison and checked the prisoners." Rolando tightened his lips in anger. "You should have checked everywhere—the morgues."

Manuel Castillo ruffled through the papers sitting before him. When he found what he wanted, he held them up. "But we did. Here are copies and notes on all our inquiries. We looked for you all over."

Rolando took several long strides to pick up the documents. He stood there, read over each inquiry, then dropped the papers in disgust on the long table before the committee.

"Look at the names of the list of prisoners."

Manuel picked up the report. He read through the names and then looked up at Rolando. "Do you see it?" said Rolando.

Manuel didn't answer. He passed it to the men on his right, who read it and shook their heads.

"I am right there on the list. They spelled my name *Ronaldo* with an "n" instead of Rolando. Still, it says I claim to be from Ybor City, Florida, and they even describe my height and red hair and that I am a cigar maker. How is it possible no one caught this?"

Manuel's color left him. "It's a terrible mistake, but you are safe at home now."

"All the time I was in prison, I was on union business. However, I was beaten, half-starved, and denied communication with our liaisons. Far worse and unforgivable, I would still be there if I hadn't escaped during a political riot to release those wrongfully imprisoned. I could have died there. What's the payment for going to Hell for this union?"

Manuel Castillo hit the gavel. "Rolando Aguirre, we have cleared your name with the Spanish authorities and the penal system. You were a wrongfully detained American, and your record has been expunged."

Manuel's boast about clearing Rolando's name infuriated him. The union did nothing. His name did not have to be expunged and did not appear on any prison records because Rolando had set fire to it and destroyed the file himself.

"You have stated your complaint, and it's a valid one. Please step outside briefly, so we can confer on how to remedy this situation."

"Remedy? No one can give me back the life I had or the one I suffered."

"I understand. This shouldn't take very long."

Rolando's breathing grew more anxious. To think he suffered such revulsions because of a few mistaken letters in his name, and would still be there if it wasn't for Javier Rivera. Rolando slapped his fist against his thigh and walked out, but had no intention of sitting outside for any great length of time. He passed through the large oak door of the cavernous meeting room with his eyes on the clock's minute hand. Incoherent murmurings slipped through the door and Rolando grew restless.

Finally, one of the committee members opened the door and asked him to come back in.

"We have come to a unanimous agreement, Rolando," said Manuel Castillo as the other men nodded.

Rolando had no patience for playing games. "What agreement?"

"When we were made aware of the horrible mix-up, we sent money for your passage home and travel. You are to get one-half of your lost wages as compensation for your unlawful stay in Barcelona's prison. It is an unforgivable tragedy, and you are more than deserving of the full amount, but funds have limits. You will meet with Pedro Alonzo, and he will help you calculate the exact amount. Since you are one of the best cigar makers, your production has always been high. It will be a healthy amount, Rolando."

Rolando waited for an unreasonable condition to be added to their *agreement*, but none came.

"I hope you will consider this payment fair."

"Fair? The day I left will never come again. The girl I love now belongs to another. Nothing, absolutely nothing will be restored. So, no, consider nothing that happened to me *fair.*"

"We will raise your compensation to three-quarters of your salary. It's the best we can do," said Castillo.

Rolando gazed at the floor for a moment. These men would never understand the enormity of what this cost him. The world would continue to spin its days and nights and money could not turn back time. He had to let this go. Time is priceless. He looked back at the committee. All eyes were on him. Rolando sighed and nodded his approval.

CHAPTER 16

ANGELINA MISSED HER SIBLINGS TERRIBLY. She was in deep thought about them when three hard knocks at the door startled her. Had Fabian forgotten something? She reached for the handle, and before she could fully open the door, she heard a familiar voice.

"Angelina, Angelina! Is me, Zio Pasquale and Pasqualino."

Her heart leaped and opened the door wide. "Zio Pasquale!"

"Angelina, I so happy to see you. Pasqualino and I come back from Key West. We see Carmen, and she say you gonna have *bambino* and to come here to find you."

Angelina threw her arms around her uncle and his little adopted son. "Oh, Zio Pasquale, it's you. I can't believe you are both here." Angelina's eyes moistened, and she put her hand on her extended stomach. "I wish my baby were here for you to hold, and my husband left ten minutes ago. I wanted you to meet him."

"I meet him next time." Pasquale looked at her midsection and made a prediction. "Is gonna be a boy."

"You think so, Zio?"

"I think so, but maybe is gonna be a girl."

Angelina laughed. "Well, you can't be wrong then." She stepped onto the porch with her uncle and looked down the street in both directions. She hadn't noticed which way her husband had gone. "I don't see Fabian." *Why was Fabian always leaving to see his friends?*

"That's a okay, Angelina, next time I come, for sure I meet him." His smile widened. "I say to Pasqualino. 'Today we no gonna stop until we find you *cugina* Angelina.'"

"Come in, sit down. I'm so happy you're here." Angelina showed them to the table.

Pasquale entered with his little, adopted Chinese son close behind.

Angelina could see by the child's bright eyes and his broad smile that Pasquale had taken good care of his son. Cleaned up with his new clothes, shoes, and a haircut, he looked nothing like the ragged street urchin Pasquale had found alone and brought home.

Angelina kissed them both and told the boy, "It's so nice to see you, Pasqualino. You've grown so much. Look at how tall you are!"

The child beamed at the mention of his height. "I go to school now."

"That's wonderful. You'll do very well." Angelina smiled at her new cousin. "So much good fortune for one little boy."

"Pasqualino gonna be a *dottore!* That's a what I say to Pasqualino, and he say okay."

"A doctor! That's wonderful." Angelina didn't have to ask if her uncle enjoyed being a father; she could see the light in his eyes.

"He so smart, just like'a you, Angelina. *Blood of my blood.*"

Angelina found her uncle's reference to their blood flowing through his adopted child as an affirmation of his big heart. "We don't have any doctors in our family. You'll be the very first, Pasqualino." Angelina patted the child's head.

"I guess your Papa's right. I used to love to study. It must be hereditary." She turned to her uncle.

Her uncle smiled his usual wide grin. "Is okay. We say hello to Fabian next time." Then with a look at Pasqualino, he nodded toward the door.

"Oh, I forgot, Papa," said the boy as he jumped up and stepped outside. A moment later, he reentered and placed two bags on the table.

Pasquale's smile never left him as he reached inside the first bag and pulled out various vegetables and two uncooked chickens. He reached inside the second bag and pulled out milk, cheese, olive oil, garlic, a warm loaf of bread, fruit, and more—a feast to Angelina's eyes.

"You do me the favor, Angelina, you take this food. We make the big mistake, and we buy too much."

She knew her uncle's generous heart, and his kindness brought a tear to her eye. "Thank you so much, Zio."

"No. Grazie to you for taking the food. You see, Pasqualino, I no tell you Angelina is the besta?"

Pasqualino nodded, a smile as wide as his adopted father's lit up his face.

Pasquale was the only person she knew with an endearing way of giving a gift and then thanking the receiver for accepting it.

"Now, I gonna cook, and is gonna be so good, you gonna ask'a for more."

It had been so long since Angelina had sat down to a meal with her family that a great sense of well-being came over her. She smiled at the joy that radiated from the smallest of families—one born Italian Catholic and one born Chinese Buddhist.

"Pasqualino and me, we like Key West so much. I work

with a my friend, Santino, and then after work, Pasqualino and I go fishing every day. Pasqualino even learn to swim."

"It sounds like a wonderful life. It must be great fun to catch and cook your meal. What kind of fish do you catch?"

"Is a called yellowtail snapper and so good." Pasquale picked up the chicken and started preparing the meal. "I gonna tell you about a miracle that'a happen to me back in Santo Stefano, Quisquina," he said punctuating his comment with by waving the bottle of olive oil in his hand.

"What miracle, Zio?" Struck with a familiar rush of warmth remembering the story of talking animals he'd told her siblings. She was eager to hear her uncle tell of yet another miracle.

"Giorgio Piscatelli, he come to see me, and he bring a chicken, justa like this one." Pasquale held it up for them to see. "But it was Friday and Lent, and we no supposed to eat the meat on Friday. Such a fine chicken. I no wanna to make Giorgio feel bad, so I cook the chicken with the garlic and olive oil. But when the chicken, she get ready to eat, something not-so-good happen. We hear a big knock at the door."

Pasquale had her attention. She didn't know what was coming, but it would surely make her laugh.

"The knock, she get louder."

"Who was at the door, Papa?" said Pasqualino, engrossed in the story.

"Patri Farrara!"

"A priest?" Angelina exclaimed.

"We no can believe, but I make the chicken so good with the garlic and olive oil that he pass by and smell it from'a the window. Patri Farrara, he get so mad. He say, 'Today is'a Friday, the day for abstinence! Nobody in Santo Stefano Quisquina, no good Catholic eat meat today, and that's a for sure!'" Pasquale paused. "But fish—she's a okay to eat."

"What happened, Papa?" Pasqualino's eyes were wide.

"Patri Farrara, he walk back and forth, and he pray very loud for Giorgio and me, so we no go to hell."

Angelina could not imagine her uncle in hell, nor could she think of one story of her uncle's that wasn't a treasure.

"Pretty soon, Patri Farrara make the sign of the cross and bless the chicken three times. He say he gonna have to take the first bite to see if God answer his prayer. Then it happened. Such a miracle, like you no can believe!"

Pasqualino gasped. "A real miracle?"

"That's a for sure. It still look justa like chicken, but it taste justa like fish! Everybody happy, and we eat it all!"

Angelina laughed. Nothing filled her with more joy than having those she loved at her table. However, even without a word spoken, the subject of family invaded the corners of the room.

As the smell of roasted chicken filled the air, Angelina remembered the many meals she shared with her family, and a pang of grief twisted inside her.

"I miss everyone."

"But how come you no tell me where you live? If I no see Carmen, I no find you."

"I didn't have your address in Key West, Zio." Angelina quickly handed him a piece of paper and fountain pen. "Please write it down before we forget."

Pasquale took the paper and handed it to his son. "You gonna see how good Pasqualino know how to write."

The boy picked up the pen and wrote every letter carefully, as if sitting in a primary class and wanting to impress his teacher. He then gave it to Angelina with a wide smile.

"Pasqualino, you are a wonderful writer."

Pasquale nodded. "*Non ti preoccupare*, Angelina. You no worry. My brother Domenico, sometimes, he make the big mistake. Sometimes, people think pride is free, but it cost too much. You forget the people you love. In Santo Stefano, Lulli, he write down everybody who make the big mistake in his libretto. He say when you fix'a the mistake, you come back, so he cross out you name."

"I wish fixing mistakes were as easy as crossing them out of a book."

"Everything gonna be justa fine."

There was something so soothing about Pasquale, like the notes of a soft melody, but one you could hear with your heart.

"You gonna like this so much, you gonna ask for more."

The room soon filled with aromas from her past. Pasquale put a dish in front of her, and for the first time in a long while, she ate with her family.

As they ate, Angelina questioned Pasquale about her siblings. He told her of her brothers' latest antics, and they laughed. Then he made his usual declaration after he cooked. "The food she is a ready. And your bambino gonna be the first Italian Presidente of L'America."

Angelina smiled at her uncle's ambition for her child. "His father is Cuban, Zio Pasquale, and what if it's a girl?"

"That'a even more special. We never see nobody in Santo Stefano Quisquina half Cuban. But in L'America, we have everybody, even a girl Presidente. God bless L'America!"

Pasquale had even made up a plate of food for Fabian, set aside for his return.

As they were about to leave, Angelina gave them an extra-long hug and watched them walk away. She marveled at how much her life had changed. The void in seeing them go had already set in. When would they see each other again?

She cleared off the tableware and discovered a small envelope underneath a dish. She opened it and found a twenty-dollar bill with a note. *Non ti preoccupare.* He never wanted anyone to worry.

Pasquale came to America thinking the streets were

paved with gold, only to discover bricks lined he streets. Angelina took the money he left her and placed it under the brick Pasquale had long ago given it to her on her sixteenth birthday. *Remember gold is a soft. And you strong—like the bricks.* His words became her staff to lean on.

CHAPTER 17

Angelina glanced up at the clock striking 10:00 and then at Señor Barria, the latest in a round of lectors, making himself comfortable, taking his seat at the podium, and picking up one of a variety of four newspapers.

"Hot and humid with no relief in sight," said Barria reading the obvious in a strong baritone voice and wiping sweat from his forehead. "The Serbian government made a treaty with Greece against Bulgaria, and the highly anticipated completion of the Panama Canal to open." For Angelina, no one seemed good enough to replace Don Carlos Madrid, and probably no one ever would.

Nearly everyone in Ybor City enjoyed surrendering a nickel or dime on a *bolita* chance and pick the winning number stamped on that one elusive little ball. But today was different.

"Now for the local news and a tragedy about someone we all know."

The cigar makers sat behind rows of long worktables riveted to their seats. And *el lector* stood up with an arm held above his head and fingers pointed to the ceiling; as if demanding everyone's attention, he read the spellbinding headlines.

"Suspected Bolita Corruption Under Investigation! Yesterday, the body of a man commonly known as Bolita Bernardo Fernandez, who wandered throughout the streets of Ybor City selling chances to win at the *bolita* number game, was found dead. He fell asleep on the tracks and was tragically struck by a train severing his body. The popular game of chance raged through Tampa, but without witnesses or evidence, no crime can be proven."

Carmen's mouth fell open. She reached across the worktable and grabbed Angelina's arm. "That can't be true. I saw him yesterday morning and bought a ticket from him."

"I don't believe how it happened." Angelina shook her head. "No one can fall asleep on steel railroad tracks. It's ridiculous and too painful. The agony alone would keep anyone awake. Bernardo has been around the neighborhood for years and would never commit suicide. He must have been dead or knocked out and left on the tracks. Once he fell and broke his leg and talked about the pain for months."

Carmen gazed at Angelina and nodded. "You're right. Murder is the only thing that makes sense. I'm shaking. Poor Bernardo. That might be the last *bolita* ticket I will ever buy."

Angelina understood the fun of trying to win by buying one chance but not risking losing by buying so many. Almost everyone in town played, so she said nothing. Far more concerning was the suspicious death of Bolita Bernardo.

Theories and opinions joined and collided until the closing bell rang.

After leaving the building, Angelina waved down a newspaper boy, gave him her coin, and bought a copy of the newspaper article. Then, while cooking Fabian's favorite dinner of yucca and sausages, she turned the pages and read the full story regarding Bolita Bernardo. The reporter set the scene, embedded his opinion into the facts, and used every word describing death except murder.

Angelina knew shocking stories never blew away, especially ones that happened in Ybor City. She had heard too many. Factory *lectors* gave their distinct flair and interpretation to current events. However, on this day, the story touched everyone. Even a few who had never bought *bolita* chances recognized the name of the skinny man shouting in a high-pitched voice to spend their coins on the next game.

The front door opened, and Fabian walked in. "Everything smells so good."

"That's because I made it, especially for you."

"Well, that deserves a kiss." Fabian came closer, and Angelina fell into his embrace.

"What do you think, Fabian? The news is terrible," said Angelina as she served the food. "The Black Hand killed poor Bolita Bernardo yesterday."

Fabian took a bite of his food and closed his eyes, savoring it. "The newspaper didn't mention the mobsters of the Black Hand; only that Bolita Bernardo was sleeping on the train tracks."

Angelina studied her husband's expression, but he kept eating without further comment.

She continued offering her opinion. "How can anyone believe that? Who can rest their head on iron train tracks? He wasn't found on the side of the tracks; his body was under the train, smashed and ripped to pieces, like someone knocked him out and laid him there."

Fabian looked pensive, but evidently, the graphic description did not affect his appetite as he cut his meat and took another bite. "*Bolita* is illegal, but the police and politicians look the other way. The *bolita* kings pay them a nice bundle to ignore their growing enterprise. Bolita Bernardo must have been doing something he wasn't supposed to do."

"Like what?"

"Like collecting money all week and not turning it over to the big man. He could have been doing a lot of things. It's very easy to steal. You put the money in your shirt and pants pockets, front and back. Then when it's time to deliver the bets to the man running the operation, you empty all your pockets but forget one."

"Maybe that's a good reason to fire him, not kill him."

"Well, perhaps someone in that mob misunderstood the order when told to 'remove him.'"

Angelina made a sobering face. "Fabian, that's terrible."

"That's reality. When dealing with big money, you're not dealing with altar boys. The men are violent and greedy. It takes a sharp mind to outsmart them. Maybe Bolita Bernardo wasn't as clever as he thought and got caught."

The article spun around in Angelina's mind, and she moved her food around on her plate without eating. "I lived by the train tracks all my life. I never saw anyone get hit by a train. Even though I have five siblings, who do things they shouldn't, they know the danger. Not to mention, who can ignore the roar and vibration of the train when it's coming? Bernardo must have been murdered."

"Well, then someone in the police department received good money to turn this murder into a sleeping beauty accident. The *bolita* criminals will pay good money for someone to take Bolita Bernardo's place."

"Why would anyone take such a dangerous job from such violent men when the last man was murdered? There's always work available at the factories."

"The Black Hand can buy anyone. They'll wave a few more dollars under the nose of the next guy so he won't be tempted to steal, or he'll also find his bed on the train tracks."

As the night went on, Fabian shared stories of the underworld, the *bolita* gambling ring, and the budding mafia element terrorizing vendors.

Angelina's face sobered, and she shook her head, recalling her fright when confronted with the Black Hand.

"They create fear. People who are afraid are easy to control. There's talk of a bookkeeper threatened if he didn't change the figures in his ledger," said Fabian.

"Threatened how?"

Fabian looked down at his food. "Things are going on out there that you can't imagine, but if we keep talking about it, I will lose my appetite, the food will get cold, and you might have a nightmare." Fabian took another bite of his dinner and closed his eyes as if savoring it or to ignore his wife. "This is very good, Angelina. What do Italians call it?"

CHAPTER 18

ANGELINA PLACED the letter she'd received from Sophia inside her box of keepsakes. Angelina had kept the letter in her pocket for a time. She enjoyed rereading about the wonderful life her childhood friend had in New York. Sophia and her fiancée were now building a new home together, and she enjoyed reading about all the details.

Angelina put aside her excitement for one old friend and exchanged it for the memory of another. Before reaching for the large volume Don Carlos Madrid had given her, she washed her hands to rid herself of the smell of tobacco leaves —confident that neither *el lector* nor William Shakespeare would have expected any less of her.

This time, Angelina did not open it to read. Instead, she pulled out the money she had secured in a little cloth bag she'd sewed, pinned to the inside of her pocket, and entrusted her earnings to the young prince for safekeeping with others she had hidden. She then set the book once again on the shelf. Angelina believed in security. Even if Fabian didn't always contribute, she saved some of her earnings for their future.

Alone, in the solitude of her home, she often thought of her mother and all she had lost with her death. It would have been a blessing to feel her love and seek her advice and encouragement in everything, especially now awaiting a child.

Angelina entered her bedroom and glanced at her framed marriage license hanging on the wall. She thought about her parent's marriage. Her father had his faults, but he treasured her mother and remained intent on pleasing her.

The front door abruptly flew open with a bang and hit the wall. Fabian came inside, even later than his usual late. "Angelina, *querida!* How was your day?"

Angelina stepped back into the kitchen. "Long, but I made my mother's minestrone soup. Since we've had Cuban dishes all week, I thought you might like it."

Fabian walked to the stove, dipped a spoon into the pot, and sipped. "It's wonderful, and you're wonderful." Although he stood close to her, his voice was a bit too loud, and the faint smell of alcohol teased the air. *He must have stopped at a bar on the way home.*

She served the minestrone, placed a loaf of bread on the table, and took a seat. "Why are you pacing? Sit down and have something to eat with me, Fabian."

Although his smile didn't leave his face, she became uncomfortable. He appeared anxious, glancing at the clock and rubbing the back of his neck until the tension overtook the room.

"Is something wrong?"

"No, of course not. What could be wrong?" He stood and walked to where he kept his whiskey. After pouring himself a glass, he dropped back into his chair.

"You know, Fabian. All the men in my family drink with their meals. They can even make the wine they drink. Priests will take a sip of wine at the altar representing the blood of

Christ. But you drink without stopping like there's a treasure at the bottom of your liquor bottles that you're anxious to find?"

Fabian laughed. "If I find it, I'll share it with you." The meal grew more awkward. He ate quickly, set down his spoon, and reached for her hand.

"Sometimes showing our trust for each other is important." He spoke quickly, and his eyes didn't meet hers.

Fabian's personality had changed. Angelina tensed and remained guarded, as though he held open a door and expected her to pass through without knowing where it led.

"Trust is never given, Fabian. It's earned." It didn't matter what she answered, because he didn't appear to pay attention.

He squeezed her hand, as if to prepare for good news. "I have a wonderful chance at good luck for us. I've forgotten where you said you put the money you've saved for us?" Now he met her eyes.

Angelina stiffened and pulled her hand away. "We agreed not to touch that money. If there's a strike, like they keep saying, it would devastate us."

"After tonight, we'll have no worries. José Valle's on his way. We're going to the cockfights with his prize rooster, *El Diablo*. This time, it's a for-sure winner. I've never seen a meaner bird. We'll double, no, more than triple our money."

Angelina squeezed her hands into fists. "Fabian, we've discussed this often. All we have to do is save what we can and be careful how we spend, and everything will be fine. We'll have nothing to worry about."

"For someone so young, you worry too much. I am being careful. Everything is on *El Diablo*. I'll quadruple it. There's no way to lose. It's for our baby." The more he spoke, the more foolish he sounded, until all his words collapsed on each other into a heap of nothing.

"Double, triple, quadruple?" Angelina jumped up and put both fists on the table as her anger pulsated. "You are the one who told me to save our money and to hide it. But Fabian, do you understand? That's all the money we have? It's for our protection in case of something unforeseen. Neither one of us has parents to turn to."

She picked up his empty bowl, placed it in the sink, and turned to face him. "I always tell you where I put it, but what's the point of saving it if you're going to take it? Everything will work out for us if we're responsible." Angelina shook her head in frustration, and her breathing became more labored. "Don Carlos told me a story about a..."

Fabian jumped up, knocking his chair to the floor. "Why did you always listen to that old fool? His nose was always in books. What did he know about real life?" Fabian stood with his feet apart, his usual stance to keep from toppling over should he sway. "Tomorrow, and all the other tomorrows, we'll do it your way, but tonight we'll bet on José's rooster."

Like all pregnant mothers, it had become instinctive for Angelina to cross her arms over her midsection to protect her child. However, Fabian closed the distance between them, pulled apart her folded arms, and shook her hard as if the money would fall from her hair. "Where are you keeping the money, Angelina?" Brittle words.

She tried to twist her body away from him, but he wouldn't release her. "Where's the money!" he shouted and shoved her against the wall with such force she bumped her head on the small shelf, and the large book fell to the floor. The pages opened, and Prince Hamlet surrendered the modest sum, like a ransom paid for her release.

Fabian's rage turned to laughter so quickly it frightened her. Uncertain and fearful of what he might do next, she didn't move.

"Of course, I should have remembered you picked Shakespeare." As rapidly as he flared up, Fabian calmed, grabbed the bills from the floor, and stuffed them into his pockets.

A loud knocking drew their attention. "Eh, Fabian. *¿Adónde estás? ¡Vámonos!*" José Valle's voice seeped through the front door like a pestilence from the Old Testament.

Fabian flashed a smile at Angelina and tried to caress her face, but she turned away. "*Querida,* forget this. It's nothing. You're still my jewel." He put his arm around her and kissed her lightly on the cheek.

She didn't react.

"Fabian, *vámonos.*" Again, the call to hurry came from outside.

"*Ya vengo.*" Fabian reassured José. In his haste to leave, he stepped on the pages of the book, crossed the room, and swung the front door open without a backward glance and pulled it closed.

Long after he'd left, Angelina remained against the wall, unable to move. He had never raised his voice or pushed her like that. She gazed down at her book and bent over to pick it up. Beneath the outline of Fabian's shoe print lay the words, *when sorrows come, they come not single spies, but in battalions.*

A deafening silence engulfed the house. Angelina felt its heaviness pressing on her skin and against her chest. She had never been around men who drank heavily, never knew how quickly the habit could become a compulsion and affect how they think.

So now what? It had taken hold of Fabian, and he'd become a stranger.

Angelina sat at the table alone, stirring the rest of her soup and recalling how the neighbors had brought soup to her home when her mother died. '*Soup replenishes our tears,*' said her old Sicilian neighbor, Signora Bertelli. The woman knew many superstitions and spells and would have said that

tonight's incident with Fabian was a forewarning of something much worse to come.

For the first time, Angelina did not care when Fabian
returned. Alone and hurt, the clock's ticking seemed to
dominate the house. She thought of setting it on the porch so
she couldn't see or hear it. In the end, she slipped into the
softness of her bed and waited for sleep to rescue her from
the thunderous silence that surrounded her, but her mind
fought back, and sleep never came.

Hours slipped away, and the front door burst open.
Angelina's heart quickened. She closed her eyes and withheld
her resentment.

Fabian entered the bedroom. He cursed the chair he
bumped into, staggered about, kicked off his shoes, and fell
into bed without undressing.

Stillness dominated the room as if she and the night held
their breath. Soon his light snoring settled into a soft
rhythm. As she lay next to her husband, one thing became
apparent—everyone was an angel when asleep. Yet, in the
darkness, with its slivers of moonlight peering through the
curtain, she could make out Fabian's form, and something
else struck her. It was possible to live with someone and still
live alone.

Throughout the night, the incident plagued her. Finally,
the early morning sun rose, and the sky shone a rich blue
devoid of clouds, but for Angelina, the day appeared
exhausted. Fabian didn't wake at his usual hour, nor did
Angelina try to stir him. She'd suffered from morning bouts
of nausea and vomiting, but they had subsided. She dressed
without being heard and left the house unnoticed.

On her way to work, Angelina thought about her life, all
her decisions, and the corners she had turned to arrive at this
point. It had never occurred to her when she married his
problems would now become hers.

Shortly after she returned home, Fabian walked through the door wearing a white shirt and tie, dressed like all cigar makers. He usually returned home much later, which made her wonder what he did with his extra time.

Fabian shook his head in a gesture of defeat. "Before you say anything, I want you to know how sorry I am. I never behaved that way before, and I will never behave that way again. It's bothered me all day. You have every right to be mad. I love everything about you, Angelina. But when I drink, I change. I don't know why." He offered his apology, like a gift he wanted her to unwrap and appreciate. "Do you understand how sorry I am?" asked Fabian.

Angelina crossed her arms. "I'm not sure. Are you explaining this or excusing yourself? Perhaps it's you, Fabian, that needs to understand the possibility that when you drink, the real you appears. You change so much, and each time it gets worse. Do you want us to be happy, or your friends to be happy?"

Fabian squeezed his eyes shut and looked stricken. "I will become a better husband."

Angelina had expected to find Fabian argumentative, defensive, unresponsive, not apologetic. "And what became of our savings?"

Fabian hung his head for a long moment and then met her eyes. "It's gone."

Though it wasn't a surprise, Angelina was stricken by all the hours working it took to save it. "My father would scream when he was angry, I won't. I'm far angrier than that. You lost everything we had. Our savings is our only protection. Do you understand? Right now, I'm working, but when the baby comes, I'll need to take some time off. I don't even know how much. If something should go wrong with you or your job, we'll have no way to pay our rent or bills or buy food. What about our baby's needs?"

Angelina passed her hand over her enlarged belly. Her time was coming closer, and she wanted to bring their child into a loving home, but she couldn't do it alone. If people can change for the worse, then shouldn't they be able to change for the better? "I can't forget how quickly you exploded. You scared me."

Fabian looked deflated. He sat on the sofa and pushed aside the newspaper next to him. "I was drinking too much."

"That's not an excuse because you control it." They had both changed. He'd grown more complex and secretive, and she'd never return to that innocent girl she had once been.

"I don't intend to drink like that again."

For the sake of her baby, she'd have to trust him. "Your hand is pressing the scale. Which way will you tilt it?" She refrained from discussing any subject concerning his drinking friends or gambling, but avoiding something does not erase it.

She could see he was straining to win a battle in his mind. "Life is passion, Angelina. That's what makes it wonderful, and that's what makes it devastating. What if my brother and mother hadn't died? What if my father hadn't abandoned us and if I hadn't been ripped from my country and everyone and everything I knew? Sometimes I shake when I think about it."

He looked up at the ceiling and blinked as though preventing tears from falling. "I used to swim every day. I fished and played. I felt safe, and my parents loved me, but one day, my childhood ended and lost everything. The wounds are deep and remain."

Angelina's frustration deflated. "I loved you more for having endured so much. Still, with every tragedy, we have a choice to grow stronger. We can either kill our past demons or allow them to kill us. If I think of my mother right now and all I've lost with her death, I'd cry all day. If I think of my father's hurtful words and how he left me no choice but to flee, I'd cry. So, what is the best solution, to give power to the tragedy or become stronger than the pain? We also have good memories. If we think only of them, they'll strengthen us."

Fabian's shoulders slumped. "Now, I'm to become a father, like my father who said many times how much he loved me and never returned." He wrung his hands. "I've heard he's still alive and knows where I am. Perhaps he found another wife and has other children. But, I belong to his past, and he's left me there."

Angelina reached for his hand. "It's a terrible story, and your father has behaved unforgivably, but the greater loss is his. He has a handsome son, and soon, he'll have a sweet grandchild. But there's another way to abandon your family without going anywhere—ignore us, make us feel unimportant, or act like we are in your way. I am here for you, but please, I need you here for me, too." She reached for his hand and placed it on her abdomen. "For us." He appeared remorseful.

Angelina struggled trying to make him understand how his behavior affected her.

"Fabian, you're gone so much with your friends. We need to prepare for this baby together. We don't even have names picked out."

Fabian passed his hand through his hair. "We'll talk about it tomorrow."

The heaviness of the last two days had taken its toll, and as they lay in bed at night, she longed to fall into a deep sleep. Angelina could feel Fabian's restlessness, while Fabian seemed troubled.

"Angelina, are you still awake?"

Angelina considered not answering and spoke with her eyes closed. "I'm awake."

"We're having a boy, so we don't need a girl's name."

"In case you're wrong, we could give her our mother's names."

"If that makes you happy."

Angelina yawned. "Well, since you insist it's a boy, would you want to name him after you, your father, or your brother, Diego?"

Fabian didn't answer. Since he had brought up the subject, she didn't understand his hesitation or why it appeared to agitate him. Instead, he sat up in bed. "I want you to know that I won't drink anymore. I'm doing it for the baby. I want to be the best father—one that will always be there, and no matter what happens in my life, I will never leave my son—as my father left me." He laid down again, and Angelina listened to his breathing until it became a soft, rhythmic snore.

She played over their conversation in her mind and his strange behavior. There was a disconnect. Although quiet, he seemed to think out loud rather than speak to her. Fabian was hiding something—something troubling him, something big.

CHAPTER 19

ANGELINA ARRIVED HOME FROM WORK, uncommonly exhausted. The nights had become a struggle to rest, so she set down her small cloth purse, reclined on the sofa, and made herself comfortable. Fabian had returned to moaning in his sleep and fighting off the drumming of sugarcane stalks in his dreams. At times like these, he drifted away like a boat without oars or an anchor.

One moment he'd swear his love for her, and then he'd turn away and drink until she counted the days of his sobriety, the way she used to sort tobacco leaves, separating the good ones from the bad—until she lost count.

Angelina had gone to the post office and mailed Sophia a letter. She about their old friends, who had married, had a child, and moved away. Sophia's life had become magical, so Angelina kept silent about worrisome or unpleasant in life in their exchange of letters.

Today, like every day, Angelina said a silent prayer and made the sign of the cross over her belly, something that had become a habit ever since she first realized a miracle was taking place inside her. The baby never stopped moving, and fatigue had become a constant companion.

Angelina had been angry with God for letting her mother and infant brother die, but she'd outgrown the feeling. The Lord had blessed her and sculpted a child—proof of His love and Divine Power. Her baby would arrive helpless and dependent on her and Fabian, and she intended to show the Lord her undying appreciation of this wondrous gift.

The scale tipped back and forth with Fabian, happy to become a father, fearful and reticent, swearing his love for her, and then turning away and drinking. Left, right, up, down.

She'd try again to trim off what frayed in her marriage and make her home a loving one for the three of them. Fabian appeared to battle within himself.

Angelina remained on the sofa and placed a small cushion under her head. She closed her eyes and envisioned the sensation of leaving her body and floating high above the earth. The sense of weightlessness eased her and her troubles grew small and existed far below. She viewed them as tiny specs in a marvelous and immense universe, and soon drifted into sleep.

Angelina saw herself younger and Rolando holding her the way he had that last day together and telling her to wait for his return. He vanished, but his words were left behind, and stretched and floated and multiplied. Angelina then found herself walking along a narrow path where a baby cried. She ran to comfort her child, but nothing relieved the infant, and the cries grew louder. She tossed about and her breathing grew strained until she awoke, still startled.

Still shaken from the dream, she feared it had been a forewarning. Signora Bertelli would have declared this a sign, but an indication of what? Hadn't Don Carlos Madrid compared her to a warrior? She had to do something.

Angelina rose from the sofa and gazed out the window. The sky had painted its canvas with a palette of grays, for the last two days, but it had remained noncommittal.

The dream lingered. Was it a premonition?

Uncommon for Florida, the day had a chill. She slipped on her light coat and left, determined to find her husband at the end of the well-worn path that led to the tavern where men indulged long into the night.

Amid all the needed preparations, it frustrated her that Fabian did nothing to help. As she walked to the bar, her resolve and anger mounted. Angelina had given much thought to her baby's name, but Fabian constantly changed the conversation when she brought up the subject. So, the selection fell on her.

As she kept walking, her frustration grew. Their child would soon come into the world, and she might as well be a widow.

Scattered droplets fell from the sky, but lost in her thoughts, Angelina took no notice as the sign *La Cantina Latina* came into view. It dangled on one hinge and flapped helplessly, like a drowning man waving an arm for help. As she approached the entrance, a sudden flash of lightning peeled across the, sky followed by the rumbling of thunder.

A large man lurched out of the bar, stumbled, and cursed. Angelina questioned her judgment and said a silent prayer that she had not come in vain.

She straightened her back, sighed deeply, and pushed the swinging door open to a mixture of pungent odors, sweat, beer, and a haze of cigar smoke. Several men turned in her direction. She passed her hand along the buttons of her blouse to ensure all were fastened and placed her arms across her swollen belly to emphasize her condition, in case someone unwelcome approached her.

The cigar smoke proved more potent than she anticipated. She waved her hand in front of her eyes to try and force it away. As she took several steps forward, Angelina reached into her pocket to grab her small fan when she almost tripped on a box on the floor. She quickly grabbed the back of a chair to steady herself and hit the shoulder of a man seated at the table. "I'm sorry I didn't see you there."

At first, he didn't move. Then as if waking from a deep sleep, he turned and appeared to be trying to focus his blood-rimmed eyes on Angelina.

Angelina never forgot a face, and this one had long ago imprinted itself in her memory. "Rico Braccio!"

He offered a dosage of mock formality. "At your service, madam."

"It's me, Angelina Pirrello. I mean, Dominguez."

"Angelina Pirrello?" He said her name as though he had to thumb through a mental journal of past acquaintants to find her listed.

He made several false tries to pull his chair out of the way until he, finally succeeded.

"Angelina Pirrello. That name has a very familiar ring."

"I think it's your head ringing, not my name."

Rico sat slumped in his seat and then squinted as if recovering his ability to focus.

"Yes. Of course, I remember."

Angelina placed her hand on a spasm in the small of her back and lowered herself into the chair across from him to try and relieve the pressure. However, it didn't matter whether she stood or sat. Comfort eluded her now.

He reached for the glass on the table and made a toast. "To my one-time fiancé." But whatever had been in the glass had been consumed. "Our fathers made all the arrangements. And then, you cleverly found a way to break our engagement and send me running. Although, had we married, I suspect you would have kept me entertained forever." Rico swayed slightly in his chair, and she took his toast as sarcasm.

"I seem to remember that you said you did not drink," said Angelina.

Rico glanced at her swollen stomach and smiled. "And I remember you said a doctor told you that you could never have children."

Angelina's face flushed. At the time, she could think of no other way to get out of her engagement with him.

"We fooled each other, Angelina."

"I see drinking hasn't affected your memory."

Rico laughed. "Drinking also has curative powers. I recommend it." Though he seemed somewhat unsteady, his memory remained clear, and he didn't slur.

"I guess you're cured then. Where's your wife, Rico?"

"I can truthfully say I don't know." He appeared unaffected.

Poor Magdalena thought Angelina. "I think you'd better go home. She's probably worried."

"She's not worried. You were right, you know."

Angelina could think of nothing profound she would have shared with him. "About what?"

"You told me if we didn't learn to love each other, we could easily learn to despise each other."

"And you were willing to take that chance. I couldn't." Angelina quickly reminded him.

Neither had forgotten that long-ago conversation. Rico leaned forward. "So, tell me, Angelina, what are you doing here? You're not one of the usual *Señoritas.*"

Why had she taken such a chance coming here? "I guess your wife and I have something in common. My husband likes to come here, as well. I'm sure Fabian's at the back of the building watching the cockfights, but I intend to make my marriage work."

"Then you gained nothing," he said.

For a moment, Angelina resisted what seemed like bait. "What does that mean?"

"We should have married. You're prettier and smarter than Magdalena, and I like your spirit." He sat up straight now. "My wife passes her time embroidering pillows and tablecloths. She accepts everything I give her and everything I say. She talks about nothing worth listening to. Perhaps I wouldn't be here if she had something worth saying, but you can't make a swan out of a chicken. Still, our parents thought it was a great match, and she lives well with every comfort. So tell me, Angelina, do you live well?"

Angelina tugged at her thin coat. "Well enough."

Rico leaned closer and met her eyes. "Did you fool me or yourself?"

Angelina avoided his stare and didn't answer.

Clearly, Rico enjoyed the exchange and seemed far less drunk than she had imagined. He waved at the bartender. "Un café con leche, por favor."

Angelina wondered, who orders coffee in a bar?

This whole discussion gave her pause, and she remained quiet as the bartender set a cup of coffee in front of Rico. He took several sips. "As I said, you should have married me."

For a moment, Angelina imagined him as her husband, but the prospect had no merit.

Rico lifted his head. "Did you know the baker told everyone you would marry him?"

Angelina stiffened. "I never agreed to that."

"So, you married someone else. That's three marriage proposals. Most women are lucky to get one." He looked away as if he caught sight of something in the distance, and then turned back. "Have you ever heard Don Carlos Madrid read in a factory?"

"Yes. Very often, actually." Angelina softened her tone. He

didn't mention her friend's death, and neither did she. The heartbreak of losing him remained painful, and she wondered why he brought up the subject.

"Were you there when he read a centuries-old Spanish story about a young man who left home?"

Angelina never forgot a story. "No, that must have been before I worked there."

Rico took another sip of his coffee and cleared his throat. "It's a fascinating story about a young man who leaves his village against his father's pleas to stay. Eager to seek his fortune and make a better life, nothing could persuade him to stay. Soon he reaches a crossroads with three paths."

Curious about why he brought up this story, Angelina listened to see where it led.

"Unsure which way to go, the villager took the road to the left. Everything goes well until, unexpectedly, the young man makes a fateful mistake. He jumps over a fence, and unaware of the danger, an angry bull charges. The Spaniard is gored to death."

Angelina listened while she pulled out her small fan and cleared the air around her of smoke.

"The author is clever here. He starts the story all over again. The man leaves his village, and his father begs him not to go. When he reaches the same crossroad, this time, he takes the road to the right. His fortune appears much better, but the tide soon turns when a man accuses him of stealing a horse. It's a case of mistaken identity, but they hung the young man or the crime."

Angelina found the story intriguing but said nothing as Rico took a few more sips of his coffee, then set it down. "Last time the Spaniard says goodbye to his father. This time he takes the center path. The journey begins anew with a completely unique experience. In a tavern, he meets several soldiers, a fight breaks out, and—within minutes—a sword ends the young man's life."

A warm flush washed over her face. "Are you saying my life would have ended badly, no matter which road I took or which man I married?"

Rico lifted his cup and finished his Cuban coffee. "You are smarter than Magdalena, but at least you'd have a warmer coat if you had married me and anything else you wanted. And who knows, I believe our marriage would have succeeded."

This ancient Spanish folktale troubled her. No matter which road she'd taken in her life or how different the refrain, the ill-fated chorus remained the same, like the glaring last notes in a tragic opera. Rico had been toying with her.

Angelina did not share his views. Rico didn't know about Rolando Aguirre. No one knew they had fallen in love. Her world had been encased in innocence when she loved him, and when he left, it all vanished, like the fumes from a cigar.

Angelina glanced at the sign, pointing to the back room inviting patrons to the cockfights. Undoubtedly, few women entered that room, and she would have to argue with Fabian in front of his friends to come home—a dismal prospect. He might want to show his friends he was the boss. She had lost her spirit to do battle and should not have come. If he preferred to stay away, then let him.

Angelina turned away to catch the eye of the bartender. "When Fabian Dominguez comes for another drink, tell him his wife was looking for him."

A swift pain seared Angelina's back. She gripped the table and tried to stretch the muscle, but it passed. She stood and gave one last glance at the man her father had wanted her to marry. "Goodbye, Rico Braccio," she said.

"Where are you going? I thought you came to find your

husband. I want to meet him. There's no reason we can't remain friends, Angelina."

"Remain friends? Our fathers promised us to each other in an arranged marriage, Rico, but we were never friends." Still reeling from his story, feeling awkward and out of place, she turned away. This reminder of another near catastrophe in her life further deflated her. With a slight push on the bar's double doors, they swung open and Angelina walked out.

CHAPTER 20

ONCE IN THE STREET, Angelina hastened her step. The sky had become angry, threatening, and
opaque. But her thoughts circled around her unexpected encounter with Rico Braccio and some things he'd said. Had she wanted a happy marriage so badly that she dismissed the gradual turning of the screw?

The pewter sky rumbled, snarled, and grew more incensed and released a riotous downpour drenching the street.

As though in unison, a sharp, crippling pain pierced Angelina's back and forced her to lean against a tree to steady herself. Pains had come and gone all month, but none with such force.

Frightened, she walked another block, and another crippling jolt whipped across her back. Her breathing grew deep and strained, and the rain mixed with the sting of her tears.

In the distance, she could see others darting in a frenzy for shelter. Afraid, she called out to them, but only the thunder answered. As the pain escalated, her breathing became more labored. She grabbed a post meant for tying horses to steady herself and willed the agony to subside.

A whirlwind of debris flew past her. Trees creaked, bent, and moaned. A violent gust of wind swung its force at a large tree branch and ripped apart its once proud limbs, grazing Angelina's arm as it fell. Angelina cried out, but the wind filled her mouth, drying her saliva and choking her.

The gale grew in intensity. The deluge thrashed about her face, forcing her to lift an arm to protect herself. She reached the familiar neighborhood of *casitas* with dirt roads. Saturated now in water, streams of mud rushed about her feet, hindering movement and threatening her balance. Why had she left the house? She accomplished nothing.

Angelina reached her porch and fumbled for the key. Like the tirade of an angry child, the tempest grew stronger and louder. She opened the door as the wind wrestled it. Losing but strength, Angelina had to force herself inside.

With trembling hands, she lit a kerosene lamp, which seemed to cast more shadows than light. Shivering now, she removed her wet shoes and clothing and put on her nightgown and two pairs of Fabian's socks. Her teeth chattered as she placed the mantle clock on her nightstand, then climbed into bed and rubbed her arms to help warm herself.

The pain subsided and then returned more determined. Over and over, the agony continued unrelenting, swaying back and forth like the pendulum of a clock.

Perspiration beaded up on Angelina's forehead. She cried out in agony and gripped the bed sheets as her fear escalated.

In her growing panic, a strange pull of long-forgotten memories and phantoms filled the room. She sensed her mother's presence, could almost smell her lilac perfume, and heard the faint whispers of her voice and the tender way she'd called her name. *Angelina.*

The dimly lit room received sporadic bursts of bright

light and a howl of thunder while the storm beat relentlessly against the windows and outside walls.

With the rhythm of her pain, vivid memories of her mother returned in flashes, the feel of her embrace and her laughter.

Angelina touched two worlds, her own and the one that held her child. She could almost hear the soft murmurings of the Sicilian lullaby she'd sung long ago to her mother when in labor with her infant brother. Now, the melody intertwined with the sounds of her cries. Still, its sweetness encircled her as though it tried to reassure her, but the memory tore at her, remembering they both had died.

"Mama, please help me," she whispered. But no words returned, only roars from the gale as obscure shadows danced across the room. The kerosene lamp flickered like a tired sentry holding a humble illumination against the darkness.

Angelina trembled the way her mother had on that summer's day that stole her from them forever. The agony must have been the same for her mother.

The rise and fall of Angelina's deep breathing and the clock's ticking were the only sounds in the house. *Too much time is passing.* Angelina remembered the words Signora Bertelli had told her father that day. But how much time is too much? And how much time had already slipped by unaccounted for?

Angelina tried to get up, but the pain constricted her movement. Although saturated in perspiration, still, a chill washed through her. If only she had followed through and gone into the back of the bar and pulled Fabian out of the cockfights, Angelina would not have been in such a predicament, but would he have left?

She remembered her father kissing her mother's hand and telling her he loved her. Angelina clasped her hands tightly together. Her father, a midwife, and a doctor had surrounded her mother to care for her, and yet the Angel of Death came and took her away. Angelina had no one. Despite the tempest's roar, she called for help, but again the storm's clamor smothered her cries.

Memories of her mother's agony returned. Angelina could see her face and hear her screams as apparitions appeared to her. It was Angelina's last recollection of child-birth, and believing now that death would also take her, she confessed her greatest sin—her desire to break her marriage vow of accepting Fabian for *better* or *worse.* The better had vanished, the worse had come to pass.

She recited an act of contrition and, in the absence of a priest, made a plea for forgiveness. Then blessing herself, Angelina offered her soul to God without Extreme Unction, the last sacred ritual given to the dying.

Her pleas for mercy came wrapped in painful bindings as she gripped the bedposts above her head and petitioned the Lord to open the gates to the next world and release her from this one. Though the rhythmic pain subsided for the moment, although her mother's presence became stronger than before, she believed the room had now filled with her mother's unmistakable scent of lilacs.

Angelina had the sensation of falling and tightened her grip on the headboard railings the way her mother had that last day. Outside, the thunderstorm pounded, and a large branch broke and slammed against the windowpane.

The air neither cooled her skin nor filled her lungs, and her ragged breathing became more labored.

At first, the banging sound did not distinguish itself from the storm. "Are you all right in there? Can you open the door?" Then, though faint, Angelina recognized Ophelia's voice.

Angelina saw her pain in a kaleidoscope of searing reds

and yellows. It twisted and changed shape and ensnared her with the anguish of her mother's death. She resisted the suffering, but its power overtook her.

What truly happened at the fall of man? Why is *'with painful labor you will give birth'* Eve's legacy to all women? It pulled Angelina deeper into torment. Screams took root inside her, then fiercely tore out of her while the scent of lilacs grew stronger.

"We're coming, Angelina! Freddy's trying to open your door for us." The voice seemed far away, as though mist from a dream.

A vague silhouette appeared before Angelina. Convinced her mother came to take her to the next life, Angelina reached out to touch her and strained her eyes in desperation to see her in the shadows.

Push. It's time to push. Again, the soothing, familiar voice made no sound but swayed in her mind. Again, she glanced around in a panic to see if someone was there. "Mama!" she called out, but no one answered. Still, Angelina sensed she was not alone.

Another rush of sweat washed over her. Her mouth dried, and she clearly remembered her mother had asked her for a glass of water on the day she died.

Push harder. Angelina could feel the voice inside her, and she obeyed. Sicilian women believed the Virgin Mary had endured this suffering and offered her compassion. Had the Virgin sent her mother to comfort her?

The pain reached a pinnacle. Angelina filled her lungs with air, released a scream that bore the depth of her agony, and it resonated in the timbre of her mother's voice.

Angelina's grueling breathing came draped in loud moans. "Mama!" she shouted again; certain her mother was there. "Mama, help me!"

The door flew open. Ophelia burst into the room with

her mother, Esmeralda, behind her. They arrived greeted by Angelina's tortured scream and the primary cry of a child entering the world.

"¡Ah, Dios mío!" said the older woman as she made the sign of the cross.

"What a time for Fabian to be gone," said Ophelia.

Esmeralda rushed to the bed, finished the delivery, and ordered Ophelia to the kitchen for a knife to cut the cord.

"Don't be afraid. It's all over. It's a blessing my husband went outside for a moment and heard your screams over all the thunder and rain," said Ophelia's mother. "Someone watched over you."

Together, the two washed away the mucus of life and wrapped the child in a blanket left in preparation for the infant's arrival.

Angelina's breathing had calmed, but she refused to release the sensation of her mother's presence. Still, no matter how hard she fought to hold on to the feeling, its vibrancy discolored.

Esmeralda laid the baby in his mother's embrace. "It's a boy, Angelina."

Tears swelled in her eyes as a sensation of pure love became overwhelming, gripping, immediate, and not like anything, she had ever known. She kissed his head and cheek, and when looking into her baby eyes, heartfelt words escaped, "I love you, my child, and I will love you forever."

Angelina had never known such an intense sensation and how, in a matter of moments, one could love their newborn infant beyond all reason, beyond the moon, the stars, and all the universe. Moments ago, she believed she stood at the threshold of death, balancing between the two worlds. Astounded, she now looked at the face of her child—God's creation—and, unlike her infant brother, her son cried out to assure her he was indeed alive.

Angelina inhaled the intoxicating scent of this new and glorious life and marveled at his splendor, the beauty of his face, the curve of his lips. She memorized the length of his fingers, the softness of his hair, and longer at the back of his neck. Confident that, should she have to identify him, she could pick him out of thousands of babies. This one child belonged to her, and after all the suffering, His creation humbled and exhilarated her.

"*Pobrecita niña*, but the pain is over, and you've been blessed with a son. He's healthy and a handsome one, *bien guapo*," said Ophelia's mother.

"Only God could produce such a wonder," Angelina sighed, still in awe of the Lord. Though the sky remained bleak and the rain steady, what happened outside didn't matter. With her child in her arms, the sun caressed her face, warm breezes brushed against her, and the earth cushioned her with its softness. She ran her fingers over her baby's forehead, down the bridge of his nose, across his cheeks, and to his lips, like her father had when he held her mother for the last time.

At this very moment that Angelina Pirrello Dominguez made her peace with God. She was both profoundly grateful for the safe arrival of her son and ashamed that she'd blamed Him for the death of her mother and brother.

"This one will make the girls cry. Look at that dimpled chin," said Esmeralda.

"If only my family were here," whispered Angelina with a deep sense of regret.

Ophelia held the baby's tiny fist. "They'll see him soon enough. You must have some powerful lungs for us to hear you over this terrible storm, Angelina."

But Angelina knew her voice could not have carried. "Did you see another woman here?"

"No." Both Ophelia and Esmeralda shook their heads.

Angelina kissed her baby again. "I'm certain someone else was here." She saw their disbelieving expressions. "It must have been the storm or the wind howling," said Angelina, but in her heart, she didn't believe that. It had been beyond extraordinary and mystifying, like a gift from her mother and God's grace in her desperation to receive help.

Angelina knew the sound of her mother's voice and her lilac scent, and she knew she had not been alone and would never speak of this again. The church teaches the spirit never dies. It has to exist somewhere. Why would the spirits not help those they loved and were still living? Signora Bertelli would insist her mother would not have abandoned her at such a time.

Angelina looked into the tiny face of her child. "Mama," she said softly and pressed against the tightness in her throat. "See what a wonderful grandson you have."

Ophelia patted the baby's head. "Are you naming him after your husband?"

Throughout her entire ordeal, Angelina had not thought of Fabian. It seemed an intimate moment between her, her mother, and her newborn. More than that, she thought of her mortality and how she might have died in childbirth, like her mother. But Angelina was not alone, and no one would ever convince her otherwise. On such a day, with God's grace, her mother returned. "I'm naming him Don Carlos, after *el lector*. He will be Don Carlos Dominguez, and like his namesake, he'll be a good man, kind, and wise. He will study poetry and literature, attend a university, and be respected."

Ophelia repeated the name, and then her hazel eyes grew larger. "Men usually want a first son named after themselves. Did your husband agree to the name?"

"No."

"Then what will he say?"

A tear slipped from the corner of Angelina's eye. "What

he always says, 'You're my jewel.'" Angelina could only offer her child a name. She had nothing else, not even a family.

Ophelia's mother straightened the bedding around Angelina. *"Mi hija,* get something for Angelina to eat."

"I don't think she wants to eat now."

"I didn't ask you if she wants to eat. I said go and get her something to eat. Bring back some fruit and some *pastelitos.* Angelina deserves a dessert after all this. It will be here for her whenever she's hungry and don't come back without *violetas* for the baby."

"Violetas?" said Angelina.

"It's a sweet, light fragrance to calm babies." Esmeralda smiled at Angelina, but Ophelia didn't move quickly enough for her mother. "Go, go."

"I'm going. I'm going."

After the door closed, Esmeralda turned to Angelina. "My children question everything I tell them, as if they know better. Hah! How is it possible they know so much, if I know so little, how?" She took a cloth and wiped the perspiration from Angelina's forehead and told her stories of when she had her children. "We all go through the same thing. So, don't worry about anything, just rest. Everything will be fine, and may you get everything you wish for."

Angelina looked at the older woman and gave her a weak smile. "My Uncle Pasquale says the Chinese have a curse. Do you know what it is?"

"No."

"May you get everything you wish for."

"Hah! That's why the Chinese live on the opposite end of the world. What kind of people can't tell a wish from a curse?" said Esmeralda.

Enchanted by her infant, Angelina turned to admire this miracle that was now hers. She remained in awe of the softness of his skin, his tender features, and how her heart burst with love. "I'm the happiest I've ever been in my life."

The door opened, and Ophelia handed her mother a small flask. "Here it is, Mama."

The older woman opened it, smelled what was inside, and smiled at Angelina. Then, with the infant still in Angelina's arms, Esmeralda leaned over and with a soft cloth, dabbed some of the scented violet water on the newborn. "Cuban mothers believe in this *agua de violetas.* They say it comforts infants and reminds them of Heaven."

Angelina saw no harm in it and no reason to object. Her mother and grandmothers believed in superstitions and spells, and no doubt Signora Bertelli would have come up with an Italian version of a similar belief.

Ophelia's mother reached over and took the baby. "Every time a child is born, it's a sign God is giving us another chance. We'll watch Don Carlos while you sleep."

The clock chimed. Fabian should have been home by now. He must be winning or drinking too much to make his way home, but this day belonged to her son, and no one and nothing could deflate the joy of such a blessed day.

"Thank you so much for everything." Angelina's words were unhurried and fatigued while this day of tensions drifted away. She soon fell into a deep sleep amid the tender sounds of her newborn, the crackling of the storm—and the fading scent of her mother's lilac perfume.

CHAPTER 21

THE FRONT DOOR opened late at night, and Fabian walked in. He went to the kitchen, moved about, dropped a pan, and the baby cried. Fabian dashed into the bedroom and gasped.

"Angelina! Oh, my God. When did this happen? Is he all right? Are you?"

He hadn't questioned if she'd had a boy or girl, but asked if *he* was all right. Overrun by emotion and still in a haze of joy from the miracle of childbirth, Angelina could not fully gather the depth of her frustration with Fabian to express herself.

He crossed the room, sat on the bed next to her, and watched them as though in wonder. Angelina saw no point in spoiling the moment. "Would you like to burp him?"

Fabian's eyes widened. He reached for his son and gently patted his back. "Angelina, I'm… His voice trailed off, and tears slid down his cheeks.

Angelina gave a weak smile. "I know how you feel. I feel the same. Our son is perfect, Fabian, down to every little finger and toe. And no child should come into this world without a name. So, without your help, I named him Don

Carlos after the most knowledgeable, and the kindest person I've known. I'm calling him Donny."

Fabian nodded his approval. "I'm sure you think I didn't care about the baby's name, but when I was four, my mother was pregnant and asked my brother and me what to name the baby. She made it a game. We picked the names, and she lost the baby. When I was six, my mother had another son. We were so excited, and we picked a name again, but Daniel was very weak and grew weaker. At four-months-old, he slipped away. When you asked me to name the baby, it felt like I might curse the baby. I couldn't do it. Don Carlos is a fine name."

"Why wouldn't you tell me when I asked? I wish you would confide in me. You hold too much inside you, and I can't read your mind."

Fabian sat next to her on the edge of the bed. She reached out and put her hand on his knee. "Fabian, we have to be closer. We have to trust each other for the sake of our child."

"I know it's an honor to name a child, and foolish not to, but the memory returned, and I couldn't do it." The baby burped, and they both laughed.

Fabian took him off his shoulder, studied his face, and choked up. "I've never been so happy. He's perfect and what a miracle to hold my son. He's my blood, my whole family."

"That's an expression my father always uses. *Sangue del mio sangue,* blood of my blood."

Angelina recounted how she went to the bar in search of him, struggled to make her way back through the storm, gave birth alone, and how the neighbors came to help. She did not mention Rico Braccio, her former fiancée, or her belief that her mother's spirit had guided her through the pain and birth.

Still embracing his child, Fabian turned to Angelina. "You're hurt and angry. I understand, but how could I have known you would give birth today? How could I know you even left the house to find me or that you would get caught outside in a terrible thunderstorm while in labor and all alone? You never said you were in pain or I would have stayed by your side through it all."

"Fabian, this is my first child. I didn't know I would give birth today, and I don't want to spoil this moment by arguing. The baby is an enormous joy to both of us. He's my whole life. So let's make a good life for all of us—a wonderful life. Don't you want that, too?"

Fabian kissed his son and tears ran down his cheeks. "After losing my whole family, maybe I've been afraid to try again. But my heart is so full with Don Carlos in my arms. I can't believe he's here."

"I know. I've been sitting here for at least two hours just looking at him. Ophelia's mother said every time a baby is born, it's like God gives us another chance to make things right."

Fabian kissed Angelina. "I'm so sorry you were alone. It's just something inside me that's so unsettled and drinking calms me."

"You sound possessed, and that scares me. Your son and I are your reason to try harder."

Still in the warm glow of Donny's birth, their conversation continued for days. It rose and diminished until all the words had been said, and nothing remained but residue.

Every day, Fabian came home, rushed to the crib, held up Donny, and beamed. *"Mi hijo!* A first-generation Cuban-American!" He kissed him, and his voice had a special softness when he spoke to his son.

With all his flaws, Angelina had to admit Fabian had proved himself a devoted father. When the baby cried, Fabian carried Donny around without complaint. He sang to him, fed him, and even changed him.

"You know, Fabian, I have no memory of my father being so attentive. I'm surprised and impressed."

He set the baby down in his crib and smiled at Angelina. "You must know I love him. How could I not?"

Fabian's love for his child never diminished, but after six weeks had passed, he took his fatherly bow, closed the curtain, and returned to the way he had been. "It's Saturday, and I promise we'll spend the day together, but first, I'm going to be gone for a few hours."

The spell had broken. Although he did not use a name, it seemed clear Fabian would meet José. If he were going anywhere else or meeting anyone else, he would have said so.

She had not found a liquor bottle hidden in the house since the first moment she placed their son in his arms, but nothing else remained the same.

"I'm not trying to be unreasonable. I understand a man taking a drink. My father had a glass of wine with his meals, and so did his father and lots of men. My family has even made wine, but this is not the same. You drink and keep drinking until you are indifferent and transformed. Don't you want to build a happy life with our little family?"

Fabian kissed her. "I've told you before; you worry too much for someone so young."

"You're only three years older than I am, Fabian."

"And you don't see me worrying."

"That's what worries me."

He blew her a kiss and closed the door behind him. Angelina gazed out the open window and watched his hurried steps. More concerning than his drinking was his drastic change in personality.

Did he rush out to bet on a cockfight? A soft breeze came through the window and brushed against her face, but it had no power to soothe her or the ominous sensation that something bad had begun.

CHAPTER 22

DONNY SMILED A LOT. He was healthy and slept through the night, and Angelina would return to work soon. She looked around her small *casita* and had no intention of spending her day staring at the walls.

She took her baby, left the house, and went down to the Cuban marketplace. The *platanos* were perfect. These thick-skinned tropical bananas had become one of her favorites. Fried in oil and the riper, the sweeter they tasted.

"Angelina! I can't remember the last time I saw you." Angelina stiffened at the sound of the woman's voice she recognized right away.

Although holding packages, Doctor Martino wasted no time approaching her with his outstretched hand. He took hold of hers and then patted the baby. "You've turned into a lovely young lady; this must be your handsome son."

The doctor appeared tired. His hair had turned gray. In contrast, Maria could not have looked more pampered and fashionable.

"It's so good to see you both," said Angelina, as she held her baby closer.

"We come to this market now and then. My father, may God rest his soul, would come here and buy groceries to cook his Cuban food. My mother remained faithful to her Italian dishes. But how interesting to run into you, Angelina. How are you doing?" The penetrating gaze on Maria's face did not match the innocence of her question.

"I'm fine. I enjoy Cuban food, so I come here often." The baby moved about in her arms. "This is my sweet baby Don Carlos Dominguez. We call him Donny. And how are your sons?"

"They're growing before our eyes. I can hardly believe it," said Maria as she lifted a hand to smooth her hair or draw attention to the latest style.

"And your husband, Angelina, how is he doing?"

Ah, there it was. How is he doing? No one asks that of a person they don't even know.

"We're all just fine. Thank you for asking?"

"Your son is the picture of health," said the doctor enthusiastically.

Angelina smiled. "I think he must be. He's so sweet and is always happy. I feel so lucky to have him."

"Why don't you come for a visit—with your husband—as soon as I get back from my trip? We had someone give us several bottles of some special wine he had brought back to us from Italy. I'm sure your husband will appreciate their flavor." *There it was again. Either Maria has grown more accommodating or clairvoyant. Otherwise, how did she know about Fabian's drinking?*

"Thank you for your kind invitation, Maria. I will tell my husband you have found a wine you especially like to drink. We'd love to come." Angelina refused to let the woman think she had struck a nerve.

"You know you're always a welcome sight." Doctor Martino spoke in the soothing voice familiar to his patients while adjusting the package in his arms. "We were picking up a few last-minute items for Maria's voyage. She sails next week to England."

"Maria's voyage? Aren't you going, too, Dottor Martino?"

Maria snapped back before he could answer. "My husband is not the kind of man to abandon his patients. However, if the patient dies, everyone thinks the doctor has killed him, but if he gets well, the saints have preserved him. Still, I wouldn't dream of pulling him away to go to England."

Angelina wondered what the woman was up to. "I've never heard of an Italian crossing the ocean to go to England. Everyone goes back to the old country."

"England is more civilized. The last time I visited Italy, they experienced a devastating earthquake." Maria pushed her handkerchief into her handbag and pulled out a fan. She flung it open and with a brisk back-and-forth movement she underscored her impatience rather than the heat.

"I am so glad Maria has this opportunity to enjoy a trip," said the doctor. "She is always so attentive to our children, her aging mother, and the rest of the family. Kindness should be rewarded."

"Of course, we should all reward kindness." Angelina had never known Maria to be kind, but she must have her moments.

"My cousin and aunt insist on seeing Buckingham Palace." Maria sighed. "I'm just going along to be accommodating, but of course, while I'm there, I might as well purchase a few things."

So, you're going on an elaborate European vacation and made it appear you're sacrificing to accommodate others. That's clever, she thought.

Everything depended on perspective. The doctor thought his wife a saint. Angelina's opinion of the woman remained unaltered from the day Maria pulled her by the hair, cursed her with *malocchio, the evil eye,* and tried to throw her out of the doctor's office while she had only come to seek help to save her dying mother.

But Maria would tell the story differently, claiming she did not know why fifteen-year-old Angelina hadn't made her reason for the visit clear. Had she only done so, Maria would have understood the gravity and been bound to help in every way.

Signora Bertelli's words returned to Angelina. *No matter how thin you slice the bread, there are always two sides.*

The doctor smiled at Angelina. "It's a pleasure to see you, my dear, but I must attend to the sick. Please remember to stop by. I'll look forward to your visit."

Angelina gave him a warm goodbye.

"And please, give our best to your husband." This was the third time Maria mentioned Fabian, someone she'd never met. Her mother is Italian, but her father was Cuban. Perhaps there's a connection, perhaps one of his relatives knew of Fabian's weakness. Interesting how not once did she acknowledge Donny right in front of her.

Angelina kissed her baby. Some things didn't matter after all.

CHAPTER 23

THE SUN APPEARED disinterested in the comings and goings beneath it, but Angelina had planned to make good use of the day. Her son was in the care of Eva Chavez, a grandmother, who seemed so excited each time she cared for him, and Fabian promised to bring home a small dresser for Donny's growing belongings. So far, lots of promises, lots of passing days, and no dresser.

When Belarmino's red and green sign came into view, Angelina approached the shop and glanced through the large picture window at a sofa, two overstuffed chairs, and a small coffee table. Nothing of particular interest caught her eye, but she knew her cousin had far more stock in his back room.

She tightened her hold on the door's brass handle, then released it as if it scorched her hand and considered the consequences of entering. Belarmino owned the store, but Belarmino's mother and Angelina's were sisters. She would have to give her cousin her address to deliver the dresser, and he would tell his mother, who would ask for a copy of her address. Zia Violetta would show up at her home with her remarkable knack for passing judgment and scrambling others' lives. With an unstable marriage and a baby to care for, Angelina saw no reason to involve Zia Violetta in her already complex situation.

She never approved of her sister's marriage to Angelina's father and would never approve of Angelina's marriage to a mere cigar maker. With her address in hand, there would be no stopping Zia Violetta from seeking her out to make her objection clear.

Unlike his mother, Belarmino had a gentle soul, but there had been an explosive scene between Violetta and Angelina's father, Domenico. Upon the death of Angelina's mother, Zia Violetta came to take all six children away from her father.

Finito! Her father yelled and slammed the door in her aunt's face. The scene weighed heavily on her memory.

Now, she stood in front of the store's entrance and looked down the street as she contemplated walking away, but why should she? She was now an adult, married, a mother, and had a mind of her own.

Angelina straightened her back, grabbed the door handle again, and walked inside. This was nothing new. She had been in the store countless times. Yet, she had a strange sensation as she walked across the room.

"Belarmino!" she called out. "Where are you?" The store had chairs piled high, sofas bumped against each other, and tables stacked with their legs removed for easy storing and reassembly. She made her way around them to a narrow aisle leading to the back, where she expected to find her cousin and a more extensive selection of furniture.

An almost breathless quiet encased the room, like that first surprising moment when something falls, breaks, or slams. Angelina turned around, and in a burst of rapid heartbeats, she gazed at the face of Rolando Aguirre.

"Angelina! Oh, my God. At last, it's you!"

"Rolando." She had not said his name in such a long time and could only murmur it now in a whisper. It seemed like she had fallen through the rabbit hole, whereby the past invaded the present in some timepiece reversal.

Was she sleepwalking, dreaming? After incalculable months of praying, worrying, waiting for any word from him or about and believing something frightful had happened, Angelina could not fully digest his sudden appearance.

She saw no sign of an injury, disfigurement, or anything noticeable that might have explained the reason for so long an absence. On the contrary, he looked wonderful. As always, he was tall, his posture straight, and his muscles from heavy lifting bulged inside his shirt. He was as she remembered him, and his sunlit red hair had metamorphosed into burnt shades of auburn.

Angelina stepped back. "I don't know what to say, Rolando." Once again, his name escaped the hidden compartment she had sealed away in her mind. She'd searched for him everywhere. Now she looked into his eyes, and a flurry of emotions exploded inside her. It reeled her back to a time of such fear for his safety and the hours of intense prayer. Angelina could not resurrect what had long ago left her devastated. Instead, she turned around to leave.

Rolando darted forward and caught her by the arm.

"Please don't go, Angelina. Don't go."

The sudden touch of his hand rekindled the familiar tug of her heart. The powerful emotion overtook her. She needed to get away. "We have nothing to say to each other, Rolando."

"Yes, we do. I have more to say."

Angelina squeezed her eyes shut, willing this cruel hallucination to vanish, but nothing happened. "Whatever you have to say, it doesn't matter now." She needed to leave before the trembling inside her became obvious and before she revealed how much he affected her. "Let me go, Rolando."

"But first, you must listen to me, please." His voice was gentle and soothing, like she remembered, and she felt herself sailing back in time. But now, at such a difficult time in her marriage, she feared a dangerous vulnerability.

Startled by her own reaction to Rolando, Angelina reached for an anchor of words to ground herself, "There is nothing to talk about, I'm married, and I have a wonderful son."

"Yes, I know about Fabian Dominguez and I'm sure you love your baby."

He knows Fabian. What does he know? Angelina's mind raced with Rolando's admission. It took her a moment to respond. "How well do you know him? No. Don't tell me. It doesn't matter."

"You deserve to hear what happened."

She looked away. "What was between us, Rolando, is in the past."

He met her eyes. "Is it?" he asked and paused. "I respect everything about you, but sometimes, the past is more alive than the present." His voice was soft and calming, like warm salve soothing a painful injury, and like before, she remembered the contrast in her father's harsh way of speaking.

Angelina stood rigid, caught in a tug-of-war of emotions.

"No matter what happens after today, and if you never want to see me again, I need to tell you why I couldn't come back to you and why you never heard from me. Give me at least that."

Rolando released her arm.

Ashamed, he could still affect her like this, Angelina stepped back. "No, I waited for you, and waited." Her voice faltered.

"Every day, I thought of you. Day after day. So many

nights, I dreamed of you. As soon as I returned, I went straight to your house. I had to make that vision I held onto come true." His words were strong and resolute, but his voice remained tender and calming.

"I don't want to hear it. You never came back. You never wrote." Angelina's throat tightened, and her voice faded.

"I couldn't come back, and I couldn't write because I was in prison." His words were heavy now, more vital, draped in frustration.

Angelina's eyes widened. "Prison? How could something like that happen to you?" There was nothing about Rolando that would bring about such a terrible fate. "Prison?" she repeated. "Why didn't someone tell me?"

"Even my family had no idea what happened. I became entangled in the effort to save a kidnapped union leader. Factory owners hired the Black Hand to create fear and threaten our plans to strike. You know they are violent men. You've seen what they can do, but this order was not to kill, so they took the head of the union Federico Galvez out of the country to Spain at gunpoint to disappear. If the union won, wages would be raised, and benefits offered. That enraged the factory moguls. Nothing matters more than the bottom line."

"I don't care. This has nothing to do with me." Angelina hit him in the chest.

"It has everything to do with both of us. This unraveled our lives. The union knew where Galvez was being held. I was born in Spain, spoke the country's Castilian dialect, and was an officer in the union. They gave me the job to rescue Galvez and return to America."

"Why didn't you admit you were going to Europe? You said you were going south to Key West, and you'd be gone for two weeks. Like a fool, I watched the passengers come off the trains for more than a year hoping to see you."

"I would never lie to you. The union intercepted my trip. I was sworn to secrecy and put on a ship to Spain that day. I thought I could send you a message when I got there, but it ended in a disaster. They arrested me within hours."

He ran his hand through his hair in obvious frustration.

"What? Why?" She fought to control the tremor in her voice.

"It had nothing to do with the cigar union. Young men were screaming about injustice and rioting in the streets. The police were on horseback, trampling people and shooting them. I was there, and that's all it took. We were rounded up and thrown in prison, and held for more time than I wish to count. I would still be there if it weren't for Javier Rivera."

"Is he an attorney or from the union?"

"No. Javier was a political prisoner, and he knew I wasn't involved with the movement. One day, rioters stormed the prison. The revolutionaries broke through the gate, and Javier led me out and helped me escape, or I would still be there."

"I can't believe no one knew what happened to you."

"And we could not communicate with anyone. The best way to get rid of political prisoners is to throw them in jail, half starve them, forget they exist and hope they die. Unfortunately, the union did nothing. They didn't work hard enough to find me."

Angelina watched every gesture, movement, and expression Rolando made. His red hair had darkened to auburn, but more than that, he appeared more determined, more independent. "I can't believe they could hold you. Didn't you have papers or something to prove you had just arrived from America and why you were there?"

"Yes, they collected them, and I never saw them again.

After all that time, it took me another two months to get home."

Stunned at what Rolando was telling her. Angelina could not believe that this single event had changed the course of her whole life. "Then how did you get home without money or papers?"

"When I escaped, I contacted the union in Spain and they booked my passage back and money to return. Before doing anything or seeing anyone, I went straight to your home to find you. I saw your father, and the moment I mentioned your name, it was like igniting a cannon. He ordered me out, and that was the end. I asked everyone where you were, but no one knew."

"I dared to try again. I had to see you. This time, your brother, Vinny, answered the door. He said your father would be furious if he saw me, but that didn't matter. I was ready to do whatever was necessary to see you again."

Angelina weakened at the revelation. She couldn't fight her tears. "Rolando, I waited, I prayed, and I cried. This is the first I've known of you in over two years. You just vanished. I thought you didn't care anymore or you'd met with a tragedy. How could I think otherwise?"

Rolando's expression softened. "I never stopped caring. The moment the prison doors opened, I sent you a letter, several letters—every chance I had."

Angelina released a painful sigh. "My father would never have given me a letter from a man in Spain, and it would not have mattered. I was married by then. I am still married." Angelina choked on her words, "Rolando, I loved you. No matter how long I would have waited for your return, I had no word. Nothing! You said you'd be gone two weeks, and I believed you." Angelina's breathing grew deeper and heavier as she confessed the powerful emotions she had suppressed. "Two weeks became four, and then eight, and twelve." She raised her voice until she nearly shouted. "Weeks became months, became years!" Hysterical now, she cried long, painful, gasping sobs and couldn't stop. "I waited an eternity."

Rolando pulled her close, and she cried against his chest. The day had turned around and turned around again. Its essence filled the room, and Angelina released all the heart-break that spilled from her heart.

This was the moment they understood each other and what lingered inside them, but they spoke cautiously, expressing their regrets of love lost but keeping it in the past where it was to remain. Their lives had become a complex puzzle, and there was no way to solve it, so they put all the pieces back in a box.

"Vinny told me you were married to Fabian Dominguez, and you were having a child." Rolando paused. "I was lost with those words, but I loved you enough not to seek you out and disrupt your life, not if you were happy."

Not if you were happy. The words were almost painful.

"Even now, it's a miracle we are together for just these moments," he spoke softly.

Angelina's emotions collided. She wanted to proclaim she was indeed happy with Fabian, and she would slam all doors that led to Rolando, but when she tried, she found herself incapable of voicing such a lie.

"You were always with me, Angelina. You will never know what I endured in that prison, caged like an animal, but you were my anchor, and because of you, I kept my sanity. Endless days blended into endless nights without distinction. No matter what torment I suffered, I held you close. Love is strange and powerful. It has no walls, no ceil-ings, or floors. It just drifts about, ever-present, like the air we breathe."

Again, Angelina wanted to pour out her heart and tell

him what she believed he wanted to hear, but this was not a line she intended to cross or tear down the barriers. "Because I lived across from the train terminal, I listened for the whistle and metal wheels grinding to a stop. I hurried to look out my window for you, but you just vanished without a word." This was all she would allow herself to say.

He had broken her heart. She'd endured searching everywhere for him? But now, what was the point?

"I know the world has moved on without me, but I'm overjoyed just seeing you."

She couldn't conceal the injustice of losing Rolando, and she voiced her anger in a moment of frustration. "What else could I believe but that you had forgotten me?"

He gazed around the room as though searching for the right words—words that wouldn't cause injury to either of them. "I couldn't write in prison. They mocked us, said everyone forgot about us." Rolando shook his head in obvious defeat. He looked pleadingly at Angelina, as though the words he wanted to would die inside him.

Angelina rubbed her arms nervously. "My own life at home grew unbearable. My father drove me out of the house by arranging marriages for me. The last one was a widower with four children, the ages of my siblings. He was wealthy, and my father felt he had arranged a good match without telling me. I had so little time and made a drastic decision right away. I left home in the middle of the night. Fabian was loving then." These words were softer but doused with regret.

"'Then? Fabian was loving *then*?'" Rolando repeated her words in the same tone she had said them.

Angelina was now certain they were both afraid to say what they were thinking. She didn't answer, and a long silence followed.

Rolando came closer and pulled her into his arms. They

stood still. Neither spoke. They didn't have to. So much heartbreak had befallen them, and after all their effort to find each other, it seemed only appropriate they be allowed this one innocent embrace.

All alone in the store with stacks of furniture piled around them, she imagined they were somewhere else, away from the world, where they could be who they were meant to be, and nothing around could penetrate the shield of this single minute in time. Rolando slipped his hand under her chin and tilted her face upward to meet his eyes as if he wanted her to know something that he couldn't say, and if either breathed too heavily, they would break the fragile gossamer wing that held them together.

Though struck by a rush of emotions, Angelina never let her thoughts escape her lips. If things had happened differently, would she still have the son she loved beyond reason?

Fate had stepped between them. This had not been a mystical story. This was her life. No matter how strong their love was, they had arrived at the end.

Angelina gently released herself from Rolando's arms. "Everything comes down to a few words—I'm married, and I have a wonderful son, Donny." Angelina could hardly bear the pain of what she knew she had to say. "Goodbye, Rolando. It's too late for us. Everything has burned. All that's left are the ashes."

She turned her back, but he put his hand on her shoulder. "From ashes, a blaze can ignite." He stepped in front of her and met her eyes. "I will never seek you out or destroy your happiness, and perhaps this is the last time we will see each other, but if you need me, I will come."

As Angelina turned her head, and her hair moved, it uncovered a glimpse of a familiar gold chain—Rolando's Saint Jude medal. Rolando reached for it and slid it out from under her collar. She said nothing.

"The saint of miracles. I gave you this the day I left and asked you to wait for me. Do you wear it because you believe miracles are possible," he paused, "or because you still care for me?"

She remained silent.

"Tell me."

Angelina didn't expect such a direct question, but why should it matter now? Their moment had perished long ago. "I've worn it a long time. It brings me comfort." She took the medal from his hand and again slipped it under her collar. Their meeting had grown too impassioned. Her eyes swelled with tears she didn't want him to see. They both knew each other's heart, but there would be no admissions, no promises, no vows.

Rolando shook his head. "Sometimes, when I look down this street, I feel a memory. It's a powerful impression. We used to walk together after work, talking and making each other laugh."

Angelina appreciated how his comment lifted the tension. "You told me how everyone in Spain loved King Ferdinand, who spoke with a lisp, and how he'd go to the ocean, fill his mouth with seashells, and try to talk without a lisp. Then, so as not to embarrass him, the entire country spoke with a lisp. And it's still spoken that way today."

Rolando smiled. "As I remember, we were only going to allow each other one question to find out about the other."

"I wanted to know what you thought of the Suffragettes," said Angelina

He snickered. "Because you had to know right away what kind of person you were talking to."

"That's right."

"Then I asked you what you thought of King Alfonso III of Spain."

Angelina laughed. "I didn't know who Alfonso was, but if he was a king, it seemed he could order the very best."

"So, you told me he smoked Perfectos and Havanas. It seems we were trying to outsmart each other."

They broke into laughter at their memories of each other, and a vibrancy filled the air the way it used to in those days gone by. Rolando and Angelina had a shared past, but after the laughter came a distressing silence. For a few fragile moments, neither spoke.

Rolando reached for her hand. "I want you to always to remember this. You waited for my return, and that means everything to me. I'm the one that let you down and didn't come back. Had I not gone on that assignment..." For a moment, his voice faded. "It doesn't matter now. Whether it was fate or destiny, things are the way they are. We lost a lot of time, and things would have been different if I had returned when I told you. I want you to be happy and know that I'll always be here for you and your son, Donny—no matter what the future brings."

Filled with overwhelming emotions she feared couldn't control, Angelina abruptly turned away and rushed out the door without a backward glance.

"Angelina!" Rolando called, "Don't go!"

But she didn't stop, answer, or look back. Flooded with memories of Rolando, tender memories, joyful memories, loving memories—but that was then. The past had no place in the present. Angelina walked away, moving more and more quickly until she ran.

CHAPTER 24

OVER AND OVER AGAIN, Angelina contemplated the strange series of events that separated her and Rolando for nearly two years. Yet, in all that time, without word, nothing sustained them.

His long-ago disappearance had once occupied all her waking hours, and now he had reappeared at the thirteenth hour when she had married and had a child. The encounter was the rarest of serendipitous moments, much like that frantic day of panic amid Florida's most destructive fire, and in all the chaos, their eyes met.

Though this time, like the first, neither sought out the other. Their unexpected happenstance unnerved her. It revived the memory of how happy she had once been with him. She shook her head as though to rid herself of any further such thoughts. She glanced at the calendar. The only thing that mattered was today, not yesterday.

She and Fabian had a wonderful child, and Angelina intended to commit herself to fortifying her marriage, thinking only of good moments, improving all the rest, and working together to build a life. Besides working full time, she kept her house spotless, cooked Fabian's favorite meals, and his clothes were washed, ironed, and ready in a day or two.

She suspected Fabian still bet on those gruesome cock-fights, but for the moment, Angelina held her tongue. That did not mean she accepted the cruel and shameful activity—on the contrary. Since they considered bullfighting an art form in many countries, what chance did a little rooster have in America?

Although they had never discussed it, she could not picture Rolando watching small animals slash each other apart, but it didn't matter. She would not complicate her life further. Angelina intended to remain faithful to the man she married.

No one was at home on the day Zio Pasquale came to town. So, he left Angelina a note to find him at Guillermo's, the Cuban café on Setima Street. Upon finding his note, Angelina dressed her son in his nicest baby clothes to meet her favorite uncle. She lost no time rushing to the restaurant where large menus in Spanish stood nailed to the wall, and bentwood chairs encircled round tables.

Angelina arrived, searched the room, and spotted her uncle talking to his friend Giorgio from their days at Garcia-Marcos Cigar Factory.

Pasquale jumped to his feet when he saw her come through the door. "Angelina! I so happy to see you." She rushed to him, and Pasquale kissed her and the baby on both cheeks.

"Oh, Zio, you do not know how good it is to find you, but I can't stay too long. I just wanted you to meet my baby. Don't you think he looks like my brothers?"

"Angelina, Angelina, and that's for sure." Pasquale laughed. "Now, you a good mother, the very besta."

Angelina laughed, and a tear slipped from the corner of her eye as she watched how gently her uncle held Donny.

"He gonna be the president We no have no presidents in our *famiglia.*"

"Are you sure?" Angelina giggled. Only her uncle would assign an infant a profession.

"I thought you said he would be the president," Angelina teased.

Pasquale took the baby from her, sat down, and bounced him gently on his knee. "He gonna be both. And that's a for sure. What you name him?"

"Don Carlos Dominguez, but we call him Donny. I know what you're thinking. No. It's not my husband's father's name, but Fabian's father abandoned the family when he was a boy."

"That is no good, but maybe he is sorry, and maybe he wanna come back soon."

That's what she loved about her uncle. He always looked for a way to put everything *bad* in the mixing bowl until it looked good.

"Next time you name the baby Domenico, after you papa, is okay, Angelina?"

Angelina nodded, but that conversation belonged to a different place and time.

"Sit down, Angelina. You remember Giorgio, no?"

Angelina smiled at Pasquale's silver-haired friend, who appeared world-weary. "It's so nice to see you, again."

Giorgio reached for her hand. "It's been a long time, Angelina, and congratulations on a fine baby boy. Such good news."

Angelina took a seat and jumped up when she realized

she sat on Giorgio's hat. "Oh, no!" Angelina handed him his crushed hat. "How careless. I am so sorry."

"It's okay. Don't worry. I will fix it." Giorgio took the hat and tried bending it back to its original shape. He did a reasonable job, but not perfect.

"I feel terrible. If I've ruined it, I'll buy you another hat, Giorgio."

Pasquale gave the hat his investigative gaze. "Such a nice fedora hat. I think it look better than before, Giorgio."

This was just the thing Pasquale would say.

"In Santo Stefano, an old man, he named Rosello and he want a fedora hat, justa like you hat, Giorgio. Then one day we have a terrible wind and a fedora hat fall down from the sky at Rosello's feet. Nobody in Santo Stefano have such a nice hat. It must have blown off the head of a rich man. But, Rosello say, 'No.' He say God give him the hat. He so proud. Every day he wear the hat everywhere he go, even inside the house when he sit down and eat and when he play pinochle with his friends."

Pasquale had captured Giorgio's attention and Angelina loved him all the more for the distraction.

"Then one day, Rosello stand up, fell down, and poor Rosello die. We bury him, and everybody in Santo Stefano cry so much. But when we go to the church, we hear a noise, like somebody knocking, but nobody see nothing. Then we go to the cemetery and the knocking come again. Everybody look at the casket the women scream and some faint. Even the priest get scared and he sprinkle the holy water on everybody. They pull open the coffin and see Rosello still dead. They close the coffin and the knocking grow louder. Then Rosello's nephew Leno, he come running. 'Wait!' he say."

"Wait?" said Giorgio. "Did the priest stop?"

"The knocking, she get louder and faster. The priest and everybody so scared. Leno wave Rosello's fedora hat and open the coffin. He put the fedora hat on Rosello's head and close the coffin. Rosello is happy and he remember he is dead and go back to sleep. No more knocking."

Both Angelina and Giorgio laughed. With everything on her mind and so much troubling her, this light moment felt like watching flowers stretch their petals and bloom.

Donny became agitated and cried in the small whimpers of the very young. "It was wonderful seeing you both, but I must go home and feed my baby." She took Donny from her uncle after he kissed the baby several times. "Zio Pasquale, I want you to visit me whenever you get a chance." Angelina got up, and Pasquale did also.

Pasquale reached into his pocket and handed her a $10 bill. "It's for the baby, Angelina, from his Zio Pasquale."

"Oh, Zio. That's way too much and not necessary." Once again, Angelina witnessed his big heart and abundance of generosity.

"It's from his Zio Pasquale who love him too much. Too, too much."

He kissed her on both cheeks. "And you kiss the baby every day from his Zio Pasquale for me, too."

It was strange how one brother offered so much love and understanding while the other resisted it and gripped his fury.

CHAPTER 25

THE TIME HAD ARRIVED for her to face her father. She dressed her son and told him all about his family. They left the house and caught the trolley.

The mild day held promise. She gazed out the trolley's window and grew impatient. Missing her family had become a chronic sadness. Still, this would not be easy. The scene played out in her mind. If she showed up with Donny in her arms, with his undeniable resemblance to her family, and the tender sounds that make babies so endearing, how could her father resist his blood?

"21st Street! Please exit from the back," came the conductor's call.

Angelina stepped off, and the air rejuvenated her. She glanced around the familiar warmth of the Italian neighborhood of her childhood as though she'd blown the dust off a picture she'd left sitting on a shelf for far too long.

Although she headed straight for her father's home, she knew she could not ignore the house with an abundance of potted plants enhancing the front porch.

Signora Bertelli must have seen her from the window,

because the door flew open as soon as she raised her hand to knock.

"Angelina, Angelina!" The woman waved her inside with a profusion of excitement. "Come, come, or the house will collapse on my head for not inviting you inside."

Italian women greeted each other with a kiss, and without a word, her old neighbor reached for the baby first and completed the custom.

"I've missed you, too, Signora Bertelli."

She followed her elderly friend into the kitchen. Cubans sat in the parlor and visited, but Italians went straight to the kitchen table with food set out before them.

"Nothing has changed. You still have lovely potted flowers by your front door."

"It keeps me humble," said Signora Bertelli. "It helps remind me that the world is a garden and we are little potted plants."

Angelina giggled. "I guess that would keep me humble, too."

Signora Bertelli bounced the baby and made him smile. "Where have you been, *bella*? Everywhere I go, everyone asks the same question. 'Where is our Angelina?' Since you've left us, my tomatoes have refused to grow any larger, and may my bones ache if I don't tell you how much I've missed you. Then again," she rolled her eyes. "No matter how hot or cold the weather, my bones always ache. Tell me, what have I done to make you a stranger?" She seemed uninterested in an answer as she kissed the baby's hands. "Look at this *bambino*. He can be no one else but yours. You must have been looking the other way when the baby stole the face right off of you. God bless him! What have you named him?"

"Don Carlos Dominguez."

"God bless Don Carlo Dominguez! The last name we can do nothing about it, but we'll drop the *s* in Carlos. Otherwise, how will anyone know he's half-Italian? And I can tell you which half will be the most important."

Angelina chuckled. "I'm sure I can guess how you'll vote."

"But where have you been hiding?" Signora Bertelli stroked Donny's head as if she'd rescued him from a lifetime of misdirected national origin. "I remember you as a baby, Angelina. It seems like yesterday." She pulled a lace hanky from her pocket and dabbed her eyes. "An angel straight from heaven you were!"

Angelina smiled as her old neighbor continued to carry on about Donny. Signora Bertelli would never come out and say a baby was beautiful. That was not the Italian way. It might be taken as the jealous curse of *malocchio*.

A woman as knowledgeable in spirits and spells would know better than to attract the Italian evil eye of *malocchio*. Instead, she reached for Angelina's hand, squeezed it, and gave a slight nod as she spoke. This was her way of letting Angelina know she thought she had a beautiful baby without releasing the words into the atmosphere and having them travel to who-knows-where. Compliments had limits. *God bless him*, and *he looks like his mother*—the best way to acknowledge attractive features without taking a risk.

Angelina looked around. Everything remained as she'd remembered it, even the smell of something good on the stove, but instead of Frank Bertelli's urn in his final resting place in the center of the kitchen table, there stood a colorful bottle of imported olive oil.

"Where are your husband's ashes, Signora Bertelli?"

"Frank's on the back steps, taking in the sun while he can. Before you arrived, I told him about his new home, and I've been waiting for a sign to confirm my decision. Then you appeared at my door. God hears all prayers."

Angelina had never quite understood everything her old friend said and had long since stopped asking. "But I thought you wanted to keep his ashes in the kitchen, close to you, and the Italian food he loved."

"Oh, he'll be very close to me, and in a way, you might say he'll also still be very close to the food he loved." A wide grin crossed her face. "More important, this new resting place is far more worthy of him. And, that reminds me, I'm releasing you from your vow to care for Frank's ashes after I'm gone."

Although it sounded liberating, Angelina could not remember taking such a vow. "What changed your mind?"

"Follow me." With Donny still in her arms, Signora Bertelli led the way to where the urn sat on the back steps. "Such a wonderful day!" She spoke with a radiant smile and waved her arm in a grand gesture, the way Italians do to make a point.

"I normally don't believe in saying, 'it's a wonderful day' until nightfall. By then, I knew for certain how it all went. But today, I'll make an exception. The sky is brilliant, the birds are singing, and my flowerbeds bloom." Signora Bertelli glanced down at the flowers, raised a skeptical eyebrow, and returned Donny to Angelina. She picked up the garden shears and, with one quick snip, eradicated a yellow leaf from a flower's stem.

"Everything must be perfect for Frank when he goes to his eternal reward."

Angelina looked up at the cloudless sky. "You're right. The day is beautiful."

"Then we shall attend to what's long overdue!" The woman put down the shears, unlocked the urn, and lifted the lid.

With a wink to Angelina, she marched across her yard, holding the urn of Francesco Leonardo Bertelli or Frank. She flung open the outhouse door and poured his once-honored remains down the hole of the commode's wooden seat, slamming the door behind her.

Angelina's eyes widened. She gasped and quickly made the sign of the cross. "Oh, my goodness, Signora Bertelli! How could you? What on earth have you done?"

"What I intended. There is something beautifully poetic in this, don't you think?" She smiled. "Oh, you're looking a little pale, *bella*. It must be the aroma of cigar leaves from your work. Never mind, I'll put color back in your cheeks. Come inside to celebrate. I made something delicious to eat."

"Celebrate?" Angelina shifted her son's weight from one hip to the other and pointed to the outhouse. "But how could you do that?"

The woman put her arm around Angelina. "It is truly a sign from above that you showed up right now. So, why don't we look at the bright side? Nothing has changed. I'll still visit Frank every day, like before, and he'll still be close to the food he loved. I see no difference." Her voice rose with obvious delight. "This whole thing has given me such an appetite."

Donny grew fussy. She followed her friend to the kitchen, where they sat at the table, and Angelina nursed her baby.

As soon as her son calmed down, Angelina could not wait another moment before she spoke, "Signora, what on earth would possess you to pour your husband's remains down the… I mean, the outhouse? If Father Cavalli ever found out —of course Father Cavalli thinks your husband's buried in the Catholic cemetery, but if he should ever find out…" Angelina held onto Donny with one hand and pulled out her small fan from her pocket, opened it, and waved it back and forth almost hysterically.

"You look as though the heat is getting to you," said Signora Bertelli as she went to the window and pulled hard to open it. "There, perhaps a little more air will help."

Angelina lowered her voice. "I mean, we are supposed to

bury our dead in hallowed ground, not in the—" She could hardly form the word. "This could be a big sin, a mortal sin, jeopardizing your soul. There's no way to ask a priest or reveal it in the confessional. What made you—? Why would —?" In shock, she inhaled deeply to regain her composure. "Oh, my goodness, Signora, how will you receive absolution for this?" Angelina believed that not marrying in the church could still be rectified, but putting your spouse down a commode might become an irretrievable sin of massive proportions.

"Angelina, Angelina, the good Lord approves."

Angelina studied the expression on the face of the woman she had known all her life and regarded by so many as spiritually wise, but this last remark seemed suspicious. "What do you mean by, 'the good Lord approves?'"

"Why, I give all the credit to Father Cavalli himself for suggesting it."

Angelina shook her head. "That's impossible. A priest would never suggest such a thing."

"Last Sunday at Mass, right in front of the entire parish, and from high in his pulpit at the altar, Father Cavalli proclaimed that everyone is entitled to 'His just reward.' Believe me; Frank has earned this."

"But, Signora Bertelli—"

The older woman continued, undeterred. "When Frank died, I packed up all his things. Times are hard, and I meant to give his clothes to the needy, but I was so emotional when he died I couldn't bring myself to say goodbye to everything. So last week, I pulled out his clothes and reached inside his black pants to be sure the pockets were empty. And what do you suppose I found?"

Angelina studied her friend's odd expression before answering. "Money?"

"I found a receipt for a costly bracelet with the inscription, 'To the woman I love, Frank.' The receipt had Frank's name but a different address. So, on that morning a Wednesday, which I now call that day of my enlightenment. I went straight to that jeweler. The man immediately remembered Frank because he was a good customer and bought other nice things for *'Mrs. Bertelli.'*" Signora Bertelli sighed and bit into an almond biscotto. "Hmm, this is very good. I insist you have one."

"Signora Bertelli, are you sure it wasn't a mistake? We all come from the same Sicilian towns, and all men name their first son after their father. My father has three cousins with his exact name. So it could have been another Frank Bertelli or you know how people always misspell and mispronounce Italian names."

"The same thing crossed my mind, Angelina. Maybe Frank had someone else's ticket in his pocket. So, I caught the trolley and went to the address on the receipt. A woman with blond hair answered the door. She had pale eyes that refused to commit to a color. They weren't brown or black, or hazel, green, or blue, like she was undecided and blended them up. So now, I ask you, how can you trust someone who can't even commit to an eye color?"

Angelina didn't want to be distracted from the subject. "What did she say?"

"'Ja!' That's what she said. Imagine that, a German! I came right to the point. 'I'm here to talk to you about Frank Bertelli.' She seemed very surprised and invited me inside, still insisting on using that German accent. I took a seat while she told me that her name was Mrs. Bertelli and asked if I had news of *her* husband."

"What did you answer?"

"Well, I certainly had." Signora Bertelli sighed. "The woman had some lovely little gold pillows on the sofa, so I fluffed one up and made myself comfortable. Then I smiled and closed my eyes until the right words came to mind. 'You married a vile, loathsome monster who is also a conniving criminal!' I said."

Angelina tried not to sound shocked. "Signora, are you sure those were *the right words?*"

"Well, it would have sounded far better in Italian with some added hand gestures, but the woman was German, so I had to say it in English!"

Still rattled, Angelina leaned forward. "And what did the woman say?"

"Not a word, but I could see shock bouncing on her like fleas, so I continued while I had her attention. 'I have been Frank Bertelli's wife for thirty-four years, right up to the day the man died. And if I'm lying, may Frank find a sliver of ice in Hell to comfort him.'" Angelina's old neighbor lifted her chin with a tinge defiance.

"The woman's face flushed red, pale, and then red again. I could tell she wanted to faint, but she must have decided against it. Can you guess what she showed me?"

Grateful Donny had fallen asleep, Angelina wasn't sure she wanted to know the answer. "No, I can't even imagine."

"Well, that German got right up, took a large Bible off the shelf, and opened it. And do you know what was inside?"

Angelina cleared her throat. "What?"

"It was the marriage license of Francesco Leonardo Bertelli, that's what! And dated eight weeks before Frank died."

None of it made sense to Angelina. "But your husband lived with you."

"I brought a picture of my Frank to compare it with a picture of her Frank. I showed her my picture. Then she showed me her picture of Frank on their wedding day—the same man wearing the same suit. The well-tailored, black one I worked so hard to make for him!"

"He married you in Sicily and married her here. Then there's no record of your marriage here. I can't believe he did this."

"I try to be generous. So, I'll tell the truth. Frank looked handsome in that suit—in both pictures. But if I hadn't found that receipt, neither of us would have ever known what he'd done. I wish I could hear how he's explaining this in God's courtroom. Signora Bertelli looked up at Heaven, and then, as if she were mistaken about the direction, looked down at the floor."

Angelina remembered Frank Bertelli as a sweet older man. This all seemed impossible.

"I told the illegal wife number two that Frank had also worn the same suit to his funeral. The woman cried, said something in German, and cried louder."

Bertelli shook her head. "Frank said he had to sell cigar bands in Key West when he wanted to go to her. Then when he wanted to come back to me, he told her he had to leave and sell cigar bands in Ybor City. Two wives and two marriage beds must have been too much for that two-faced, two-timing man. The two of them are in Hell."

"What two?"

"Frank and his friend Judas. Like Frank, he also gave a kiss of betrayal. Well—that's *too* bad."

Angelina never realized her old friend knew so many American expressions. "I'm so sorry. You were always the very best wife to him."

"My dear little Angelina, remember what I tell you. There are good men and bad. The bad ones can't keep secrets. They leave clues, and like dogs, they shed them everywhere. Overlook nothing men do or say, or you'll end up like me."

A sudden chill of uneasiness pricked Angelina.

"My husband said his love for me was an overflowing

well. Strange, I dropped my pail into that well and I heard a loud thump. Can you believe it?"

Angelina had no response.

"Neither one of us wives suspected Frank," she said, and placed a tray of cookies in front of Angelina. The middle-aged woman reached for a cookie and took a bite. "Who would have thought it? First, I reduce my husband to ashes. Next, he returns as the skeleton in my closet."

Angelina considered the state of the other wife. "So, this woman didn't know your husband.... Her husband.... Signore Bertelli had died?"

"That's right. The illegal Signora Bertelli lived on the other side of town, and Frank had been cautious not to mix his friends from the north with those from the south—something he must have learned had worked during the Civil War. She thought he'd abandoned her, but he was so 'loving,' she said. It just couldn't be true. So, she worried something bad had happened."

"What did you say?"

"He's dead. Most would consider that something bad. But at least he had the decency to die in our bed. It was the least he could do after over thirty years of marriage. Still, a maggot dipped in honey is still a maggot."

"Who else knows about this?"

"I'm only telling you because of your vow to watch over Frank's ashes. Now you where they are.

Again, Angelina did not remember such a vow.

"However, I pride myself on being compassionate, so I told this lady if she wanted to come and pay her respects to Franks Bertelli's remains, to please come over, I'd be happy to escort her personally to his final resting place."

Angelina gasped. "No! Oh, no! You didn't?"

"It's the only decent thing to do, *bella.* She's coming

tomorrow at noon." Signora Bertelli took another bite of her cookie and closed her eyes, obviously savoring it.

Once again, Angelina could not think of an appropriate reply.

"I always prayed Frank would outlive me." She raised her eyebrows. "Isn't it wonderful how the Lord answers our prayers by not answering them?" She gazed up at the ceiling and made the sign of the cross, presumably in gratitude. "All this excitement has given me such an appetite. I insist you and the baby stay right where you are. I made the most delicious artichoke frittata. It will make you proud you're Italian —and not one of those Germans. And if I'm lying, may the devil offer a teaspoon of water to men with two wives."

Angelina opened her mouth but could not think of a suitable response.

"I know, I know," said Signora Bertelli. "The good Lord says we should forgive, but I checked the scriptures, and there is no mention of how long we can take to do it. So, with no deadline specified, I say, what's the rush?"

I'll face Papa another day, thought Angelina.

CHAPTER 26

ANGELINA STUDIED her husband's stoic expression. Something about his demeanor reminded her of the day they'd met. Women's heads turned when they saw him, including her own. Something inside her resisted him back then, and she felt the same odd sensation. Although, nothing had changed. Fabian's looks were still striking; however, life was never about good looks but good hearts. He closed the distance between them, embraced, and kissed her.

"Angelina, I know I told you to take the baby to Eva's so we can have a little time alone together, and we will, but just for a little while. My friends and I have something to do today

and—."

A loud knocking drew their attention. Fabian released his hold on Angelina, took hurried strides to reach the door, and swung it open. *"Bienvenidos, amigos."*

"¿Acere, que bola?" His friends greeted Fabian with their usual Cuban spin on Spanish for *'What's up?'* His friends slapped Fabian on the back and tipped their caps to Angelina, who greeted them more warmly than she felt. Certain one or

CHAPTER 26 | 193

more had concealed a bottle of spirits, she offered everyone some food and pastries to help dilute whatever they intended to drink.

"*Hola,* Angelina. How do you like your new furniture?" José Valle had the same disheveled look as before.

Angelina gave Fabian a stern look. Hurt, he had not even given her enough time to respond to his change of plans, which ruined the day. "It's wonderful, José. Thank you again for helping my husband bring it home."

He nodded. *"De nada."*

She excused herself to the bedroom. As she suspected, they brought out some liquor, laughed, told jokes, and sang Cuban songs. Although her door remained closed, the walls were thin, and their voices were loud.

How could he do this to me? Angelina stretched out on the bed and listened to the rhythmic way Cubans clipped the tails of their words—they dropped the "s" sound, and the "d" also seemed endangered. She had long since mastered Spanish, but Rolando had taught her to listen for the distinct sounds of dialects.

It had been a long time since she thought of Rolando and everything he'd shared. *Spanish is the official language in over twenty countries and each with its unique interpretation.* She could almost hear the timbre of Rolando's voice whenever he taught her something new. He told her never to forget him, and she believed that was one promise she could keep.

At that moment, the bedroom door burst open. Noise and the smell of alcohol wafted in. Angelina tensed.

"We're going to Marcos' house. I'll be back before you realize it, *querida.* I promise we'll do something wonderful today."

Angelina didn't want to cause a scene in front of these men. However, even if Fabian could not see it, their marriage would reach a breaking point. She couldn't save it by herself.

Fabian blew her a kiss as he left with his friends. The thud of the front door slamming reverberated through the *casita*.

Without her leaving the house, Angelina could hear their chorus of laughter coming from the street and when they broke into a Cuban song. They appeared to be bouncing the universe like a ball.

How often had Fabian assured her that she and the baby meant everything to him? Of course, she wanted to believe him, but her father had said trust only what you see.

Frustrated, she sat alone. If she had taken off and left Fabian at home, the world would condemn her, but men had privilege.

Angelina glanced at her calendar where she'd circled the date. No one could have missed the oversized poster, trimmed in purple, yellow, and white ribbons and hanging on the wall near the flower shop. The Suffragette's colors were distinct, and Suffragettes had no intention of being ignored. But, as always, ratifying the Constitution to give women the vote would need women's collective stamina to ignite a fire against this unjust oppression.

Angelina left her house and knocked on her neighbor's door. "It's me, Ophelia—Angelina."

The door swung open, and to Angelina's surprise, Carmen appeared. "Well, welcome, hello, and *bienvenida*."

"This is wonderful. I didn't realize you were visiting Ophelia, Carmen."

Carmen shook her head. "It's not visiting. It's called manual labor. I'm helping her paint, and that's what's known as the abuse of a relative."

Ophelia came from behind and rolled her eyes. "Come in, Angelina, and don't believe her. The painting was Carmen's idea, and she's only here to take all the credit."

Angelina stepped inside and glanced at a gallon container of paint. "You can paint later," said Angelina. "I have a better idea. Let's go to the Suffragette meeting and show our support."

Carmen turned to her cousin. "You might as well get used to this. It's all Angelina talks about at work."

"Well, I went to a Suffragette meeting about a year ago, and it was so inspiring. There's one today, and I would like you both to go with me. You'll enjoy it, and when we get the vote, you can tell your grandchildren you were there."

Carmen turned to Ophelia. "Don't we have to have children before we have grandchildren?"

"That's what I thought," said Ophelia. "Anyway, Angelina, I don't understand how this works. If we can't vote, how do we vote to get the vote?"

"That's an excellent question." Angelina giggled. "Let's go to the meeting and find out."

Carmen picked up a paintbrush. "I don't know. There's a lot of painting to do."

"They serve cake," said Angelina, still smiling.

"Painting can wait. I wouldn't want the Suffragettes to feel disappointed in the turnout."

There was no mistaking the location or the women. Though typical for a march or parade, many women wore white with purple and green sashes.

As soon as they arrived, Angelina proudly led the way through the large double doors of the meeting hall. It had been a long time since Angelina had attended a meeting, but her belief in the cause had not changed.

"Angelina Pirrello, where have you been?" said a woman behind her. Angelina turned around and immediately recognized Gladys Parker as the president of the chapter she'd attended long ago.

"Oh, Mrs. Parker, it's wonderful to see you again. I saw your picture in the newspapers leading a march down the main business district in Tampa. You've been so inspirational to the movement."

"Well, thank you, my dear. You also gave a powerful talk at our meeting that day, and we couldn't be happier to see you again."

"I talk about our cause with other women, and I'm always with you in spirit, but my personal life has been challenging. However, I brought my friends to the meeting. May I introduce Carmen and Ophelia. It's their first meeting."

"Welcome, young women. It's our honor to have you. This fight has been ongoing for over fifty years, but the world is changing, and we will get the vote."

"Angelina is convinced we'll get the vote," said Carmen.

"The men have stopped ignoring us and getting rebellious. Perhaps that's good and we are finally making sense."

Someone nudged Parker from behind. "It's time, Gladys."

"Again, I'm so happy to see you. We'll talk more later." She turned toward the front of the room and walked to the podium. "Welcome, sisters. Please take your seats. We have so much to discuss this afternoon."

Gladys Parker smiled at everyone when the room settled down, but the news would be far from consoling. "First, I want to say that nothing will stop us from getting what should be ours. It's been many decades since we first campaigned for our right to vote. And here we are still challenging the Constitution for a fundamental human right. Not just men are created equal, but *men and women*."

Gladys Parker could still inspire a room of Suffragettes, and Angelina was glad she came.

"I can think of nothing a man can do that a woman cannot learn to do."

"And we can do it better," whispered Carmen. Ophelia nodded.

"And we can give birth to a new generation that will have

greater respect for their mothers, sisters, and wives. But what kind of a world is it when our daughters must live with their hands tied and their mouths have no voice?"

A hand went up, and Gladys nodded. "Tell them about the march."

"Yes. It's important to know what happened. We held a peaceful march three weeks ago, but the newspapers failed to report how we were treated. As we marched, we were cursed, jeered, and spit on. Men threw rocks at us. We were hurt and arrested. And what was our charge? *Disturbing the Peace.* We did no such thing. We marched peacefully and were arrested, while the men who caused the riotous disruption of a peaceful march walked off without incident."

Gladys sighed deeply. "When went got to jail, guards pushed and knocked us down, and worms infested our meals. So it's essential to know—."

A sudden and terrible smash echoed throughout the cavernous room. Women jumped from their seats screaming while large stones came barreling through the windows, breaking glass that flew in every direction and drawing blood from several women sitting nearby.

"Oh, God, what is happening" Ophelia screamed.

"Sisters, help! A large rock struck Miriam Hendricks's head. She needs medical aid. Blood is gushing from the wound," shouted a woman Angelina didn't know. "Miriam, Miriam, can you hear me?" She tried tapping her face to get her to respond, but Miriam did not move."

"Quick," said Gladys, "lock the doors, so they can't get inside and do worse."

Ophelia and Angelina rushed to the doors and turned the large lever that locked the doors.

"We have to get help." Came another scream.

A cake sat on display at the back of the room, ready to offer members at the end of the meeting. Carmen dashed over, grabbed the neatly folded napkins, and pressed them against Miriam's wound to stop the bleeding.

"Keep it on the wound," said Angelina to the woman, cradling Miriam's head.

Though crying, the woman nodded, she would do it.

Another crash and more debris flew through the air. "Oh, Lord, someone help us," Ophelia cried.

Angelina feared for the child she carried. "These men are growing more dangerous. They don't even care where they're aiming." Several more rocks came flying across the hall.

Gladys Parker met Angelina's eyes. "I was always afraid this day would come, but I hoped I was wrong." She grabbed a bag behind the podium and pulled out a gun.

Startled to see the weapon, Angelina grew more fearful. "What are you going to do?"

"What I must. No one came here today to be terrorized or attacked."

Parker went to the front entrance, released the lock, and she flung open the door, and shot three rounds into the air. "You are mistaken about us. We are armed, and after what you've done, any shot I fired now will be considered self-defense! If you don't believe me, come forward now."

Angelina thought of her baby. She could not take a chance and stood away from the windows and doors, but the screaming of both the women hurt inside and the men outside threatening to do worse echoed in every direction.

"Go home, old bag. No one cares what you think. It's a man's world. We rule it, and no petticoats take going to take over."

Carmen came up behind Angelina. "We've got to get out of here before someone gets killed. There are three women already bleeding badly."

"You, of all people, cannot take a chance with your unborn child."

"Yes, I know."

"I just spotted a side door where they must get deliveries. Let's use it and get out," said Ophelia.

Angelina nodded. She knew Ophelia was right but she also wanted to help Gladys Parker.

"You can't help," said Carmen as though she could read her mind. "I'm sure those men have guns, too."

"This way," said Ophelia.

Together they exited through the side door, and several women followed. As soon as they reached the street, Angelina had a clear view of the men breaking windows and throwing rocks and gasped when she saw the one wearing a brown cap. "Fabian!" Angelina screamed. "How can you do this?"

Fabian met her eyes and dropped a rock, and whatever he said was lost amid screaming women and shouting men.

Carmen and Ophelia turned toward Angelina. *"Aye, Dios mio!* It is Fabian," said Carmen. "Let's get out of here." They grabbed Angelina by the arms and ran down the street with her, crying hysterically.

CHAPTER 27

"I WAS DRUNK. Can't you understand, I just went along with it."

"So, you go along with whatever your friends do when your drunk? It's beyond appalling." Angelina could not believe her own husband had taken part in the attack on the Suffragettes' meeting—a movement she believed in, and attended by her invited friends.

"Can't you understand I was drinking? It wasn't something I would have done if sober."

"Is that really an excuse?" Offended, embarrassed, and angry were just part of the enormity of her feelings. How could Fabian do something so violent and irresponsible, drinking or sober? "You didn't get drunk by looking at a bottle of liquor. You poured it in a glass, took the first drink, and the second, and on and on. Then you went to go to a Suffragette meeting and threw rocks through the windows— at women." A hot flush of anger ran through Angelina's body

"You act like the bottle has a life of its own and poured itself down your throat."

Their argument went deep into the night with nothing

resolved. Fabian said he was sorry and washed his hands of it. Heartbroken that everyone recognized him and it reflected on her. She could never show her face at another Suffragette meeting. So drinking was the culprit, and the shame of it belonged to her.

The scene haunted her all night and day. Angelina was not ready to let this go, but life goes on. They had to eat. She could not deny Fabian had a natural talent for growing plants. With a well-stocked variety of vegetables, they had enough for his Tia Lourdes and some for the neighbors.

Since Fabian hadn't arrived yet, she saw no reason to delay starting dinner for the lack of a few potatoes. After the recent rain, a trowel would slide easily through the ground. She went outside and uncovered the dirt, but she soon hit something far larger and harder than a potato.

Confused, Angelina pulled out a strange object wrapped in newspaper and string. An ominous feeling came over her as she removed the wrapping. Her hands trembled, and her heartbeat quickened as she held something ominous, something she'd never touched or thought she ever would —a gun.

It had a strange rigid, coldness, and its weight was heavier than she imagined. Yet, she held it in one hand, and with a bit of pressure from one finger, it could end the life of a human being. Perhaps this gun had already killed someone or more than one person.

The only way to reach the garden was through the house, where her husband spent countless hours. *No one but Fabian could have buried this.* The thought terrified Angelina, and she fought back a rising wave of panic. Only something terrible required the use of a gun. Was something being planned, or had it already happened?

She brushed off the dirt from the newspaper for a clue. Several pages remained smudged and tattered. Still, the date and words were clear enough. 'Bolita Bernardo, Run Over by Train.'

She had never dug up anything in Fabian's garden, and he must have felt certain she never would.

Angelina's imagination raced with frightening possibilities, but she had no proof.

However, unlike hunting rifles, pistols were meant to shoot and terrify people. Still stunned, she stared at the firearm, uncertain how to handle her discovery. It might be dangerous for Fabian to realize she knew about it. She needed time to think, but there was not much time. After some nervous minutes, Angelina wrapped the gun back up, tie it with the same string, and bury it where she found it.

She reentered through the back door as Donny became fussy and cried. "Shh, shh, my little one." Angelina sang to him until he fell asleep in her arms, and slipped him into his crib, but her mind had never stopped racing.

She paced back and forth, glancing at the time. The clock's minutes now inched closer and closer to the moment Fabian would arrive.

In a sudden burst of anguish, Angelina dashed back to the garden and dug up the gun once more. Again, she ripped off the string and newspaper, but this time, she took the firearm into the house, intending to do whatever it took to protect herself and her child. If Fabian didn't care enough about his family, Angelina had no intention of waiting for a tragedy to happen.

She went to the stove and stirred the stew she had prepared, but the distraction did not quiet her nerves, and her anger continued to rise. To think she had only discovered the gun because she wanted to add some potatoes to her meal. What else lay under the dirt?

The door swung open, and Angelina jumped, but Fabian

didn't notice her reaction. He walked in beaming. "Hello, my little family."

The incident at the Suffragette meeting could not be forgotten or justified. Angelina could still see the faces of Fabian with all his drunken friends attacking helpless women at their meeting. Now with another terrifying discovery about Fabian, she had no idea how much more she could take. She remembered how he could keep a straight face even when he told her a funny story, which made her laugh all the more. Now, he drank often, smiled a lot, and spent more and more time away from his 'little family.'

"Hello, yourself, Fabian."

Still seething, she stared at him in disbelief. If only she could rip off his mask and expose who was hiding? Her father had warned her many times to observe everything and everyone.

Fabian gave her a quick kiss and then went to the crib to gaze at his son, who was sleeping. "My God, he's perfect."

Angelina wanted to rid herself of the frustrating thoughts consuming her. "You must be hungry. Sit down, and I'll get you a plate. This meal is a very special, Fabian—one you won't forget."

"No one can take that away from you, Angelina. You're a wonderful cook."

Angelina set an empty dish in front of her husband and dropped the gun on the plate with a thud.

Fabian jumped up from his chair. "What the h—!"

"Funny, that was my reaction, too."

The blood rose in Fabian, and his face flushed with anger.

"I found the gun where you buried it." Angelina tightened her hands into fists. "What are you doing that requires you to bury a gun?"

Fabian stared at her and did not answer. Angelina did not take her eyes off him until he did.

He shrugged his shoulders. "It's for a friend."

"No friend would ask you to bury a gun especially not where your family lives."

As the pressure kept building, Angelina saw no reason to dismiss her distress. "Is this worth the risk of what you can lose? You are dancing like a marionette, and these men are pulling the strings. When they tire of you, they'll cut the strings. People are loyal to themselves first. Everyone fears men like that, but obviously—not you. You already have something wonderful. Your son smiles when he sees you. So why are you walking away?"

Fabian's eyes narrowed into angry slits. "Do I not come home every day? You are my wife and have no right to question me." He slammed a fist against the wall.

He must believe in his Tia Lourdes philosophy that women should be submissive to their men. Angelina burned with anger and had no intention of backing down.

"That's right. I *am* your wife, and I don't care what lawmakers think of women or how we're denied basic rights. I am your equal, and have every right to know what is going on, since it affects my life and our son."

Fabian clasped his hand around her arm. "The gun is not mine. That's all you need to know."

Angelina twisted her arm free and met Fabian's eyes. "You are making a mistake with me. If I was the kind that simply obeyed orders, I would never have left my father's home."

Fabian turned around, grabbed the gun, put it in his pocket, and walked out the door.

Angelina fumed with anger as she watched him leave.

ALTHOUGH THE SUN REMAINED CONSTANT, and nothing much changed in Ybor City, Angelina's and Fabian's conversations straddled among fewer words. They stood rigid, unwilling to accept the other's viewpoint.

For Angelina, this meant far more than an argument, but the stones and arrows that shattered lives and marriages. Fabian had to know she would never tolerate his involvement. However, his Tia Lourdes had raised him to believe women should hold a broom in one hand and a baby in the other. Above all, to support their men in everything without question or comment.

Nothing in Angelina's mind could dismiss the incident of the gun. It lingered and plagued her.

Fabian left for work before she did. As soon as she dressed, she reached for her pendant watch in the back of the bureau. Beautifully crafted, it once belonged to her grandmother and brought Angelina a measure of comfort when she was anxious.

Angelina glanced at the clock. The noisy ticking urged her to leave. She fumbled around the drawer, and to her shock and confusion, it wasn't there. *Could I have put it somewhere else?*

Angelina opened all the dresser's drawers, moving things around, pulling things out, and searching without success. She had always been so careful with her gift from this grandmother she had never known.

In a panic, she searched everywhere—her handbag, in the pockets of her clothing, under their bed, beneath the bureau, until the clock's ticking grew increasingly urgent. Frustrated and anxious, she had no choice. Angelina dashed out of the house and hurried to work with a heavy knot in her stomach and one thought: *Where is it?*

CHAPTER 28

CARMEN TOOK her usual seat next to Angelina. "So, next Saturday, come to Ophelia's at 2:00. It's her birthday, and my aunt's making a special meal. We'll eat, sing some Cuban songs, and I'll teach you how to salsa."

Angelina didn't want to tell anyone of her fears with Fabian and was not in the mood to celebrate anything, but that wasn't Carmen's or Ophelia's fault. "How old will she be?"

"Twenty-three. I hear twenty-three is the finest year in a Cuban's life because we receive a blast of great wisdom."

Angelina laughed. "Well, I wouldn't want to miss such a special celebration."

Carmen splayed her fingers, balled them into a fist, and stretched them out again. She then picked an assortment of tobacco leaves.

Dolores appeared, bent down, placed her elbow on the worktable, and dropped a coin and a piece of paper in front of Angelina. She glanced at the paper and looked up at the woman.

All three had worked at Garcia-Marcos before the fire

destroyed the building. Still, since the woman had the habit of insulting others, making trouble, and behaving badly, Angelina and Carmen made certain they sat on the opposite side of the room from Dolores.

"Tell Fabian to put this dime on number seventeen! Last night I dreamt of a bull with yellow eyes. Everyone knows a bull's the symbol for the number seventeen."

Had Fabian found another way to infuriate her? Angelina glanced at the coin as though it swarmed with maggots. How did this woman even know she was married to Fabian? Did he tell her to give the bet to his wife, Angelina?

To accept it would make her a party to the *bolita* gambling syndicate. "Pick up your money, Dolores. If my husband's taking bets on *bolita,* then he'll have to do it without my help."

"You can't cheat me out of my bet. Carlota Gomez found a stray cat on her porch, a sign to bet on number one. Now, she's twenty dollars richer." Dolores liked to control the conversation with neither good sense nor good manners, and Angelina lacked the patience to put up with her.

"Go away, Dolores," said Carmen. "Besides, everyone knows a bull stands for number fifteen, not seventeen."

"*¡Cállate!*" Dolores raised her fist in anger. "This is none of your business, Carmen."

Angelina picked up the coin and walked to the window. "It might interest you that for Italians, the number seventeen is terrible luck. In Roman numeral means *I have lived.* In other words, I'm dead. I can either give you back your money or toss it to the wind."

"*¡Mierda!*" Dolores spat. She dashed toward Angelina and yanked the coin from her hand. "Tell Fabian—"

"I don't deliver messages either."

Angelina rubbed her hands together to rid herself of the feel of the coin, but Carmen leaned over the moment she took her seat. "I have some news about that *sin verguenza* you married," she whispered.

Carmen was right. Fabian had no shame, but she had been careful not to share her marital troubles. Her father had always said *dirty laundry is washed at home*. So, she had said nothing about his drinking, gambling, or possession of a gun to anyone, but her growing sadness grew harder to conceal.

"What news, Carmen?"

Carmen lowered her voice. "I don't want anyone to over-hear. I planned on telling you at the break," she whispered.

El lector appeared and stepped up to the rostrum to deliver his reading local newspapers that also reported on international events. *La tabaquería* grew hushed in antic-ipation.

Angelina now believed her life held more conflict and tension than any news story. Her mind remained cluttered with thoughts of Fabian. How could she have misjudged him so badly? He had made her laugh. He said he loved her and in time she loved him, too. They had a wonderful son. But happiness needed sustenance, or its sweetness dissolved, like the weight of salt in water.

At the break, Angelina quickly hurried out of the building with Carmen. "I can't believe you left me in suspense for all this time. What has happened?"

"I don't know everything, just bits and pieces dipped in gunpowder. It has something to do with the *bolita* bets. I think Fabian could be in big trouble."

Her words fueled both fear and anger inside Angelina. "Exactly what do you mean?"

"My brother works in the kitchen at that Costa Rican Restaurant. I stood near the back door waiting for food to take home when I overheard some men arguing outside. They spoke about their dealings with your husband and that no-good friend of his—"

"José Valle?" interrupted Angelina.

"That's the one. They call him *El Gallo* because he's like the head rooster who collects the money and runs the cock-fights. I couldn't hear every word, but it sounded like Fabian and José were stealing money from the *bolita* kings."

Angelina stiffened. "Stealing?" She had to force the word out.

Carmen glanced over at Dolores, watching them. "Let's sit at the far end of that table." Once again, Carmen continued her story. "I hear *El Gallo* and your husband are rigging *bolita.* If I heard it, others are hearing it too."

Angelina tried to picture it, but the strain unnerved her. "How can that be? It's just a hundred numbered balls in a bag. They reach into the bag and pull out the winner. How can they cheat at that? Besides, Fabian should be scared. He said Bolita Bernardo was killed because he stole the money selling chances, but cheating at the actual game? How?"

"You're a smart girl, Angelina. The problem is, you're missing a criminal mind. I'm sure you'd figure it out if you gave it some serious thought."

"I still can't understand why one chance in one hundred tempts anyone."

"Shh. Don't let the cigar makers hear that. Every week they pay *el cafetero* for their Cuban coffee, *el lector* to read to them, and *el bolitero* for at least one chance in a hundred. But they don't know about Fabian and José—yet."

"What is it?"

"*El Gallo* and your very handsome husband are playing a dangerous game."

"Carmen, stop giving me little spoonfuls at a time. Just say it."

Her friend leaned closer. "One of the men found Fabian icing a ball."

"And what is that supposed to mean?"

"Just like it sounds. He chooses the winning number and freezes that ball. Then, when it's time, he just puts his hand in the bag, feels around for the little frozen ball, and pulls it out as the winner."

Angelina widened her eyes in astonishment. "Why would he take such a chance? Someone could touch the ball before it thaws or find it freezing in ice before he places it in the bag, or someone could see him doing it."

"Someone did, and José and Fabian must have paid him well to keep his mouth shut. After that, they stayed clear of the ice wagon."

"So, it's over."

"Angelina, there's one thing I've learned about men. A good one can go bad, but a bad one only gets worse. These men at the restaurant said *El Gallo* and Fabian began another swindle. They drilled a hole in the winning ball and filled it with lead. The heaviest ball falls to the bottom of the bag. They reach in and pull it out as the winner."

Angelina's heart raced. "How could he play such a dangerous game? We even talked about Bolita Bernardo after they found his mangled body on the railroad tracks. He should be terrified."

"You won't find *boliteros* at church on Sunday unless they're planning to steal the collection plate. They probably went to church to pull money out of the donation basket as kids, but I didn't hear everything these men said. So, maybe I'm wrong."

Angelina shook her head. "Nothing is that hard to believe anymore."

"Did someone put Fabian and *El Gallo* up to fixing the game? Who is crazy enough to hire men, teach them to steal, and trust them to keep quiet?"

Carmen narrowed her eyes. "I don't want to scare you,

but your husband and his friend might end up like those roosters they bet on: beaten, bloody, or dead."

Angelina could feel the hair rising on her arms. "I want no part of this. He could put us in real danger."

"Here's something else you should think about, Señora Angelina Dominguez. Every day, *el lector* reads the news. What if a lector arrives, opens the newspaper, and reads about Fabian Dominguez's criminal activity while you're sitting in the room? What if your father makes the connection?"

Angelina stiffened. "I couldn't bear it. I'd die of humiliation." Such a disgrace played over in her mind. She couldn't accept she had married a man who had changed so drastically. Had she been too blind and naïve? "If only there had been some signs before I married him. When I met Fabian at Rosa's wedding, he was calm, charming, and even clever. He's become someone else."

"Everyone should be very good at something. Your husband, Fabian, is very good at being *no good*. That takes some talent."

Angelina looked down at the ground to shut out everything while she absorbed the danger. "I don't understand. Fabian brings home the right amount of pay every week. If he's stealing money, his pockets would be full. If he's gambling, they'd be empty."

"Or he pretends the *bolita* money is his pay. Swindlers become more dangerous when they're swindled."

"And what if someone's angry or thinks they've been cheated and believes I'm involved and think they've been cheated or angry about something? They could hurt my son and me."

"Go to your father's house, *chica,* and stay there. You'll be safe. Or you can come to my house."

"Thank you, but if I was truly at risk, I would never go to your house and put you and your family in danger or my father." A numb feeling invaded Angelina. She pictured herself arriving at her father's house, facing him, and confessing that everything he'd worried about had come true—but much worse.

"It's just luck that I overheard that conversation at the Costa Rican restaurant."

Carmen and Angelina turned back toward the factory entrance. "Fabian drinks too much. I don't speak to him when he's drinking and evenings, we don't speak at all, but if he's into something that could threaten Donny and me…" Angelina tried to shake off the chill from the alarming thought.

"On his deathbed, my father asked my mother to make a bet. My mother bought the ticket and put it in his coffin. She said if he wins, the *diablo* can cash it for him in hell. If he loses, it will remind him of all the money he wasted when he was alive. After his funeral, when everyone left, she told us the nicest thing my father ever did for her in all the years they were married was to make her a widow."

Carmen shook her head. "He had a list of excuses for everything he did wrong. I'm pretty sure those excuses were first written on prehistoric cave walls to preserve them for future generations of men." Carmen paused and put her arm around Angelina.

"I don't know, Carmen. He didn't always behave like that. Once, he was wonderful." Angelina didn't want to believe she had misjudged and mismanaged her life so terribly. Still, a horrible sense of dread infused her. "Something isn't right. I'm going to tell Lopez I'm going home. He's not going to like it, but I don't care. I hope he's not there."

"And what if Fabian is there counting *bolita* tickets or *bolita* money? Maybe it's not such a good idea for you to go alone. I'll go with you."

"Thank you, but there's no reason for you to lose work, too."

"But, I—"

Angelina shook her head, "If he's doing something this bad, I don't want you involved." She hugged her friend, made her excuse to her supervisor, and hurried down the street. She thought of all the times Fabian made her laugh, he'd loved her, and how hard it was for both of them to leave their child in the care of Eva Chavez each morning. Neither wanted to leave him. Angelina fortified herself by thinking only of the good, but the tightening in her stomach persisted.

She rounded the corner and casually glanced through the store windows she passed until she reached Gilchrest's Pawn Shop and stopped abruptly. She gasped incredulous, at the item on exhibit. *It just can't be. My pendant watch!* It now sat on a cushion of black velvet on display in a store window. Angelina stared at the watch in disbelief. It had a gold setting and unique design, and was made by an Italian craftsman. What were the chances there were two identical Italian-made in this little corner of Tampa known as Ybor City?

Angelina reached for the door, burst inside, and made her way straight to the watch.

The shopkeeper peered over his glasses. "Please look around, miss. I'll be with you in a moment." He then continued to attend to his customer.

The words meant nothing. Angelina reached for the pendant, knocking over the cushion it sat on, and studied the watch closely. She knew at once with absolute certainty it was her grandmother's gift. She had kept it safe and wore it mostly on special occasions. There could be no reasonable explanation for why it was here.

"Thank you for coming in, and come back soon." The shopkeeper offered his customer a quick, obligatory smile, deposited several bills into his cash register, and then turned to Angelina.

"Hans Gilchrest at your service. I see you're admiring the gold pendant watch. It's quite beautiful, is it not? The workmanship is exceptional." His voice had a weather-worn peal to it, as though he'd long since grown accustomed to parroting the same recitation.

Angelina mistrusted him and held up the watch. "This belongs to me. How did you get it?"

He squinted. "I have nothing to hide. This is a legitimate business."

Her voice trembled. "How did you get it?"

"A young man needed money for a trip back to Cuba. That kind of thing happens every day in this shop."

Perhaps it was stolen. What else could it be? "Whoever sold it to you stole it from me. What's the name of this man?"

"Now, now, there's no reason to get upset. I'll look over my records."

As Angelina waited, her breathing became precariously shallow. Carmen had just said Fabian was a thief, but to think he would steal something that he knew meant so much to her seemed beyond improbable. Perhaps it was one of his friends. Someone he brought to the house gave him a drink and saw the opportunity.

Gilchrest went behind the counter, pulled out a large ledger and turned the pages while repeatedly adjusting his glasses. "Ah, yes, here it is. I remember now, a very nice-looking young man, very personable, also. It's Fabian Dominguez. Do you know him?"

Angelina closed her eyes tightly as the sound of Fabian's name erupted inside her, along with a repressed scream. If it was possible to die from anger, this was it. It raged through her whole being.

The shopkeeper adjusted the black velvet cushion and

reached for the pendant in Angelina's hand, but she pulled back.

He gave her a frustrated sigh. "If you're sure it's yours," he said, "you'll have to prove somebody robbed you. Do you have a receipt for its purchase?"

"I only have to prove you received stolen property." The angrier she became, the louder she spoke.

Gilchrest mumbled little annoyances.

Angelina's eyes burned as she read the name written in Fabian's familiar, fluid script.

"Well?"

"He is my husband, Mr. Gilchrest."

"Then, it's not a robbery, is it? Everything that belongs to a wife becomes her husband's property upon marriage. That's the law. He may dispose of it any way he chooses. Your consent is not required."

Angelina looked at the man for the first time—medium height and thin with an angular face that appeared dwarfed against an oversized beard. The wire-rimmed spectacles he wore magnified his eyes. "How much do you want for it?" Her words could have choked her.

"Now you see reason," the shopkeeper gave a wry smile. "The watch is exquisite, but I'm sure you know that, Mrs. Dominguez. I could not sell it for less than $50.00. It's a treasure, and that's a bargain."

"That's robbery, a king's ransom, especially when you know it belongs to me."

"No, it *belonged* to you. It belongs to me now."

"I'll give you eight dollars."

"It's a rare antique, a well-crafted European watch set in 24-karat gold with a beautiful hand-carved design with precious stones. Eight dollars? You can't be serious. It's worth much more."

Angelina disliked this man. "Twelve dollars."

"How can you expect me to part with an heirloom for such a paltry amount?"

Angelina's hands doubled into fists as she seethed with anger at Fabian's betrayal.

"Fifteen."

"You insult me," Gilchrest stared at her through his spectacles. "Do you realize this piece is probably one of a kind, custom-made—scarce indeed? Italians are known for their fine artistry. Think of Michelangelo, da Vinci, Donatello, and Bernini, the sculptor. These artists inebriate us with exquisite works."

Angelina suspected Fabian had been there often, and the man knew him much better than he wanted her to believe.

"Do you appreciate and understand art, *Señora* Dominguez?"

"Do you? Art is making something wonderful out of nothing, but you do the opposite, Mr. Gilchrest. You buy something wonderful from those in need and pretend it's nothing, then you declare it exquisite, of fine artistry, and you ransom it. Isn't that right? What did you pay Fabian for my pendant?"

"I am sorry, but my files are confidential."

Angelina did not believe him. She leaned forward. "Fifteen dollars, and that's my final offer. Take it or not."

He didn't answer.

"Then keep it." She turned toward the door.

"Wait! I have a charitable disposition. And since you did own it once—"

The very words exasperated her. "Once? I never relinquished my ownership."

He rolled his eyes in apparent frustration and picked up his pen. "All right, I'll let it go for an unbelievable seventeen dollars, but please, you must tell no one. It would ruin my business if anyone found out about my generous nature. I have my reputation to protect."

Angelina doubted anyone held his reputation in high regard. "My name is Angelina Dominguez. My address is the same as the one in your records for Fabian. While I don't have the entire amount, I will pay you three dollars or more every week until you are paid in full. Surely, you've heard of this. Haggerty's Furniture Emporium calls it the *Divided Payment System,* and they are a larger and more innovative establishment than your pawn shop, wouldn't you agree?" Angelina was not interested in his answer. "You will keep the watch until I pay for it in full. Here's my first payment of three dollars. I want a receipt showing my payment and my balance. I'll be back every week until it's paid in full."

"Well, as long as I am in possession of the watch, that sounds quite agreeable. Very clever of Haggerty's to think of it." Gilchrest's shrewd smile reappeared. "However, as you can see, I have many other lovely things. Is there anything else you'd like to see?"

"Yes, I'd like to see my receipt."

His face sobered, and he wrote out the ticket as Angelina fumed over Fabian's unbelievable betrayal and how she had to resort to Haggerty's ridiculous payment contrivance to regain what had always belonged to her.

Gilchrest handed Angelina the ticket. Furious, she crushed it in her hand and rushed out of the pawnshop, taking long, hurried strides to reach home.

Still clutching the receipt in her hand, Angelina cut through the dirt road of an alley. It sat behind store buildings where the earth cast a shadow and exhaled stale, pungent odors of garbage and urine mixed with the day's usual infusion of heat. Angelina took shallow breaths to escape the stench and turned around to judge the distance to return, but it measured the same to reach the end of the alley.

A burly man burst through a backdoor, stepped against the building, and urinated. He glanced back at her, and his indifference chilled her. Angelina lifted her long skirt to her calves and ran as fast as her feet would move while trying to hold her breath to escape the foul air.

The sanctuary of her home came into view as she kept running and hurried up her porch steps catching her breath. Angelina reached for her key. The door appeared closed, but it had not been closed enough to catch the latch. With a slight push, it slid open.

She stepped over the threshold without making a sound. Nothing appeared out of place. Still, the house had an unsettled feeling. She made her way to the kitchen and grabbed a skillet from the stove.

She heard a faint noise, like leaves swishing in the breeze or sheets ruffling, and then the sound of muffled voices. Angelina's pulse raced. She approached her bedroom. This door was closed but did not block the aromatic scent of jasmine perfume.

"You're my jewel." Fabian's familiar phrase came floating back to her, oiled with a woman's laughter. Words he'd spoken so many times as he vowed his love to his wife. Now his words floated about like tainted vapor to seduce a strange woman in Angelina's bed.

The skillet dropped from her hand with a loud thud, and as quickly as a flash of lightning, everything she lived for, knew, and held sacred ceased to exist. Angelina trembled in her anger, slammed open the door that bounced against the wall, and stepped inside.

A raven-haired beauty held a glass of wine, and when the woman turned her head, nothing could have prepared Angelina for the face of her husband's lover.

The earth crumbled beneath Angelina, and the shock was so strong it gave her a sense of falling.

CHAPTER 29

"Sophia!"

Fabian jumped out of bed without releasing the neck of his wine bottle and grabbed the blanket. "What are you doing home?"

"What are *you* doing home?" The sensation of wild horses stampeding through her heart and trampling the remnants of the love she had once cherished for her husband.

Fabian attempted to plead. "Listen…I…"

But he could not finish or penetrate the iron barrier Angelina quickly erected in her mind. In a state of shock, she shrieked in a voice that she didn't know she had, a voice that came from some untapped place of revulsion.

Fabian reached out. "Sophia came to see you. She said you were like sisters, so I told her to wait."

"So, all she had to do was knock on the door, and you threw away our marriage?"

Although unsteady, Fabian managed to step closer. Sophia's strong perfume, the aroma of liquor, and the vile, unmistakable scent of adultery encompassed the room. For the second time, and without moving an inch, Angelina returned to the foulness of the alley.

"You have to believe me, Angelina. This means nothing."

Angelina gazed at the scattered clothing on the floor and turned to Fabian. "No. This means the end of everything."

Frantic thoughts raced through Angelina's mind. *Had his love for me ever existed, or did he just grow tired of me?*

Sophia reached for her clothes. "I'm so sorry, Angelina. I'm not trying to steal your husband. I have a fiancé back in New York—a doctor—I love."

"Love? That's impossible!" Angelina doubted Sophia could love anyone any more than Fabian did. "Get out of my house!"

Fabian's hand shook as he set down his bottle of liquor. "Wh-what you see, Angelina, it's not anything—nothing."

Fabian wavered as he stood, shifting his weight. He then leaned on the bureau to steady himself, as if the shock of seeing his wife had thrown him off his course, and unsure how to regain his footing.

Sophia rose from the bed, spilling her wine goblet. Deep burgundy rolled across the white sheets.

Sophia dressed. Her movements appeared routine and practiced for such a wretched occasion. Angelina had known her far too long and understood her implied confidence. Fabian had not been her only conquest and surely not destined to become her last.

"Angelina," said Sophia calmly. "You know I love you. I never meant for this to happen."

"Then it would never have happened." Angelina saw no distinction between the two of them. The betrayal could not have taken place without the willingness of the other.

The air seemed thin, and Angelina found it harder to breathe. Her friendship, her marriage, and her love for both evaporated.

Fabian came closer and staggered to kiss her, but in his condition, Angelina easily pushed away his Judas kiss. *"E finita!"* she shouted, echoing the finality of her marriage. She turned to her husband. "Get out, Fabian, and take your jewel with you." She waved the pawnshop receipt in Fabian's face, but her fury strangled her words, and the offense had shriveled compared to his affair.

Nothing between them was true. Angelina continued to feel her breathing grow strained and heavy. Again and again her chest rose and collapsed until she could force out what should have been unmistakable to him. "It's over, Fabian."

"It's the liquor." Fabian's frustration grew into fury, and he punched the plaster wall and screamed. Blood dripped from his knuckles. His face contorted in either fury or pain, as if searching for an excuse.

Angelina studied her husband's muddled expression. Each of his words held a different weight, and when strung together, they were uneven and profane. He seemed unaware of the finality of his actions.

"Where are you hiding your soul, Fabian? I'm through trying to find it. Something deep inside you has broken, and you allowed it to destroy your life, but I will not let you destroy my life or our son's. Not today, not ever. I've been holding onto something that didn't exist." She glanced once more at Sophia. "Both of you get out!"

Fabian reached for her. "I'm sorry, Angelina, this won't happen again."

"We agree on something."

His eyes were pleading, and his ramblings predictable, like weak muscles flinching under greater pressure. "We have a son. We're a family," said Fabian.

"No. From now on, Donny and I are a family. You have abandoned us, just like your father abandoned you. Drinking, gambling, unholy activities, and possession of a gun—

that's your family." Angelina released him from her heart. "I refuse to let Donny become a replica of his father. What worthwhile lesson could you possibly teach him? He's far too precious."

"You don't mean that. I've loved no one but you and our son. Believe me." Sweat beaded profusely on Fabian's forehead as if he'd never considered his actions had consequences.

Sophia mumbled absurd apologies and then hurriedly stole her way out the door carrying her shoes.

Angelina pulled the stained sheets from the bed and threw them at Fabian. "I don't need you anymore." Pasquale's brick sat on the dresser. Angelina reached for it and had a surge of strength. Her words came more easily now. "I am strong, Fabian, and I will never need you again." The muscles in her arm flexed and with a scream of rage, she threw the brick across the room and shattered the glass frame on the wall, purchased with joy to preserve their marriage license.

Though unsteady with drink, Fabian seemed to awaken to the seriousness of his adultery. "Please, Angelina. We'll try again."

"You never tried in the first place." Her words burned and wounded her. "You've stolen my grandmother's pendant watch, gambled away our savings, drank bottle after bottle, exposed us to the violence of the *bolita* criminals. Now, you've taken Sophia to the bed where *I sleep.* She was like a sister, someone I have known nearly all my life. I guess it didn't concern either of you. There's nothing left to destroy, Fabian. I think you've covered everything. You've destroyed all that mattered to me."

"I love *you*, Angelina."

She raised her hand to her temple. "Stop, Fabian! You're only sorry you've been caught. It was you who has been dimming the lamp of our marriage. Now we stand in total darkness. There are no rainbows in the dark. Take whatever you need. Don't be here when I come back."

"Angelina, please don't take this so seriously. I swear Sophia means nothing to me. It's you, I love. Why can't you believe me?" Fabian pulled on his pants as he spoke.

Angelina didn't listen to the rattling of Fabian's words but to the spaces between them, where the actual truth was out of breath and gasping heavily, unable to survive.

"Sometimes it's hard to know when something begins, Fabian, but there is no mistaking when it ends." She stormed out the door.

He followed her outside. "Come back. Where are you going? This is your home, and you're my wife." His voice grew more intense and threatening. "You have nowhere to go. Your father will never let you return." His words crashed hard and loud and would echo inside her for days.

"You did this to us. So, you leave. Donny and I will stay."

With no explanation, the stench of the alleyway once again returned to her, along with the torturous vision of Sophia and Fabian in their adulterous embrace. Angelina believed Fabian. Sophia meant nothing to him, and she was about to marry someone else, so the affair meant nothing to her, either. However, it meant everything to Angelina. She looked pleadingly at the sky, hoping to see a sign from her mother, but the sun appeared feeble and dimmed its luster.

The thought of it curdled inside her. She became nauseated until she could no longer support it and had to bend over and vomit her disgust onto the street.

An older woman walking her dog called out, "Are you sick, *chica?* Do you need my help?"

Angelina rejected the stranger's voice, shook her head, and hurried away. People were not always what they seemed.

CHAPTER 30

A MONTH after Fabian's betrayal, Angelina walked up the same steps of the courthouse where she'd married Fabian and where the Justice of the Peace had repeatedly asked if she'd take this man for her husband, '*Sí o no?*' Looking back at her wedding day, her hesitation must have been a premonition. Perhaps somewhere deep inside her, a voice shouted, *"No!"*

As she stepped inside the courthouse office, an unnerving feeling overcame her. Everything seemed frozen in time; even the little man who married them wore the same indifferent expression, brown suit with the same oblong stain on his lapel. He appeared lost in time, as though he resided there unaffected by the outside world, like the desks and rows of wooden file cabinets.

It had been well over two years since her greatest mistake in judgment. Now, anxious to unravel her union, she stood among couples eager to say their vows.

Angelina went straight to the rival counter on the left and glanced up at the sign posted on the wall stating the filing fee for Dissolution of Marriage. In comparison, it was less lucrative for the state of Florida to perform marriages and far more profitable to dissolve them.

"I want a divorce. Where do I file, pay, and sign?"

"Where's your husband?" said the young man behind the counter, snapping his suspenders and sporting a jamboree of upper lip fuzz.

"Does it matter?" She'd already lost a part of her life with Fabian, and his whereabouts no longer interested her. "I live in our *casita* with our son, and I pay the rent. He took every-thing that belongs to him, including a large bureau." Angelina reached for a fountain pen, dipped it in the inkwell, and scribbled something. "I don't know or care where he lives, but here's the address of his Tia Lourdes. He's there or she knows where."

The young man read the address, removed his spectacles, and glared at Angelina. She surmised he wore them only to appear knowledgeable because he looked less imposing without them. "It takes two of you to marry, and two of you to get divorced," he stated as if this would scare her off.

Angelina had no intention of backing down. "It only takes one person to destroy a marriage, and that person is Fabian Dominguez. And it only takes one person to say *that's it, no more, I'm done,* and I'm *that* person, Angelina Dominguez. So where do I sign?"

Although this man was much younger than the one who had married them, she saw many similarities, except this one seemed set on impressing her with his expertise.

"I have the power to decide how this should be handled and where and if to file for divorce. Divorce is against the public's interest."

"Public interest?" In anger, Angelina tightened her right hand into a fist and pressed it against the thick glass counter.

Her son meant the world to her, and at least he was in her care. Beyond that, she had not fully recovered since discovering Fabian and Sophia together and all the gradual torments that preceded it. The knowledge that the only thing binding her to Fabian was a single piece of paper buried in an official file tormented her.

She took a frustrated breath, pursed her lips, and picked up the nameplate in front of her that read *Mr. Raul Neri.* She set it down and spoke more determined than ever. "No one knows what goes on behind closed doors, least of all the public. I want a divorce, not because I don't understand my husband, but because I do."

Neri made an unnecessary and unappealing noise reminiscent of rusty hinges creaking, and then, with less authority than Angelina believed he possessed, he issued his official statement. "The court only grants divorce if there is evidence that one party violated the other."

"And what do you consider a violation?"

He straightened his back and lifted his chin, looking down at Angelina while she folded her arms, ready to resist whatever was on his mind.

"The terms for divorce are very clear, and there is no way to misinterpret them. There's abandonment, cruelty, madness, and adultery." He lifted an eyebrow. "Do any of these apply?"

"Yes!"

"Which ones?"

"All of them!" Angelina returned his gaping stare. "Fabian Dominguez *abandoned* the sanctity of our marriage. His behavior has been beyond *cruel.* He needs a doctor specializing in disorders of the mind because he could not remember we have to pay rent and buy food, so he foolishly gambled away our money. Evidently, he also forgot he was married, or what I look like, because he mistakenly took another woman to our bed—an obvious sign of *madness,* more commonly known in the Bible as the offense of *adultery*. As the injured party, I want a swift divorce."

"Marriage is swift. Divorce is not. We will need all the pertinent information and must notify your husband. He has the right to contest it."

Angelina reached across the counter and pulled out a blank form from a wire basket labeled *Dissolution of Marriage*.

She ignored the mumblings of the clerk as she scribbled out relevant information, signed it, and slid the form across the counter with her filing fee sitting on top. "It's been a month since he left. I have the house and our son and he has his Tia Lourdes home, who I'm sure welcomed him back with open arms. You can notify him there and here is where he works—sometimes, maybe. I wrote down both addresses. Please advise him that either way, he no longer has a wife, and the sooner it's official, the better."

Angelina met the clerk's gaze for one intense moment. *Why is he stalling?* Did he plan on denying her the right to live free of this man who broke every marriage vow and left her and her child without funds and n potential danger? What more did he need to hear? *Should I mention the gun?*

The clerk said nothing more, and Angelina said everything she meant to. With no reason to be there any longer, the room became stifling, and beads of perspiration gathered on Angelina's forehead. Overwhelmed by an urgent need to leave, she rushed past the lines of hopeful brides and grooms, past innocuous file cabinets, desks, and chairs. She grabbed the brass handle of the heavy wooden door and drew it wide open.

Once outside, she filled her lungs with a long, cleansing breath and hurried away from the building where the two most important events of her life had taken place. This one ended the dream that her marriage would last a lifetime. Yet, she still had a sense of foreboding she couldn't shake.

In a burst of energy, she went straight to the home of Eva Chavez who cared for her child. When Eva opened the door, Angelina stepped inside and scooped up her son and held him close. "Eva, thank you for all your help, but if anything happens to me, you must take my son to his grandfather, and if anything happens to both my father and me, take him to Signora Bertelli. She'll know what to do."

"What about the boy's father?" the woman said.

Angelina saw no reason to discuss Fabian's failings. "He's never picked him up, has he?" The woman shook her head.

"He has a job that doesn't allow him to care for a child, and it would be too dangerous for Donny."

Angelina took a torn envelope from her handbag, wrote on the back, and handed the woman a slip of paper with her father's and Signora Bertelli's addresses. "This is just in case something serious or unexpected takes place."

"You aren't expecting something serious or unexpected, are you?"

The question weighed heavily. "No.... I mean, just in case."

Angelina picked up Donny and said goodbye to Eva. She had such a sense of contentment with her child in her arms. All the way home, she sang him his favorite songs and recited little children's poems.

"Hey, Diddle Diddle, the cat, and the fiddle—" Donny laughed. Her son was her universe now. "And the dish ran away with the spoon." He clapped his hands and smiled, revealing his two teeth.

When they reached home, she fed him and read him some simple stories until he yawned and rubbed his eyes. Angelina sang a few lullabies until he fell asleep. For a time, she sat by his crib and watched him in slumber. Such a precious gift, she thought.

Angelina took out her Saint Jude medal from under her

clothing and tightened her hand around its shape and texture. He was the saint of miracles. The time had come. She would take Donny home to meet the family.

Throughout the night, a sense of urgency overtook Angelina's thoughts. She paced as she practiced what to say to her father. It seemed now that the walls were closing in. She believed in family and had longed to say, *Papa, this is your grandson.*

There was no more time to waste. The next morning, she first dressed Donny in his little sailor suit she bought to take his picture. However, the purpose of the visit was for her father to realize the resemblance between his sons and grandson, so in the end, she dressed him in a more casual outfit with striped pants similar to one of Vinny's baby pictures.

With Donny in her arms and hoping to soften her father's heart, Angelina jumped on the trolley to her old neighborhood before her courage faded. She looked out the window, but with each familiar street drawing her closer to her father's house, her heartbeat raced.

At last, the colorful sign, *Domenico's Fine Italian Food,* came into view. Angelina drew in a deep breath. It had taken her a long time to make the commitment to face her father, and this was not the time to hesitate.

She stepped off the trolley with her son in her arms and trepidation in her heart. As she reached the store's entrance, she heard a familiar voice.

"Angie, Angie!" her little sister, Lily, rushed over in such a hurry she tripped and almost lost her balance. "Where have you been? I've missed you so much. I cried for you every day."

If only Angelina could be sure her father felt the same. Balancing Donny with one arm, she placed the other around her sister and kissed her. The child's honey-colored hair had darkened, but her smile remained brilliant.

"Oh, Lily, I've dreamt of this moment for so long. How you've grown."

"I had another birthday. I'm nine now!" she shouted.

"Well, happy birthday." Angelina held out her son for Lily to see. "And now you're an aunt. This is Don Carlos Dominguez. I call him Donny. If you sit down, you can hold him."

Lily rushed inside and sat on a chair with her arms outstretched while Angelina carefully placed her son in her sister's lap. It seemed like just yesterday they shared the same bed, and she would read Lily stories until she fell asleep. Nothing remained the same.

Angelina looked around the usual well-stocked shelves. She could never mistake the figure at the rear of the store. Even with his back to her, Angelina could tell which brother restocked the shelves.

"Vinny!" she hollered more loudly than she meant to.

Vincenzo turned around and his face lit up. Although he'd never been very affectionate, he rushed to give her a hug meant for a bear. As though under a spell, and if only for a moment, the essence of her childhood returned.

Vinny kissed her on the top of her head. Angelina didn't miss his attempt to make it clear he was now taller. It seemed like a lifetime ago, when verbally sparring with her brothers had been a family sport.

Angelina pointed to her son. "Remember your nephew, Donny."

Vinny broke into a wider grin, took the baby from Lily, and held him up for a better look. Angelina was delighted by his response.

"Anyone can see he looks just like me. Handsome, huh?"

"Don't let Signora Bertelli hear you compliment him. She'll think you're trying to curse him."

Vinny made a scuffing sound and a gesture of dismissal. "Oh, that old superstition. Why be silent about incredibly good looks."

Angelina couldn't contain her joy. "You'll never know how much I've missed all of you. I wanted so much to let you know where I lived so you could come for a visit whenever you wanted, but if Papa found out, I was afraid of what he might do."

"All of us understand. We're still waiting for him to realize it's the 20th century, and this is America."

Angelina gazed around the store again. As always, everything had a place, but the unanswered question weighed heavily. "How is Papa?"

"He still can't get the pomegranates to grow." Lily giggled.

Vincenzo shook his head. "Nothing changes. He's still as angry as ever."

His remark saddened her. It had been so long. Indeed, it was time to make amends.

"Everybody misses you. Yeah, even me." But her brother's smile lost its illumination as he glanced out at the street, then turned to her. "Papa went to pick up some supplies. He'll be back soon." Vinny's apprehension could not have been any clearer.

Yet, Angelina could not imagine how much more courage she'd have to gather if she allowed more time to pass. She had made so many excuses, fearing his anger. Would she be brave enough and strong enough to do this again?

Everything in the store reminded her of her father. Almost mechanically, Angelina checked the products on the shelves and reached for a can of tomatoes. She turned it around, so the label faced the aisle and seen more clearly. "Sometimes, it feels like I'm still here." If only she'd sent one of those letters, she'd written and addressed. It was her fault. She allowed her father to intimidate her, but perhaps, after all this time, he'd softened and missed her, too.

"My son reminds me of all of you. Papa will love him, too. How many times has he said, 'Blood of my Blood?'"

The door opened, and Salvatore came in holding a case of olive oil. "Angie!" He set it down, rushed over, and tightened his arms around her, lifting her off the floor and spinning her around.

Angelina laughed. Her siblings missed her as much as she missed them.

"Look at Angie's baby. He's good-looking like me," said Vinny.

Sal slipped his arm around the child and took him from his brother. "And smart like me, right?"

"Of course," said Angelina.

As Vinny had done, Salvatore quickly glanced out the window. "Don't stay now. Come Tuesday nights. Papa goes to his friend's house. A bunch of Sicilian spaghetti-benders like to play pinochle, so come back at 7:00. He's not here then, and the other children wouldn't be upset they didn't see you." He lost his usual playfulness. "I'm serious. Papa will be here any minute."

Donny raised his arms and Angelina picked him up. "I'm staying. I must see him."

From the large picture window, they all saw Domenico approaching the house. For one tense moment, no one spoke. With every step closer, her panic elevated. But what was the point of avoiding him? Certain her father's heart would melt at the sight of his first grandchild, Angelina stiffened her resolve and braced herself for the critical moment as she watched her father's rigid posture approaching. With his every step growing closer, her brother's anxiety became almost tangible, piercing the air.

Vinny placed his hands on Angelina's shoulders and squeezed as a warning. "Go, Angie, go, go. Go!"

Though a nervous tremor engulfed her, she didn't move. "No matter what happens, I love all of you," she said, "and I will love you forever."

Her father's footsteps grew louder as he approached the store's entrance.

Sal stepped closer to her, pointed to the back door, and whispered, "Angie, please, go. Don't do this!"

She had waited too long and thought about it too much. It had to happen. Still, her heartbeat quickened as the footsteps grew louder. Angelina closed her eyes at that critical moment when Domenico twisted the knob and a trifling squeak warned the door was opening.

CHAPTER 31

DOMENICO HAD ALWAYS BEEN a creature of habit, a man of unwavering beliefs who lived in a world of black and white. The haze of compromise did not exist for Angelina's father, and the fear of what might happen caused her resolve to crumble.

Gray hairs now salted his temples, and he stood more rigid than she remembered. Without the slightest softening of his expression, Domenico faced his firstborn child.

"Hello, Papa. I came to see you. I wanted to say... I mean, I wanted to show you." Her words faltered under his stare. She cleared her throat. "This is... it's Donny, your grandson."

A tempest, both soundless and unseen, tore through the room. It left Angelina weakened by its force, but Domenico appeared bolstered by its strength. The muscles in his jaw visibly tightened, but he said nothing. As they faced each other, the ticking of the pendulum clock kept pace with the drumming of Angelina's heart and unnerved her.

"Papa, I know I hurt you, and I'm so sorry, leaving seemed like my only escape to prevent a loveless marriage." Though heartfelt and true, her words seemed lacking as they scattered like litter at her father's feet. "I miss my family so much. You mean everything to me. Please, Papa, I love you, but it's hard to ask forgiveness for not marrying a man I disliked, nearly double my age, and with four children. Why can't you see that? You made marriage arrangements without even asking me or considering how it would affect my entire life. You gave me no choice but to escape."

She sighed and, holding her child; she dared to close the distance between them. "I need you and my family now more than ever."

Domenico did not react. He had never been an especially affectionate man, but Angelina desperately longed for his embrace, and not receiving it seemed a cruelty she wasn't certain she could bear.

Domenico's breathing grew heavy, like a volcano spouting smoke before it erupted. "You made your decision. You left and should stay away."

"Papa, try to understand. I didn't care for Umberto Rizzo. I couldn't marry a man I didn't care for, who had already lived half his life with his first wife. He must be set in his ways and beliefs. I'm barely beginning to live my own life. I wanted to discover married life with a man I loved and who I believed loved me."

"The baker would have offered you security."

"But I need love. I wanted a husband, not another father. I wanted to experience motherhood and have my own children. You said he was not expecting to have any more than the four children he already had. I wanted my own children and to discover with my husband which way the world spins for us." She paused. It was almost too much to go on. Why was this so hard to understand?

"There's no excuse for the way you left. None!" The vein in his neck pulsated.

"It was a mistake marrying Fabian Dominguez, but I truly

cared for him and believed he loved me. I thought I found happiness, someone to spend my whole life with." Angelina sensed she'd stepped into a trap, and her words of regret and explanation had drifted into ash.

She grew desperate and turned her son around so her father could see him more clearly. "Papa, this is the one thing I do not regret." Surely her father could see the love and pride she had for her son. "This beautiful little boy is your grandson, Don Carlos. You have to admit how much he looks like our family. Don't you think you could love him, too?" Angelina exerted more energy than necessary to make a point that should have been obvious. "My son needs the love of a grandfather and the love of all his uncles and little aunt as much as I need all your love."

Domenico glanced at the child and then at Angelina. "I warned you many times what would happen if you dishonored me. I have other children to raise and protect, and it was you who left our family. We're Italian, and you should have married your own kind. An egg knows better than to dance with a stone." His words were glazed in bitterness.

Fearful of what went on in her father's mind, she braced for what he might say next.

But Domenico stroked the cheek of his grandson, kissed his hand, and gently pulled him from Angelina's embrace. "We both lost something, Angelina, but your loss is the greater. You disrespected me by leaving like a thief in the night. The difference between you and me is I lost one child, but I still had five more. You lost your only remaining parent."

Angelina couldn't move. Her father spoke as if she'd died. The notion of such a declaration sickened her.

"However, I accept your child as my blood. You're right, he resembles your brothers, and we will love him."

The threatening cloud of rejection lifted. The weight of

all her pent-up tension evaporated, and her heartbeat again. Nothing could have thrilled Angelina more. Her father had received her child as his family. She threw her arms around him.

"You have made me so happy, Papa." She wanted to say more, but tears of joy caught in her throat.

"He is one of us and should learn our ways. I'll take good care of him and raise him like he's my own."

An alarm went off inside her. Her joy turned to shock. Domenico's words had conjured up a lovely melody, and he now banged the piano keys with his fists.

He had six living children, and he wanted to take away the only child she had. She could think of nothing she had done to make him think she'd accept such a contemptuous arrangement. His offer infuriated her. He intended to leave a mother without her child. She could not believe his words that throbbed inside her head. "No! Never!" Angelina erupted.

She pulled her son from her father's arms, and they met each other's gaze.

With a stern expression, Domenico slammed his fist on the end table and took one step toward her.

Hugging her son tightly, Angelina stepped back.

"I did not remove you from this family. You did that to yourself," said Domenico. "You knew exactly what would happen when you left my house. Dirty water can never be washed clean, Angelina. How many times have I told you that?"

Before Angelina could respond, her father moved forward again, forcing her to step back. She'd witnessed this maneuver when her mother's sisters came to take his children from him. Domenico had rid himself of them with this tactic and heated words.

"Nothing can change what you've done," her father said.

"The past is written in stone. You are dead to me, Angelina, and there's no passage back from the dead." Domenico continued to spout out anger and step forward until finally forcing Angelina outside, where he slammed the door in the face of his oldest child shouting his farewell.

"*È finita!*"

He reverted to Italian when he intended it as a command when daring anyone to challenge him. Her father severed all ties to her with a single word—*finished!*

The worst had come to pass, and Angelina grew strangely calm. "No, Papa. *Non è finita.*"

The door remained closed. "It's not finished. There's too much between us. I want my son to know his family, but not without his mother. How can you think like that? It would break his heart and mine."

She could hear Lily crying. Sal and Vinny came to her defense and begged their father to let her in, but it was not Domenico's way.

Why couldn't her father find it in his heart to forgive her? With her arms wrapped around her baby, Angelina sobbed hysterically. If only her mother were here. If only her father could forgive. *If only* crushed her heart.

The day had withered with anguish. Colors faded, slipped into nightfall, and shadows filled the streets.

For a time, Angelina lacked the strength to move. She lingered outside, hoping her father would reconsider, but the door remained closed.

Kerosene lamps flickered inside the house. A wedge of light escaped through the curtains and spilled like a puddle in front of her. For a moment, Angelina stared at it and then stepped into its faint illumination and cried.

It was all she had left of her father.

CHAPTER 32

FOR WEEKS, Domenico's hurtful words returned to his eldest child. Angelina could not dispel the sound of her father slamming the door in her face. She could hear it echoing in her mind. She picked up Pasquale's brick and held it close when she needed a reminder of her strength. Her young son was the center of her life, her single focus, and pierced all sorrow.

Angelina sat at her worktable as the closing bell rang. The day had been long. She put down the *chaveta* knife used to trim cigars and cleaned off her workplace.

"Here, Angelina. Take these mangos. My neighbor gave me too many." Carmen placed them on her workstation.

Angelina looked up at Carmen and smiled. "Thank you. I love mangos, like nature's candy."

So much had gone wrong, but Angelina enjoyed Carmen's company, who always danced her way to the bright side of everything. She had uncomplicated philosophies and a verbal bucket of water to extinguish emotional fires. "Now that Fabian moved out and vanished, why don't you come over, Carmen? I'll make us dinner."

"Well, let me check my calendar of events, current dinner

invitations, upcoming fiestas, and those dances at the social club where the music is so loud and young men fight over who's going to spin me around on the dance floor." She glanced into her skirt pocket. "Hmm. You're in luck. I seem to be free tonight. There must have been a cancellation."

"I'm so glad." At least tonight, thought Angelina, Carmen was sure to distract her with a lively exchange.

"It's true. I spread joy wherever I go." Carmen gave an exaggerated sigh.

"We'll stop at my house and leave these mangos, then go two more blocks and pick up Donny."

"Good idea. These mangos are giving me muscles," said Carmen.

They left the factory building, with Carmen still chattering as they walked.

"I told Luis he was far too greedy for my taste. So, I handed him back his love and told him to pass it on to the next *señorita* standing in line. That's when he said, 'If you leave me, I'll kill myself.' Can you believe it? What an actor."

Inviting Carmen to eat dinner already uplifted Angelina's spirits. Her friend could make anyone laugh and push away their troubles. "What did you say to that?"

"What could I say? I offered him my condolences. I mean, it's not often you can offer solace to someone just before they're a corpse, right?" Carmen sighed. "The earth is mostly ocean. It's like God found sea life less annoying than men walking around on land. I mean, that's pretty obvious."

Angelina enjoyed how Carmen always reloaded the gun with the same bullet her boyfriend shot at her.

"The next week, I hear Luis is out with Consuela Torrez. She's pretty and pretty dumb, too. Beauty comes and goes, but stupid sticks around and glues itself inside the brain where no doctor can remove it."

"I thought you liked Luis in the beginning."

"The problem with the beginning is that it always comes first, and that's when we don't know too much. However, the end always comes at the end. Now I ask, when are the beginning and end the same? The answer is *never*." Carmen raised her eyebrows as if daring Angelina to dispute this. "However, I have to say, an opportunity presented itself. Since Luis graciously offered to kill himself if I didn't come back to him, I sent him my sharpest kitchen knife with a note attached to the blade: 'This should come in handy, and you're welcome!'"

Angelina laughed. "I wish I could have seen his face when it arrived."

"I know." Carmen took in a deep breath. "Life is filled with precious little moments, and I hate it when I miss one. We all have a sensible corner of our hearts, but the not-so-smart corner overruns it. I'm telling you that Luis is a master of lies and comes dressed in the elaborate costumes of a good guy that conceal the truth. If there were a Sistine Chapel for Liars, he'd be canonized its saint."

Angelina thought of Fabian and Sophia. "We all know people who talk without thinking, but just as many who actually think without thinking."

"Think without thinking? Well, now, that's something to think about. The world is full of terrible liars."

Angelina nodded. "I read the Greeks rulers were smart liars. They called their lies *myths*, then they invented gods for their myths and built them temples, and then everyone had to worship and offer gifts to the gods."

"And who got the gifts?"

Angelina smiled. "Who do you think? Didn't I just say the Greeks rulers were smart."

"Gotta hand it to those Greeks."

Angelina glanced down the street. "You know what? On the next block is a blue house with a wonderful avocado tree. I know the owner's daughter, Elena. She said we could go through the backyard and take all the avocados we wanted. I brought a bag with me."

"Avocados, huh? Did I ever tell you how to make Cuban-style avocado salad?"

"Not yet."

"Trust me. You don't want to die without knowing my recipe."

"Okay, I promise to stay alive until you give me the recipe." Angelina enjoyed her friend's way of describing the most ordinary things.

"A wise decision. Give me two ripe avocados, salt, cilantro, a tomato, garlic, and olive oil. Nothing will ever make you feel so happy you're alive."

"It's always good to know I'm alive." They turned the corner, and Angelina pointed to a distance house. "It's that blue one on the next block with the big window in the attic."

Carmen stopped, and her smile vanished. "I can't go near that place."

"Why not? No one lives there."

"That's what people think, but inside there is a woman who cries all day and night, and I don't want to see or hear her."

"You must be thinking of another house. This one's empty. Elena told me her mother owns it, so no one's home or crying."

"She's always home and always crying."

"Now, that's just as good as a Greek myth. Even if someone were there—which there's not—she wouldn't still be crying."

"Well, that depends." Carmen raised her eyebrows and gave Angelina a sobering glance.

"Depends on what?"

"You don't think people die, and lie around at the cemetery watching the worms dig holes, do you? There are many stories about spirits who live among us right here in Ybor City, but I know this spirit is real because my mother knew Graciela."

"I'll show you the empty house. Elena told me the key to the house is where she hid the key to the gate."

"And I'm telling you, a young woman who fell in love lived in that house. But not just a little in love, like I always do when I'm with Carlos, Enrique, and what's his name? No, not like me. Graciela Hernandez fell in love, like a heavy bucket of bricks fell on her head and knocked her out cold, and it happened with that man Santiago."

"What man, Santiago?"

"Angelina, you have lived here all your life, and never heard of *Good-for-Nothing-Santiago? Santiago-sin-Verguenzo? Miserable-Heart-of-Stone Santiago?* He told Graciela he loved her and left her pregnant, promising to return. All lies. She waited and waited, but he never came back. Poor Graciela stopped eating until, one day, she wasted away and died of a broken heart or hunger or both."

Angelina rubbed away an unexplained chill from her arms. Santiago's last words were eerily similar to Rolando's promise to return to her. He'd also loved her, and leaving her filled with love for him. Angelina believed she had an affinity with Graciela. At least she now knew Rolando could not return to her and never stopped caring. Still, the events altered her life. She shook her head to rid herself of such thoughts. "That must have happened a long time ago, Carmen."

"It happened before I was born, so no, not very long ago, since I'm still quite young." Carmen gave one of her devilish grins.

"I don't believe in ghosts, Carmen."

"Shh, shh, shh. Oh, my goodness. Never take a chance and say out loud they don't exist. They are everywhere, in the air, the trees, the grass beneath our feet, looming around our heads. Worse, they have big ears. You'll insult them, and they'll conspire to prove you wrong. Nothing's more frightening than a ghost with an axe to grind."

Angelina grinned. "All right, but if you find a spell to make Graciela leave the house, delicious avocados are waiting for us."

"It's a shame, too. I love avocados."

"Well, then?" Angelina fixed her gaze on Carmen. "You have about half a block to stop believing in ghosts. I mean, what's more important, Cuban avocado salad or ghosts?" Angelina didn't want an answer. "We are not going inside the house. We'll go to the tree in the backyard, fill up a bag, and leave—quickly. Then we'll go to my house where you can show me your avocado recipe—so I can die in peace." Angelina grinned. "Or you can watch me eat delicious avocado sandwiches for lunch all week."

"You are making this hard. Why aren't you afraid? Ghosts are dangerous."

"I only know one story about ghosts."

Carmen's eyes lit up. "What is it?"

"My old neighbor, *Signora* Bertelli told me that back in Santo Stefano Quisquina, there was an abandoned village next to where she and my family lived. So many people had packed up and boarded a ship to America. Only the very old were left behind."

"Did something happen?"

"The streetlamps lit up at night in the dark by themselves. Everyone believed it was the ghosts of those who once lived there and walked out of their graves at the cemetery to light the torches."

Carmen nodded. "You see. There's no other way to explain that."

"I think someone played a trick. The dead are dead.

Anyway, ghosts used to be people. Some were good people, and some were bad—like when they were alive. So, tomorrow we'll pick some avocados, leave after a few minutes, and be gone before Graciela knows we came."

Carmen wrinkled her brow as if the bag of free avocados weighed heavily on her mind and then marched past the house in question without glancing at it.

"See, nothing happened," said Angelina. "That's because ghosts are nocturnal. They sleep all day and haunt at night. I've heard they're related to bats and skunks."

"How is that a pleasing comparison?" Carmen flashed a somber face.

"I thought you knew all things regarding phantoms." Angelina could no longer hold back her amusement, and then they both laughed.

They reached Angelina's home and laughed as they climbed onto the porch. Angelina placed the key in the lock, but the door swung open with a push.

Angelina stepped inside, and in one agonizing moment, she saw everything she owned tossed and trampled. The bag of mangos fell from her arms and rolled across the floor as the most horrifying thought materialized, and she screamed.

The house was in terrible disarray with everything tossed everywhere. Drawers jutted or dangled out of their cabinets, and furniture knocked over or pushed out of place.

"*Aye, Dios mio!*" shouted Carmen. "Could this be the Black Hand?"

Gripped by fright, Angelina rushed to the bedroom. Her clothes were flung about in every direction. She ran to the closet.

"Oh, God, all of Donny's belongings were gone!" Angelina screamed in horror, as though her body had caught fire. After all Fabian had done to her, she never imagined he would do something this repulsive.

"Fabian's stolen my baby, Carmen. All that's left is this little blanket. He would never have taken all our child's things if he hadn't taken the baby from Eva."

"*Maria Santisima!* He's even worse than Graciela's Santiago."

"Maybe it's not too late. I have to reach Eva's house before Fabian."

Angelina darted from the house and ran down the street.

Carmen followed her. "I never heard of anyone doing this. Fabian's pure evil?"

Carmen struggled to keep up with Angelina, who lifted her long skirt and ran faster than she ever had. The fear of losing her child propelled her through the street. How could it have occurred to her that he would do something so low, so despicable?

When they reached the white-shuttered home of Eva Chavez, they both knocked furiously. The woman inside sprang to answer the door. "Aye, Angelina. It was horrible. I tried to stop him, but there were two of them. I had no defense against these men. They just burst in."

"What do you mean?" Angelina rubbed her arms to try and stop the uncontrollable tremors rushing through her body.

"Fabian pushed me aside, came in, and grabbed your boy about an hour ago. I couldn't stop him."

A terrible pressure pushed against Angelina's heart. She had no illusions about Fabian or his capabilities, but he'd reached a new low.

"The *sin verguenzo.* Where did he go?" shouted Carmen.

With tears streaming down her face, Angelina blurted out her desperation. "I can't lose my baby. How did this happen?"

"He came to the door with another man. When I opened it, he told me his name, mentioned you, and said he wanted his son. He pushed his way through the door and picked up

Donny. You told me to take the baby to your father's house if anything happened to you. Your husband never once picked up Donny. You just said he had a job that didn't allow him to care for a child. I told him to leave Donny, but he just laughed and said Donny was his child, not mine."

Just the thought of all that could go wrong with Fabian as a caretaker frightened her. "All these months, he's never picked him up. Not once. I never imagined this. He must be drunk."

"I don't see how you'll catch them, Angelina. He threw some money at me and said Donny wouldn't be coming back. As they left, I heard the other man say they better hurry if they were going to catch the 6:30 to Cuba."

"Cuba!" The word almost burned Angelina's lips to say it. "How would I ever find my baby in a country of millions? It can't be true."

"I'm so sorry, but that's what he said, and there was no way to stop him."

Angelina turned away and ran. "Wait for me," said Carmen, who strained to keep up.

"You're not going alone. I'm going with you. If this is true, this Eva woman should have come searching for you," said Carmen between gasps.

Angelina ran as fast as her mind and heart were racing.

"Wait. Why are you turning? We need to catch a trolley."

"I don't have time to wait for one. The police station is not that far away," Horrific thoughts of Fabian neglecting their son grew more vivid.

"That will take time. Let's go straight to the docks," said Carmen as she gasped.

"We can't reach the docks before the police can drive us there, and more importantly, only they can stop Fabian. If we find him on our own, we'll still have to call them for help. If he went through this much to steal my baby, he would not just hand him back to me."

"The shortest route to the station is this way," said Carmen.

With no time to lose, they darted through an obstacle course of pedestrians, wagons, and street vendors.

"Maybe that Eva woman is lying. Maybe Fabian isn't leaving the country," said Carmen, still gasping as they ran.

"I believe her. It makes sense. Fabian needs to escape from the *bolita* gangsters. They'll tear Ybor City apart looking for him, and what will become of my baby if he's with his father when they find him?" She shook her head to rid herself of the frightening thought. "I told Fabian I would not let Donny grow up like him. I even told him I didn't want our son around him. So, now he's taken him away from me. I have to get him back. He's all I have left of a family, and I won't be able to bear my life without him."

The police station came into view. Angelina caught her second wind and hurried up the cement stairs, through the heavy door, and rushed to the front desk. "I need help. I'm so scared for my baby."

But the officer on duty continued to write. Angelina glanced at the name on his badge. "Sergeant John O'Hare, my son is in danger. His father kidnapped him and is taking him out of the country."

The sergeant looked up and lifted a bushy eyebrow. "Kidnapping is a serious crime, but if your husband has him, that's not a crime. What makes you think your baby is in actual danger?" Sergeant O'Hare slowly reached for a form.

"My husband is Fabian Dominguez, an alcoholic associated with cruel and violent criminals. He even has a gun. My child is in terrible danger."

"What does he look like? How old is your baby, and what's his name? Is your baby American or Cuban?"

Carmen shot the answers right back. "This is Angelina Dominguez, Fabian Dominguez is her very ex-husband. He looks like all bastards, good-looking, with a big smile. His hair and eyes are dark, and everything else is ho-hum and so-so. He hates the police and uses them as the butt of all his jokes. You should lock him up and forget to feed him. The child is nine months old, nothing like the father, and as American as Abraham Lincoln. That's obvious by his name: Don Carlos Dominguez. He has dark curls and fair skin. Why are you still sitting here, sergeant? The boat with our stolen child leaves at 6:30!"

"Well, if it's the child's father, I can do nothing. We cannot legally prevent a father from taking his own son."

Angelina's mind raced. Desperate to get their support and save her child, she said the only thing she could think of. "My husband has a gun, and I'm sure he plans to use it. He's with another violent man. My child is in extreme danger. He's been taken from the arms of the woman who watches him. She said he was about to take the child to Cuba, where the father was born. My husband has never picked him up, so this woman could not confidently say who picked him up. It could have been someone posing as the father. Please help me." Her chest heaved, and tears rolled down her cheeks. "My son is all I have."

Sergeant O'Hare appeared concerned, enough to fill out a report, but not enough to enlist some officers to the case.

Although Angelina took pride in her honesty, there was no line she would not cross for her child's life. In that moment of panic, she had to say something to make any father jump to action. "You don't understand. My baby is very ill. He needs his medication to stay alive. I have it. My husband does not. My child might die without it."

Carmen appeared stunned at Angelina's announcement, but her resolve did not skip a beat either, and she turned to the sergeant. "Are you going to have it on your conscience that you left a baby in mortal danger and did nothing? There's very little time left. The boat leaves at 6:30."

Sergeant O'Hare straightened up, called two officers, and ordered them to take Angelina and Carmen in the police wagon to the docks. He then turned to the women. "If I find your baby and he has been passed on to another man or woman to be taken out of the country, they will be immediately arrested for kidnapping. I must warn you, but if the child is with his father, the law does not consider it kidnapping, and we can do nothing. It will be up to you to prove that he has knowingly endangered your child's life. Do you understand?"

Angelina's head drummed with anxiety. "Yes. Yes. Yes. I understand," she said. *What an outrageous law.* Her fright reached new heights, and she cried out. "You wouldn't sit here and talk so much if it was your child."

The officers, Angelina and Carmen, rushed out, and when the endless ride halted, Angelina was the first to jump out onto the docks. Ships and boats soared in every direction.

"I'm checking the passenger registries. A man traveling with his baby boy shouldn't be hard to find," an officer said, "I'll have the other officer check passengers entering the boats."

Carmen turned to Angelina. "They don't know what Fabian or the baby look like, but we do."

"I'll run this way, Carmen, and you can run the other way. There can't be that many boats going to Cuba," she said anxiously.

They both rushed toward the lines of passengers and searched the mass of faces. Nowhere appeared a man with a baby. *La Reina Del Mar* slipped away from the docks. Passengers pressed against the boat's deck and waved farewell to those on land. The long summer day blazed about them, but the sun's dying rays burned and obscured their vision.

Carmen rushed to where she stood. "Don't tell me that Fabian's on that boat!"

"It has to be. It's sailing to the right country at the right time." Angelina stared out at sea in horror. "He loves his son, but he is no caregiver. He's only doing this to hurt me."

The officers appeared, and one pointed to a boat out to sea. "We've checked. That was the only one leaving for Cuba. Since you believe your husband has your child, we have no authority to try and stop the boat. We also have no certainty that your husband has no medication for your child or that he is actually on that particular boat."

They all stood and watched the boat move toward the horizon. Angelina released a flood of tears. Everyone she loved had slipped away, like dark shadows vanishing into obscurity.

"My child's my life, my whole family." The air withered around her. Although outdoors, she existed inside a stifling room without doors or windows. Her breathing became strained—she exhaled deep, painful breaths. "How can I survive this, too?" Angelina spoke in a fractured voice. Her knees grew weak, and she fell to the ground.

Carmen bent down, put her arm around her friend, and held her. "You'll survive this. You're the strongest person I know. I want you to come and stay with us. Please come. You shouldn't be alone after something this terrible. And as for Fabian, may they bury that *hijo de puta* face down, staring at the devil's face in Hell."

CHAPTER 33

THREE MONTHS HAD PASSED since Angelina found Fabian with Sophia and one week after that, her father renounced her, but the loss of her son could not be measured by ordinary bricks of time and its weight of this insufferable loss pressed against heavily against her heart.

Angelina withdrew from her life. She stopped working, rose early, and when too exhausted to keep her eyes open, she fell into an almost comatose sleep. Convinced that somewhere in her memory were clues to rescue her child, she meticulously wrote down every memory she had of Fabian's drinking partners. She boldly entered the local *cantinas*, questioned the customers and bartenders, even dared to enter the male gatherings during cock fights. Always searching for familiar faces with always the same response. Fabian had vanished.

As soon as the sun lit the sky, Angelina hurried to Fabian's cigar factory and stood outside the employee entrance.

"Have you seen Fabian Dominguez? He has taken my son. Do you know anything to help me find my child?"

Without any results and desperate, Angelina walked

along the streets until she reached Tia Lourdes' home. She appeared to adore Fabian, but still, she was a mother and surely, she understood that her nephew had committed an abominable crime by stealing a baby from his mother.

Angelina trembled as she knocked twice. She could hear muffled voices inside, but not what was said. She knocked again, and then again.

Lourdes opened the door, not wide enough to invite Angelina inside, but just enough to allow the woman to stand at the opening and block her from entering. *"Hola,* Angelina, what can I do for you." Her words, her expression, and her stance punctuated her indifference. It was already clear that Lourdes was not about to betray her nephew, no matter what crime he had committed.

"I want my son back in my arms. Fabian has kidnapped him." Angelina trembled as she choked down the tears and spoke.

"As I told you once before, women are supposed to support and serve their men. Perhaps you failed in your duty and he took action to protect his son." She raised her chin and looked down on her niece through marriage.

"My baby needs me. Please, tell me where to find him. I am begging you." Angelina could not hold back her tears. "Tia Lourdes, please help me. He's so small and needs his mother."

Lourdes took one step back into her house and reached for the doorknob. "That's not possible, I know nothing about it." She pulled the door closed.

Everything in Lourdes' demeanor contradicted her words. Of course, she knew Fabian had the child. Why else was she so cold, accusatory, and defensive? It was beyond belief. A mature woman helping her nephew kidnap his child from the mother. Where was her compassion for at least the child? Sickened at the woman's lack of concern, anger mixed with punishing sadness. Angelina sobbed uncontrollably.

∽

DAY AFTER DAY, Angelina traveled up and down the streets. Like a tragic opera, she asked the same questions of everyone she met. Futile minutes and hours left her imprisoned by despair until she no longer had the means to sustain her existence without returning to rolling cigars.

It was on the darkest of nights that Angelina Pirrello Dominguez lost all hope. She looked around her home. It appeared hollow, like a bell without the critical component to ring. In the silence of such a small house, an enormous void had begun to move about like a fog. The vapor of this dense cloud coiled around the rooms, moist, impassable, and maddening.

On the bureau sat the book of nursery rhymes she read to her baby. She opened it and glanced at the last line of the one that her baby loved best. The one where she tickled him and he laughed. Her voice quivered as she read: *And the dish ran away with the spoon.* In her present state, the words somehow seemed a twisted prophesy. *Fabian ran away with my son.*

'It's not a good idea to stay in that house alone. Stay with one of us.' Carmen and her cousin Ophelia pleaded almost daily, but Angelina had no desire for company, and no well-meaning words would quell her grief. She now blamed herself for not realizing the depth of Fabian's affinity for deceit. Did she believe that her marriage would be the same as her parents?

Mother, father, husband, and child—God-given relationships, those meant to be the strongest, the closest, the most intimate, were all lost to her. Had she committed some unforgivable wrong that made her unworthy to receive the deepest kind of love, loves sanctioned to endure a lifetime and follow her through the veil into death?

Angelina imagined her heart misshapen from the assault and forced to endure this dark purgatory. All that remained were the charred embers of her anguish. As a mother, she was cast into the unimaginable—condemned to exist at the very hem of Heaven without her child.

She looked around her three-room *casita* with a sense of disconnect, as if trapped in a cubicle of non-presence. Something shiny jutting from beneath the bed caught her eye, Fabian's silver-handled razor. He must have dropped it in his haste to pack up and steal their child.

Angelina reached for it and could almost feel the imprint of Fabian's hand. She now understood the desperation that plagues a person to end it. She trembled as she slid the shield off the blade's sharpness, and slowly pressed the razor's edge to her flesh. A crimson droplet rolled down the curve of her neck. It would be so easy to free her spirit from this snare.

With Fabian's razor in her trembling hand, she gazed up at the shelf that held the book Don Carlos Madrid had given her so long ago. Shakespeare's young prince had agonized over the same dilemma. *Whether tis nobler in the mind to suffer the slings and arrows of outrageous fortune or to take arms against a sea of troubles and by opposing end them.*

End them. She'd repeated the soliloquy so many times, but not until now did those words have such a powerful draw.

Angelina squeezed her fingers tightly around the silver handle. It remained rigid, unyielding, and awkward in a woman's hand. Yet, with just the right amount of pressure against an artery she could, *Shuffle off this mortal coil.* And why not? Should she prolong her suffering amid *the whips and scorns of time?*

Zio Pasquale's brick lay propped against the bedroom door. She had reached for its surge of strength when she'd found Fabian with Sophia. Could it brace her now? Angelina stared at it as the clock ticked away nervous minutes. She meekly picked up the brick.

With the slightest breath, she blew out the kerosene lantern and a profound darkness enveloped the room. Even the customary ghostly shadows abandoned her, and like the sky and the room, everything went dark inside her.

A strange heaviness pressed against her skin, entered her body, and surrounded her heart as if imploring it to stop beating. Lost in this eerie, obscure nothingness, Angelina grew fearful of her own thoughts.

Overcome with grief, she fell onto her bed where she kept her son's blanket and laid against its softness in a desperate need to touch him. Once again, she had to endure another devastating heartbreak while the phantoms of those she loved encircled her. She released neither brick nor razor. They swayed like a pendulum in her mind.

She rummaged through time and thought of Claudio Garcia's dreadful funeral with the wails and cries of the paid mourners, and Father Cavalli's pronouncement that Claudio was condemned to Hell for his unforgivable mortal sin of suicide. The priest was wrong, and if the church believed that, then the church had made a grave mistake. A loving God would never do such a thing for one weak moment out of a lifetime of moments.

Angelina's body quivered. Life had broken her, the way it had Claudio Garcia when his factory burned down and he lost everything. She closed her eyes, and from her open window, she listened to the wind rustling through the trees. The calming sound did its best to lure her back from this dark place.

She desperately ached for her mother and longed to drift into an endless slumber to reach her. *Ah, there's the rub. For in that sleep of death what dreams may come?* Shakespeare had said it. What assurance was there that death granted peace?

Angelina cried softly at first, then in painful, wrenching sobs. The days of her life had piled on top of each other and hardened into an impenetrable barricade that separated her from those she loved. A solitary cry against the universe and all that had befallen her erupted deep inside her.

Once again, Angelina squeezed the razor and could almost feel the texture of death. She had taken on a powerful opponent, and it took every particle of her strength to inch its force away. With Pasquale's brick cradled against her chest, she inhaled a great breath that cleansed and filled her being while echoes of her uncle's words returned, 'Remember you strong. Everything gonna be okay. *Non ti preoccupare.*'

In that instant, whether real or imagined, her mother's lilac scent permeated the room. Angelina opened her eyes wide. "Mama!" She inhaled the perfume and allowed its sensation to embrace her and awaken something inside her. With the blade still in her hand, she flung the silver-handled razor across the room. Angelina had experienced the painful agony of losing her mother. She would not allow her child to suffer the same fate.

CHAPTER 34

ANGELINA'S PERSISTENCE in searching for her only child had no end. She kept a ledger of who she spoke to, and when, and what they said. Not one day passed without several entries and when she entered a name, she would approach them once again in case they remembered something, heard something new, or were ready to tell her the truth of what they knew. Every night, she read the ledger over and over, careful to talk to everyone she encountered, those she knew and those she didn't, until she fell asleep still gripping the ledger in her hands.

There was only one person she purposely had never contacted since that one emotional day in the furniture store, the one Angelina yearned to see and reach out to above all the rest. She had no idea how Rolando would react, but she had to try everything and everyone to find her child and he was a logical choice. He knew Fabian; perhaps he would know something to help her, unlike all of Fabian's friends who claimed they knew nothing.

Angelina reached for the door handle and marched into *Belarmino's Used Furniture* store. This was Rolando's day off at the cigar factory and he told her he'd be at Belarmino's helping him with his inventory if she ever needed him. She'd see her cousin Belarmino also, but this time, it had no effect on her, what he'd tell his mother about her, or what her Zia Violetta would tell everyone else. Only one thing mattered —Donny.

She hurried to the store, quickly greeted her cousin, and then, with a mixture of emotions, faced Rolando. "Something terrible has happened. You said you know Fabian Dominguez, but how well do you know him?"

Rolando's expression of concern was immediate. "Why do you ask? What's happened?"

"He's kidnapped my son." Frantic, her words nearly constricted in her throat. "I've been everywhere, spoken to everyone that knows Fabian or might have seen him. I must get my son back. Men will more easily tell another man what they know. If you should discover even a hint of Fabian's whereabouts, promise me you'll tell me. Promise me, Rolando." No mother should ever have to utter such words. Just saying this made her feel light-headed.

"When did this happen?"

"A month ago."

"Angelina, why did you wait so long to come for me?"

"I thought if I stopped everything and spent my days approaching everyone, I could discover where to find my son on my own. Fabian's taken Donny to Cuba, but where in Cuba? I'm so afraid I'll never see him again." She could no longer hold back her emotion and sobbed uncontrollably.

Rolando's eyes widened in alarm. "Oh, my God, Angelina. I can't believe you've been through all this alone. You should have come to me first. And, yes, I know Fabian Dominguez very well. He has two faces, one handsome and another unpleasant and hidden." He pulled Angelina into his arms as she continued to cry. "I will get your son back. I promise."

Rolando flashed Belarmino an urgent glance as he took Angelina's arm. He gently guided her out the door and across the street to the alcove where no one could see them, the same place where they had first kissed.

Her emotions grew stronger against that tender and vivid memory colliding with her present horrible reality. "Oh, Rolando, I can't take this heartbreak. It's stronger than I am." She spoke through her tears.

"Whatever has happened to you, Angelina, has happened to me, as well. Calm your breathing and tell me everything. What do you mean Fabian has kidnapped your son?"

"I divorced him, and he stole our son. I saw his boat leave for Cuba, but it was too late to stop it."

Rolando raised both his hands in frustration. *"Dios mio*, who rips a baby from his mother? The man is crazy. Why didn't you come to me right away?"

"I didn't want to involve you in my problem, but I'm desperate and scared. I don't know who Fabian is anymore. He even has a gun."

Rolando looked around the alcove walls at its crumbling brick and faded paint. "Together, we'll find your baby, and I'll bring him back to you."

Angelina shook her head. "I have to go to Cuba. I have to—"

"No. It's far too dangerous. You follow up on Fabian's contacts here. I know much more about Fabian than you think. I also know his friends in Cuba. Around here, so much has changed. You would be more helpful here asking around until I get back."

"But if he's in Cuba, I could help you there."

"Fabian is associated with men making a lot of money doing something illegal, and they're not going to let a strange American woman draw attention to their dealings just because she wants to find her son. You would put yourself and even Donny in danger."

She stared at Rolando, trying to digest and justify what he was saying.

"If they see you coming, they'll pass Donny around and drop him in anyone's lap, just to keep you away and make sure you stop looking for him. I'm not saying Fabian would allow it, but he can't be everywhere. These men are evil."

Angelina's legs weakened. "I will never stop looking for him. Never."

"Which is why you cannot go. Just talking about Donny, you start crying. I lived in Cuba for a while. I know my way around, and I'll be on the next boat for Havana, but you *must* stay here. Fabian is back in his own country. He has long-time connections, and we don't know how far his reach is in the Cuban underworld."

Rolando pulled her gently into his embrace. "You have been my world for a long time, and now Donny is, too. I can't worry every day that something tragic might happen to you because of what I might have overlooked or misjudged. I couldn't bear it. You stay here. I'll go."

Angelina raised her head and met his eyes. For one glorious moment, a wondrous feeling came over her. He wanted to protect her.

Rolando pulled a handkerchief from his pocket and wiped her tears. "I know what it is to yearn for someone with all your heart and feel helpless. I swear I'll find him."

THE BREEZE BLEW HARD that afternoon at the docks. Rolando wasted no time, and Angelina insisted on seeing him off before he embarked. She slipped something special into his hand and closed his fingers around it. "It's your turn to keep this."

Rolando opened his hand and saw the Saint Jude medal of miracles he gave Angelina so long ago as his promise to return to her.

He pulled her close and held her. In his eyes, she could see how it moved him.

"Please stay safe for both of us. I have prayed every day to find Donny, and we only need one miracle. May Saint Jude make it this one."

"Saint Jude brought us back to each other, and he can do it again." The ship sounded its horn, and Rolando held Angelina close. "It almost hurts to let you go. This time, nothing will come between us."

Angelina longed to believe him, but the world had an appetite for peril.

CHAPTER 35

"CIGAR WORKERS STRIKE. Get your Sunday Tampa Tribune!" The high-pitched soprano of a young paperboy's voice rose above the clamor of the streets. Within moments, those that depended on the cigar factories rushed toward the boy and paid their coin while angry rumblings grew among the crowd.

"Oh, my God, no! Not now," whispered Angelina. Cigar makers always spoke of a strike. Now, with her livelihood so uncertain, she'd need money to survive. But it wouldn't be right to give Rolando all the responsibility of finding her son and then burden him with her finances. She had to do her part. She would sell the extra vegetables and few other things and she would find work.

Every day, Angelina searched for Fabian's companions, but when she found one, they claimed to know nothing. She suspected she had crossed into the world of the violent *bolita* syndicate. If Fabian did not fear criminals, he must have become as dangerous.

If she failed to discover information, would Rolando be able to find her baby without her help?

Angelina picked up a discarded newspaper and read the article below the headline. Details of the strike churned like rancid butter across the front page and smeared onto the next. The heat and humidity enhanced the agitation and anger between the union and the cigar barons. Both sides had short tempers, and as she feared, the owners were less negotiable and the workers more demanding. Angelina recalled her father's long-ago prediction of a strike. *People will go hungry.* His words of warning came to pass.

Angry voices filled the streets, incriminating fingers were pointed, and critical issues came under scrutiny, argued, and pulled apart without a solution. The dismal occurrence heightened. With no reason to come together at work, Angelina feared people would scatter and be harder to locate and question them about finding her son.

ANGELINA LIVED for Rolando's letters. She suspected he tried to keep her from worrying and knew much more than what he shared, but it also sounded like he must be protecting her. *Don't worry, Angelina. I will only leave Cuba when I have Donny in my arms, and that day is coming.* Angelina held each letter of reassurance she received against her heart, and at night, she placed them under her pillow to keep her hope alive.

Every day had twenty-four hours, and the world kept spinning on its axis, but the longing for things to resolve had become insufferable. Added to her stress, Angelina had to find a way to survive without a job. Negotiations between union leaders and the factory elite moved like a pushcart with its wheels trudging through mud and the days raining with despair. Even some enterprises that relied on the patronage of the thousands of cigar workers were threatening to close.

Even though Rolando had asked her repeatedly if she needed money, she always said no. He had gone to Cuba to rescue her child, and she would do nothing to distract him from his mission or deplete his finances or energy worrying about her.

Angelina's life greatly changed with the strike, but she would never tell Rolando she took in washing and mending, cleaned houses, sold the vegetables from her garden, and anything else she could spare. For a few coins, she also offered her skill in English, Italian, and Spanish, reading mail and writing letters for those who couldn't. Amid the arduous days and nights of exhaustion, she kept her hope alive, but one terrifying dread persisted. *My son, my little son, how am I supposed to go on if Rolando can't find you?*

To distract herself, Angelina set up a system of washing—one tub to wash, one for the first rinse, and one for the final. Water splashed in all three. The harsh rhythm of pushing and pulling so much laundry across the washboard's corrugated surface caused her back and arms to ache. Her hands reddened, and with such prolonged intervals in water, it took time before she regained the feel of the natural oils on her skin.

At last, she placed the freshly laundered, ironed, and folded clothes in a wagon and set out to deliver them.

The two-story, red-brick house with its bright white shutters casts a towering presence. Angelina gazed up at the balcony. Having never been inside a house with two floors, much less one with a balcony, she wondered about the sensation of standing out on the extended ledge, looking down at people below and looking up at the clouds. One day, she'd know the feeling. *One day, but not today.*

Angelina reached for the ornate brass lion's head knocker. As she waited, she looked over the impeccably kept garden. Every flower appeared as a glorious design of nature.

A large man opened the door. He glanced at Angelina and at the clothes basket with a tired look of disinterest. Then, without a word, he turned his back and shouted, "Anna! The washerwoman is here." The label stung and echoed in Angelina's mind. *Washerwoman.* She'd become the symbol of poverty her father had feared—with her love of classic literature, her goal of receiving a higher education, and her mastery of three languages—her hopes and dreams now lay submerged in tubs of soap and water.

When the man's wife appeared, Angelina forced a smile, handed her the neatly folded clothes, collected her coins, and wondered if the woman ever noticed the stains she'd struggled to remove or the loose buttons she'd tightened. Did the woman remember her name, or did she also call her *the washerwoman?* Deflated by life, Angelina pulled her hand wagon away, whispering her fatigued prayer for her son's return.

A sudden cackling of loud Sicilian voices drew her attention across the street. A man had been grabbed by the collar and thrown out of a store. When he struggled to get up, another brawny man punched his face, shouted a demand in Italian, and knocked him down again.

The man on the ground choked out his words in panic. "Tell Nico I will have his cash tonight." His fear inflamed his face, and though surrounded by witnesses, no one came to his defense or helped him get up. Nico had become the king of the Black Hand, the worst of the Mafia. Honest men were afraid to tell the authorities what they saw, and the truth became a commodity purchased with fear.

Angelina turned away in disgust and pulled her wagon behind her. She offered a prayer for the man on the ground. If she could see the fear in the Sicilian community, why couldn't the police?

With all her bundles of clean clothes delivered, she took a shortcut through the park where older men dragged benches and pushed crates together to play pinochle. She took a seat for a moment across from Joe Sergi's Tailor Shop with its familiar sign. *The only difference between the rich and poor is a good suit of clothes. Step inside and walk out a rich man!*

A sudden, soft breeze lifted her hair and refreshed her while a discarded newspaper blew against her skirt. Without the reader at work, she'd rarely heard the news, but these headlines blared: "UNSINKABLE TITANIC SINKS INTO THE OCEAN."

A picture of a large ocean liner with an oval photograph inserted of its captain dominated the front page. The report described the ocean tragedy on the ship dubbed not only the most luxurious but unsinkable.

Angelina hadn't eaten all day and pulled a slice of an apple from her pocket and took a bite as she read the names of the American passengers listed in alphabetical order. Lewis, Lopez, Lizetti, Martin, Martino. *Martino?* The name jumped off the page, and her apple fell into her lap. Angelina's shock exceeded her hunger. With a gasp, she read the name again, certain she had imagined it. *Martino, Maria, wife of Dr. Martino of Ybor City, Florida.*

It just couldn't be. Angelina's eyes grew large at the sight of Maria's name. Maria's comment about Italy being unsafe and Britain far more civilized now seemed ironic. Maria liked the best, and she would have certainly booked her return voyage on the acclaimed ship. Angelina read the entire article, even glancing through the entire list of those who met their '*untimely death in the cold, ruthless sea.*'

Her mouth became dry, leaving her almost parched. She'd considered this woman exempt from injury and harm of any kind, yet it gave her no pleasure to think otherwise. *Poor Dottore Martino.*

She recalled her own mother saying that the living should remember the dead in their best light. Think only of their good deeds. But Angelina had no good memories of Maria Martino. Nevertheless, she had sons and losing their mother was a great tragedy. And as a mother who lost her own son, though not perished, Angelina understood the crippling pain of Maria's mother.

No one should die young, not her own mother, not her infant brother, not Claudio Garcia, and not even his sister, Maria Martino. The news truly saddened her. She made the sign of the cross and said a sincere "Hail Mary" for the soul of the woman who had cursed her with *malocchio* when her own mother died.

Thoughts of Maria's poor mother struck Angelina even harder. The old woman had lost her only son to suicide, and now, to lose her remaining child to another unnatural occurrence could only be called unthinkable. First, the priest had refused the mother's wish to bury her son in a plot on sacred ground because he had committed suicide. Now, with her daughter Maria lost at sea, without a body, Maria wouldn't be buried at all. No mother expected to outlive her children.

She kept the paper with her and read the article twice more, but could not visualize the magnitude of Maria Martino falling overboard in frigid water. What went through her mind in those last moments? Angelina's hands trembled as she lowered the newspaper and looked out into the distance.

Zio Pasquale had told her Maria might appear to be going through life with every privilege and carrying a light bag of sponges, but one day, sponges will get wet, and their weight would become too heavy a burden to bear.

Angelina shook her head in disbelief and prayed again for the fierce soul of Maria Martino. In contrast, Zio Pasquale told Angelina that even though she believed she went through life carrying heavy bags of salt, he promised it wouldn't last. One day, she would cross a river. The salt would get wet and vanish. The water would dissolve her troubles. Could it be true? Angelina wiped a tear.

Her hardships continued, and the day grew old. She had to hurry home, fill her washtubs once again, and push clothes back and forth across the washboard as if grating cheese in her father's store.

It would be a long time until she would cease to think about Maria, with no need to wonder if her own father knew of the tragedy. Before the story appeared in the newspapers, he would have known about the doctor's wife. In the tight Sicilian district of Ybor City, customers would have come in all day to discuss the enormous calamity of a sinking ship and losing someone so prominent in their neighborhood.

After doing the laundry, Angelina peeled a potato for her dinner. It didn't stop her hunger pains, but helped to survive the crisis. She could not get Maria Martino out of her mind. Who could have imagined such a fate? Grieve welled up for Maria's children if not for the woman herself. They needed the love of their mother—something Angelina understood intimately. It seemed the world had no shortage of separated mother and child.

Contemplating her troubles, she poured herself a glass of water. Her hand trembled when she picked it up. Frustration, pain, loss, and heartbreak had affected her in so many ways.

Angelina stepped outside to clear her lungs. She snipped three wild roses halfway down their stems and placed them in a jar on the kitchen table. A moment later, the clouds released a shower while the sun remained bright in the sky— she was reminded her of her mother's belief. *If it rains while the sun is shining, the devil's getting married.* But regarding her laundry business, the devil's nuptials were a nuisance, interfering with the delivery and payment necessary for her endurance.

She pushed her kitchen table against the wall, climbed on

top, and nailed up seven lines of thin rope. Soon washing draped the room in parallel lines to dry, while the devil's wedding raged on outside.

She climbed down, sat at the kitchen table, and stared at the roses she'd picked and placed in a jar. Their small offering of scarlet petals softened the room and gave her courage. If such a delicate flower could find the will to bloom amid so many thorns—so could she.

CHAPTER 36

ANGELINA ROSE at daybreak to do her growing piles of her customer's laundry and avoid the summer's assault of heat and humidity. Still, by midday, her energy had depleted, and she collapsed on her bed, exhausted. Once again, she wondered how she did not notice the little fires of Fabian's character.

Rolando was an even better man than she had imagined. His letters came almost daily while on his self-imposed expedition to Cuba, a country not his, searching for a child who was also not his. He even tried to leave her with money to live on. She didn't mention that Fabian had stolen it.

If Rolando intended to lose work to find her child, she had no intention of adding to his burden by supporting her.

Angelina recalled the many arguments at the courthouse before winning her divorce decree. Fortunately, Fabian must have wanted his freedom. She collected the frame she had once purchased to display her marriage license proudly. It made no difference that she had broken the glass. The frame remained intact, so she inserted her official *Dissolution of Marriage* document inside. She then hung it up, not in her bedroom as before, but in a prominent spot near the front door. It would be the first thing she saw when entering her home and the last thing when she left. Once Rolando brought back her son, she vowed Fabian would never cross her mind again.

Day after day, Angelina tried everything to find her son, except contacting the one powerful person who had the muscle to resolve the matter. Yet, each time she thought of him, she forced herself to dismiss the frightening thought. The newspapers were full of the latest criminal activity that pointed to Nico Trezza and his crew, but like always, no one had been brave enough to testify against them.

How could anyone sane trust the man who murdered a mobster in the street in broad daylight?

Angelina's prayers grew more and more desperate. "Oh, dear God, please help me know what to do," she said out loud. The Mafia had entered her father's grocery store, torn the place up, and demanded protection money. The incident still made her shake. But, although devastated, she under-stood even more now the real danger. He had the reputation of a ruthless killer and would remain her last resort.

Angelina could only think of one other way to locate her child. So, without wasting another moment, she jumped up and left the house.

She had every confidence in Rolando. Still, she worried about his safety. If something dangerous happened to him while trying to rescue Donny, Angelina would never forgive herself. She walked along the avenue with a nervous gait as fear consumed her thoughts, until she noticed a large sign depicting a magnifying glass. It held her attention with its bold, black lettering and perpendicular placement over the entrance of a detective agency—all meant to capture the notice on both sides of the street.

This could prove a powerful key in supporting Rolando's

search to find Donny. The words on the slogan garnered her full attention. *We Never Sleep Until the Case is Solved.* Angelina never slept either, so she accepted the invitation painted on the door—Welcome.

The large office appeared triumphant in masculinity. Chaotic piles of paperwork sat on file cabinets. The strong scent of cigars wafted in the air, and the ashtrays overflowed. A row of desks flanked the room, but only two men sat behind them. One remained disinterested. The other raised his bushy eyebrows and stared at Angelina as if he had pinned her to a display board of dead butterflies.

He cleared his throat. "Our agency is the largest in the country, and we solve whatever is unsolved. Our record is superb, and your trust is well placed." He then spits into a brass cuspidor at the foot of his desk. "Why have you come?"

Since he did not introduce himself, ask her name, or extend his hand in greeting, Angelina mimicked his detachment and came to the point. "My husband stole our son and fled to Cuba. I must get my child back. How much money would I need to hire you to find him?"

The detective raised his chin. "We charge fifty dollars to begin an investigation and another fifty to one hundred when the job is complete, plus any expenses we may incur."

Despite her exasperation with the man's lack of concern, Angelina had not expected so high a cost.

"Let me give you part of the money now and all of it when the cigar factory strike is over. Until then, I'm willing to work for you every day with no pay, run errands and research whatever you need. I'm quick to learn, and can help in every way. I speak, read, and write three languages and will organize your files, wash your windows, clean your office, go to your homes, and clean them as well as. I'll even do your laundry and mending." She slid her fingers across his desk and showed him the dust. "Everything in your office will shine."

"We have too many customers that don't want to pay, can't pay, forget to pay. And your son is not even lost. He's with his father. If we take him from his father, we are the kidnappers."

"He needs his mother."

"We don't steal children from one parent only to give them to another." He resumed his paperwork as though she'd never been there.

"You'd be returning him to the one who cares for him. He's a baby and needs his mother."

"Close the door on your way out," he grumbled without looking up.

Angelina could hardly restrain herself. "Sir, I've done everything I know how. I need professional help. You don't seem to understand. My boy could be in danger. His father is extremely irresponsible."

"I'm sorry to hear that. Come back after the strike when you have more money. Maybe we'll consider your situation then."

Angelina pushed back harder. "Why don't I work for you first? Then you'll receive full payment before you even know my son's name—you can begin the investigation and start after I've paid your price. You have nothing to lose."

The man shooed her away with his hand.

Had she been talking to a wall? In the end, she'd lost all patience and raised her voice. "You're trained to find people. I need someone trained."

The man expelled his exasperation with a sigh. "Close the door as you leave."

His condescension pierced her heart. Her eyes moistened, but Angelina refused to let this horrible man see tears fall. Why couldn't he understand a mother's desperation?

Angelina doubled her fist and slammed it on his desk the way she'd seen her father do so often. Furious at her treatment, she went to the entrance; and turned to face him with one foot out the door. "My son is my whole life. I came here because you're trained, but an organ grinder's monkey is also trained, and they just dance around and look busy."

He jumped to his feet.

Angelina pushed the door hard. A loud click and bang sounded as the door shouted her fury at him.

"Get out!" he said.

But Angelina had already turned her back and walked away.

THAT NIGHT, she read Rolando's encouraging letter. He had found an important connection and expected to discover her child's whereabouts soon. Angelina kissed the letter. No one else had offered to help her to the extreme as Rolando.

Love could not be defined. There were many kinds of love, and Rolando's sailed above the rest. He had walked away from everything and left the country to search for her child. He had won her heart many times, but this surpassed all the rest.

Angelina tossed and turned throughout the night. When she thought of Fabian, one thing kept her awake. If Fabian had so many questionable friends in Ybor City and he kept a gun hidden for one or more of them, as he claimed, then they trusted him. He must be part of some nefarious business dealing going on under the watchful eye of the police.

Knowing him as she did, it didn't seem likely that he would walk away from something financially lucrative. It also didn't seem possible that he would stay in Cuba and try to do it from such a distance. He would return.

"Hello, hello," Carmen's voice seeped through the door. "Your army is here."

Angelina pulled open the door and greeted Carmen and Ophelia. "I was hoping you would come."

"Of course," said Ophelia.

"When have we ever failed you?" said Carmen as they stepped inside and hugged Angelina. "What is it you need us to do?"

Angelina reached for several tablets of paper, and three fountain pens, and led the girls to the kitchen. "I'm leaving work and going straight to the last place Fabian worked and asking as many as possible if they know where Fabian is, whether he's in Florida or Cuba. I was hoping you could help me write down my information and describe Donny. Most of them already know Fabian. If someone can help me get my baby back, I'll give them my pendant watch as a reward. It's beautiful, crafted in Italy, pure gold, with lovely stones."

"Is that the same pendant watch you worked so hard to buy back from that good-for-nothing pawn shop thief?" said Carmen.

"That's right, but it's not worth more than my son."

"But isn't this what the police department is for?" said Ophelia.

"That's right, again. But they act like Fabian took our son on vacation. In this world, men have all the rights. Women can't even vote out all the bad laws and useless politicians." Her anxiety seasoned her words.

Carmen waved her hand in the air. "You heard her, Ophelia, the world isn't fair. Keep writing."

EVERY WORKDAY, when the last bell rang, Angelina rushed ahead of everyone and made her way to Fabian's old cigar factory. Stopping as many cigar workers as she could, she passed out her hand-written notices recounting the great calamity of her life and her offer of a reward for information in locating her child.

But the days ran together, leaving her exhausted without success. After mounting expressions of sympathy, it became apparent that Fabian had not returned. Adding to her distress, she worried about Rolando. He might be in more danger than either of them realized. Rolando assured her he had friends in Cuba that would help him, but Fabian had been born Cuban, which could be far more perilous for Rolando.

Her desperation grew along with her fears until she dared to return to *La Cantina Latina*. The bar had not changed. The sign still dangled helplessly on one hinge, and when she again dared to enter, the same mixture of pungent odors of sweat, liquor, and cigar smoke greeted her. Angelina had no intention of wasting time. She went straight to the two men serving at the bar and set down her notices of the kidnapping.

"I am a mother desperate to be reunited with my son. He was stolen from me by his father, Fabian Dominguez. If you or anyone here has any information that will help me locate my child, I will give you a valuable piece of jewelry." She saw no reason to say it was a woman's watch. "My son's name is Don Carlos Dominguez, and he's eleven months old now. No decent man would want to see such a young child taken from his mother."

"We know Fabian Dominguez. He came here often, but we haven't seen him in a long time."

Angelina could not hold back her tears. One bartender reached underneath the counter and handed her a small paper napkin he gave out when serving drinks. She wiped her tears.

"But if he returns, I will have my wife go to your address and tell you."

Angelina had faith in Rolando's determination to find her child, but she could not stand the feeling of doing nothing to help.

She arrived home drained of energy. Too tired to cook, she took a few bites of bread, went to bed, and tossed about. Wrapped in a blanket of misery, Angelina now stood on the brink of a steep cliff. Only one drastic and dangerous option remained.

CHAPTER 37

By MORNING, Angelina had gone over her plan yet again, convinced she had no other avenue left.

Time might run out to save her child, and she had no guarantee Fabian would remain in Cuba. He could take Donny and travel somewhere else, to South or Central America, before Rolando reached him.

The day's humidity added to her frustration. She went to the window and opened it, hoping a breeze might offer some relief when she saw Carmen running toward her house. The moment Carmen saw her, she waved both hands furiously. She shouted something Angelina couldn't make out. Judging from the fierce expression on her friend's face, Angelina dashed out to meet her.

"Angelina, Angelina!" Carmen gasped. "They're going to lynch your Uncle Pasquale!"

"What? Oh, my God!" Angelina had known fear many times in her life, but for the first time, she faced extreme shock. "Murder! No! It can't be! Pasquale is in Key West."

"I swear on my mother's eyes it's true," said Carmen. "The men said Pirrello and someone else's name murdered some cigar factory bookkeeper. They're dragging them to Grand Central and Howard."

"Impossible!" Wild panic overcame Angelina. She ran with Carmen, desperate to reverse time, protect her uncle, and save him from this unspeakable madness.

The rows of cigar factories ended where the street intersected at Howard, where imposing trees had stretched their roots and offered an occasional bystander some welcome shade.

Angelina frantically waved down a carriage and gave the man all the money she had in her pocket to rush them to where the mob had gathered on Howard Street.

When they arrived, a large body of angry men blocked the street. Angelina jumped out before the carriage stopped and pushed her way through the unholy assembly of men, forming a barrier. She could hear them shouting that these two men had caused the death of a cigar factory bookkeeper.

"Angelina!" yelled Carmen in alarm. Angelina didn't stop. She couldn't, afraid she'd arrive too late to help Pasquale.

Men with blank eyes shouted in thundering voices. All were crackers, white, Anglo-Saxon, and probably churchgoing. These strangers to Ybor City had crazed looks in their eyes. She pushed her way through the wall of men.

They pushed back, and she fell. Angelina got up and again fought her way through the crush of bodies. In the madness, she refused to lose momentum and looked over the shoulders of two men, when an incredulous sight appeared before her.

"Fabian!" she screamed. Appalled, she bellowed his name again and again, "Fabian! Fabian!"

He met her eyes for one astonishing and inconceivable second as blood raced through her veins. Then he turned and pushed his way through the crowd.

Not since Donny's kidnapping had Angelina known such

a horrifying moment. She had to reach Fabian and get her son back, and she had to reach her uncle to try to save his life. A large man shouting obscenities came from behind, knocking her over with the force of his elbow. Frantically, she pulled herself up and looked in every direction but lost sight of Fabian. Unwilling to give up, she fought her way through the crowd, but he'd vanished.

Perspiration beaded on her forehead, but she shivered amid the chill of insanity surrounding her. *Did my mind play a trick on me? Had I imagined seeing Fabian? I couldn't have...or?* Doused in terror, she had fallen into a vat of repulsion, and nothing around her appeared real.

Angelina reached the edge of the field and stood frozen. She had arrived too late. On the nearest tree, side-by-side, hung two bodies—well-groomed men—in white shirts, pressed pants, and ties, but their hands and feet were bound with leather belts. Neither one could have foreseen a hangman's noose when they dressed that morning.

The scene astounded Angelina, and the pressure inside her grew so intense urine ran down her legs, hidden by her long skirt.

The victims' faces appeared distorted. Angelina wanted to run, but she had to know the truth and forced herself closer until the name on the signs around their necks were clear— Angelo Barbaro and Frank Pirrello. Fear for her uncle had overwhelmed her and constricted inside her. She fell to her knees, limp from its release.

Neither man was Zio Pasquale. Her heart kept racing. She now desperately ached to throw her arms around her uncle.

Still, a price had to be paid for viewing the bodies of murdered men, and the universe took its toll. The scene had etched itself into Angelina's memory, and she knew this vision would return over and over throughout her lifetime.

The horror of the murders had vilified the air, and those

present inhaled its vulgarity. A man passed Angelina with a sign. He tied it to the feet of one victim and then shouted its message: "This is Our Justice."

A hefty, fair-haired man laughed as he removed the belt tied to a dead man's legs and looped it back through his pants. The sight of these men shaking hands and patting each other on the back caused bile to rise inside Angelina.

Angelina's saliva became dry and turned to foam as she watched the smiles exchanged between men who didn't belong to Ybor City.

"That's showing them," someone yelled. They were mad dogs following a scent and committed a sin that surpassed penance. Certainly, no act of contrition could cleanse them. Angelina shivered as she walked among those who broke the most sacred commandment and were surely condemned to Hell.

The image of the dead men consumed her mind, like a massive weight capable of taking her to the bottom of the sea. She had never met him, but she could not deny one man was Frank Pirrello. Her father spoke of this cousin, Fabrizio Pirrello, a cigar maker who changed his first name to Frank. They had come to America together. Out of respect, it seemed important now to remember everything her father had said about him.

A silent eulogy rushed about inside Angelina. Her father had said he and Fabrizio had endured poverty and hunger. His mother had tied a loaf of bread to the ceiling so no one would eat before the family. Fabrizio had angered his cousin Domenico when he allowed the American officials to change his name, and her father cursed him for it: 'May they bury you with that name,' he'd said.

Angelina watched complacent reporters position their cameras toward the two dead men hanging from a tree and then interview the lawless and sanctimonious without emotion. No one seemed appalled that Fabrizio Pirrello and Angelo Barbaro had been murdered. No one blamed anyone for the despicable act. Instead, several families had spread blankets in the field to eat lunch and watch the hanging. No one investigated if they were truly guilty of the death of a cigar factory bookkeeper. No one wanted to hear the facts or their defense.

Angelina fell twice as she strained to get away and hurried to the far end of the open field. Fabrizio's blood ran through her veins as well. Her father called it *sangue del mio sangue,* blood of my blood.

As the tall grass swayed about her, she wrapped her arms around herself and looked up at the galaxies.

Nothing could have been be so wicked and heartless. Still shaking, Angelina looked up at the heavens and wondered how many worlds inhabited the universe. How many had the heartbreak of this one?

CHAPTER 38

THE NEWSPAPERS PLASTERED pictures of the two men hanging from a tree. Vision of the lynching induced nightmares and haunted Angelina's waking hours.

The day's newspapers reported the murdered men had left wives and children without a breadwinner. Worse, the men had not committed the crime. Now, the two guilty men were in custody for the murder, and neither was Italian.

The mob knew nothing and threw the blame on the Italians, any Italians. *May those who tied the knots around the two victims die of their shame.*

Angelina reached inside the mailbox. It contained an envelope letter from Rolando. She eagerly opened it, read it, and ran to Carmen's. Angelina knocked on the door harder than usual.

"What's the matter?" said Carmen, surprised.

"I just wanted someone to know what I'm about to do," said Angelina.

"Well, you came to the right place. I'm wise beyond my years and will let you know if what you are about to do is smart or not so much."

Angelina rubbed her hands together nervously. "I've decided it takes being scared to death to draw out every ounce of courage inside you. I'm going to see Nico Trezza."

"What! Are you crazy? He's the most dangerous man around. I'm not even Sicilian, and I know that."

"That's right. Fabian isn't Sicilian either, and Nico Trezza is not a mystery. Everyone knows what he's capable of doing. If Fabian goes back and forth to Cuba, Nico will grab him either way."

"Rolando's smart. Can't you wait to see what he can do to find Donny?"

"What if Rolando can't find my son? Fabian thinks like a criminal, and his friends are the same. Nico Trezza's father is a sweet old man who lives next door to my family. I've delivered meals to him for years, and because of it, Nico does not allow his men to extort protection payments from my father's grocery store. He respects my family. I think he'll help me."

Carmen shook her head. "Those men are savages, Angelina. They take showers in other people's blood."

"Fabian's not in Cuba. He's here. I saw him at that horrible lynching and when he saw me, he turned and pushed his way through the mob of people. I screamed at him, but the crowd was so loud and thick, I couldn't break away quick enough."

"What? he's back? With both the criminals and cops searching for him, that man must be bordering on the edge of insanity."

"I think he goes back and forth to Cuba." It cost Angelina to talk about it. Her voice quivered in anger. "I can't stand this anymore. Rolando is helping me, but if Fabian's growing more and more dangerous. He's capable of anything."

"Still, of all people, Nico Trezza? He's cruel—a man without a conscience. You're frightening me, Angelina."

"I'm counting on that. If people think Nico wanted my baby returned, they'd be afraid to hold back information."

Carmen's eyes were wide with fear. "I know for a fact that you're a very smart girl, but today, of all days, why is it you aren't smart enough to realize how smart you are? Perhaps you work too hard all day, worry too much all night, and now, you can't think clearly." Carmen turned around and walked away, then turned back to Angelina. "You cannot approach that man. He is crazy, and violent, and crazy violent. He must have been born without a soul."

Angelina reached for Carmen's hand. "Time is running out for me, Carmen. I can feel it. Fabian leads a treacherous life. If something unexpected and tragic happens to him, someone else will take my child. Babies change so much. How long do I have before I don't even recognize my own flesh and blood if he passes me on the street?"

Carmen blinked nervously. "Angelina, maybe you don't know this, but I've heard Trezza kills people, even has them tortured while he smokes cigars, drinks wine, and watches. You're making a bargain with the devil, and I can't believe you're not afraid."

"Of course, I'm afraid, but what choice do I have? I'm more afraid of losing my son forever." Angelina had vivid recollections etched in her mind, like the day they murdered a mobster in the street and Nico pulled an envelope from the dead man's pocket with one hand and held a gun with the other.

"Nico pushed a man off a roof, and our friend Rosa from the factory told me her husband's pregnant first wife sat in a restaurant waiting for her husband when Trezza bombed it. Yet, no one would testify against this mobster out of fear for their own lives."

"Those stories are beyond horrible. I can't believe you're willing to take such a chance."

"The decision didn't come easily, but all the prayers and petitions to saints have remained unanswered. I have to do something."

"I thought you went to that detective agency."

"They charge more than I have and won't help without full payment. Even worse, they think like the police. If my child is with his father, then it's not a rescue, but a crime to take Donny from his father."

Angelina grew visibly nervous. "I know Fabian does not intimidate Rolando, but I just received a letter from him telling me something terrifying. Fabian lives near the sugarcane plantations. It's where Fabian grew up. It's where his brother lost his way and died. There are endless fields of tall sugarcane, and the ocean's strong wind pounds them against each other like loud drums, drowning out all other sounds. It's a death trap. No different from falling in a well and no one hearing your screams for help. At this time of year, the sugarcane is high. No one found the little body of Fabian's brother until the harvest."

"That's horrible, but can it be that unsafe for a grown man?"

"Inside those fields, men have gone undiscovered. What if they force Rolando into those fields? What if no one is watching, and my baby wanders in there?" Angelina rubbed her arms nervously. "Fabian is insane and irresponsible. Nico Trezza is my last hope."

"*Maria Santísima!*" Carmen crossed herself. "Not Trezza. The cemeteries are full of those who make bargains with such men. Bad men never change. It's like they came into the world, and their mothers gave them a gun and a knife for a rattle." Carmen looked around the room as though searching for inspiration to convince Angelina to avoid Trezza.

"Once, at *la tabaquería*, a girl named Emilia worked with us. You don't know her because she left long before you arrived. She was born in Sicily and, as a child, caught a young boy named Cesare trying to cut the head off a cat. Emilia screamed, and the cat got away, but maybe it died later."

Angelina wrinkled her brow in disgust. "That's horrible."

"More than horrible. Their fathers did business together, but Emilia avoided him after that. The years passed, and when they were grown, Cesare went to Emilia's home with his father. He was very nice to everyone, and the fathers agreed that Cesare and Emilia should marry."

"Then he changed?"

"Emilia believed he'd changed, but people are who they are."

Angelina shook her head. "Why do fathers do that?"

"I'm sure Emilia wishes she'd been as smart as you. She married him. A few months after her daughter was born, Cesare went to America alone. When the baby was nine months, he sent them a ticket for passage. All that week, she and her mother couldn't stop crying. With so many people trying to get to America, anyone would have taken her ticket, but Cesare's father and brothers came to her house to ensure she got on the boat. The trip became a nightmare."

Angelina had heard many stories of such a trip. "Steerage means below the deck, in packed quarters, a place meant originally to store cargo. It's dark, lots of sick people, and terrible. No, it's much worse than terrible."

"I believe it because her baby got very sick and died the day before they docked."

The words struck close to Angelina's heart. "Oh, Carmen. I feel so sorry for her."

Carmen nodded in agreement. "Do you know what they do with the dead on a ship?" She didn't wait for Angelina to answer. "They throw them in the sea. Emilia couldn't stand the thought of her child being eaten by fish. So, she pretended her baby was alive and was nursing or sleeping until the ship docked and she could bury her child in a grave."

Saddened by the story, Angelina imagined it was a good thing she had never met Emilia. Together, their sorrow would have multiplied and have become too much for either to bear.

"When the ship landed, Cesare was waiting with a big smile and a doll for his daughter. But when he saw the baby was dead, he threw the doll into the ocean and blamed Emilia for the tragedy. When they reached the rooms he'd rented, his anger grew worse, and he beat her so badly, she said she doubted her mother would have recognized her."

"What a horrible man and a horrible welcome after such a long and painful journey. How could he not realize it was Emilia's loss, too?"

"That's my point. Some men are born evil and never change. It's something inside them we can't see until it's too late. Nico Trezza is the worst kind of dangerous man, Angelina. He can't even pretend to be nice, like Cesare. He wants everyone to fear him and does terrible things, so they don't change their minds."

"I have no choice," said Angelina.

Carmen, visibly nervous, crossed and uncrossed her arms. "I can't imagine what the Pope would say about this."

Angelina straightened her posture. "The Pope is the Holy Father, but a father isn't a mother. I must find my child or reach inside my heart and pull out my love for him from the roots. Fabian steals my child. The law will do nothing, but if they caught Rolando with my son, he will go to prison for kidnapping, and the penalty will be severe when all he's doing is trying to help me. I may never see him again. Every day, the threat of what can happen to Rolando terrifies me more and more. If I can bargain with Nico, I can save my baby and Rolando."

"Are you sure there is no other way? I'm so scared for all of you."

"Everything is so urgent. No matter what it takes, I have to get my son back, but I'm also afraid for Rolando. Fabian has a gun. What if he uses it? I'd never forgive myself."

"Oh, Angelina, Angelina. I can't stand this. My heart is in a high-speed just thinking of this. How did your life get so complicated? I'm going to church and will light a candle for you with every saint I see."

IT WAS no surprise that such a man as Nico Trezza dined at Anselmo's Restaurant, not because violent men gathered there, but because of its fine wines and exceptional cuisine. He'd been seen there often, seated at a corner table in the back, sharing a meal with men wearing hardened expressions and loosely concealed weapons.

Angelina hurried to the restaurant but then paced outside, mentally rehearsing what she planned to say and how to say it with the most impact. She was sure the owner and his chef must be inside preparing a special meal for this notorious criminal, not because he feared displeasing Nico; it was more likely an extortion payment of protection.

Angelina stepped inside Sam Anselmo's restaurant and asked to speak to the owner.

When he appeared, she took a determined stance.

"*Signor,* I am Rosa's friend. I was a guest at her wedding, remember? You told me once, 'If you put good things into a pot, good things come out.'"

"That's true, and I never forget a guest. You're Angelina."

"Yes, and it's very important I speak to Nico Trezza. If you tell me when he arrives, a good thing will come out of it."

His expression did not flinch, nor did he answer her right away. But when she glanced at the waiter behind Anselmo, he held up three fingers, which she understood meant Nico would arrive at 3:00 or did it mean there would be three of them arriving?

"Many people come here to dine. I pay attention to the food, not the people."

He did not fool Angelina. If he remembered her face and name from two years ago, he would not forget such a well-known criminal entering his restaurant days ago.

She glanced over Anselmo's shoulder at the waiter again; he gave a quick nod. She had checked the time before entering and knew it was 1:30. "Your food smells wonderful, *Signor*, perhaps I'll come back later and have something to eat."

"Of course, it's the finest restaurant in town."

"I can see that." Angelina excused herself and slipped out. But she didn't dare leave the block if Nico showed up early. She walked up and down the street, out of view, but always with her eyes on the restaurant.

A few pigeons flew about. They all knew Anselmo's Restaurant's routine of disposing of food scraps. They flapped their wings and kept watch for the exact moment. A few more pigeons arrived of varying colors. Most had gray-blue iridescent feathers around their necks and chest. They pecked their way in a desperate search for crumbs. Angelina arrived as anxious as the pigeons.

Zio Pasquale's stories of his belief in miracles swirled around her. This would be a good time for a miracle to take place.

An automobile pulled up, not like the standard Model-Ts she'd seen, but gift-wrapped in elegance. He'd obviously enjoyed his money wherever he got it. Nico stepped out, and Angelina watched him from a distance. After a time, she walked past the restaurant and glanced through the large picture window. He sat at the furthest table from the entrance with a white napkin over his tie and shirt and lifted his wineglass. She could not imagine committing violent acts of extortion all day and still having an enormous appetite. The scene reminded her of DiLeto's dog. It growled if anyone went near it while eating. To disturb a dangerous and hungry man during his dinner would be risky.

Angelina wore her pendant watch and kept an eye on the time. Nico ample time to eat. She then stepped inside and took a seat, as if waiting to be called to a table. She caught sight of one of Nico's men standing near the entrance and realized she knew one of them—someone from her old neighborhood, someone she'd known from school.

"Eduardo?" she said, louder than she meant to.

She stood and offered her hand to greet him. It had been a long time since he'd grown into a man, but not even his height or mustache could hide his features or that familiar intensity in his hazel eyes. After all, they'd been classmates since childhood.

He took her hand and shook it as if in greeting, but he applied far more pressure than necessary, as though he tried to pass on a message like he did when he wanted her to give him a test answer in school. But this time, it seemed Eduardo held the answer and tried to pass it on to her. Angelina was immediately unsettled, but this was too important, and she had come too far.

"I want to talk to Signor Nico Trezza. I need his help."

Eduardo guided her a little further away from the other men. "Nothing comes free in life, Angelina." His eyes were intense, as though he wanted her to read his thoughts.

Eduardo had always been quite clever. But she knew him well enough from childhood to recognize he wanted her to understand something secretive. Still, this was not a game for her.

Angelina kept her voice low. "What do you know that I don't?"

Once again, he moved her a bit further from the others, and his voice was almost as low as hers. "A few years ago, my father needed a favor, too, and because of that favor, this is where you find me now." With no further explanation, Eduardo turned away, leaving her to decipher his unclear message. "Sit right here," he said loud enough to be heard by the other men.

Angelina took a seat, still mystified by Eduardo and his comment.

Another man appeared, clearly disinterested in her. "Nico Trezza will see you now."

She followed him to the corner table at the rear, arrayed in fine linens. She glanced back at Eduardo. His expression remained intense and cryptic. She turned to Trezza as her resolve withered. "Signor Trezza, I am..."

"I know who you are. If I didn't know, you wouldn't be standing here. It's bad business to meet strangers when I'm seated with only a fork in my hand. Someone might try to take advantage of me. Are you here to try to take advantage of me?" He glanced at her and laughed.

Angelina did not flinch as she faced the man who had swallowed up the entire Italian neighborhood with his propensity to ignite terror. She was there to make her request, explain why she was so desperate, and leave.

"I heard your son was taken."

Then he understands my desperation. "Yes."

"And what is it you expect me to do?" Trezza appeared impatient, unwilling to listen to a complex story.

"Please, find him and bring him back. You're my only hope."

Nico smiled, but it was not a smile to put her fears at ease. His smile appeared to mock her. "Then you'll have to repay me."

Angelina's confidence drained with this sudden shift to a business deal—something for something.

Nico took a sip of wine. "Your father has done my father a kindness. He's watched over my father for years; I owe him my respect."

She weighed every word and dared to hope.

"But I hear your father has washed his hands of you, so out of respect, I must do the same."

A burst of flames ran through Angelina, incinerating all hope. She stared at this man who disregarded civil law and attacked and terrified innocent Sicilians. Of all the things he could have said, she never expected him to refuse her out of respect for anyone.

Nico took another sip of his wine and continued, "You've grown into a beautiful woman, Angelina."

She tensed and shifted her weight from her left foot to her right as if readying herself to run if necessary. Nico's words ignited a memory. Bettino had said the same thing the day he burst into her father's store and reached for her breast.

It took a long time to collect enough courage to face this man she suspected of murdering Bettino, a man she'd seen wave his gun at those in the street, a man who'd shouted the Sicilian warning of *omertà*—you talk, you die.

Angelina had a great love for her son, a mother's unconditional love, a love meant to transcend time and reach the next world. But how far could she extend her courage? Could she allow Nico to have his way with her, shame her, and degrade her for the love of her child, thus degrading her child also?

I am strong, like Pasquale's brick.

Would God consider this a mortal sin, or would she wear the crown of a martyr? Either way, she would never become a sacrificial lamb for the pleasure of a man who terrified her —any man.

"How old is your son?" Nico's smile fueled her mounting uneasiness. Was this a commonplace question or a calculated move?

Angelina didn't answer. At this one moment, she understood the meaning of Eduardo's crushing handshake crystalized.

"I'm a patient man, and there are many ways to repay a favor."

The contemptuous threat had not been disguised. She would remain in his debt, and so would her son. Overcome by the extent of their peril, she took several steps back. "I've made a terrible mistake, Signor Trezza. I'm sorry I bothered you."

Before he said another word, Angelina turned, rushed past his bodyguards, out of the restaurant, and down the street as if a pack of rabid dogs, foaming at the mouth, were chasing her. Every second mattered. Only after reaching far enough away did she dare look over her shoulder. Still trembling, she had to remind herself she'd made no bargain. There'd be no debt to pay to the devil. Her soul was still her own and so was her child's.

As soon as Angelina saw Carmen on the front porch, she hurried to close the distance and they quickly hugged each other.

"Oh, Angelina, I've been sick with worry. What happened?"

"I couldn't do it, and I pray God will shield me from ever seeing that man again."

"*Gracias a Dios.* I rushed to church and lit a candle for your protection. But, please, before I faint, what exactly happened with Trezza? Speak fast because I'm growing weak."

"Before I spoke to Nico Trezza, I saw Eduardo, someone I've known since we were children, and now he's involved with the Black Hand."

"Did he tell you to leave or lure you to Trezza?"

"He passed me a message, like a riddle, but at first, I couldn't put it together. I thought Nico Trezza would be eager to help me because I've helped his elderly father since I was a child, but he's given all the credit to my father. So repayment for me was my son's soul or mine. 'Nothing comes free in life,' Eduardo had said. I'm sure it's what happened to him because of his own father, who liked to gamble and mostly lost."

"*Ay, Dios mío,*" said Carmen. She put her arm around Angelina. "I'm so glad you walked out."

"I didn't walk, Carmen, but ran and ran, almost as fast as my heart was beating. I may be out of breath for months every time I think about this."

"Like wolves, those men stand together. They move in a pack because they are nothing alone, always threatening the innocent," said Carmen. "I am still trembling from the courage it took for you to go there."

"I will never go near Nico Trezza again, and I will never let him near my child. I've learned something valuable."

"What's that?"

"Fear is powerful—it teaches us who we are. And the line we refuse to cross."

CHAPTER 39

ANGELINA WALKED ALONG THE AVENUE, desperate and uncertain what to do next. Two weeks had passed since she had approached Nico Trezza. It wasn't what happened but the uncertainty of what might have happened that gave her horrid nightmares.

Danger ignited in every direction. Angelina wrote Rolando and warned him to stay away from the sugarcane fields, posted the letter, came home, and wrote him again to make sure he understood how easily one could lose their way when the wind pounded the stocks until the sound became deafening.

She needed to talk to someone who knew her well, someone who knew more about the world than she did. Signora Bertelli went to confession on Saturday evenings and arrived early to avoid the danger of waiting her turn and standing behind someone with an unreasonable number of sins to confess. Angelina arrived on time to catch her.

The confessional booths, for the convenience of sinners, lined the east and west wall of the church. They stood like centurions, two on each side, for the concealment of parishioners' peccadillos. Angelina sat near the middle aisle to keep watch on all four confessionals.

To her delight, her friend stepped out of an east booth, and Angelina rushed to her.

"Signora Bertelli! Signora Bertelli!" She was careful not to speak above a hush.

"Just one look at you, Angelina, and the sky rains gold."

"I need to talk to you, but I'll wait for you at the back of the church so you can say your penance."

"All right *bella*. I won't be long. My biggest sin is I forgot to water the flowers."

Angelina gave her a nervous smile and glanced in the direction of those in line to confess. This was no time for Father Cavalli to recognize her voice. He might hurry out of the confessional and lecture her for marrying outside the church, and now with a divorce and a child, he'd make her recite the whole rosary as penance.

Angelina dipped her hand in the font of holy water, blessed herself, and pleaded with God for guidance.

Signora Bertelli appeared and together they stepped outside. Her old friend kissed Angelina's cheek, and warm memories flooded back to a simpler time that now seemed so long ago. She hid her panic so not startle the older woman. "How have you been, Signora?"

"What can I say? My bones have rusty hinges now. Sometimes I think I can even hear them asking for oil. But while I wait for my trolley, let's sit on this bench before my shoes start killing me."

Angelina followed her lead.

Her old neighbor put her hand over her heart. "I tell you, there's something quite distasteful about new shoes. When I have the money to buy a new pair, my feet hurt when I first wear them. It's my punishment when so many don't have shoes."

Angelina smiled. It was a light-hearted complaint and took her back to how innocent life had once been when she was young.

Signora Bertelli rolled her eyes. "When I was a child in Sicily, my sister and I shared one pair of shoes. We went barefoot in summer, and when the weather became too cold, my father would carve wooden shoes for all of us from large tree branches. I don't know why they didn't hurt, or maybe they did, and we were just happy to have something on our feet. I didn't get my first pair of real shoes until I was ten, and even then, they were not new. Life was hard."

"Life is so much better here in America. We all have shoes," said Angelina.

"So many memories, little Angelina." She sighed. "But no one really leaves home behind, you know. Home is always inside us, and take it wherever we go."

"That's a beautiful thought."

"Yes, life is better here." Signora Bertelli nodded. "Yet, Sicily had mountains, fields, and the deep, blue of the Mediterranean. It's so beautiful, but when you're hungry, you can't eat *beautiful.*" She sighed again. "Well, that's enough about me. So, tell me, which saint should I pray to, so I may see you more often? Are you doing well, *bella?*"

Angelina shook her head. "Oh, Signora, I can't even accept the reality of what has happened when all I wanted was a normal life."

"Oh, my poor, sweet Angelina. There is no such thing as a normal life. It doesn't exist. There is just life. But don't worry. God knows everything! For everything we suffer in life, there's a remedy. Only death has no remedy. But when you are ready for the answer, you don't even have to go to church to receive His blessing. He comes right to your home and delivers it. God's Sicilian, you know! But let's not discuss the obvious. Tell me exactly what has happened, and talk as fast as you like. I never miss a word."

The story weighed heavily on Angelina, and it frustrated her even more as she shared her journey through time with Fabian Dominguez. He had left a trail of warning that sparked a blaze. "I trusted him, but I should have paid more attention and packed my baby and my bags right away instead of trying to save our marriage. Fabian seemed such a good husband at first, but he concealed his darkness."

"Never forget that the devil was once an angel." Signora Bertelli sobered at the story, and her smile withered. "The man is a curse. I pride myself on the removal of curses."

"When he drank, little by little, everything changed. He was a cigar maker and did well. Without telling me, he took a job collecting *bolita* bets, and even worse, cheated the criminals that hired him. He took one of my childhood friend, Sophia, to his bed, but the most truly unforgivable; he's stolen our son." The words were harder to say every time she repeated them. Nothing mattered anymore except Donny.

Signora Bertelli's eyes opened wide, and she pressed a fist against her teeth as though she bit her hand—the Italian gesture for anger. "Your son! Holy Mary, mother of God! Mark my words. Your husband will sit on hot coals in Hell one day." She shook her head in frustration. "There are good men, but don't let your guard down. You were right to leave him because if you waited longer, could leave him."

"What do you mean?"

"I have known many women who live with bad men. They give them one more chance, then two. They have one child and then more, stay home, have no money of their own, and are trapped. It's a horrible life, but you left early."

"I've never known anyone who changed so much."

"Oh, Angelina, Angelina, what can I say? Some men give us light, and some give us darkness. Our job is to recognize the different shades." Signora Bertelli raised her head toward Heaven as if sending a prayer stamped *urgent*. "I have never understood why we must die so many times during our life and then go on living covered in wounds."

Angelina didn't want her friend to wander off the subject. "I believed him back then; now I cry every day for my son in the care of a father who has become a criminal and is always drunk."

The older woman, still visibly infuriated, placed her hand over her heart. "May the curse of your husband's ancestors befall him."

"What curse?"

"There's always a curse. In ancient times with nothing to do, people placed curses on each other to pass the time. The Catholic Church removes original sin, but they overlook curses. If no one removes them, they stick and drip down from one generation to the next. That's why we see entire families with so many troubles."

Her old neighbor never altered her view of the ancient world. "Can you see my fate?"

"In the Old Testament… or is it… Anyway, it says somewhere that all rivers run into the sea, yet the sea is not full. Like the difficulties that flow into our lives, when we think we can't take anymore—more come. Hah!" Signora Bertelli rolled her eyes at the revelation.

"Remember when you came to my home, and I put my husband's ashes where they belong, down the hole in the outhouse? Well, now you understand. There's nothing worse than a man who breaks your heart. Mine was clever. He reached out from his grave and broke my heart *post-mortem*. Now was that totally necessary?"

After all the unforgivably cruel acts Fabian had committed against her, Angelina had to admit pouring a husband's remains down the outhouse was not as ghastly as she had once believed.

Again, her old friend gazed at the sky as if receiving inspiration from the universe. "You must promise to pay special attention to what I tell you now, because it's very important."

Angelina leaned forward, eager for any instruction that would give her peace and improve the outcome of her life.

"Ah, but you already know what to do, Angelina."

"No, I don't."

"Our lives can change completely in a single moment."

The trolley approached, and Signora Bertelli kissed Angelina again. "I must go home immediately to clear you of what's standing in your way. Misfortune never comes alone, you know. It brings a friend."

"What should I do, Signora?" Angelina reached for her friend's hand. She needed more time with her old neighbor.

The woman patted her head as she did when Angelina was a child. "You're like my blood, and I wouldn't say this if it wasn't true. Not a raindrop falls from the sky that God didn't put there, and nothing that happens is wasted. All experiences are necessary, and that's a good thing. I believe you have a special gift, Angelina. Here's the trolley. I must do my part to help you, or the earth will swallow me up through my kitchen floor."

She climbed onto the trolley and took a seat by an open window, reached out, and touched Angelina's cheek.

"You already know what to do. You have no reason to be afraid. The time is almost here."

"Can't you tell me what it is?"

"I promise, the answer is already on its way and may even come right to your door."

The trolley clanged its bell and pulled away. Her old neighbor blew her a kiss. Angelina waved goodbye. Though sweet and caring, Signora Bertelli had always viewed the workings of the world through an unusual pair of spectacles, and Angelina was never entirely clear about interpreting her advice. Was it nonsense or psychic wisdom?

Angelina walked home deflated. The passing of time was growing more and more urgent. Worse, Rolando, who had been writing her of his progress three times a week, had stopped, and it terrified her.

"CIGAR STRIKE OVER! Read all about it."

Thrilled and astonished, Angelina rushed to buy a newspaper. At last, the strike had ended and its claims of victory, negotiations, and changes to come, sold out newspapers. The story spilled onto several pages with accusations, underworld figures, murder, lynching, and kidnappings. How could anything be settled with such shocking occurrences? Angelina had survived the ordeal. Now she could earn the money to hire a legitimate private investigator to find Donny. If it was not kidnapping for a father to take his son, it would not be kidnapping for the mother, either.

MONDAY MORNING WAS the first day back to work and at higher wages. Angelina stepped inside the factory to the now familiar scent of tobacco permeating the air. It seemed like a lifetime had passed since she had first arrived at work in a cigar factory and had to dash to the window, almost too dizzy to catch her breath. Now it seemed the means to an end, a blessing to fulfill her biggest dream.

Each worker told their story of lessons learned, of how

they sacrificed, and their fears. But when Carmen walked in, Angelina jumped to her feet and threw her arms around her.

"See that. Bad weather doesn't last forever, and neither does bad luck," said Carmen.

"I've missed your daily petals of wisdom, and I hope you're right. I'm waiting for Rolando's next letter, but there's a hurricane passing through Cuba right now. Roads are washed out, the sea is choppy, and it's hard to get mail and supplies. So, I just have to be patient and not think of the worse because I can't take much more."

"So, you finally admit to yourself that you love Rolando? Everyone at the factory could see you and Rolando Aguirre were in love, then you marry that Señor, Pretty Face Fabian, but No Good for Nothing."

Angelina nodded in agreement. "Everyone is entitled to one miracle and one big mistake in their lifetime. I had my big mistake, and now it's time for my miracle."

"And since your mistake was such a big one, your miracle should knock down the streetlamps."

Angelina forced a grin. "Once, my mother told me there are no mistakes in life. They are only lessons. If we don't learn the first time, we will get the lesson again." Angelina remained reflective. "You know, Carmen, pay attention to everything a man does and says. I should have noticed the minor differences between Rolando and Fabian. Instead, I only saw what I wanted to see." Angelina had never admitted her true feelings for Rolando, but now it burst inside her.

Carmen shook her head. "We aren't all blind like you think we are. When Rolando returns, you better not let him go this time, or that will be two big mistakes you've made, and that disqualifies you for your one entitled miracle."

CHAPTER 40

ANGELINA WENT HOME as the daylight had begun its spiral into darkness. She lit her kerosene lamp and dropped onto the sofa, exhausted.

A sudden knock at the door broke her concentration, but she was too tired for an idle conversation with a neighbor and decided not to answer.

The knock grew louder and in more rapid succession. She wished she had not lit the lamp as the illumination now flicked across the window. With a sigh, Angelina forced herself to get up, reached for the handle, and pulled open the door.

A storm of angry emotions immediately tore through her. It had been at least a year since that ill-fated day, but a year did not lessen the pain. Angelina wanted no part of whatever Sophia Esposito had to say, unwilling to see her or force herself or to exhume the weight of her betrayal.

But the woman arrived radiant, fashionably dressed, and carried an elegant silk-embroidered shawl to make a statement since the summer's heat swarmed about her. However,

Angelina focused on the mask Sophia wore, concealing the canyon of her deceit.

"Fabian doesn't live here anymore, but, of course, who knows that better than you?"

"Angelina, I must talk to you."

The last time they met, Sophia was in bed with Fabian. This was not a vision Angelina wanted to remember, and now it had reappeared. For what purpose? The woman outwitted respectability and had learned to perfect an expression of innocence.

Unnerved by Sophia's boldness, Angelina focused on the mask and tried to slam the door, but Sophia raised her hand, grabbed the edge of the door, and blocked her.

"Listen to me. I know where to find your son."

Angelina immediately released the door's handle and stepped out onto the porch. She gazed at this woman she'd known all her life, yet didn't know at all. "Where is he?"

"When Fabian took him to Cuba, he walked right past the police you sent to find him. They let him through because he dressed your son as a girl, with a bonnet tied with ribbons, a dress full of bows, and he called Donny 'Mary.'"

"Maria?"

Sophia shook her head. "No, Mary."

Nothing concerning Fabian was logical. "The whole thing sounds incredible."

Angelina met Sophia's eyes. She could not believe the level of irony. How was it possible that the only person who could help her find her son was the one who betrayed her?

"Fabian came back last week, and I saw your son. He brought Donny with him because of some business deal with his friends. If it works out, he is going to stay in Florida. He loves that boy, but if it doesn't happen, he's returning to Cuba with his child."

"No! He is my child!" The hoarse, raspy sound of Angelina's voice and her breathing grew strained and audible. "Is he all right?"

"Donny looks well enough. Fabian leaves him in the care of the woman next door and her eighteen-year-old daughter, who's engaged. The girl takes him back and forth between houses to play with his toys and nap. Fabian said you saw him at that terrible lynching, and if it weren't for the large crowd of people between you, you would have reached him."

Angelina became aggravated that it had certainly been Fabian that day, proving him the coward Angelina knew him to be.

"Anyway, no sense in thinking about it now," said Sophia.

Angelina noted Sophia's pauses, inflections, and hand gestures. If a trick, this would be unspeakably cruel and pointless. She had nothing left of value. Still, the woman had acquired a talent for duplicity. Angelina saw no reason to believe her. Hadn't she rushed to New York for her big wedding right after she'd been with Fabian? But that was a year ago, and if she'd returned to Ybor City and knew where Donny was, then she must have returned to Fabian's arms.

"Here's the address." Sophia ripped a page from the same little book with pink embossed flowers in which Angelina had made the prophetic mistake of writing her own address. "Go there tomorrow. Fabian will leave at 4:00."

"How do you know all this? How do you know the exact time?"

"I heard them making their plans. If they go by trolley, they will leave on time. If they go by automobile, they'll have more time. I know what I am talking about. They have to meet someone, and they will not want to miss that meeting."

"It seems strange to be getting this information from you."

"I promise what I am telling you is the truth." Sophia nodded for emphasis. "You'll find your son alone with a young woman about our age. Fabian is the only one that knows what you look like. So that is your moment to take Donny, but after 5:00, it won't matter what you look like. After 5:00, the house will be full of people, and they won't let you take him. Fabian only brought Donny because he has something going and is not sure he will return to Cuba and doesn't want to leave his son behind."

"So, he is passing him off on this young woman about our age who doesn't work?"

Sophia ignored the remark. "I have to warn you, you'll never catch a glimpse of your Donny if you try to go before 4:00 in the afternoon or after 5:00. It's critical you understand not a moment more or less. It's your only chance. Fabian is becoming dangerous. So remain calm when you go, and do nothing that would raise suspicion. Do you understand?"

Angelina withheld the tears threatening to spill. She ached to hold Donny, and her longing almost broke her resolve. "Why are you doing this?"

"It's part of my penance for hurting you. You wrote me such affectionate letters. You did nothing to deserve what we did to you. When I came that day to visit, I found Fabian—drunk, charming, and incredibly handsome and couldn't resist him. You always thought I was a saint. I'd already been with my fiancé, John Greenfield and Eduardo, from school. You remember him, don't you? Well, he certainly grew up that last year we studied together." Angelina remembered Eduardo's ambiguous warning about Nico Trezza. But it wasn't as easy to picture him with Sophia.

"It was just something unexpected that happened with Fabian. Every urge ignited, and I reached out to him."

It didn't matter about Fabian anymore. All that mattered was the address on the piece of paper. It then occurred to Angelina that Rolando must have tracked Fabian and must also be on a boat back from Cuba. She looked at Sophia for signs of deceit. "What do you mean, this was part of your penance? What's the other part?"

Sophia hesitated for a moment. "I must be sure Fabian never finds out I had his child. I pushed up my wedding date because I'd only been with Fabian while I was here." Sophia paused.

Angelina leaned against the doorframe to feel something solid behind her. It had been a year since she had last seen Sophia, and the repulsion of her affair appeared to have no end.

"If you never want Fabian to know about your child, why are you telling me?"

"Fabian doesn't know about my child because I'm afraid he'll do something outrageous as he did with your son. You and I, Angelina, were so close for so many years. I think it's important you know your son has a younger brother."

Angelina could not imagine anything more startling, but she said nothing.

"Your Donny was only four months when I was with Fabian. So, our sons are around seventeen months apart. He has my husband's name, John Greenfield."

Again, Angelina did not react.

"I never meant to hurt you, Angelina."

Angelina wondered if Sophia had changed so much, or in her own innocence, had she never noticed this trait as they grew up? "Your wedding was a social event. Everyone talked about it here, married in church at High Mass, conducted by no less than the bishop of the archdiocese. Did you confess your sin or condition to a priest?" Angelina knew the answer, and Sophia ignored the question.

"Maybe one day, when they're grown, and Fabian can't steal either one, the two brothers can meet," said Sophia.

Angelina's maternal instinct told her this should never

happen. "You had better think this through. If you tell your son that my child is his brother, then you tell him his father is not his father, and his mother couldn't control her 'urges' with men, even with the husband of her oldest friend who helped her all through school. Why would you want to tell your son his paternal grandparents, uncles, cousins, and aunts are not his relatives? Do you think he'll appreciate this story better if you tell him he was conceived while his real father was very drunk but charming and incredibly hand-some and married to someone else?" The heavy moment lingered in silence, yet Angelina saw no emotion in Sophia. "He could hate you for it, and you could lose both your son and husband."

"Sometimes, things happen no one planned."

"And sometimes we have to make a plan, Sophia? Life is hard enough. There will be many things to explain to my son, but there is no reason to break your son's heart or mine. Anything you tell your son will only hurt and confuse him. You take a big chance with a husband who's a respected doctor. Fabian can only offer shame. You disrupt all three lives. Let your family be happy for as long as life allows."

Angelina had known Sophia nearly all her life, and she saw this as only a maneuver to ease her conscience, but with possible dire consequences. What good would come of exposing her child to Sophia's world or Sophia's son to his true father?

"You can't be mad forever, Angelina."

"Haven't you changed my life forever?" Angelina held on tight to the address in her hand, although she had already memorized it. "When I gave you my address and invited you to my home, I was so happy you said you'd come." Then she paused and realized the memory was more painful than she thought.

"Fabian and I had a strained marriage, but you stepped in

and shattered it beyond repair. Because of that, he stole my child. I'm so grateful for these directions. My son means everything to me, and I want him back more than life itself. But it's preposterous to thank you, Sophia. You and Fabian have broken my heart. I loved you both, and you left me with such intense anguish I once considered taking my life, but that will never happen again. I'm stronger than even I thought."

Sophia gazed at Angelina without expression or comment.

"Now, I'm supposed to be grateful you want to help me and reclaim our friendship. But, once again, I'll cry myself to sleep tonight because I still don't have my child." Angelina sighed. "We are all young, and life is long. Perhaps I will forgive you one day, but that day is not today."

"Do you understand I wasn't thinking? I meant no harm?"

"I understand all our years as friends meant nothing to you, and you even had a baby with my husband." Angelina let her words sink in. "There are people in this world who refuse to accept the responsibility of their actions, people who blame others for their bad deeds." Angelina wondered if the world had assigned a clinical name for people like Sophia.

"You married quickly to trick your husband and son."

Sophia shrugged off the criticism and changed the subject. "Angelina, you are putting too much into this. It's turned out for the best for everyone. No harm has been done, and no one will ever know."

"No harm?" How easily Sophia remained detached by her actions. Yet, she lacked something necessary in compassionate human beings, and Angelina suspected she'd have many more men in her lifetime. "Is this everything you came to say?"

"One day, you'll see I'm just trying to help, and you'll

forget all this, like the childhood games of our youth. I'll write you."

"Games? This is not a game. It's my life."

Apparently unaffected, Sophia relaxed. She spoke unhurriedly and even took a moment to remove a bit of lint from her skirt. "I know it doesn't seem true, but I meant no actual harm."

"Then you fooled yourself."

Signora Bertelli's last words had returned many times—how God would deliver a blessing to her door. The slip of paper was a blessing. Her old neighbor also said when the time came, Angelina would know what to do—and her old friend was right.

With all her beauty, jewels, and fine clothes, Sophia appeared lacking. At that moment, Angelina believed that after losing Rolando, the pain had intensified to where she had conjured up her love for Fabian in her mind. However, love doesn't exist in the mind. It blooms deep inside the heart, where it's meant to flourish, breathe, and live forever, or the petals will fall.

"We were like sisters, Sophia. So, I'll give you some good advice. Please don't hurt your son or put such a strain on your marriage. They may not forgive you. You've been blessed; just be grateful." Angelina took in a nervous breath. "We've both grown up and outgrown each other. I'm eternally grateful for this address to find my Donny, but—" She paused. "Wait, a moment."

Angelina stepped inside her house and returned with something in her hand. "I'm certain this belongs to you. You mentioned your fiancée had given you another expensive gift and described the earrings in one of your letters." Angelina opened her hand and revealed a diamond earring.

Sophia raised her eyebrows in surprise, reached for it, and gazed up at Angelina, but didn't say a word.

"Yes, that's right. You lost it when you were in my bed with my husband. I've been working hard washing and mending clothes for whatever coins I could gather to live. It would have been easy and more than justified to have sold the diamond earring and kept the money. But I've never taken anything that doesn't belong to me." She gave Sophia a hard look. "And especially not someone else's husband." Again, Sophia remained silent. "So now I've returned your earring, and we have nothing more to say to each other. Goodbye, Sophia."

Angelina stepped inside, closed the door, and pressed her back against it to keep it closed.

"I know we will be friends once again, Angelina. You'll see." Sophia's voice was light, confident, almost musical as it seeped through the door—like pestilence wrapped in French perfume.

For a moment, Sophia waited, and then her heels clicked as she crossed the porch and went down the steps. The sound diminished as the woman walked away.

Angelina's breathing grew heavy. Her chest pounded with anxiety. So many thoughts collided in her mind. She could not move—not an inch. Tears rolled down her cheeks. Perhaps one day, she would forgive Sophia. But for now, she could not release the weight of her betrayal or Fabian's.

Angelina inhaled deeply and then exhaled a cleansing breath meant to force out all thoughts of the two of them. She twisted the door lock closed. *"Finita,"* she said in a firm voice. Her father would have trumpeted the meaning in Italian. *It's finished!*

Still, Sophia gave her no proof she was telling the truth or guarantee Angelina could really get her child back. No guarantee at all.

CHAPTER 41

ANGELINA LAY AWAKE. Sleep had been impossible, even the night held its breath. Her life would soon change completely —either become exceedingly worse or happier beyond her imagination.

After all the tossing and turning, she climbed out of bed, went to the window, and gazed at the full moon. When young, she had been told not to go out when a full moon appeared. She might encounter *Lupo* Mannaro—a man in an Italian children's tale who becomes a werewolf when the moon changes phases. It seemed unbelievable that throughout the world, in all cultures, and for countless centuries, adults thought it was fitting to tell children stories of evil queens, cruel stepmothers, big bad wolves, and wicked witches. *What a strange civilization we are.*

Small birds chirped their soft serenade while the moon took its final bow. Whether the day's end would be wondrous or devastating, the sun showered its brilliance across the sky with a storm of thunderous beauty.

Every minute has a purpose, Angelina thought. She prayed she had considered every possibility.

Angelina glanced at the sizable well-read book. *'Discretion is the better part of valor.'* Shakespeare's words fortified her resolve.

'You are a warrior, Angelina,' Don Carlos Madrid's words offered courage. The story he told now seemed appropriate. She had burned her ship, and everything depended on what happened next.

Angelina tucked Rolando's last letter in her pocket. He said he had important news and was returning to Tampa right away. What important news? Would he arrive today in time to help her rescue her son? He must know that Fabian came back with the baby. Or was it something else? Or was Sophia lying, since she still had contact with Fabian? Questions and more questions.

Rolando needed to know that Sophia had allegedly given her the key to finding her son. With no other avenue to follow, Angelina could not dismiss this one frantic possibility of rescuing her child. With such a narrow corridor to accomplish it, she would do it alone. Rolando might draw too much attention. He was taller than most, had unmistakable red hair, and Fabian would certainly recognize him. Worse, Fabian always had his friends with him, and Rolando would be alone.

On such a warm day, Angelina rubbed the chill from her arms. Her mind raced. She selected a shawl she planned to wear over her head to help avoid recognition. She left it out on the chest and slipped back into bed. Throughout the night, Angelina had prayed all would go well and that the Lord would have mercy on her frantic quest to regain her child.

She had no appetite but made coffee to keep her alert on such a fearsome day, but nothing corralled her nervousness. Her hands shook as she wound up her grandmother's pendant watch. Timing could not be more critical today. Angelina pinned the watch securely on her dress.

For hours, Sophia's ominous warning raced through Angelina's mind. *You'll never catch a glimpse of your Donny if you try to go before 4:00 in the afternoon or after 5:00.* Was this a warning or a trap? Still, what choice did she have? After all her exhaustive searching, no one could help her.

The fear of making a mistake during this thin sliver of one hour almost paralyzed her. Still, she needed her wits about her to present herself as calm and unaffected, or Angelina would undoubtedly draw suspicion and fail.

With an iron resolve to complete her task, Angelina imagined how much her son must have grown since she saw him last. She entered the dry goods store when they opened, bought what her son would need, and returned to the house to add it to her travel bag. Angelina packed, unpacked, and repacked it, reassuring herself she had forgotten nothing.

Finally, Angelina went down to the terminal, bought the train tickets for herself and Donny and entered on the side of the station, not visible from her father's house. Her visit needed to wait until later. For the moment, she could not risk being detained or losing her concentration.

All day she paced, wrote what she would do, what she would say, and if confronted, to remain composed. She tried to think of every occurrence and not overreact, panic, or draw suspicion.

After all her excitement that their *casita* become a happy home, it remained a house—a sad, empty house, a ghostly mausoleum of what might have been. Angelina recalled the day they moved in when a long-ago memory returned. She pulled out a kitchen drawer and reached back. The tiny paperclip she had placed there on her wedding day, meant to represent *something new,* was still there. It appeared a relic now from her long-ago innocence, from when she believed marriage would last *until death do us part.*

The time came to leave. Angelina said the last of her prayers, opened the front door, and paused a moment where Fabian had carried her over the threshold. She never intended to return and gazed at the *casita* one last time and listened to the ticking of the mantle clock. The clock had been there when they moved in. It had marked all the minutes of her marriage and the birth of her son, and now it marked the moment of her departure.

Angelina walked out, closed the door, and dropped the paperclip in a trash barrel at the foot of the porch without looking back.

In the street, the day blurred and swelled all around her as people hurried about their business, but for Angelina, only a warning alarm sounded in her mind. It would reach the pinnacle of panic while every passing minute drew her closer to the moment of crisis.

She reached Carmen's house, hurried up the porch steps where she knocked, and then knocked harder.

"Okay, okay, I'm coming."

The door opened, and Angelina stepped inside. "I'm so glad you're home. I have to leave my satchel here and pick it up later."

Carmen took it from her and groaned. "What's inside, gold bricks?"

"One brick, better than gold."

"Clothes? Why?"

Angelina deliberated on how much to say, but what was the point? The truth was never palatable by the spoonful. "Oh, Carmen, I have only one chance to rescue my son."

Carmen's eyes grew wide. "You found him!"

"I don't know, but if it's true, I'm not returning home. Fabian's proven he'll do whatever he can to take my child from me, so I'll leave for New York to be with my father's family there. I'll be safe and write you with my address. Here's the key to my house, you can keep everything. Will you do it?"

Carmen rubbed her arms nervously. "Of course, but I can't bear the thought of you leaving."

"It wasn't an easy decision, but it was the only one. It's far too dangerous for me to stay." Angelina pulled out a paper from her pocket. "In case something should happen, I've written down the address of where I am going and what time I'm supposed to be there."

"Now you are frightening me."

"I've been up all night planning every move. I will not make a mistake, but if I am not back by 6:00, call the police and give them this address that Sophia gave me."

Carmen shook her head. "No, you can't do this. Wait for Rolando. He can go instead."

"I just received a letter saying he was returning, but when was he arriving? I can't wait. I have only one hour to grab my baby." Angelina's voice cracked. "One hour, Carmen. That's all. Then he might be lost to me forever."

"Let me go with you."

"I knew you'd want to help, but I'll draw less attention if alone. Even if Rolando were here, I couldn't tell him where I was going. He'd insist on going with me. In a moment of excitement, if both men faced each other, they could…." Angelina couldn't finish the sentence.

"I should leave. I'll be back for the satchel. I've packed enough to get us to New York."

"But why so far away?"

"It's far enough from Fabian to make me feel safe and New York is big enough to get lost. I've thought about this all night and can't imagine him finding us."

"Do you need some money? I have a bit saved. You can have it all."

"You are the best friend I could ever have, but since the strike, I learned to live on almost nothing, and now that we returned to work, I kept to that Spartan life and saved all I could to pay investigators to find Donny. Now, I'll use that money to escape."

Carmen threw her arms around Angelina. "I can't believe this is happening. Nothing will be the same if you leave." Her voice filled with emotion, and her eyes moistened.

"And if I stay, I'd be looking over my shoulder every minute, afraid to leave my son, afraid to go to work, afraid my son will be forced from my arms. To rescue him, I checked everything, including streetcar and train schedules. I had to practice what to say and how long it took to say it. I've even timed myself on how long it takes me to walk an average block."

Carmen put her hand on Angelina's shoulder. "I can't imagine being more prepared."

"I can't think of anything but getting my baby back right now. I'm so scared I've overlooked something. As soon as I return, I'll grab my bag and jump on the train out of Ybor City."

"I think you are making a mistake going alone. Let me go, too."

"No matter which way I turn, peril is facing me. I won't bring you into this." The streetcar approached, and Angelina gave Carmen a quick hug, rushed to the trolley, and waved from the window as it pulled away.

EVERY MINUTE HAD BEEN ASSIGNED a purpose. Angelina took her seat on the trolley. Although humidity drugged the air and made most people tired, it had no time to lose her focus. Again and again, she checked her watch. With no room for error, she exited the trolley near a whitewashed home with numbers as close to the ones on Sophia's slip of paper.

Angelina kept to the west side of the street, convinced the sun's afternoon glare could obstruct Fabian's vision—should he look in her direction.

It seemed impossible to be so frantic on the inside yet have to appear so tranquil on the outside. It was now 4:10 PM, and Fabian had not appeared. Had Sophia tricked her? Every lost minute meant she had to move even quicker. Her senses heightened as she watched those coming and going and repeatedly checked the time. 4:22.

Never one for punctuality, at 4:25, Fabian stepped out of the house with his friend, José. From across the street, Angelina glared at the man who had shattered her life. After all he'd done to her, the anguish of seeing him again was almost physically painful. He had tossed away their little family without remorse, and there he stood, grinning and carefree as if he was still bouncing the universe like a ball.

She wanted to run toward him and scream, throw something at him for all the misery he'd brought her, but this moment was not about Fabian. She never intended to think of this man again after today.

Angelina watched from a distance as Fabian jovially slapped José on the back. They shared a deep belly laugh. Painful memories of her marriage flooded Angelina's mind. Either he wore a mask now or back then. Nothing bad lasts forever. Likewise, nothing good can be deemed to endure forever. Everything takes effort. Fabian's once strikingly handsome looks appeared to have faded, like the way leaves lose their vibrancy, wither, and fall from the tree, leaving it bare. Or perhaps people see what they want to see.

The two men stepped inside a Model T and drove off.

Angelina checked her pendant watch. With minutes lost, she had 35 minutes to find her son, grab him, and run for the streetcar. Or did this mean Fabian would be back in an hour from when he left? She could not take a chance. The urgency of not knowing exploded like alarm bells in her mind. In her agony, she whispered a heartfelt Hail Mary.

CHAPTER 42

ANGELINA SQUEEZED her hand around her pendant watch. Another seven minutes lost. Finally, Angelina spotted the house, and her breathing became labored, but she would not allow herself to lose focus.

It took a great effort to relax. Angelina took in a deep, cleansing breath and forced herself to walk calmly toward the house.

Someone had painted this *casita* an unbecoming shade of green to conceal peeling white paint, but then abandoned the job and the house looked disfigured. If there had ever been flowers and a lawn in the yard, the weeds now hid all traces.

Once again, Angelina verified the address of the house, that appeared angry with its heaping graveyard of discarded and broken objects.

Angelina stood at the front door and instinctively placed her hand over her heart, fearing its pounding might become noticeable. A young woman about Angelina's age answered and held the door handle as though ready to close it.

Angelina smiled and took care to appear friendly and tranquil as she spoke. "Hello, so sorry I'm late. I'm here to pick up little Don Carlos and take him to visit my family. Señor Dominguez told me he'd be gone at 4:00 and to come then." Angelina gently pushed against the barrier that separated her from her son to ensure the door wouldn't slam shut.

The girl's brown eyes grew larger. Left alone and in charge, she appeared confused. Angelina used the moment to open the door even wider and slip inside. "He did tell you Donny was going with Alicia, right?"

"No, Señor Dominguez said nothing like that."

"He said he'd leave with José Valle. Did they leave together?"

The girl nodded.

"Did he tell you they'd go around 4:00?"

The girl nodded again.

"Well, then, I wouldn't know if he didn't tell me, would I?" Angelina smiled.

The babbling sounds of her son graced the air and caused her pulse to race. She followed the sounds from the disarray to the far end of the front room, where she saw her son's face. Seeing him left her almost dizzy with excitement but stricken with fear.

Donny's eyes opened wide when he saw his mother, and he raised his arms. He smiled and clapped, but whimpered when Angelina didn't pick him up. Certain he recognized her, she could hardly keep her composure. He had just learned to say *mama* when Fabian kidnapped him, and now she was terrified he might say the word, trigger an alarm and dislodge all her prayers.

"My mother's next door. I'd better ask if you can take him."

A shiver passed through Angelina. She'd come too far to let this girl stop her. "Yes. Go ask your mother." She spoke softly. "I'll play with him until you get back."

If the girl picked up the child to leave, Angelina would stop her. If she hollered out a window for her mother, Angelina would grab her son and run out, but Angelina did not allow herself to react. Instead, she remained like a jungle cat in wait, ready to leap forward to protect her young.

The girl stood there momentarily, looking back at the child as if deciding what to do. "Wait here. I'll go next door to ask."

Angelina nodded. "Yes, that's best."

The moment the young woman left through the front door, Angelina grabbed her son, held him close, and pressed a desperate, long-dreamed-of kiss on his forehead. "You'll never know how much I love you," she whispered.

All *casitas* had the same design and Angelina knew just how to reach the back door. With Don Carlos in her arms, she dashed through the house and out to the yard. She crossed over a broken fence to a neighbor's lawn but a dog started barking from behind another fence. His continuous barking brought a woman to her window.

"*Que estas haciendo, chica?* Hey, that's Fabian's son." The woman's shrill voice grew louder. "Somebody, stop her!"

Angelina ran. *Oh please, God, help me.* Terrified, she held her child protectively and moved with a surge of energy she didn't know she possessed.

Angelina had to reach the trolley two blocks away before the clock struck, 5:00 or the same people keeping her from her son might pull up.

"Kidnapper! Someone, stop her! I'll have you arrested!"

Angelina knew the distant voice was directed at her, but minutes and seconds counted. Even though she was the child's mother, several women could overpower her and take her son. She would not lose time by looking back, but feared the baby's weight might slow her down.

In the distance, she could hear the trolley ringing its bell.

Another sudden burst of nervous energy sustained her as she rounded the corner, pushing her strength beyond what she believed possible. Nearly out of breath, she ran toward the trolley and was stunned at the sight of Rolando jumping off and rushing toward her. *Please, God, help me reach him before we're stranded.*

Angelina's energy falter when Rolando reached her and pulled the child from her arms, allowing her to run faster. Then, without a word spoken, they hurried to catch the trolley as the metal wheels were slowly beginning to churn and pull away.

They jumped on and made their way to a pair of seats. Still heaving with exhaustion, Angelina dared to look out the window at the sight of a large woman running up the street screaming.

Shaking and still panting from the ordeal, she took her son from Rolando, held him close, and buried her head in his softness. Amid the terror and struggle, the love and joy of at last holding her son again, and the thrill at seeing Rolando made it all worth it. All her emotions had erupted at once, and Angelina had never felt more alive.

Rolando placed his arm around her as she released her pent-up tears. "It's over, Angelina. You're both safe."

After all the harrowing weeks of searching, she had her child in her arms again. She drank in every feature. He'd grown more animated; his hair had thickened. His clothes were ill-fitted and stained. She doubted Fabian knew their son's size or how to care for his clothes.

Angelina gazed up at Rolando, who answered her question before she asked it.

"I arrived today, and Carmen came rushing to find me, screaming as if her house was on fire. She gave me the paper you gave her and told me what you said. How could you think to try something like this alone?"

"I planned every minute and went over and over it in my mind. I grew so desperate, I had to do it."

"It was a dangerous move. So many things could have gone wrong. You should have waited for me." Rolando sighed and kissed her forehead. "I learned of Fabian's plan in Cuba. He tried to recruit a man I knew. I intended to rescue Donny, but my contact said he'd returned to Ybor City near the factory."

"Sophia told me I had to act quickly."

"How am I supposed to be your hero when you take on such a dangerous venture without me? I will lose my union card with the Knights in Shining Armor."

Overjoyed, it was over but weary from the emotional and physical stress. Angelina could not hold back her tears. He put his arm around her. "We'll have plenty of time to talk when you're ready."

She looked down at her child, almost afraid to take her eyes off him, fearing he would vanish again. Had the separation broken the bond between mother and child? Yet, when her son put his small hand gently on her face and touched her tears, Angelina's heart soared. She showered him with her kisses and held him protectively until the three stepped off the trolley.

But the ordeal wasn't over. In not too long, Fabian would realize what she had done and come after her. He also had an automobile, which meant he could reach her quickly and there was only way to leave in a hurry—the train station. She had to move faster.

Donny must have sensed all the tension. He cried and squirmed, and Rolando had to hold him as they hurried to reach Carmen, who waved from her porch.

"Thank God. I've had no peace since you left, and you have little Don Carlos! He looks well." She kissed the baby as tears swelled in her eyes when she handed over the satchel.

"I'm sorry, Angelina, but I had to find Rolando. I couldn't just sit here and hope you were safe."

"It was a blessing. Rolando took Donny from my arms, and I could run faster. I don't even want to imagine what would have happened if I had missed the trolley."

Carmen, who had a quip for every occasion, looked shaken. "What Fabian did to you, he's done to all of us. He changed all our lives." She shook her head, as if rejecting the answer to her question. "Is this goodbye, then?"

Angelina embraced her best friend. "It has to be. Look at what he's capable of."

"He will never hurt you again as long as I'm here," said Rolando.

"But there is no way for you to be here with me every hour, and we all know what Fabian's like. If I stay, I'll live in fear. I have no choice but to get away and blend in some-where else. Everyone says America's a melting pot."

"So, you're going to New York to melt?"

Rolando smiled. "Melt in summer, freeze in winter. Have you thought of that?"

"I have family in New York. I'll feel safer there." She turned to Carmen. "I want you to know I treasure you. I could never have found a better friend, and as soon as I get settled, come visit me for a week, a month, or forever." Angelina kissed Carmen's cheek.

"I'll miss you so much, Angelina. It's like losing an arm."

"If you ever want that arm back, come to New York. I know we'll be together again. You'll see." Angelina hugged her tightly.

Rolando hugged her, too. "I will never forget how you came running to find me, and I'll always be grateful for that."

Angelina glanced out into the distance. "It's not over. Fabian was supposed to return at 5:00. Even if he's late, he'll return soon and has an automobile. It won't take him long to figure out I have his son."

They all turned when the sound of metal wheels ground its way along the tracks. Angelina checked her watch. "This trolley will take us right to the train station."

They hurried onboard, and Angelina blew Carmen a kiss from the window.

Rolando carried Donny and the satchel. It seemed so natural for him to relieve her anxiety.

Angelina had checked every train schedule. There would be many stops, but only one train line headed to New York City. As soon as they arrived at the terminal, she checked their tickets and gazed at the sign she had seen all her life— *Domenico's Fine Italian Food.*

Rolando looked around. "The last time we stood here together, I was leaving you."

"Yes, but this time, I'm going, and you'll be coming to join me."

"No one could keep me away," said Rolando

"How soon can you settle everything here?"

"Very soon."

She tilted her head and kissed him with all her pent-up love and passion. After everything they had been through, eternity would not have been enough time together. Angelina pulled reluctantly away.

"Donny and I are in danger if I don't leave right away. I packed everything last night. Please come to me as soon as you can." She glanced at her father's grocery store with a connecting door to the family home. "So many that I love are in that home. I have to say goodbye to my father and my siblings."

"I'll be here when you come out."

She spoke with a heavy heart as she reached for her son

and lifted him into her arms. "This is something I have to do. I'll be back."

"Yes, I understand. However, I have already met your father, and he is not looking forward to meeting me again."

Angelina nodded her understanding. "I can't be long, or the train will leave without me."

"Choo-choo." Donny chattered and pointed to the train.

"We're going to see your *nonno,* Donny." She drove away all discouraging thoughts and summoned her strength. Still, before she stepped inside the little grocery store, she whispered a final Hail Mary. She inhaled deeply, hesitated, and then pushed open the grocery door. The little bell rang, announcing her entrance and showering Angelina with a lifetime of memories.

She found her father in his usual chair behind the counter, working on his libretto. He looked up and came to his feet. Angelina's heart stopped.

"What are you doing here?" His voice was harsh.

She had practiced everything she wanted to say. Now that the moment had arrived, only disjointed fragments of well-rehearsed phrases survived and ran through her mind. Angelina stood in silence, with only the muffled sounds of people scurrying about outside to catch their trains.

This would be her last chance to speak to him. By tomorrow, Ybor City and all she knew would fade. Angelina held her child close and gathered her courage. "Papa, before you order me away, shout or ignore me, I need to say something."

Donny squirmed in her arms. She tried to calm him, but still, he wiggled out of her grasp and hollered as he tried to wander off.

"Angie, Angie!" Lily appeared, rushed across the room, and hugged her. "Can I play with him? Please."

Her sister's shouts brought her brothers to the doorway. "Take the little one into the house," her father said to them.

330 | THE WEIGHT OF BETRAYAL

Her visit would be short, but she had gone through so much, suffered so much, and was no longer a child. She had to say what she felt.

"You don't have to speak to me, Papa. All you have to do is listen. Since I left your house, certain things you predicted came true. But you know what you know because you took a chance and experienced life." Angelina swallowed hard. "I also know what I know because I took a chance. I've had my dreams shattered and my heart broken. I am not sure you would believe all I have suffered and survived alone." She'd never spoken to him like this. "You left Sicily in the early morning hours when you were only seventeen and without your family knowing. I left the same way and only one year older."

"I tried to protect you," her father grumbled.

This was no time to unearth the soil for old arguments. "We both threw open our arms to capture our lives because neither of us was willing to live wondering what might have been."

Her father didn't answer or argue.

"After a lifetime of listening to the sounds of the trains, today I'm stepping onto one. I've packed up all my dreams, and I'm taking them to New York, where I'll start over." Naturally, this would not impress her father. "I'm returning to your last name and giving it to my son. I'll live among the Sicilians in the Lower East Side of Manhattan and contact our family there." This would please her father, but she wasn't doing it for this purpose. The entire reason remained far too long and complex. "I'll blend into a world, a language, and people I understand. You always said, 'Italians protected each other.' No matter what the outcome of my life, Papa, I know who I am—*sangue del mio sangue*. We are blood."

Her father's stern expression remained. "We cling to who

we are, or are nothing," he said. Angelina understood his words served as an anchor for his old-world beliefs.

The train whistle sounded in the distance. She glanced at her pendant watch.

Angelina leaned over to kiss her father's cheek and expected him to pull back, but he didn't. For the first time, her father had listened without discounting, turning his back, slamming the door, or pounding a fist on the table. She regarded this as a token of unspoken absolution, but her days of needing his approval had passed. Angelina was no longer an obedient child, hoping to please. She had suffered many trials, grown stronger, and intended to live without permission.

"I carry you in my heart, Papa, where you will always remain." She believed he had begun to forgive her, not in the usual way as perhaps another father might, because Domenico had pride. His forgiveness would come in small droplets, but would one day fill a flask.

The train's metal wheels screeched louder as it approached. Angelina kissed her father again and hurried into the next room to pick up her child and hug her siblings.

"Don't get too mushy, Angie," said Vincenzo, and then he grabbed and kissed her. Her siblings spoke over each other as Angelina reached out and kissed each one with a tearful goodbye.

She glanced at her father, who had now busied himself. Pride was a burdensome thing, Angelina concluded. "Goodbye, Papa. I want you to know that I know how it feels to lose a child, and even if you never say it, I believe you love me." Angelina expected his denial, but it never came. "And I know you will love me forever," she added as she walked out the door.

For the first time in her life, Angelina was unrestrained with the power of independence which soared inside her.

As she left the house, she saw her uncle walking toward her with Pasqualino. Elated, Angelina shouted, "Zio Pasquale!"

"You came to see you, Papa? Now everybody so happy."

"Yes, Zio, but I am leaving. I have to catch this train. It's very important. I will write and tell you everything. I only stopped for a few minutes to say goodbye."

"Goodbye? Goodbye, take two hours, no a few minutes."

Angelina grinned. "Two hours?"

"And that'sa for sure." He reached for Donny and took him out of her arms. "First, I have to say hello to you *bambino*. He is so handsome." Pasquale kissed the child and then showed him to his son. "This is your cousin, Pasqualino. You can call him, President Donny."

The boy held Donny's hand and smiled. "Is he really gonna be the President Papa?"

"I never say a lie." Pasquale turned to his niece. "Angelina, first we say goodbye. Then we go inside, eat something, and say goodbye again. Then we make a toast for you to have a good trip, we sit down and visit, and we talk about Santo Stefano Quisquina, Sicilia, and all the people that come to America, and about the family, so we no forget nobody. And then it's okay we kiss goodbye."

Her uncle could always make her laugh, but knowing she was leaving everyone so far behind frightened her and heightened her anger with Fabian. "I love you, Zio Pasquale, and I wish I had two hours to say goodbye, but it's urgent. I can't miss the train." She kissed her uncle and her little cousin, Pasqualino.

She could hear the train's whistle and rushed across the street before she broke down entirely for leaving everyone she loved. When she reached the train, she heard someone shout, "Hey, Angie!" She looked behind her. All her family stood on the porch calling her name and waving, and her father stood with them stoic, expressionless—but there.

She understood now how time and passions were measured differently by each generation, and each followed its path, and each thought they were the ones that discovered how to love.

Angelina blew them all a kiss and walked toward the train. Nothing could stop her. Even the air seemed to push her toward a new vibrancy. She stood at the end of the line of those boarding. Again, her son squirmed. She set him down a moment and held his hand.

"Angelina!"

She glanced across the platform and saw Rolando in the distance, waving and making his way through the crowd. "Rolando," she whispered.

As soon as he reached her, he put his arm protectively around her. "There's a crowd on the platform today. I was afraid I might lose you."

He reached down, picked up her son, and stroked the child's hair.

"Everything happened so fast, and I could not reach you. I know you have to settle things here, pack your belongings, give notice at your job, and the union counts on you, but please do whatever it takes to leave and come to New York as soon as possible. I've risked everything, Rolando, lost so much, and now I've come to where I can almost touch my dream. I'm starting my life over."

Rolando set down the child, "Well, isn't that a coincidence? I've been thinking about starting my life over again, too."

Angelina choked on her tears. "I can't stay. I'm getting on the train. It's the only way to save my son from his father. Promise me you'll follow as soon as you can settle things. I need you with me, Rolando. I do."

Rolando pulled her close and gave her such a meaningful kiss, it lingered after he released her. "Love is a funny thing, Angelina, it's like falling through the universe. It grows in barren land, without rain or sun and in a hellhole of a prison. Yet, even deprived, you realize who are the most important people in your life. Our love never died. It loomed about in splendor and awaited our return." His words entranced Angelina.

Rolando reached beneath his collar and pulled out the St. Jude medal. "Remember when I gave this to you? I was leaving, and it was my promise to return. Now you're leaving, and the medal will keep its promise I will return to you."

"Oh, Rolando. Please come as soon as you can. I don't think I can bear life without you." The words caught in her throat. Angelina could not stand the anguish of losing once again, the one she knew she was destined to love. "Goodbye, but just for now," she said with tears streaming down her cheeks.

"The medal always keeps its promise," said Rolando.

Angelina turned away. It was all too painful; what if it happened like before, and he disappeared again? She turned away, picked up her child, and hurried toward the train. She now knew the different kinds of love, and she loved Rolando fiercely and grieved the enormity of not having him with her. However, Angelina had to be realistic. This might be her only chance to save her child. She'd come too far, sacrificed too much to risk Fabian finding her.

The train's whistle blew, and the conductor shouted the last call.

Angelina hurried, got on board, made her way down the aisle, and took a seat. The train's whistle blew again, and with a great sigh of relief, the doors locked, and the train trembled its forewarning that it was about to embark on its journey.

Angelina looked out the window at the little grocery store and waved, but in that fraction of time, too small to have a name, her sense of triumph erupted into flames of panic.

Fabian! she screamed his name in her mind. To her horror, she saw him racing toward her father's house. Her family remained outside, and the younger children were still waving. Seeing them, Fabian turned in the direction they were looking and rushed toward the train. He ran along the side of the cars, gazing into windows.

She froze, and her mouth went dry. She could only whisper, "Oh, please, God. No."

Fabian's searing hot rage was visible and as undeniable as Angelina's intense will to save her child from his father. The tidal wave of Fabian's insane determination terrified her.

Overcome with panic, she held her son securely in her embrace and shut her eyes. A crushing sensation of fear that something might go wrong came over her as if she might fall through time and space.

The iron wheels churned. Fabian's face flushed crimson with rage as he tried to grab the train. For one horrifying moment, their eyes met, and Angelina stopped breathing.

Fabian slammed the side of the railroad car with both fists and said something obliterated by the train's garish whistle. Still, he delivered his message with one venomous glance—he intended to come after her.

The train picked up speed, and he vanished, but the experience left Angelina shaking with a terrible piercing sensation as her mind fought to sort out the stream of rapid occurrences reliving in her mind. *The woman chasing me must have reached Fabian and told him. Since he stole Donny, he must know I won't stay and risk losing him again. And what's faster than a train to leave?*

She reminded herself that Fabian had yet to learn her destination, at which terminal she might step off or if she

336 | THE WEIGHT OF BETRAYAL

would change trains several times. Angelina let this calming thought linger and rescue her from a landslide of nerves.

Now, as on that night, she'd left her father's house so long ago, Angelina once again felt that time had shifted—the present and all she had endured now became the past. The train's wheels moved steadily, and through the window, she saw everything familiar she had known all her life spin madly by and vanished.

Her child yawned, rubbed his eyes, and the train's vibration lulled him to sleep. Angelina set him down on the seat facing her and, for a time, watched him breathe. In this little child lay her whole life. Everything she did would be for him.

"It looks like the seat next to you hasn't been taken," said a man's voice.

Angelina looked up and jumped to her feet. "Rolando! What on earth are you doing here?"

His brilliant grin widened. "You didn't honestly think I would let you get away from me a second time? I'm going wherever you're going. Sooner or later, something wonderful happens to all of us that changes our lives forever, and you, my Angelina, are what happened to me. I've waited a long time to be with you. I will not lose you again. We'll start life over together. I'll help you achieve everything you want."

"You just bought a ticket and jumped on the train? You have no suitcase, no clothes, and what about the union?"

"What about the union? Did they warn me I was in danger? Did they try hard to find me? Because of them, I lost you and an outrageous amount of time in a horrid Spanish prison. What do I owe them?"

"But you have nothing with you!"

Rolando took her in his arms and kissed her as if no one else in the world existed, and then he whispered in her ear, "You're wrong, Angelina. I have everything. I have *you*."

EPILOGUE

A RAGING fire burned inside Fabian, and his face flushed red with its blaze. He fiercely watched the train carrying his child as it gained speed, grew smaller, and vanished into the distance.

With his muscles constricted and his hands squeezed into tight fists, Fabian shouted Spanish curses and pushed through the crowd, bumping into anyone in his way. His rage grew, furious that Angelina, a woman, had outsmarted him. Fabian had greatly misjudged her ability to plan such a minute-by-minute escape, but Angelina was never foolish.

Fabian raced to the ticket office, forced his way through the back door, grabbed the clerk by the collar, pulled him to his feet, and shoved him to the back wall where the office was not visible to customers. He then pulled a gun from his pocket and pressed it against the ticket clerk's ribs.

"Don't tell me you don't know Angelina Pirrello Dominguez. She lived across the street all her life, and everyone around here knows the Pirrello family and their grocery store. She bought a ticket, and I want to know where she's going." His momentary pause chilled. "Now!"

Sweat broke out on the clerk's forehead as he glanced down at the gun pressing deeper into his ribs. "I don't know, exactly."

"Well, that's a shame because I expect you to tell me *exactly*." Fabian raised the gun and placed it under the man's chin.

The clerk's limbs shook. He widened his eyes behind his glasses. "She's going back East somewhere, I think."

"You think? You better think harder because I don't like games, and God help you if I return to hunt you down!"

The pressure of the gun hard-pressed against the clerk's ribs intensified. His breathing grew labored until he choked out the words.

"Grand Central Station, New York City, New York."

ABOUT THE AUTHOR

Sandra Montanino Sandra Montanino lived in three different countries by the age of eight. These rich exposures gave her a wealth of appreciation for her own multicultural heritage. Inspired by the life of her Sicilian grandmother, Sandra has penned The Weight of Salt from the richness of family stories instrumental in igniting her imagination of a time that once was.

Encouraged by the publication of her article in Ancestry Magazine, Sandra has won numerous literary awards from the League of Utah Writers and is the recipient of the Southern California Outstanding Fiction Award. *The Weight of Salt* is her debut novel and the first in her series. Originally from Southern California and the mother of five, she now lives in Utah between the lake and the mountains with her husband Gennaro of many years, a cat who loves to sleep, and a big dog who thinks he's a puppy.

Sandra Montanino can be found online at: www.sandramontanino.com

Please Also join my mailing list at: https://landing.mailerlite.com/webforms/landing/y1s5m1

Made in United States
North Haven, CT
05 May 2023

36270825R10207